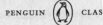
WEIR OF HERMISTON

ROBERT LOUIS STEVENSON was born in Edinburgh in 1850. The son of a prosperous civil engineer, he was expected to follow the family profession but finally was allowed to study law at Edinburgh University. Stevenson reacted violently against the Presbyterian respectability of the city's professional classes and this led to painful clashes with his parents. In his early twenties he became afflicted with a severe respiratory illness from which he was to suffer for the rest of his life; it was at this time that he determined to become a professional writer. The harsh nature of the Scottish climate forced him to spend long periods abroad and he eventually settled in Samoa, where he died on 3 December 1894.

Stevenson's Calvinistic upbringing gave him a preoccupation with predestination and a fascination with the presence of evil. In *Dr Jekyll and Mr Hyde* he explores the darker side of the human psyche, and the character of the Master in *The Master of Ballantrae* (1889) was intended to be 'all I know of the Devil'. Stevenson is well-known for his novels of historical adventure, including *Treasure Island* (1883), *Kidnapped* (1886) and *Catriona* (1893). As Walter Allen in *The English Novel* comments, 'His rediscovery of the art of narrative, of conscious and cunning calculation in telling a story so that the maximum effect of clarity and suspense is achieved, meant the birth of the novel of action as we know it.' But these works also reveal his knowledge and feeling for the Scottish cultural past. During the last years of his life Stevenson's creative range developed considerably and *The Beach of Falesá* brought to fiction the kind of scene now associated with Conrad and Maugham. At the time of his death Robert Louis Stevenson was working on his unfinished masterpiece, *Weir of Hermiston*, which is at once a romantic historical novel and an emotional reworking of one of Stevenson's own most distressing experiences, the conflict between father and son.

PAUL BINDING, who spent his early childhood in Germany and was educated in Yorkshire, the Home Counties and Oxford, is a novelist and critic. His work includes *Separate Country: A Literary Journey Through the American South* (1979) and *Lorca: The Gay Imagination* (1986), the novels *Harmonica's Bridegroom* (1984) and *Kingfisher Weather* (1982), and

St Martin's Ride (1990), a memoir of Germany and personal reflections on changing Europe, which won the J. R. Ackerley Prize in 1991. Forthcoming are *Rolled Over on Europe*, a sequel to the latter book, and a study of Eudora Welty. He was Eudora Welty Visiting Professor of Southern Studies in Jackson, Mississippi (1985–6), has lectured in Sweden, the Netherlands and Italy, and is an enthusiastic animal rights activist.

ROBERT LOUIS STEVENSON

WEIR OF HERMISTON
and Other Stories

SELECTED AND EDITED
WITH AN INTRODUCTION BY
PAUL BINDING

PENGUIN BOOKS

PENGUIN BOOKS

Published by the Penguin Group
Penguin Books Ltd, 27 Wrights Lane, London W8 5TZ, England
Penguin Books USA Inc., 375 Hudson Street, New York, New York 10014, USA
Penguin Books Australia Ltd, Ringwood, Victoria, Australia
Penguin Books Canada Ltd, 10 Alcorn Avenue, Toronto, Ontario, Canada M4V 3B2
Penguin Books (NZ) Ltd, 182–190 Wairau Road, Auckland 10, New Zealand

Penguin Books Ltd, Registered Offices: Harmondsworth, Middlesex, England

This selection first published in Penguin English Library 1979
Reprinted in Penguin Classics 1992
5 7 9 10 8 6 4

Printed in England by Clays Ltd, St Ives plc
Set in Linotype Pilgrim

CONTENTS

INTRODUCTION

I

Weir of Hermiston, on the ninth chapter of which Stevenson was engaged the day he died, stands in an extraordinary relation to the rest of his work. Indeed, it provides perhaps the only example of an unfinished, posthumously published novel not only surpassing all its author's previous literary performances but belonging to an altogether different category of achievement from even the best of them.

Its unfinished state does not by any means make it unique in the Stevenson canon. Stevenson often had three or four books on hand at once, resuming work on one when weary with another, and he left behind him seven unfinished books of which two others apart from *Weir* are of sufficient length and substance to stand up for themselves – *St Ives* (later completed by Sir Arthur Quiller-Couch) and *Records of a Family of Engineers*, a history of his own family. During the year of his death, Stevenson was occupied with at least four ambitious works of fiction. While the letters he wrote when he first started work on *Weir* show the high hopes he entertained for it, it was not until he took it up anew, after labouring at other projects, that it took hold of his imagination in a way no previous novel had done. He wrote in an agitated, possessed state of mind, and it seems more than probable that, his physical condition being what it was, the intensity of his work on *Weir* brought about his death. A fatal brain haemorrhage attacked him on the evening of Monday, 3 December 1894, in the morning of which day he'd dictated to his stepdaughter an account of the anguished love problems of his hero, problems which bore a marked resemblance to those he had faced in his own youth.

The acute excitement which pervaded Stevenson while writing *Weir* is perhaps best conveyed through an account his stepson, Lloyd Osbourne, has left of those days:

One evening, after dinner, he read the first chapters of *Weir* aloud. I had my usual pencil and paper for the notes I always took on such occasions, but that night I made none. It was so superbly written that I listened to it in a sort of spell. It seemed absolutely beyond criticism; seemed the very zenith of anything he had ever accomplished; it flowed with such an inevitability and emotion, such a sureness and perfection, that the words seemed to strike against my heart. When he had finished, I sat dumb. I knew I should have spoken, but I could not. The others praised it ... but I was in a dream from which I could not awake ... Then the party broke up and we dispersed on our different ways to bed ... I had hardly passed the threshold of the door, however, when I heard Stevenson behind me. He was in a state of frightful agitation; was trembling; breathless, almost beside himself. 'My God, you shall not go like that!' he cried out, seizing me by the arm, and his thin fingers closing on it like a vice. 'What! Not a single note, not a single word, not even the courtesy of a lie! You, the only one whose opinion I depend on, and all you can say is "Goodnight, Louis!" So that is your opinion, is it? Just "Goodnight, Louis" – like a blow in the face!'

The bitterness and passion he put into these words is beyond any power of mine to describe ...

Then I tried to tell him the truth, but with difficulty, realizing how unpardonably I had hurt his pride ... That it was a masterpiece; that never before had he written anything comparable with *Weir*, that it promised to be the greatest novel in the English language.

We were in the dark. I could not see his face. But I believe he listened with stupefaction. The reaction when it came was too great for his sorely strained nerves; tears rained from his eyes – and mine, too, streamed. Never had I known him to be so moved; never had I been so moved myself; and in the all-pervading darkness we were for once free to be ourselves, unashamed. Thus we sat, with our arms about each other, talking far into the night. Even after thirty years, I should not care to divulge anything so sacred as those confidences; the revelation of that tortured soul; the falterings of its Calvary ... To me his heroism took on new proportions, and I now was thankful I had refused an important post to stay with him. 'It will not be for long,' he said.

This passage surely gives us the key to what makes *Weir* so significantly different from its author's other books: in writing it, Stevenson was plundering his most secret and cherished storehouse of memories, was drawing on the most significant emotional experiences of his life.

Yet *Weir*, like all Stevenson's major fiction, is an historical novel, the genesis of which was his fascinated contemplation of an actual historical person, Robert MacQueen, Lord Braxfield. Writing to his cousin Bob at the outset of work on it, Stevenson described *Weir* as 'an attempt at a real historical novel, to present a whole field of time'. This in itself indicates a *total* seriousness of intent, which was not the case with the earlier novels. *Weir* is a fusion of the two most creatively significant strands in Stevenson's imagination – in it his interest in and understanding of Scottish history are united with a full confrontation of his own personal, psychological and moral history.

In order to see how this union came about, we should look first at this personal history of Stevenson's, and more particularly at that of his youth and young manhood.

Robert Louis Stevenson was born in Edinburgh on 13 November 1850. The Stevensons were a distinguished, prosperous family of lighthouse engineers. He was later to write of them:

We rose out of obscurity in a clap. My father and Uncle David made the third generation ... of direct descendants who had been engineers to the Board of Northern Lights; there is scarce a deep sea light from the Isle of Man north about to Berwick, but one of my blood designed it; and I have often thought that to find a family to compare with ours in the promise of immortal memory, we must go back to the Egyptian Pharaohs: upon so many reefs and forelands that not very elegant name of Stevenson is engraved with a pen of iron upon granite. My name is as well-known as that of the Duke of Argyle among the fishers, the skippers, the seamen, and the masons of my native land. Whenever I smell salt water, I know I am not far from the works of my ancestors. The Bell Rock stands monument for my grandfather, the Skerry Vohr for my

Uncle Alan; and when the lights come out at sundown along the shores of Scotland, I am proud to think they burn more brightly for the genius of my father.

Louis was a delicate, highly-strung, imaginative child; he had inherited from his mother's family a lung condition which later developed into consumption;* and a principal result of so much ill-health was a cultivation of a lively faculty for make-believe. An only son, he was the object of undivided affection and attention from his parents and nurse. His schooling was an erratic affair, his mother and father early recognizing their offspring's brilliance, and he was allowed to pursue his private interests to a most unusual extent.

When Louis was seven years old, his parents moved into 17 Heriot Row in the heart of the New Town of Edinburgh, that beautiful monument to the Silver Age of Scotland, to the Scottish 'haute bourgeoisie's' enlightenment and, too, to their belief in order and the need for a firm structure to life in society. Apart from holidays – during which he grew to know and love the Lowlands countryside and seashore – Stevenson spent all his life up to and including his early maturity in Edinburgh. No city proclaims the past so dramatically as the Scottish capital. From the Greyfriars cemetery where the Covenanters lie buried and where the youthful Stevenson loved broodingly to wander, to the Grassmarket, site of the old Tolbooth prison, from the towering, crowded tenements of the Old Town to such elegant creations of the Adam brothers as Charlotte Square and George Street in the New, one is continually aware of the lives and sentiments of people of the past. Essays, autobiographical fragments, an early topographical book, *Edinburgh: Picturesque Notes*, as well as some of the most memorable pages of his fictional works, all pay tribute to the enormous influence the city had on his sensibility. To paraphrase V. S. Pritchett's remarks on Scott, the historical passion

* It perhaps should be said that there are those who deny that Stevenson was consumptive; from his early twenties onwards he was prone to haemorrhage, and it was of a brain haemorrhage that he died.

was to be the engine of Stevenson's creative impulse. Later, indeed, Stevenson came to see this passion as itself a deeply Scottish characteristic; as he says in *Weir of Hermiston*:

For that is the mark of the Scot of all classes: that he stands in an attitude to the past unthinkable to Englishmen, and remembers and cherishes the memory of his forebears, good or bad; and there burns alive in him a sense of identity with the dead even to the twentieth generation.

Stevenson was to become increasingly aware of the essential Scottishness of his early life, and something he says in an essay, 'The Foreigner at Home', is pertinent here in our discussion of this period:

About the very cradle of the Scot there goes a hum of metaphysical divinity; and the whole of two divergent systems is summed up, not merely speciously, in the two first questions of the rival catechisms, the English tritely inquiring, 'What is your name?', the Scottish striking at the very roots of life with, 'What is the chief end of man?' and answering nobly, if obscurely, 'To glorify God and to enjoy Him for ever.' I do not wish to make an idol of the Shorter Catechism; but the fact of such a question being asked opens to us Scotch a great field of speculation; and the fact that it is asked of all of us, from the peer to the ploughboy, binds us more nearly together.

The role played by religion in Stevenson's development cannot be underestimated. As a small child, Stevenson came under the influence principally of his nurse, Cummy, to whom he remained devoted through his life, calling her in the dedicatory verses of *A Child's Garden of Verses*:

My second Mother, my first Wife,
The angel of my infant life.

Cummy belonged to an extreme Calvinist sect which had broken away from the established Church of Scotland to which Louis' parents belonged. Her heroes were the seventeenth-century Covenanters, who came, particularly during his boyhood, to dominate Louis' imagination. It was because of

Cummy, then, with her stories of the Covenanters' doomed, hunted last days and her readings of devotional works, including a poem 'The Cameronian Dream' which according to Balfour's *Life* was 'the earliest piece of literature which awakened in him the sentiment of romantic Scottish history', that Stevenson spent what he later often referred to as a 'Covenanting childhood'.

But along with tales of their noble stands, Cummy had preserved the Covenanters' fanatical faith, with its obsessive insistence on predestined election and damnation, and little Louis was brought up to be a pious, virtuous, God-fearing child. Of these childish 'high-strung, religious ecstacies and terrors', Stevenson said in an autobiographical fragment (written in California when he thought himself to be dying):

It is my nurse that I owe these last: my mother was shocked, when, in days long after, she heard what I had suffered. I would not only lie awake to weep for Jesus, which I have done many a time, but I would fear to trust myself to slumber lest I was not accepted and should slip, ere I awoke, into eternal ruin. I remember repeatedly ... waking from a dream of Hell, clinging to the horizontal bar of the bed, with my knees and chin together, my soul shaken, my body convulsed with agony. It is not a pleasant subject. I piped and snivelled over the Bible, with an earnestness that had been talked into me. I would say nothing without adding 'If I am spared', as though to disarm fate by a show of submission; and some of this feeling still remains upon me in my thirtieth year ...

I was lovingly, but not always wisely treated, the great fault being Cummy's over-haste to make me a religious pattern. I have touched already upon the cruelty of bringing a child among the awful shadows of man's life; but, it must not be forgotten, it is also unwise, and a good way to defeat the educator's purpose. The idea of sin, attached to particular actions absolutely, far from repelling, soon exerts an attraction on young minds. Probably few over-pious children have not been tempted, sometime or other and by way of dire experiment, to deny God in set terms. The horror of the act, performed in solitude, under the blue sky; the smallness of the voice uttered in the stillness of noon; the panic flight from the scene of the bravado: all these will not have been forgotten. But the worst consequence is the romance conferred on doubtful actions; until the child grows to think nothing more glorious than to be struck dead in the act of some surprising wickedness. I can never again take so much interest in anything, as I took, in childhood, in doing for its own sake what I believed to be sinful.

This preoccupation with sin and guilt, rooted in his psyche at an early age, was reinforced most strongly by his difficult relationship with his father. This was in fact the most important relationship of his life, certainly from the point of view of his art, and it provided the driving emotional force of *Weir*, his one great novel.

Thomas Stevenson (1818–87) was a man of complex and difficult personality, as much so as his famous son. A dreamy boy and something of an idler at school, he grew up to become the most eminent of all the engineers produced by his distinguished family, making an important contribution to optics as applied to lighthouse illumination. His achievement in his chosen field of science was later recognized in 1884 by his being elected President of the Royal Society of Edinburgh. Nor was science the only domain in which he excelled. A devout member of the Church of Scotland, he wrote several works of Christian apologetic, which he valued above all else he had accomplished. Yet his stern sense of professional and religious duty, though it dominated all he did, did not totally banish his boyhood self. He sent himself to sleep with stories of adventurous journeys, shipwrecks, and escapes, and he amused his young son during his so frequent bouts of illness with such narratives. He was later to greet Louis' first readings aloud of *Treasure Island* with elation. It also must be mentioned that Thomas Stevenson suffered from increasingly protracted bouts of depression, which encompassed a morbid sense of his own unworthiness and acute fears of death. Louis described him in his memorial essay to him as possessing:

... a blended sternness and softness that was wholly Scottish and at first somewhat bewildering; with a profound essential melancholy of disposition and (what often accompanies it) the most humorous geniality in company; shrewd and childish; passionately attached; passionately prejudiced ...

The conflict between father and son, though doubtless incipient even in earlier years, began in earnest in Louis' late teens, when, a student at Edinburgh University, he showed the inevitable inclination to break from a peculiarly protected and restricted mode of life and explore both his own inclinations and the varieties of attitude and behaviour he now found at hand. Battle raged over the questions of Louis' religious beliefs, of Louis' morals and choice of company, and of his future career. Disagreement over religion pervaded, indeed at times dictated disagreement over the other matters, but it also became a mask for disguising deeper psychological tension – the father seeking to dominate and determine, the son desperately striving to free himself of what was, even by the standards of his time, country and class, a particularly heavy parental yoke. Religion indeed became, on an unconscious level no doubt, Thomas Stevenson's most powerful weapon, since it aroused in the rebellious son a guilt that never was wholly to leave him.

As a matter of fact, as regards the actual dogma professed, Thomas Stevenson was not a bigot. In 1843 the Church of Scotland suffered its famous Disruption – two-thirds of its ministers formed an independent Free Church which became the home of the stricter Calvinists, the Covenanters' spiritual heirs. Thomas Stevenson, however, was a Moderate. But though he may have differed from his more conservative contemporaries on certain points of doctrinal emphasis, he was most intransigent in his attitude to those who would not or could not accept Christianity. Like so many young intellectuals of his time, Louis was influenced by two movements which seemed to undermine the whole rational foundations of the Christian faith: Darwinism and the new historical/critical scrutiny of the Scriptures. The doubts these implanted combined with a young man's psychological dissatisfaction with the specific form of Christianity he had been presented with – Puritanism with its suspicion of the life of the senses and a sexual ethic with which Louis, like so many others, found it impossible to comply. Thomas Stevenson, it would appear, showed little sympathy with his son's problems, preferring to regard all manifestations of independence and intellectual questioning of received opinions as wilful perversity. We find Stevenson, at the age of twenty-two, writing to a close friend:

The thunderbolt has fallen with a vengeance now. You know the aspect of a house in which somebody is still waiting burial: the quiet step, the hushed voices and rare conversation, the religious literature that holds a temporary monopoly, the grim, wretched faces; all is here reproduced in this family circle in honour of my (what is it?) atheism or blasphemy. On Friday night after leaving you, in the course of conversation, my father put me one or two questions as to beliefs, which I candidly answered. I really hate all lying so much now – a new-found honesty that has somehow come out of my late illness – that I could not so much as hesitate at the time; but if I had foreseen the real Hell of everything since, I think I should have lied, as I have done so often before. I so far thought of my father, but I had forgotten my mother. And now! they are both ill, both silent, both as down in the mouth as if – I can find no simile. You may fancy how happy it is for me. If it were not too late, I think I could almost find it in my heart to retract, but it is too late; and again, am I to live my whole life as one falsehood? Of course, it is rougher than Hell upon my father, but can I help it? They don't see either that my game is not the light-hearted scoffer, that I am not (as they call me) a careless infidel. I believe as much as they do, only generally in the inverse ratio; I am, I think, as honest as they can be in what I hold. I have not come hastily to my views. I reserve (as I told them) many points until I acquire fuller information. I do not think I am thus justly to be called a 'horrible atheist'; and I confess I cannot exactly swallow my father's purpose of praying down continuous afflictions on my head.

Now, what is to take place? What a damned curse I am to my parents! As my father said, 'You have rendered my whole life a failure!' As my mother said, 'This is the heaviest affliction that has ever befallen me.' And, O Lord, what a pleasant thing it is to have just *damned* the happiness of (probably) the only two people who care a damn about you in the world.

Guilt was the principal legacy also of Louis' most serious youthful emotional involvement. The exact identity of Claire as she has come to be called after the eponymous heroine of a novel Louis wrote later in his life and at his wife's instigation destroyed, has been the subject of much biographical speculation.* We can be fairly certain, however, that she was a girl of a far humbler social class than Louis', that Louis' parents disapproved intensely of the connection, that Louis wished to marry her and that he, despite his adolescent ardour, gave into his family, and broke off the affair. In his early manhood, Stevenson wrote poems to relieve his sadness, his sense of loss:

> That sun is set. My heart is widowed now
> Of that companion-thought. Alone I plough
> The seas of life, and trace
> A separate furrow far from her and grace.

And even more poignantly:

> Love – what is love? A great aching heart,
> Wrung hands; and silence; and a long despair.
> Life – what is life? Upon a moorland bare
> To see love coming and see love depart.

The sexual dissipation in which Stevenson indulged during his young manhood after parting from Claire can only have reinforced his sense of guilt.

The struggle to assert himself against his father over his career was scarcely less painful than those over religion and love. Thomas Stevenson intended Louis to join the family engineering concern, and Engineering was the subject Louis first read at Edinburgh University. Louis also accompanied his father on several enterprises of construction on the Scottish coast. Hard as he tried to think as an engineer, capable though he was of writing a prize-winning essay on a 'New Form of Intermittent Light for Lighthouses', Stevenson found this work incompatible

---

* Studies of Stevenson at one time suffered from an overdose of speculation on this topic. Now, however, the tide has turned, for James Pope-Hennessy's *Robert Louis Stevenson* (1974) does not mention the 'Claire' involvement at all. Despite the lack of circumstantial evidence, I still believe – in the light of his writings – in an intense sexual relationship in Stevenson's youth; 'Claire' is a convenient shorthand for this.

with his deepest preoccupations. From his early adolescence onwards his ambitions were literary, and these were treated by his father with suspicion. Nevertheless, during a walk to Cramond on 8 April 1871, a walk later spoken of as 'dreadful', Louis managed to tell his father that he did not intend to become an engineer. Thomas, albeit reluctantly, agreed, yet said that Louis must have a profession to fall back on. The Law was decided on, and Louis proceeded to study this subject at the University. He did indeed read with success for the Scottish Bar, but made little attempt to practise. The Law interested him very nearly as little as Engineering.

The intimate relationship between all these conflicts, their many points of unity, cannot be over-emphasized. Weber's classic thesis has made us all familiar with the connection between Puritanism and worldly/economic success. Stevenson's rebellion against orthodox Christianity and his defiance of the values and life-styles of professional-class Edinburgh were really, from the psychological point of view, one and the same, the constricting philosophies being embodied in a single figure, his father. Even Scotland itself, whose past remained the very centre of his imaginative life, came to be seen by the youthful Stevenson as an oppressive father-correlative. Yet afterwards, in exile in the South Seas, he was to return, in his mind, obsessively, compulsively, to Scotland and in particular to those times of exhausting conflict:

> Do you remember – can we e'er forget? –
> How, in the coiled perplexities of youth,
> In our wild climate, in our scowling town,
> We gloomed and shivered, sorrowed, sobbed and feared?
> The belching winter wind, the missile rain,
> The rare and welcome silence of the snows,
> The laggard morn, the haggard day, the night,
> The grimy spell of the nocturnal town,
> Do you remember? – Ah, could one forget!
>
> As when the fevered sick that all night long
> Listed the wind intone, and hear at last
> The ever-welcome voice of chanticleer

Sing in the bitter hour before the dawn,
With sudden ardour, these desire the day:
So sang in the gloom of youth the bird of hope;
So we, exulting, hearkened and desired.
For lo! as in the palace porch of life
We huddled with chimeras, from within –
How sweet to hear! – the music swelled and fell,
And through the breach of the revolving doors
What dreams of splendour blinded us and fled!

I have since then contended and rejoiced;
Amid the glories of the house of life
Profoundly entered, and the shrine beheld:
Yet when the lamp from my expiring eyes
Shall dwindle and recede, the voice of love
Fall insignificant on my closing ears,
What sound shall come but the old cry of the wind
In our inclement city? what return
But the image of the emptiness of youth,
Filled with the sound of footsteps and that voice
Of discontent and rapture and despair?
So, as in darkness, from the magic lamp,
The momentary pictures gleam and fade
And perish, and the night resurges – these
Shall I remember, and then all forget.

It was in something of the spirit of this poem (written in 1890) that Stevenson created *Weir of Hermiston*.

The song 'the bird of hope' sang to Stevenson in his 'gloom of youth' was of an artist's life in which his emotional and sensual yearnings could be satisfied and his desire to devote his energies to his literary craft taken seriously. Artists constituted for him a palatable alternative society, and his twenties were consumed by attempts – fairly successful ones – to inhabit such a world. He took himself off for many months of several years to the artists' colonies of the Forest of Fontainebleau; '... it is not so much for its beauty that the forest makes a claim upon men's hearts, as for that subtle something, that quality of the air, that emanation from the old trees, that so wonderfully changes and renews a weary spirit ... You forget all your scruples and live a while in peace and freedom, and for the moment only. For here, all is absent that can stimulate to moral feeling.' And here he met an American divorcée, almost eleven years his senior, with whom he fell deeply in love, and whom against violent opposition from friends, and above all from his family, he pursued to the States. His journey to America, emigrant class, made irreparable his already very bad health; it led too to his being temporarily disinherited from his father and caused a major physical and psychological breakdown. News of this last led to forgiveness and to a financial generosity from Thomas Stevenson. Louis married Mrs Osbourne, mother of two surviving children, became a stepfather to her son, to whom he was already devoted, and returned to Scotland.

Before his breakdown, Stevenson wrote to the same friend to whom he had described the falling of the 'thunderbolt' after his announcement of religious apostasy:

... how for God's sake about my father? Tell me, please, Charles. Since I have gone away I have found out for the first time how much I love that man: he is dearer to me than all except F. [Mrs Osbourne]

Back in Britain, Stevenson was able openly to profess this love, a task made easier by the affection that swiftly grew up between his father and his wife, and, surely intimately bound up with this, was able as never before to acknowledge his own Scottishness and the importance of his native country to him. Had this return and reconciliation never taken place, we should never have had even the lighter, popular books, such as *Treasure Island* (1882), begun a year after he came back from America, in the Scottish Highlands. For psychologically he could not have survived without parental approval and affection; the intense emotional bonds, of love and hatred, with his father may have made rebellion and freedom almost imperative, but to survive in perpetual estrangement would have gone against his deepest-seated needs and impulses. The marriage, so curiously embarked on, turned out on the whole a happy one, and the security of the home Fanny made for him can be thanked for his being able to devote himself so whole-heartedly to his writing. But the balance and sanity of viewpoint that prevails in these writings, above all in *Weir of Hermiston*, we owe to the fact that he was received back into his family, that his conscience and affections were, as far as the present was concerned at any rate, gratified without his feeling he had surrendered any of his integrity. The pains of the past were, of course, another matter, and Louis took almost the whole of his tragically short life to confront them whole-sightedly in his fiction.

The tensions of Stevenson's life up to his thirtieth year were responsible for, I believe, four significant features of the work he was to produce from that time to his death in 1894.

First there is the manifest professionalism of his work. Though this can in part be attributed to a strong desire for a success which would vindicate him in the eyes of his parents, basically it stems from a belief, instilled in him from the earliest age, in the necessity of the patient perfecting of an inherited skill, in the value of care over detail and the taking of pains, in achievement being the result of loving yet unremitting hard work. This professionalism had both good and bad effects on Stevenson's writings. On the one hand, it produced an anxiety to secure markets, leading to the turning out of pot-boilers, to the pandering to a philistine public. On the other, it meant that his work, including many of his lightest productions, is distinguished by a wonderful artistry, which won him the admiration of, among others, Henry James. All Stevenson's novels from *Treasure Island* to *Weir* are carefully and beautifully constructed, and told in a graceful and yet highly economical style. And the most considerable of them were preceded by intensely hard preparation and documentation.

Secondly, there is the preoccupation with sin and guilt. His childhood as a 'religious pattern', his rebellious adolescence, left him with an obsession with what one can see in Miltonic terms as evil as the act of self-assertion or *non serviam*; we can certainly detect in his earlier work a fascination with the desire to carry out gratuitously wicked acts, a fascination which drove him to write, after a strange dream, his famous fable of man's duality : *Dr Jekyll and Mr Hyde* (1886). His hero finds himself unable to cope with his evil impulses, and discovering that a drug can enable him to become another person for periods of his time, decides to use this second body for the isolation of these impulses. Dr Jekyll describes in his confessions the sensations he experienced a few minutes after having become Hyde :

... within I was conscious of a heady recklessness, a current of disordered sensual images running like a mill-race in my fancy, a solution of the bonds of obligation, an unknown but not an innocent freedom of the soul. I knew myself, at the first breath of this new life, to be more wicked, tenfold more wicked, sold a slave to my original evil;

Jekyll's scheme goes wrong; he finds he cannot escape from the evil body, the evil turns against itself, and Hyde consequently destroys himself. So the fable suggests the essentially self-destructive nature of evil, an idea of course at the heart of orthodox Christianity.

Some modern criticism of Stevenson – for example Leslie Fieldler's essay in *No! in Thunder* – has tended to concentrate on these interests of Stevenson's, a concentration that seems to me mistaken, for those works in which he most relentlessly pursues them are lacking in density, are indeed little more than a working through of psychological tensions bequeathed by earlier experience. *Dr Jekyll and Mr Hyde* is interesting if we are thinking of Stevenson as a 'case'; in its own right, it is a somewhat thin work in which the author has all too often to fall back on the rhetoric of popular fiction for effect. Stevenson's most ambitious expression of this preoccupation was *The Master of Ballantrae* (1884); indeed, after this book it would appear, in overt form at any rate, to have burned itself out. The Master himself was intended to be 'all I know of the devil'. But he remains a character psychologically implausible, whose utterances are rarely other than theatrical and who seems cardboard beside the other superbly-rendered figures, such as his brother and the Grieve of Durisdeer. Certainly Stevenson was indeed brilliantly able to pursue and render dichotomies within a single personality but this only when he broke away from the simplistic notion of Dualism. In other words, his most incisive insights into the complexity of the human personality were achieved, when, still keenly aware of the existence of good and evil, he ceased to see the first force in charge of one set of actions, the second of another and opposing one, but saw them, confused and jostling, throughout the psyche.

Thirdly, there is his peculiar relationship to Scotland; all Stevenson's most valuable work is concerned with the Scottish past. If we read through his letters, we can come to realize that it was in analysing the culture and history of Scotland that his intellect was most fully exercised. The belles-lettres and romances he produced may have satisfied his desire to win fame but never the strongest demands of his mind. In 1881, with such well-known works as *Travels with a Donkey in the Cevennes*, *Virginibus Puerisque* and some of the stories of *New Arabian Nights* behind him, and a growing reputation before him, Stevenson put himself forward as a candidate for the professorship of History at Edinburgh University. Writing to Colvin (later editor of his works and letters) Stevenson said:

In short, sir, I mean to try for this chair. I do believe I can make something out of it. It will be a pulpit in a sense, for I am nothing if not moral, as you know. My works are unfortunately so light and trifling they may interfere ... it would be a good thing for me, out and out good. Help me to live, help me to work, for I am the better for pressure, and help me to say what I want about God, man and life.

These lines are most revealing. They suggest a dissatisfaction with his literary efforts, a feeling that they do not constitute true 'work', and that they prevent him from speaking his mind about three major subjects. Stevenson was not successful in his application; it was in his fiction that he was to carry out his most penetrating explorations of Scottish history. *Thrawn Janet*, included in this volume, is the result of extensive study of the phenomenon of witchcraft, the role of the Kirk, and the nature of Lowlands village life in the early eighteenth century. *Kidnapped* (1886) and *Catriona* (1893) began with Stevenson's interest in the Appin Murder and its historical significance. From this specific event he was led on to depict the tensions and political strains within Scotland in the years following the Forty-Five. And *Weir of Hermiston* originated in Stevenson's many-years-old fascination with the figure of Lord Braxfield. Fictionalizing him resulted, as we shall see, in the portrayal and analysis of many and diverse aspects of Scottish cultural life.

Finally, these years were responsible for the father–son conflict being a leading motif throughout Stevenson's work. Two nouvelles, *The Story of a Lie* (1880) and *The Misadventures of John Nicholson* (1887), have it as a central theme; the father plays a crucial role in *The Master of Ballantrae* and a father-figure is of considerable importance in *Catriona* (1893). But *Weir of Hermiston* is its apotheosis.

As I have said, a young man's struggle against his father is intimately bound up with his relationship to his society's *status quo* and it inevitably involves a search for a faith by which to live and for an acceptable social philosophy. His reaction against authority – as novels by authors other than Stevenson will bear out – leads to a complicated and often deeply ambiguous state of mind. For all that he feels he must work out for himself a personally satisfactory *Weltanschauung*, he remains forever bound to his elders because of the very intensity of his relation to them. Thus just as Archie in *Weir of Hermiston* discovers after his act of rebellion against his father how much he admires him, so in the actual writing of the novel Stevenson found himself describing with compassion and understanding, as well as with critical insight, those very cultural patterns and values he had earlier protested against. But ambiguity is of fiction's very essence, and without it *Weir* would not be the dense, rich novel it is.

Four short works have been chosen as literary postscripts to *Weir of Hermiston*.

Will o' the Mill first appeared in Leslie Stephen's periodical the *Cornhill* in January 1878 and reflects Stevenson's early admiration for Meredith in its setting, in its philosophy that life must be lived to the full, and even in its style, which is far less spare than was usual with him. It is, however, a poetic and artistically-wrought fable of the conflict in man's nature between his questing spirit and his desire for security. The tale has considerable bearing on Louis' emotional predicament in his late twenties. Will, the central figure, longs to leave his mountain home for the wide mysterious world of the plains, yet settles for a life of regularity and stability, justifying himself by a gentle sense of resignation and a quietist philosophy. Yet before he dies, an old man, he re-experiences – in a beautiful passage, one of the finest flowers of Stevenson's early art – all the troubling, exciting promptings and epiphanies of his youth. No man, Stevenson is saying, can escape confrontation with the mysterious forces behind life, no matter how hard he tries to protect himself. *Will o' the Mill* can be seen as Stevenson's defence of himself to burgher Edinburgh. Whatever his failures and inadequacies, he must have felt, at least he had made a bold attempt to explore the heights and depths of life as, secretly, every human being longs to do. And the story reflects too Stevenson's concern with the passing of time, something his perpetual ill-health must have made him abnormally aware of.

Thrawn Janet, one of Stevenson's most famous short stories, was written in the Highlands in 1881, one year after his return from America. It was his first Scottish tale, and provides therefore the first indication of his extraordinary ability to render the Scottish past in fictional terms. It also is the first manifestation of his lively sense of the terror latent in life and, too, of his almost uncanny narrative skill. Indeed these last two attributes have perhaps worked a little against it; too often has it been regarded as a mere 'horror-story'.

The story indeed demands fuller discussion than *Will o' the Mill*, among other reasons because appreciation of it requires some knowledge of Scottish history (relevant historical information is provided in the Notes). Of this weakness, Stevenson, who was proud of the tale, was aware, for he wrote in an introductory note:

Thrawn Janet has two defects; it is true only historically, true for a hill-parish in Scotland in the old days, not true for mankind and the world.

Stevenson is being, I think, a little hard on himself here; the story does have universality of application. But we can see from the above-quoted lines that Stevenson too did not regard *Thrawn Janet* as a mere horror-story. It must be admitted, however, that he intended it as the first part of the title-story of a volume of what he called 'crawlers': *The Black Man and Other Stories*. The second part, 'The Devil on Cramond Sands', has been lost. The name of this title-story is important. A black man, as Stevenson himself points out in a footnote in *Thrawn Janet*, was the most frequent form in which the devil manifested himself to Scottish witches, a fact which can be verified from other sources. In *Thrawn Janet* we read of the presumed devil: 'He was of a great stature, an' black as hell, and his e'en were singular to see. Mr Soulis had heard tell o' black men, mony's the time; but there was something unco' about this black man that daunted him.' Stevenson, therefore, absorbed as he was in Scottish folklore, takes this centuries-old belief about the devil as his creative starting-point. The way in which the tale is told is all-important to his purpose; first we have a passage describing the personality of the Minister of Balweary in his later days and presenting his curious relationship to the parish and then comes the explanation for these, the sinister episode of Jenet McClour, related by 'one of the older folk'. The speaker's anonymity and the Scottish dialect stress the fact that we are being offered a piece of folk-history. The narrator believes his tale, fantastic though it seems, to be true. The horror *Thrawn Janet* possesses springs above all from the credulity, superstition and devil-obsession of his mind.

The story is given a specific setting in time as well as place. The climax occurs 'the nicht o' the seeventeenth o' August, seeventeen hun'er' an' twal', at the tail-end of the period (beginning roughly 1560) of intense persecution of witches in Scotland, a persecution implemented by the mass hysteria and communal sadism excited by the rhetoric of obsessed preachers. Knowing as we do Stevenson's own sufferings under the yoke of Calvinism, we can perhaps see the more clearly his detestation of the villagers' irrationally vindictive behaviour towards Janet. Her dottiness is the result of protracted isolation owing to her shady past: she has had a child by a passing dragoon. The lines describing the cruel treatment meted out to her transcend in their compassion the specific predicament in question, and make us think of the plight of all outcasts branded by popular ideology-backed hysteria:

... at the hinder end, the guidwives up an' claught haud of her, an' clawed the coats aff her back, and pu'd her doun the clachan to the water o' Dule, to see if she were a witch or no, soom or droun. The carline skirled till ye could hear her at the Hangin' Shaw, an' she focht like ten; there was mony a guidwife bure the mark o' her neist day an' mony a lang day after; an' just in the hettest o' the collieshangie, wha suld come up (for his sins) but the new minister.

'Women,' said he (an' he had a grand voice), 'I charge you in the Lord's name to let her go.'

Janet ran to him – she was fair wud wi' terror – an' clang to him, an' prayed him, for Christ's sake, save her frae the cummers; an' they, for their pairt, tauld him a' that was ken't, an' maybe mair.

'Woman,' says he to Janet, 'is this true?'

'As the Lord sees me,' says she, 'as the Lord made me, no' a word o't. Forbye the bairn,' says she, 'I've been a decent woman a' my days.'

We can gain further (and important) insight into Stevenson's vision of Janet if we look at her appearance in his late and unfinished work: *Heathercat*. Set, like *Thrawn Janet* and *Weir of Hermiston*, in the fictitious Lowlands Parish of Balweary, it takes place during the 'Killing-Time', those terrible last days of the Covenanters – the 1680s. We catch here a glimpse of Janet

26

McClour in her girlhood – gay, friendly, amoral, animal, superstitious and eccentric, and the object of the clergyman's amorous
attentions. We read of the Curate that he :

... went on with his little, brisk steps to the corner of a dyke, and
stopped and whistled and waved upon a lassie that was herding
cattle there. This Janet M'Clour was a big lass, being taller than
the curate; and what made her look the more so, she was kilted
very high. It seemed for a whole she would not come, and Francie
heard her calling Haddo [the Curate] a 'daft auld fule,' and saw
her running and dodging him among the whins and hags until he
was fairly blown. But at the last he gets a bottle from his plaid-
neuk and holds it up to her; whereupon she came at once into a
composition, and the pair sat, drinking of the bottle, and daffing and
laughing together, on a mound of heather. The boy had scarce heard
of these vanities, or he might have been minded of a nymph and a
satyr, if anybody could have taken long-leggit Janet for a nymph.
But they seemed to be huge friends, he thought; and was the more
surprised, when the curate had taken his leave, to see the lassie
fling stones after him with screeches of laughter, and Haddo turn
about and caper, and shake his staff at her, and laugh louder than
herself. A wonderful merry pair they seemed.

The tragic years of ostracism by the community that must
have passed between this time in Janet's life, and that described
in *Thrawn Janet* itself, we can imagine for ourselves.

And what of the other central character in the story, the
Minister? The tale would appear to be told in order to explain
Mr Soulis's present lonely, haunted state. Stevenson speaks in
the introductory note of Mr Soulis's 'conversation', and of a
certain ambiguity which he felt was present in the story as to
the merits or desirability of this. *Thrawn Janet* is set 'before
the days of the Moderates', that is, before the relaxation of
certain of its more intransigent practices and emphases took
place within the Church of Scotland. The young Mr Soulis,
then, is something of a Moderate before his time, and for this
reason despised by his flock as a 'callant', 'fu' o' book-learnin'
an' grand at the exposition, but ... wi' nae leevin' experience
in religion'. He and his like would have done 'mair an' better
sittin' in a peat-bog, like their forbears of the persecution, wi'

a Bible under their oxter an' a speerit of prayer in their heart'. Unlike the other villagers he treats Janet kindly, and it is he who, in common with many other Scottish ministers of the time, and earlier, performs the (authentic) exorcism of the devil from Janet, which is to have so terrible a result. It seems likely from the knowledge we have of the adult Stevenson's dislike of the Covenanting faith that he would sympathize with the Minister as he is in his youth. His development from ardent scholarly young man into the 'severe, bleak-faced old man, dreadful to his hearers', who lives 'without relative or servant or any human company', and whose 'eye was wild, scared and uncertain', would seem to be wholly tragic. Yet the young minister is called 'self-deceived' by his elders in his parish, and events would appear to vindicate their judgement. The phenomenon of witchcraft and its persecution constitutes one of the most extraordinary and terrifying features of seventeenth- and early eighteenth-century Europe, and can, of course, be paralleled by various activities of other times, including our own. Is not Stevenson, then, suggesting in his story the inadequacy of young Mr Soulis's vision of life that leads him to disregard the psychic inner destruction of Janet? It is of little importance what metaphysical vocabulary one uses; recognition of the possibility of a human being's succumbing to forces of irrational evil must be made. This Mr Soulis in his early years of ministry does not do. This aspect of the story does indeed take us in our minds far beyond a Scottish hill-parish in 1712.

The Misadventures of John Nicholson (1887) is an unjustly neglected work, which has been out of print for many years. It is Stevenson's only story set in the Scotland of his own lifetime. It also comes the closest of all his works to a direct treatment of the prolonged strained relationship between Thomas and Louis Stevenson; indeed, Mr Nicholson is far nearer to a portrait of Thomas than is the father of *Weir of Hermiston*. Not that this story has *Weir*'s emotional power, but it does show Stevenson making an attempt to face up to elements in his own life; it even includes the hero's guilty flight to America, his disinherited sojourn there, and his return and ultimate reconciliation.

The first two paragraphs of this nouvelle describe respectively the son, John Nicholson, and the father, David. Mr Nicholson has much in common with Thomas Stevenson: religious zealotry, rigid attachment to professional-class values, and that brand of emotionalism that masks as anti-emotionalism and principally exercises itself on the suppression of the tenderer or less socially acceptable feelings, as well as on the conversion of self-denial into a positive rather than a negative virtue. The context of Mr Nicholson's attitudes, that of the Church of Scotland, is made very clear:

About the period when the Churches convene at Edinburgh in their annual assemblies, he was to be seen descending the Mound in the company of divers red-headed clergymen: these voluble, he only contributing oracular nods, brief negatives, and the austere spectacle of his stretched upper lip ... A stranger to the tight little theological kingdom of Scotland might have listened and gathered literally nothing. And Mr Nicholson (who was not a dull man) knew this, and raged at it. He knew there was a vast world outside, to whom the Disruption Principles were as the chatter of tree-top apes ... it was an evil, wild rebellious world, lying sunk in *dozenedness*, for nothing short of a Scot's word will paint this Scotsman's feelings. And when he entered his own house in Randolph Crescent (south side) and shut the door behind him, his heart swelled with security ... Here was a family where prayers came at the same hour, where the Sabbath literature was unimpeachably selected, where the guest who should have leaned to any false opinion was instantly set down, and over which there reigned all week, and grew denser on Sundays, a silence that was agreeable to his ear, and a gloom that he found comfortable.

The last phrase is surely a perceptive and telling one. It suggests that rigid protestantism, such as Mr Nicholson's and Thomas Stevenson's, is so often a form of hugged cosiness – its virtues are those that encourage and support economic success and worldly position; it results in a fear of disruption of any kind, whether from within or without, and leads the devotee into self-congratulation, intolerance and self-suppression. Moreover, by attaching such paramount importance to such qualities as industry, restraint, carefulness, etc., it leads to a refusal to consider, let alone accept, an individual for what he is. Mr Nicholson cannot see beyond John's stupidity and laziness to his real and lovable personality.

In the midst of these [the family], imagine that natural, clumsy, unintelligent and mirthful animal, John; mighty well-behaved in comparison with other lads, although not up to the mark of the house in Randolph Crescent; full of a sort of blundering affection, full of caresses which were never very warmly received; full of sudden and loud laughter which rang out in that still house like curses. Mr Nicholson himself had a great fund of humour, of the Scots order – intellectual, turning on the observation of men; his own character, for instance – if he could have seen it in another – would have been a rare feast to him; but his son's empty guffaws over a broken plate, and empty, almost light-hearted remarks, struck him with pain as the indices of a weak mind.

The Puritan father ignores or seeks to put down a boy's whole complex of instinctive reactions and emotions. When the boy becomes a young man, the problems resulting from such wilful blindness and repression are greatly increased. John has little in common with Louis Stevenson, but I think that in this short work we come the nearest we ever do in his fiction to an aspect of the conflict, undoubtedly there but not mentioned in those letters collected by Sidney Colvin: Thomas Stevenson's moral harshness towards Louis' early sexual development. How much Thomas Stevenson knew about Louis' visits to the Leith and Lothian Streets of Edinburgh, whether in fact these amounted to all that much, what action he actually took over 'Claire', these are interesting subjects for conjecture. But we can be sure that the disagreements between father and son must have received fuel from differences over sexual morality, and John Nicholson's innocent sensualities – his visits to Collette's, for example – though not specifically sexual – seem to represent this source of dissension. The inability of Puritanism to accept the need of the evolving personality to explore different experiences is well portrayed in Mr Nicholson's conduct. What is even more strongly castigated in this nouvelle, though, is the way in which an adamant, metaphysically-backed morality leads to a hardening of the heart. Mr Nicholson finds it near-impossible to forgive. Tenderer emotions have for so long taken inferior place to adherence to a severe moral law that he finds it exceedingly hard to yield to them. His forgiving of John is a long time coming and not, I might add, particularly convincing when it does. This is because Mr Nicholson is an accurately-sketched rather than a fully-drawn character. The father and son in the story are, of course, nothing like as complex personalities as Thomas and Louis Stevenson; moreover, the story contains no differences on intellectual matters, which were of such supreme importance in the original case, one of the *données* of the story being that John is stupid. We must also remember that *The Misadventures of John Nicholson* was conceived as a Christmas tale; it is powerful almost in spite of itself rather than by intention. The central relationship is, however, an interesting one, and the background of professional-class Edinburgh superbly rendered.

The wonderful *The House of Eld* (posthumously published 1896), one of a series of fables which Stevenson, immersed in Polynesian folklore, wrote in Samoa, scarcely needs comment, so economic and incisive is it, so powerful an address to the depths of the imagination does it form. It performs, indeed, the function of the greatest folk-tale, conveying by a sparely-narrated logical sequence of events a universal truth about man's nature. It also sheds light on the psychological and intellectual progress of Stevenson's life, that which culminated in the writing of *Weir of Hermiston*. In succinct and allegorical form it states the case that one can never wholly escape the creeds taught one in childhood. Calvinism may have seemed a hideous and repressive thing, but would not any of the later faiths Stevenson was drawn to – Bohemianism, Socialism, Tolstoyanism – have ultimately proved equally restricting to the human spirit? The fable suggests too that relationships with parents, striven against though they may have to be, endure always, and that no rebellion that maims those who have given one life can altogether be justified. This is surely the meaning of the haunting poem with which the story ends:

> Old is the tree and the fruit good,
> Very old and thick the wood.
> Woodman, is your courage stout?
> Beware! the root is wrapped about
> Your mother's heart, your father's bones;
> And like the mandrake comes with groans.

It is the presence of the 'mother's heart', the 'father's bones' that gives *Weir of Hermiston* its power, gives it too the universal charity which a great novel always displays.

Weir of Hermiston brings together Stevenson's creative strengths and confronts, in fully-assimilated fictional form, all the significant experiences of his early life. The plot is dominated, indeed determined, by the father–son conflict. We see the younger man seeking a kinder, richer philosophy than his father's – or his father's society's – and how, though loving him, he defies him, is punished by him, and goes into exile. The novel's setting is first Edinburgh, then the Lowlands countryside, both landscapes of the greatest personal importance to Stevenson. The hero's love-affair parallels Stevenson's romantic, physical involvement with 'Claire', and includes in its progress a renunciation on the grounds of expediency.

Weir of Hermiston contains therefore emotional matter of such a nature that Stevenson's sustained unremitting seriousness was ensured. We find in the novel the interest in man's questing quality, in the search for an acceptable *Weltanschauung* that was present in *Will o' the Mill* and *The House of Eld*. We find too the fascination with the divided personality that is so recurring a feature of the Stevenson *oeuvre*. We have revealed as never before that knowledge and feeling for the Scottish cultural past which so distinguished *Thrawn Janet*, *Kidnapped* and *Catriona*. And *Weir of Hermiston* is a testimony, too, to Stevenson's belief in the transfiguring nature of artistic form. A disciplined control is exercised over the diverse material. Unfinished though it is, the novel triumphs partly through its beauty of form.

Stevenson first saw *Weir of Hermiston* as a novel about Robert MacQueen, Lord Braxfield (1722–99), whose strange and terrifying figure had haunted him ever since his adolescence. Braxfield – like so many eminent Scots of his day – had had his portrait painted by the great Scottish artist, Raeburn. This can be seen today in the Scottish National Portrait Gallery in Edinburgh. Stevenson had long been familiar with the picture, and in *Virginibus Puerisque* (1881), in an essay on Raeburn's work, he spoke of the impact it had had on his sensibility and of Braxfield's own almost legendary personality. 'He has left behind him', he wrote, 'a reputation for rough and cruel speech; and to this day his name smacks of the gallows.' Nevertheless, the portrait did not depict a complete monster. Stevenson noted a 'tart, rosy, humorous look'; he thought the nose resembled a cudgel, and he observed that 'a peculiarly subtle expression haunts the lower part of his face, sensual and incredulous, like that of a man tasting good Bordeaux with half a fancy it has been somewhat too long uncorked'.

But the main source for his knowledge of Braxfield was Lord Cockburn's *Memorial of His Time* (published 1856). Stevenson re-read this book while writing *Weir of Hermiston*. What Cockburn has to say about Braxfield is therefore of relevance to our appreciation of Stevenson's novel:

But the giant of the bench was Braxfield. His very name makes people start yet. Strong built and dark, with rough eyebrows, powerful eyes, threatening lips, and a low growling voice, he was like a formidable blacksmith. His accent and dialect were exaggerated Scotch; his language, like his thoughts, short, strong, and conclusive.

... within the range of feudal and the civil branches [of jurisprudence], and in every matter depending on natural ability and practical sense, he was very great; and his power arose more from the force of his reasoning and his vigorous application of principle, than from either the extent or the accuracy of his learning ...

With this intellectual force, as applied to law, his merits, I fear, cease. Illiterate and without any taste for refined enjoyment, strength of understanding, which gave him power without cultivation, only encouraged him to a more contemptuous disdain of all natures less coarse than his own. Despising the growing improvement of manners, he shocked the feelings even of an age which, with more of the formality, had far less of the substance of decorum than our own. Thousands of his sayings have been preserved, and the staple of them is indecency; which he succeeded in making many people enjoy, or at least endure, by hearty laughter, energy of manner, and rough humour ...

It is impossible to condemn his conduct as a criminal judge too gravely, or too severely. It was a disgrace to the age. A dexterous and practical trier of ordinary cases, he was harsh to prisoners even in his jocularity, and to every counsel whom he chose to dislike ... It may be doubted if he was ever so much in his element as when tauntingly repelling the last despairing claim of a wretched culprit, and sending him to Botany Bay or the gallows with an insulting jest; over which he would chuckle the more from observing that correct people were shocked. Yet this was not from cruelty, for which he was too strong and too jovial, but from cherished coarseness.

This union of talent with a passion for rude predomination, exercised in a very discretionary court, tended to form a formidable and dangerous judicial character. This appeared too often in ordinary cases: but all stains on his administration of the common business of his court disappear in the indelible iniquity of the political trials of 1793 and 1794. In these he was the Jeffreys of Scotland. He, as the head of the Court, and the only very powerful man it contained, was the real director of its proceedings. The reports make his abuse of the judgment seat bad enough; but his misconduct was not so fully disclosed in formal decisions and charges, as it transpired in casual remarks and general manner.

Braxfield was the subject of many anecdotes with which Stevenson – who, it must be remembered, had himself read for the Scottish Bar – would have been familiar. When a defendant charged with radical sedition justified himself by saying that all great men have been great reformers of one kind or another, 'even our Saviour himself', Braxfield's reply was: 'Muckle he made o' that, he was hanget.' Another prisoner was told by him: 'Ye're a verra clever chiel, man, but ye wad be nane the waur o' a hanging.' At the same time he has been recognized as a man of enormous capability, indeed of dedication, and it must always be borne in mind that Lord Cockburn's was a biased Whiggish account of the Judge. With the more favourable stories of his intelligence and integrity Stevenson would also be familiar.

Stevenson brings Braxfield to fictional life as my Lord Hermiston very vividly, by a hundred small strokes. His rude sarcasm, his pure dedication to the almost abstract study of Law, his coarse conversation when deep in his cups, his quickness of mind, his contempt for culture and its professors ('He had a word of contempt for the whole crowd of poets, painters, fiddlers, and their admirers, the bastard race of amateurs, which was continually on his lips. "Signor Feedle-eerie!" he would say. "Oh, for Goad's sake, no more of the Signor!"'), his faltering attempts at gentler intercourse with his fellow-men, his frightening public personality – all are brought before us. Perhaps the scene which impresses itself most upon our imaginations is his trying of Duncan Jopp. We watch him in the courtroom levelling jibes and cruel expostulations at the pathetic mean wretch of a criminal and his down-at-heel mistress. His behaviour is a great shock to his son who has entered the court to witness procedure, and later Archie tells his father:

I was present while Jopp was tried. It was a hideous business. Father, it was a hideous thing! Grant he was vile, why should you hunt him with a vileness equal to his own? It was done with glee – that is the word – you did it with glee, and I looked on. God help me! with horror.

We share Archie's horror, and yet later on in the novel, when Lord Glenalmond refers to Lord Hermiston's behaviour as 'Perhaps not a pleasant spectacle. And yet, do you know, I think somehow a great one', we can – if reluctantly – agree with him. His son admits that he is something 'very big' – his is a complex personality which cannot be adequately disposed of by trite judgements. (The impossibility indeed of accurate judgement of another human being is one of the dominant ideas of *Weir of Hermiston*.) Lord Glenalmond criticizing Archie for his censure of his father and half-defending the latter for his treatment of Jopp, says:

... There was a word of yours just now that impressed me a little when you asked me who we were to know all the springs of God's unfortunate creatures. You applied that, as I understood, to capital cases only. But does it – I ask myself – does it not apply all through? Is it any less difficult to judge of a good man or of a half-good man, than of the worst criminal at the bar? And may not each have relevant excuses?

We do not step inside Hermiston's mind; we see him for the greater part through the eyes of his son, for it is with his tensions and ambiguities of attitude that we are really concerned. As has already been said, this relationship owes its fictional force to Louis' with Thomas. Braxfield/Hermiston may seem a long way from Thomas Stevenson, but a closer examination can narrow the gap. Lord Braxfield/Hermiston is an extremely successful man in the world's eyes – so was Thomas Stevenson. Success naturally leads to an acceptance of the *status quo*. Thomas Stevenson was a 'strong Conservative, or as he preferred to call it, a Tory'. Lord Braxfield was a famous anti-Radical, and his most notorious case was that of Thomas Muir in 1793. (This is actually ascribed to Hermiston in the novel.) Muir, a Glasgow lawyer, had been virtual leader of a middle-class radical group, the Friends of the People. The members of this fraternity were followers of Tom Paine (1737–1809), whose *Rights of Man* had appeared in 1791; they were influenced by the French Revolution, called for reform of suffrage and property distribution. Lord Braxfield had this to say about Muir's relationship with the French:

I never liked the French all my days, but now I hate them ... A Government in any country should be like a corporation; and in this country it is made up of the landed interest which alone has a right to be represented. As for the rabble who have nothing but personal property, what hold has the nation of them? They may pack up their property on their backs and leave the country in the twinkling of an eye.

When, in the novel, the Lord Hermiston finds out about Archie's public denunciation of the execution he himself has commanded, he accuses his son of French-style radicalism:

'Father, let me go to the Peninsula,' said Archie. 'That's all I'm fit for – to fight.'

'All? quo' he!' returned the Judge. 'And it would be enough too, if I thought it. But I'll never trust ye so near the French, you that's so Frenchifeed.'

'You do me injustice there, sir,' said Archie. 'I am loyal; I will not boast; but any interest I may have ever felt in the French –'

'Have ye been so loyal to me?' interrupted his father.

And before the denunciation we are told of Archie:

Seductive Jacobin figments ... swam up in his mind and startled him as with voices; and he seemed to himself to walk accompanied by an almost tangible presence of new beliefs and duties.

Political difference is the equivalent in *Weir of Hermiston* of the religious difference of the Stevensons. Both Archie and Louis reacted against their fathers for holding philosophies that seemed to them intolerant, repressive, uncompassionate. Both Adam Weir and Thomas Stevenson believed their sons to be committed to subversive ideas that, if followed through, would lead to a disruption of society, an abandonment of standards that could at the very least be termed efficacious.

We can see a further connection between *Weir of Hermiston* and Stevenson's own early life if we see capital punishment as represented in the hanging of Duncan Jopp and Archie's revulsion against it as metaphors for Calvinism and Louis' reaction against that. The cruelty of the hanging, its finality, the fact that the sentence authorizing it takes note of only one particular in a man's character and career, its denial of any opportunities to reform, its approval by the greater part of society, its endorsement of the *status quo*, its keeping of order by fear, all unite to make it an excellent symbol of a rigid life-denying faith. And when Archie calls out in disgust: 'I defy this God-defying murder', we are made to wonder whether so stern a faith as Calvinism does not also defy God by murdering the charity and compassion which the founder of Christianity commanded. The thought is again brought into our minds when we read Lord Hermiston's scornful questioning of Archie about what profession he would be suited for; in this speech we can surely hear echoes of the dissensions of the Stevenson family:

What do ye fancy ye'll be fit for? The pulpit? Na, they could never get diveenity into that bloackhead. Him that the law of man whammles is no' likely to do muckle better by the law of God. What would ye make of hell? Wouldna your gorge rise at that? Na, there's no room for splairgers under the fower quarters of John Calvin.

So often, in father–son disputes, it would seem, from literature and from life, the older man finds the younger lacking in what he thinks of as masculinity, while the son is appalled by the father's absence of tenderness. Neither vision is really justified, for the father, product of an earlier society, has been taught to repress tenderer emotions, while the very courage the son displays in standing up to him testifies to his being a true heir of traditional male values: enterprise, strength of mind, pride and a lack of concern with comfort.

Lord Hermiston underrates these qualities in his son, but Archie is equally unfair to his father. He doubts that he feels any love towards him. From Dr Gregory, an actual famous physician of the period, Archie learns how wrong he is:

'When you had the measles, Mr Archibald, you had them gey and ill; and I thought you were going to slip between my fingers,' he said. 'Well, your father was anxious. How did I know it? says you. Simply because I am a trained observer. The sign that I saw him make ten thousand would have missed; and perhaps – *perhaps*, I say, because he's a hard man to judge of – but perhaps he never made another. A strange thing to consider! It was this. One day I came to him: "Hermiston," said I, "there's a change." He never said a word, just glowered at me (if ye'll pardon the phrase) like a wild beast. "A change for the better," said I. And I distinctly heard him take his breath.'

We, on the other hand, are not so surprised at this revelation, for we have been told by Stevenson of the Judge's diffident attempts at a less austere relationship:

As time went on, the tough and rough old sinner felt himself drawn to the son of his loins and sole continuator of his new family, with softnesses of sentiment that he could hardly credit and was wholly impotent to express. With a face, voice, and manner trained through forty years to terrify and repel, Rhadamanthus may be great, but he will scarce be engaging. It is a fact that he tried to propitiate Archie, but a fact that cannot be too lightly taken; the attempt was so unconspicuously made, the failure so stoically supported.

Inside Archie himself there is a dichotomy between the stern and the tender. Stevenson sees this as the result of his being the product of a marriage between two very different people. The legacy of two such strongly divergent personalities has rendered Archie a youth apart. 'It should seem he must become the centre of a crowd of friends; but something that was in part the delicacy of his mother, in part the austerity of his father, held him aloof from all.' We have seen the kind of man Archie's father is; his mother is all gentle emotional piety and tenderness. The upbringing she gives her son influences him greatly:

There is a corner of the policy of Hermiston, where you come suddenly in view of the summit of Black Fell, sometimes like the mere grass top of a hill, sometimes (and this is her own expression) like a precious jewel in the heavens. On such days, upon the sudden view of it, her hand would tighten on the child's fingers, her voice rise like a song. 'I to the hills!' she would repeat. 'And O, Erchie, arena these like the hills of Naphtali?' and her easy tears would flow.

Upon an impressionable child the effect of this continual and pretty accompaniment to life was deep. The woman's quietism and piety passed on to his different nature undiminished; but whereas in her it was a native sentiment, in him it was only an implanted dogma.

Exactly so! Archie's philosophy of life is a gentle one, full of a compassion inherited from his mother, but it is held with an intransigence derived from his father. This aspect of Archie's nature, unbeknown to him, has been commented on by his school – and university – companions. 'It is a fact, and a strange one, that among his contemporaries Hermiston's son was thought to be a chip of the old block.' It is this element inside him that causes him to make the original denunciation and, after exile in the country, to steel himself to a life of independence and solitude in which he can work out for himself his true beliefs and feelings.

Archie, like the hero of a German *Bildungsroman*, a genus Stevenson admired, is educated by love. It is his experiences in this domain that lead him to a richer, fuller philosophy and viewpoint. The scenes between Archie and Kirstie are intensely moving, and the novel shows Archie developing from a somewhat austere Puritan youth towards true manhood, in which he will not deny the full life of the psyche and the body, their dictates, their yearnings :

His heart perhaps beat in time to some vast in-dwelling rhythm of the universe. By the time he came to a corner of the valley and could see the kirk, he had so lingered by the way that the first psalm was finishing. The nasal psalmody, full of turns and trills and graceless graces, seemed the essential voice of the kirk itself upraised in thanksgiving. 'Everything's alive,' he said; and again cries it aloud, 'Thank God, everything's alive!' ...

He went up the aisle reverently, and took his place in the pew with lowered eyes ... He could not follow the prayer, not even the heads of it. Brightness of azure, clouds of fragrance, a tinkle of falling water and singing birds, rose like exhalations from some deeper, aboriginal memory, that was not his, but belonged to the flesh on his bones. His body remembered; and it seemed to him that his body was in no way gross, but ethereal and perishable like a strain of music; and he felt for it an exquisite tenderness as for a child, an innocent, full of beautiful instincts and destined to an early death.

This passage is characterized by a yea-saying attitude to life learnt from Meredith, and which we have noted in *Will o' the Mill*. But just as Stevenson was intellectually a child of his

time, so Archie is of his. Sidney Colvin in his editorial note
wonders why Stevenson set his story in the year preceding
Waterloo. There seem to me to be very good reasons for this.
We can work out from the book that Archie was born in 1795.
He thus grew up in the first generation that was familiar with
the ideas of Rousseau and the French Revolution, just as we
have seen that Stevenson belonged to the first post-Darwin
generation. During Archie's nineteen years of life he would
be aware of the career of Napoleon, the philosophy of Goethe,
the world of the Romantic poets. Archie's feelings are utterly
consistent with those of a young man who has read Wordsworth, Scott and Byron in the days when their poetry was a
fresh element in human experience. Indeed the two latter
writers are mentioned in the text. There is, Stevenson seems to
be implying, a similarity between Archie Weir's generation and
his own, post-Darwinian one. Both sought freedom from the
bondage of a society conditioned by a sterile philosophy. Had
Stevenson finished the novel, we know it would have contained
a scene in which Archie was liberated from prison by force. We
think therefore of the storming of the Bastille, of Byron and
the Château de Chillon, and above all of the superb scene of
the storming of the Tolbooth in Scott's *Heart of Midlothian*
(1818). Forced entry into prison has obvious but nonetheless
powerful symbolic significance.

Through his exile in Hermiston, Archie discovers more about
Scottish life and history than he has ever known before. By
becoming Laird of Hermiston he becomes part of the Scottish
scene. This parallels Stevenson's own – later – discovery of
Scotland, of how truly Scottish he was. Archie's association
with the Elliott brothers links him to Border history, his
attendance at Torrance's Church to the country kirk, and his
falling in love with Kirstie, instinct-driven fusion of urban and
rural Scotland, can stand for a renewal of love for his own
country in all its complexity (cf. David Balfour's love for
Catriona). Indeed, the characters and scenes of *Weir of Hermiston* form a paradigm of Scottish history and culture.

Let us begin with the relationship between my Lord Hermiston and his wife. Though Adam Weir is representative of the ambitious, thrusting, self-made Scot, his actual style of living is almost patrician. He has married into an old-established Border family, the Rutherfords of Hermiston, thus showing his fundamental belief in rank and privilege. The contrast between himself and his wife is an acute one – in depicting this, Stevenson drew upon the relationships between his great-grandmother and her second husband and between his grandfather and grandmother. (The interested reader is referred to *Records of a Family of Engineers*.) Both couples followed the same pattern, the women gentle and pious, half-fearful, half-admiring of the – to them – worldly males. The men, Stevenson writes, were:

conscious, like all Scots, of the fragility and unreality of that scene in which we play our uncomprehended parts; like all Scots, realising daily and hourly the sense of another will than ours and a perpetual direction in the affairs of life. But the current of their endeavours flowed in a more obvious channel. They had got on so far; to get on further was their next ambition – to gather wealth, to rise in society ...

How closely Stevenson followed his forebears' lives can be seen in the anecdote of Lord Hermiston complaining about his wife's food; this is based on a family incident. For, absorbed in piety as she is, Mrs Weir is incapable of organizing a household, incapable indeed of really facing up to the harsh realities and responsibilities of life. Stevenson suggests in the first chapter that the relationship between the Judge and his wife could easily be paralleled in other Scottish couples of their time, and class. We can remember here the opening pages of Hogg's *Confessions of a Justified Sinner* (published 1834, but set at the end of the seventeenth century). Lady Dalcastle cannot face the disagreeable actuality of her husband's sexual demands, nor the administrative position of the lady of the household. She retreats into a life of piety strongly coloured by fanaticism under the direction of a clergyman, Mr Wringhim. Her father sides with her husband. Mrs Weir is a far more sympathetic figure, her rhapsodic faith is described movingly as is the whole texture of her life and the nature of her death. But Stevenson makes it clear that her religion is only just saved from fanaticism by the tenderness of her personality, that it prevails because her life lacks any other kind of stimuli, and that it constitutes a turning-away from life. 'She was a true enthusiast,' Stevenson says of her, using the word in its more literal eighteenth-century sense, 'and would have made the sunshine and glory of a cloister.'

Through Mrs Weir we enter, of course, one of the main arteries of Scottish tradition – that of the Covenanters – and here we can see put into literary form Stevenson's relationship to Cummy and her faith. Mrs Weir repeats Cummy's practice of regaling the small boy with tales of the Covenanters' bravery and divine election:

> It was a common practice of hers ... that she would carry the child to the Deil's Hags, sit with him on the Praying Weaver's stone and talk to the Covenanters till their tears ran down. Her view of history was wholly artless, a design in snow and ink; upon the one side, tender innocents with psalms upon their lips; upon the other the persecutors, booted, bloody-minded, flushed with wine: a suffering Christ, a raging Beelzebub.

The memory of the Covenanters is a perpetual exemplar to Mrs Weir – and to her son too. His defiance of the execution of Duncan Jopp is of a piece with the last stands of the Covenanters. The Covenanters haunt the novel in other ways also. Archie is to kill Frank by the Weaver's Stone and thus incur the death penalty; it was by this stone that Claverhouse – Bonnie Dundee, persecutor-in-chief of the Covenanters – personally killed a devout good man, the Praying Weaver. Frank and Archie have Claverhouse and the Weaver respectively behind them. One of the Four Black Brothers, Gib, is the head of a sect, God's Remnant, who preserve the faith of the defeated Cameronians/Covenanters as a protest against the moderatism of the eighteenth-century Scottish Kirk: '"I've had a great gale of prayer upon my speerit," said he, "I cannot mind sae muckle's what I had for denner."' Yet his seemingly gentle habits conceal a fierceness that has once manifested itself and is to do so again later.

Returning to Archie's father, we note that the Lord Justice-Clerk is also my Lord of Hermiston and that when Archie cannot, because of the denunciation, become a lawyer he is sent to be a laird. There was the closest connection in the last part of the eighteenth century between lawyers and the country gentry. Most lawyers bought themselves estates in the south of Scotland or the Lothians if they were successful – and they were welcomed rather than shunned by the ordinary landowners, who were glad for marital connections to be made between legal and landowning families (see Adam Weir's marriage into the Rutherfords). Weir himself, so full of contempt for so many people, has nothing but respect for a laird; it is a position he, and later Archie himself, take very seriously, and we must remember that the gentry and larger-scale farmers (such as Hob Elliott, the eldest of the Four Black Brothers) in late eighteenth-century Scotland were very progressive-minded, applying the so-called 'English' methods long before their general adoption in the country of origin. Archie's move out of Edinburgh was not into a wilderness but into an important economic and cultural area of his country. But of course the move has symbolic connotations as well, for the profession of law which Archie has deserted stands more than any other for the high mark of urban culture Scotland attained in the late eighteenth century. Ever since the Age of Stair (begun with the publication of the *Institutions* in 1681), lawyers played a dominant role in Scottish life and were of all professions perhaps the most revered and learned. Their contribution to the cultural life of Edinburgh's Golden Age was enormous, they set the tone of the New Town. Lord Glenalmond in *Weir of Hermiston* is an example of the refinement of a distinguished Edinburgh lawyer. And it was in the second half of the eighteenth century that the debating club, the Speculative Society, of which both Archie and Louis Stevenson were such enthusiastic members and which was so excellent a training-ground for lawyers, was allowed its own room in the University. Thus Archie is leaving a very sophisticated culture for a more elemental one in which he can discover more about himself and the well-springs of life.

The Four Black Brothers also contribute to the paradigm of Scottish culture. Hob is the serious farmer, his wife being materially-minded and socially ambitious. Gib is not only the torch-bearer for the Covenanting tradition but also a weaver, and weavers in the 1790s were among the keenest radicals in Scotland. We are told that Gib had been a supporter of the French Revolution, and Lord Hermiston himself refers to Radicalism as 'weaver's poalitics'. Weavers were also notorious sectarians in religion and so Gib's character and views are utterly consistent with his profession. Of the other brothers, Dand is a shepherd, a poet, a wild man with the girls and with drink. He represents an older more primitive Border society such as largely died after the 1707 Union. His going from farm to farm entertaining company with his songs and flirting with the women might seem then a survival from an earlier age. But he is a figure of his time too:

Walter Scott owed to Dandie the text of the 'Raid of Wearie' in the *Minstrelsy* and made him welcome at his house, and appreciated his talents, such as they were, with all his usual generosity. The Ettrick Shepherd [James Hogg] was his sworn crony; they would meet, drink to excess, roar out their lyrics in each other's faces, and quarrel and make it up again till bedtime.

The remaining brother, Clem, looks forward to the newer Scotland. He is a Glasgow entrepreneur. Glasgow was a rapidly-expanding town during the period in which the novel is set, and consequently a source of increasing wealth. It grew from a place of only 23,000 people in 1755 to a city of over 77,000 in 1801. Clem could have bought out his brother, the Laird, 'six times over', he is a worldly man 'with no more religion than Claverhouse'. His sister Kirstie, who lives with him, has the pertness, the confidence and the semi-sophistication of a city-girl combined with the wilder passionate impulses of one of her own Border ancestors.

I have dwelt on this sociological aspect of *Weir of Hermiston* because I wish to stress the solid foundation on which this work of great emotional force and brooding tragic power stands. This side of Stevenson's achievement has never been stressed enough. In *Weir of Hermiston* he shows himself a master of significant representative detail the cumulative effect of which presents us with a portrait-in-depth of a society. To this we must add the distinctive tone of the novel. It is one of complete authority, suggesting the careful compassionate weighing of considerations and knowledge concerning the people of the book: it is in other words the tone of a fair judge. Stevenson's legal training was to bear fine fruit after all. And yet we are always left with the feeling that the characters escape full summary, full judgement. There is something mysterious, unknowable about all of them.

For it is in the presentation of the characters as autonomous beings, as creatures whose existence is utterly independent of their creator's, and who are at the same time viewed as being in the grip of destiny that the true greatness of Stevenson's last novel is revealed. I would like to draw the reader's particular attention to the characters of Frank Innes and the older Kirstie.

Frank is the agent of Archie's downfall and his most significant speeches and deeds are informed by a malignant jealousy. Yet the reader feels a certain charm emanate from him and feels too (a rare feat in fiction) the effect of his particular brand of good looks. It comes as no surprise either that the otherwise fastidious Archie could have him as a friend or that the younger Kirstie will fall victim to his seductive powers. 'It was his practice', we read of him, 'to approach any one person at the expense of some one else. He offered you an alliance against the some one else; he flattered you by slighting him; you were drawn into a small intrigue against him before you knew how.' The reader will have met in the course of his life a number of people who are in varying degrees guilty of this unpleasant social habit. Stevenson's ability in his delineation of Frank is to see beyond the social to the spiritual, to reveal how the trait is a symptom of a sickness of the soul which brings pain both to others and to the person himself. Stevenson's tracing of the course of Frank's treacherous behaviour towards Archie and Kirstie is masterly, because it does not omit exposure of the real weaknesses of the more sympathetic characters, weaknesses to which Frank is able to apply his talents. And we see these actions of his both as they must have appeared to Frank himself, so largely ignorant of his own nasty motives, and how they should look to an impartial yet never coldly-detached observer of the human scene.

The older Kirstie is another triumph of analysis combined with sympathy – fundamentally passionate, frustrated in her life, clear-headed in her management of her affairs yet self-deceived and not above a certain servitude to envy, but withal warm-hearted. Stevenson tells us that 'she carried her thwarted ardours into housework, she washed floors with her empty heart. If she could not win the love of one with love, she must dominate all by her temper'. Hence her strained relations with her neighbours and kinfolk. But when Archie comes to live at Hermiston, she finds, to use Stevenson's beautiful and penetrating phrase, 'in the Indian summer of her heart', an adequate object for her emotional nature:

Her passion, for it was nothing less, entirely filled her. It was a rich physical pleasure to make his bed or light his lamp for him when he was absent, to pull off his wet boots or wait on him at dinner when he returned. A young man who should have so doted on the idea, moral and physical, of any woman, might be properly described as being in love, head and heels, and would have behaved himself accordingly. But Kirstie – though her heart leaped at his coming footsteps – though, when he patted her shoulder, her face brightened for the day – had not a hope or thought beyond the present moment and its perpetuation to the end of time. Till the end of time she would have had nothing altered, but still continue delightedly to serve her idol, and be repaid (say twice in the month) with a clap on the shoulder.

Flesh and blood people as Stevenson's creations seem, brought to life by so many touches of observation and empathy, we also see them *sub specie aeternitatis*, forming patterns of be-

47

haviour and self-perpetuating relationships, acting on drives and impulses and having, too often unwittingly, to face the consequences of these, caught up in events that seem truly inevitable. We feel while reading *Weir* that we are witnessing the gradual unfolding of history, just as we do when we read *War and Peace* or *Vanity Fair*.

And yet, even after having said this, one has not perhaps cited what makes the novel a great one. For like *War and Peace*, *Weir* also moves us. Mrs Weir's death, Duncan Jopp's behaviour when on trial, Archie's interview with his father after his act of rebellion, his evening talk with Lord Glenalmond, Kirstie's nocturnal visit to Archie's room, the younger Kirstie's distress at what she takes for Archie's sudden coolness towards her – after many readings, these scenes – and others – touch our hearts and seem to become part of our own experience while reminding us of the complexities and diversities of human beings and of their need for love.

Though Stevenson died after writing the ninth chapter, we know what he intended to happen from notes that he left. This – as recounted by Stevenson's executor, Sidney Colvin – is appended to this volume. Stevenson himself wondered whether he could keep up the inspired quality of what he had written. Others have wondered the same. Whether he could have done so seems to me pointless to speculate. *Weir of Hermiston* though literally incomplete is complete in spirit and is one of the most persistently overlooked first-rate novels in our language.

NOTE ON THE TEXT

WEIR OF HERMISTON: first published posthumously by Chatto and Windus (1896)

WILL O' THE MILL: first published in the *Cornhill Magazine* in January 1878. First published in book form in *The Merry Men and Other Tales* (1887)

THRAWN JANET: first published in the *Cornhill Magazine* in October 1881. First published in book form in *The Merry Men and Other Tales* (1887)

THE MISADVENTURES OF JOHN NICHOLSON: first published in *Yule-Tide*, Cassell's Christmas Annual (1887). First published in book form in the *Collected Works* (1894–8)

THE HOUSE OF ELD: uncertain date of composition. Stevenson wrote a series of fables between 1887–8 and then added to their number when in Samoa. *The House of Eld* was appended with other fables to the volume containing *Dr Jekyll and Mr Hyde* in the *Collected Works* (1894–8)

Text follows that of *Collected Works* (1894–8) edited by Sir Sidney Colvin, Stevenson's literary executor.

WEIR OF HERMISTON

TO MY WIFE

I saw rain falling and the rainbow drawn
On Lammermuir. Hearkening I heard again
In my precipitous city beaten bells. And here afar,
Intent on my own race and place, I wrote.
    Take thou the writing: thine it is. For who
Burnished the sword, blew on the drowsy coal,
Held still the target higher, chary of praise
And prodigal of counsel – who but thou?
So now, in the end, if this the least be good,
If any deed be done, if any fire
Burn in the imperfect page, the praise be thine.

INTRODUCTORY

In the wild end of a moorland parish, far out of the sight of any house, there stands a cairn among the heather, and a little by east of it, in the going down of the braeside, a monument with some verses half defaced. It was here that Claverhouse shot with his own hand the Praying Weaver of Balweary, and the chisel of Old Mortality has clinked on that lonely grave-stone. Public and domestic history have thus marked with a bloody finger this hollow among the hills; and since the Cameronian gave his life there, two hundred years ago, in a glorious folly, and without comprehension or regret, the silence of the moss has been broken once again by the report of fire-arms and the cry of the dying.[1]

The Deil's Hags was the old name. But the place is now called Francie's Cairn. For a while it was told that Francie walked.[2] Aggie Hogg met him in the gloaming by the cairnside, and he spoke to her, with chattering teeth, so that his words were lost. He pursued Rob Todd (if any one could have believed Robbie) for the space of half a mile with pitiful entreaties. But the age is one of incredulity; these superstitious decorations speedily fell off; and the facts of the story itself, like the bones of a giant buried there and half dug up, survived, naked and imperfect, in the memory of the scattered neighbours. To this day, of winter nights, when the sleet is on the window and the cattle are quiet in the byre, there will be told again, amid the silence of the young and the additions and corrections of the old, the tale of the Justice-Clerk and of his son, young Hermiston, that vanished from men's knowledge; of the Two Kirsties and the Four Black Brothers of the Cauldstaneslap; and of Frank Innes, 'the young fool advocate,' that came into these moorland parts to find his destiny.

CHAPTER I

LIFE AND DEATH OF MRS WEIR

THE Lord Justice-Clerk[1] was a stranger in that part of the country; but his lady wife was known there from a child, as her race had been before her. The old 'riding Rutherfords of Hermiston,' of whom she was the last descendant, had been famous men of yore, ill neighbours, ill subjects, and ill husbands to their wives though not their properties. Tales of them were rife for twenty miles about; and their name was even printed in the page of our Scots histories, not always to their credit. One bit the dust at Flodden; one was hanged at his peel door by James the Fifth; another fell dead in a carouse with Tom Dalyell; while a fourth (and that was Jean's own father) died presiding at a Hell-Fire Club, of which he was the founder.[2] There were many heads shaken in Crossmichael at that judgment; the more so as the man had a villainous reputation among high and low, and both with the godly and the worldly. At that very hour of his demise, he had ten going pleas before the session, eight of them oppressive. And the same doom extended even to his agents; his grieve, that had been his right hand in many a left-hand business, being cast from his horse one night and drowned in a peat-hag on the Kye-skairs; and his very doer (although lawyers have long spoons) surviving him not long, and dying on a sudden in a bloody flux.

In all these generations, while a male Rutherford was in the saddle with his lads, or brawling in a change-house, there would be always a white-faced wife immured at home in the old peel or the later mansion-house. It seemed this succession of martyrs bided long, but took their vengeance in the end, and that was in the person of the last descendant, Jean. She bore the name of the Rutherfords, but she was the daughter of their trembling

wives. At the first she was not wholly without charm. Neighbours recalled in her, as a child, a strain of elfin wilfulness,
gentle little mutinies, sad little gaieties, even a morning gleam
of beauty that was not to be fulfilled. She withered in the growing, and (whether it was the sins of her sires or the sorrows of
her mothers) came to her maturity depressed, and, as it were,
defaced; no blood of life in her, no grasp or gaiety; pious,
anxious, tender, tearful, and incompetent.

It was a wonder to many that she had married – seeming
so wholly of the stuff that makes old maids. But chance cast
her in the path of Adam Weir, then the new Lord Advocate,[3]
a recognised, risen man, the conqueror of many obstacles, and
thus late in the day beginning to think upon a wife. He was one
who looked rather to obedience than beauty, yet it would seem
he was struck with her at the first look. 'Wha's she?' he said,
turning to his host; and, when he had been told, 'Ay,' says he,
'she looks menseful. She minds me –'; and then, after a pause
(which some have been daring enough to set down to senti-
mental recollections), 'Is she releegious?' he asked, and was
shortly after, at his own request, presented. The acquaintance,
which it seems profane to call a courtship, was pursued with
Mr Weir's accustomed industry, and was long a legend, or
rather a source of legends, in the Parliament House. He was
described coming, rosy with much port, into the drawing-room,
walking direct up to the lady, and assailing her with pleasantries,
to which the embarrassed fair one responded, in what seemed
a kind of agony, 'Eh, Mr Weir!' or 'O, Mr Weir!' or 'Keep me,
Mr Weir!' On the very eve of their engagement it was related
that one had drawn near to the tender couple, and had over-
heard the lady cry out, with the tones of one who talked for the
sake of talking, 'Keep me, Mr Weir, and what became of him?'
and the profound accents of the suitor's reply, 'Haangit, mem,
haangit.' The motives upon either side were much debated. Mr
Weir must have supposed his bride to be somehow suitable;
perhaps he belonged to that class of men who think a weak
head the ornament of women – an opinion invariably punished
in this life. Her descent and her estate were beyond question.

Her wayfaring ancestors and her litigious father had done well by Jean. There was ready money and there were broad acres, ready to fall wholly to the husband, to lend dignity to his descendants, and to himself a title, when he should be called upon the Bench. On the side of Jean, there was perhaps some fascination of curiosity as to this unknown male animal that approached her with the roughness of a ploughman and the *aplomb* of an advocate. Being so trenchantly opposed to all she knew, loved, or understood, he may well have seemed to her the extreme, if scarcely the ideal, of his sex. And besides, he was an ill man to refuse. A little over forty at the period of his marriage, he looked already older, and to the force of manhood added the senatorial dignity of years; it was, perhaps, with an unreverend awe, but he was awful. The Bench, the Bar, and the most experienced and reluctant witness, bowed to his authority – and why not Jeannie Rutherford?

The heresy about foolish women is always punished, I have said, and Lord Hermiston began to pay the penalty at once. His house in George Square was wretchedly ill-guided; nothing answerable to the expense of maintenance but the cellar, which was his own private care. When things went wrong at dinner, as they continually did, my lord would look up the table at his wife: 'I think these broth would be better to sweem in than to sup.' Or else to the butler: 'Here, M'Killop, awa' wi' this Raadical gigot – tak' it to the French, man, and bring me some puddocks! It seems rather a sore kind of business that I should be all day in Court haanging Raadicals, and get nawthing to my denner.' Of course this was but a manner of speaking, and he had never hanged a man for being a Radical in his life; the law, of which he was the faithful minister, directing otherwise. And of course these growls were in the nature of pleasantry, but it was of a recondite sort; and uttered as they were in his resounding voice, and commented on by that expression which they called in the Parliament House 'Hermiston's hanging face' – they struck mere dismay into the wife. She sat before him speechless and fluttering; at each dish, as at a fresh ordeal, her eye hovered toward my lord's countenance and fell again;

if he ate in silence, unspeakable relief was her portion; if there were complaint, the world was darkened. She would seek out the cook, who was always her *sister in the Lord*. 'O my dear, this is the most dreidful thing that my lord can never be contented in his own house!' she would begin; and weep and pray with the cook; and then the cook would pray with Mrs Weir; and the next day's meal would never be a penny the better – and the next cook (when she came) would be worse, if anything, but just as pious. It was often wondered that Lord Hermiston bore it as he did; indeed he was a stoical old voluptuary, contented with sound wine and plenty of it. But there were moments when he overflowed. Perhaps half a dozen times in the history of his married life – 'Here! tak' it awa', and bring me a piece of bread and kebbuck!' he had exclaimed, with an appalling explosion of his voice and rare gestures. None thought to dispute or to make excuses; the service was arrested; Mrs Weir sat at the head of the table whimpering without disguise; and his lordship opposite munched his bread and cheese in ostentatious disregard. Once only Mrs Weir had ventured to appeal. He was passing her chair on his way into the study.

'O, Edom!' she wailed, in a voice tragic with tears, and reaching out to him both hands, in one of which she held a sopping pocket-handkerchief.

He paused and looked upon her with a face of wrath, into which there stole, as he looked, a twinkle of humour.

'Noansense!' he said. 'You and your noansense! What do I want with a Christian faim'ly? I want Christian broth! Get me a lass that can plain-boil a potato, if she was a whüre off the streets.' And with these words, which echoed in her tender ears like blasphemy, he had passed on to his study and shut the door behind him.

Such was the housewifery in George Square. It was better at Hermiston, where Kirstie Elliot, the sister of a neighbouring bonnet-laird, and an eighteenth cousin of the lady's, bore the charge of all, and kept a trim house and a good country table. Kirstie was a woman in a thousand, clean, capable, notable;

once a moorland Helen, and still comely as a blood horse and
healthy as the hill wind. High in flesh and voice and colour, she
ran the house with her whole intemperate soul, in a bustle, not
without buffets. Scarce more pious than decency in those days
required, she was the cause of many an anxious thought and
many a tearful prayer to Mrs Weir. Housekeeper and mistress
renewed the parts of Martha and Mary; and though with a
pricking conscience Mary reposed on Martha's strength as on a
rock. Even Lord Hermiston held Kirstie in a particular regard.
There were few with whom he unbent so gladly, few whom
he favoured with so many pleasantries. 'Kirstie and me maun
have our joke,' he would declare, in high good-humour, as he
buttered Kirstie's scones and she waited at table. A man who
had no need either of love or of popularity, a keen reader of
men and of events, there was perhaps only one truth for which
he was quite unprepared: he would have been quite unprepared to learn that Kirstie hated him. He thought maid and
master were well matched; hard, handy, healthy, broad Scots
folk, without a hair of nonsense to the pair of them. And the
fact was that she made a goddess and an only child of the effete
and tearful lady and even as she waited at table her hands would
sometimes itch for my lord's ears.

Thus, at least, when the family were at Hermiston, not only
my lord, but Mrs Weir too, enjoyed a holiday. Free from the
dreadful looking-for of the miscarried dinner, she would mind
her seam, read her piety books, and take her walk (which was
my lord's orders), sometimes by herself, sometimes with Archie,
the only child of that scarce natural union. The child was her
next bond to life. Her frosted sentiment bloomed again, she
breathed deep of life, she let loose her heart, in that society. The
miracle of her motherhood was ever new to her. The sight of the
little man at her skirt intoxicated her with the sense of power,
and froze her with the consciousness of her responsibility. She
looked forward, and, seeing him in fancy grow up and play
his diverse part on the world's theatre, caught in her breath and
lifted up her courage with a lively effort. It was only with the
child that she forgot herself and was at moments natural; yet

it was only with the child that she had conceived and managed to pursue a scheme of conduct. Archie was to be a great man and a good; a minister if possible, a saint for certain. She tried to engage his mind upon her favourite books, Rutherford's 'Letters,' Scougal's 'Grace Abounding,' and the like.[4] It was a common practice of hers (and strange to remember now) that she would carry the child to the Deil's Hags, sit with him on the Praying Weaver's stone and talk of the Covenanters till their tears ran down. Her view of history was wholly artless a design in snow and ink; upon the one side, tender innocents with psalms upon their lips; upon the other the persecutors, booted, bloody-minded, flushed with wine: a suffering Christ, a raging Beelzebub. *Persecutor* was a word that knocked upon the woman's heart; it was her highest thought of wickedness, and the mark of it was on her house. Her great-great-grandfather had drawn the sword against the Lord's anointed on the field of Rullion Green, and breathed his last (tradition said) in the arms of the detestable Dalyell. Nor could she blind herself to this, that had they lived in those old days, Hermiston himself would have been numbered alongside of Bloody Mackenzie and the politic Lauderdale and Rothes, in the band of God's immediate enemies.[5] The sense of this moved her to the more fervour; she had a voice for that name of *persecutor* that thrilled in the child's marrow; and when one day the mob hooted and hissed them all in my lord's travelling carriage, and cried, 'Down with the persecutor! down with Hanging Hermiston!' and mamma covered her eyes and wept, and papa let down the glass and looked out upon the rabble with his droll formidable face, bitter and smiling, as they said he sometimes looked when he gave sentence, Archie was for the moment too much amazed to be alarmed, but he had scarce got his mother by herself before his shrill voice was raised demanding an explanation: Why had they called papa a persecutor?

'Keep me, my precious!' she exclaimed. 'Keep me, my dear! this is poleetical. Ye must never ask me anything poleetical, Erchie. Your faither is a great man, my dear, and it's no for me or you to be judging him. It would be telling us all, if we behaved ourselves in our several stations the way your faither does in his high office; and let me hear no more of any such disrespectful and undutiful questions! No that you meant to be undutiful, my lamb; your mother kens that – she kens it well, dearie!' and so slid off to safer topics, and left on the mind of the child an obscure but ineradicable sense of something wrong.

Mrs Weir's philosophy of life was summed in one expression – tenderness. In her view of the universe, which was all lighted up with a glow out of the doors of hell, good people must walk there in a kind of ecstasy of tenderness. The beasts and plants had no souls; they were here but for a day, and let their day pass gently! And as for the immortal men, on what black, downward path were many of them wending, and to what a horror of an immortality! 'Are not two sparrows,' 'Whosoever shall smite thee,' 'God sendeth His rain,' 'Judge not that ye be not judged' – these texts made her body of divinity; she put them on in the morning with her clothes and lay down to sleep with them at night; they haunted her like a favourite air, they clung about her like a favourite perfume. Their minister was a marrowy expounder of the law, and my lord sat under him with relish; but Mrs Weir respected him from afar off; heard him (like the cannon of a beleaguered city) usefully booming outside on the dogmatic ramparts; and meanwhile, within and out of shot, dwelt in her private garden, which she watered with grateful tears. It seems strange to say of this colourless and ineffectual woman, but she was a true enthusiast, and might have made the sunshine and the glory of a cloister. Perhaps none but Archie knew she could be eloquent; perhaps none but he had seen her – her colour raised, her hands clasped or quivering – glow with gentle ardour. There is a corner of the policy of Hermiston, where you come suddenly in view of the summit of Black Fell, sometimes like the mere grass top of a hill, sometimes (and this is her own expression) like a precious jewel in the heavens. On such days, upon the sudden view of it, her hand would tighten on the child's fingers, her voice rise like a song. 'I to the hills!' she would repeat. 'And O, Erchie, arena these like the hills of Naphtali?' and her easy tears would flow.[6]

Upon an impressionable child the effect of this continual and pretty accompaniment to life was deep. The woman's quietism and piety passed on to his different nature undiminished; but whereas in her it was a native sentiment, in him it was only an implanted dogma. Nature and the child's pugnacity at times revolted. A cad from the Potterrow once struck him in the mouth; he struck back, the pair fought it out in the back stable lane towards the Meadows, and Archie returned with a considerable decline in the number of his front teeth, and unregenerately boasting of the losses of the foe. It was a sore day for Mrs Weir; she wept and prayed over the infant backslider until my lord was due from Court, and she must resume that air of tremulous composure with which she always greeted him. The judge was that day in an observant mood, and remarked upon the absent teeth.

'I am afraid Erchie will have been fechting with some of they blagyard lads,' said Mrs Weir.

My lord's voice rang out as it did seldom in the privacy of his own house. 'I'll have nonn of that, sir!' he cried. 'Do you hear me? – nonn of that! No son of mine shall be speldering in the glaur with any dirty raibble.'

The anxious mother was grateful for so much support; she had even feared the contrary. And that night when she put the child to bed – 'Now, my dear, ye see!' she said, 'I told you what your faither would think of it, if he heard ye had fallen into this dreidful sin; and let you and me pray to God that ye may be keepit from the like temptation or stren'thened to resist it!'

The womanly falsity of this was thrown away. Ice and iron cannot be welded; and the points of view of the Justice-Clerk and Mrs Weir were not less unassimilable. The character and position of his father had long been a stumbling-block to Archie, and with every year of his age the difficulty grew more instant. The man was mostly silent; when he spoke at all, it was to speak of the things of the world, always in a worldly spirit, often in language that the child had been schooled to think coarse, and sometimes with words that he knew to be sins in themselves. Tenderness was the first duty, and my lord was invariably harsh. God was love; the name of my lord (to all who knew him) was fear. In the world, as schematised for Archie by his mother, the place was marked for such a creature. There were some whom it was good to pity and well (though very likely useless) to pray for; they were named reprobates, goats, God's enemies, brands for the burning; and Archie tallied every mark of identification, and drew the inevitable private inference that the Lord Justice-Clerk was the chief of sinners.

The mother's honesty was scarce complete. There was one influence she feared for the child and still secretly combated; that was my lord's; and half unconsciously, half in a wilful blindness, she continued to undermine her husband with his son. As long as Archie remained silent, she did so ruthlessly, with a single eye to heaven and the child's salvation; but the day came when Archie spoke. It was 1801, and Archie was seven, and beyond his years for curiosity and logic, when he brought the case up openly. If judging were sinful and forbidden, how came papa to be a judge? to have that sin for a trade? to bear the name of it for a distinction?

'I can't see it,' said the little Rabbi, and wagged his head.

Mrs Weir abounded in commonplace replies.

'No, I canna see it,' reiterated Archie. 'And I'll tell you what, mamma, I don't think you and me's justifeed in staying with him.'

The woman awoke to remorse; she saw herself disloyal to her man, her sovereign and bread-winner, in whom (with what she had of worldliness) she took a certain subdued pride. She expatiated in reply on my lord's honour and greatness; his useful services in this world of sorrow and wrong, and the place in which he stood, far above where babes and innocents could hope to see or criticise. But she had builded too well – Archie had his answers pat: Were not babes and innocents the type of the kingdom of heaven? Were not honour and greatness the badges of the world? And at any rate, how about the mob that had once seethed about the carriage?

'It's all very fine,' he concluded, 'but in my opinion, papa has no right to be it. And it seems that's not the worst yet of it. It seems he's called "the Hanging Judge" – it seems he's crooool. I'll tell you what it is, mamma, there's a tex' borne in upon me: It were better for that man if a mile-stone were bound upon his back and him flung into the deepestmost pairts of the sea.'

'O my lamb, ye must never say the like of that!' she cried. 'Ye're to honour faither and mother, dear, that your days may be long in the land. It's Atheists that cry out against him – French Atheists, Erchie![7] Ye would never surely even your-self down to be saying the same thing as French Atheists? It would break my heart to think that of you. And O, Erchie, here arena *you* setting up to *judge*? And have ye no' forgot God's plain command – the First with Promise, dear? Mind you upon the beam and the mote!'

Having thus carried the war into the enemy's camp, the terrified lady breathed again. And no doubt it is easy thus to circumvent a child with catchwords, but it may be questioned how far it is effectual. An instinct in his breast detects the quibble, and a voice condemns it. He will instantly submit, privately hold the same opinion. For even in this simple and antique relation of the mother and the child, hypocrisies are multiplied.

When the Court rose that year and the family returned to Hermiston, it was a common remark in all the country that the lady was sore failed. She seemed to lose and seize again her touch with life, now sitting inert in a sort of durable bewilder-ment, anon waking to feverish and weak activity. She dawdled about the lasses at their work, looking stupidly on; she fell to rummaging in old cabinets and presses, and desisted when half through; she would begin remarks with an air of animation and drop them without a struggle. Her common appearance was of one who has forgotten something and is trying to re-member; and when she overhauled, one after another, the worthless and touching mementoes of her youth, she might have been seeking the clue to that lost thought. During this period she gave many gifts to the neighbours and house lassies, giving them with a manner of regret that embarrassed the recipients.

The last night of all she was busy on some female work, and toiled upon it with so manifest and painful a devotion that my lord (who was not often curious) inquired as to its nature.

She blushed to the eyes. 'O, Edom, it's for you!' she said. 'It's slippers. I – I hae never made ye any.'

'Ye daft auld wife!' returned his lordship. 'A bonny figure I would be, palmering about in bauchles!'

The next day, at the hour of her walk, Kirstie interfered. Kirstie took this decay of her mistress very hard; bore her a grudge, quarrelled with and railed upon her, the anxiety of a genuine love wearing the disguise of temper. This day of all days she insisted disrespectfully, with rustic fury, that Mrs Weir should stay at home. But, 'No, no,' she said, 'it's my lord's orders,' and set forth as usual. Archie was visible in the acre bog, engaged upon some childish enterprise, the instrument of which was mire; and she stood and looked at him a while like one about to call; then thought otherwise, sighed, and shook her head, and proceeded on her rounds alone. The house lasses were at the burnside washing, and saw her pass with her loose, weary, dowdy gait.

'She's a terrible feckless wife, the mistress!' said the one.

'Tut,' said the other, 'the wumman's seeck.'

'Weel, I canna see nae differ in her,' returned the first. 'A füshionless quean, a feckless carline.'

The poor creature thus discussed rambled a while in the grounds without a purpose. Tides in her mind ebbed and flowed, and carried her to and fro like seaweed. She tried a path, paused, returned, and tried another; questing, forgetting her quest; the spirit of choice extinct in her bosom, or devoid of sequency. On a sudden, it appeared as though she had remembered, or had formed a resolution, wheeled about, returned with hurried steps, and appeared in the dining-room, where Kirstie was at the cleaning, like one charged with an important errand.

'Kirstie!' she began, and paused; and then with conviction, 'Mr Weir isna speeritually minded, but he has been a good man to me.'

It was perhaps the first time since her husband's elevation that she had forgotten the handle to his name, of which the tender, inconsistent woman was not a little proud. And when Kirstie looked up at the speaker's face, she was aware of a change.

'Godsake, what's the maitter wi' ye, mem?' cried the housekeeper, starting from the rug.

'I do not ken,' answered her mistress, shaking her head. 'But he is not speeritually minded, my dear.'

'Here, sit down with ye! Godsake, what ails the wife?' cried Kirstie, and helped and forced her into my lord's own chair by the cheek of the hearth.

'Keep me, what's this?' she gasped. 'Kirstie, what's this? I'm frich'ened.'

They were her last words.

It was the lowering nightfall when my lord returned. He had the sunset in his back, all clouds and glory; and before him, by the wayside, spied Kirstie Elliott waiting. She was dissolved in tears, and addressed him in the high, false note of barbarous mourning, such as still lingers modified among Scots heather.

'The Lord peety ye, Hermiston! the Lord prepare ye!' she keened out. 'Weary upon me, that I should have to tell it!'

He reined in his horse and looked upon her with the hanging face.

'Has the French landit?' cried he.

'Man, man,' she said, 'is that a' ye can think of? The Lord prepare ye, the Lord comfort and support ye!'

'Is onybody deid?' says his lordship. 'It's no Erchie?'

'Bethankit, no!' exclaimed the woman, startled into a more natural tone. 'Na, na, it's no sae bad as that. It's the mistress,

my lord; she just fair flittit before my e'en. She just gi'ed a
sab and was by wi' it. Eh, my bonny Miss Jeannie, that I mind
sae weel!' And forth again upon that pouring tide of lamentation in which women of her class excel and over-abound.

Lord Hermiston sat in the saddle, beholding her. Then he
seemed to recover command upon himself.

'Weel, it's something of the suddenest,' said he. 'But she was
a dwaibly body from the first.'

And he rode home at a precipitate amble with Kirstie at his
horse's heels.

Dressed as she was for her last walk, they had laid the dead
lady on her bed. She was never interesting in life; in death she
was not impressive; and as her husband stood before her, with
his hands crossed behind his powerful back, that which he
looked upon was the very image of the insignificant.

'Her and me were never cut out for one another,' he remarked
at last. 'It was a daft-like marriage.' And then, with a most
unusual gentleness of tone, 'Puir bitch,' said he, 'puir bitch!'
Then suddenly: 'Where's Erchie?'

Kirstie had decoyed him to her room and given him 'a jeely-
piece.'

'Ye have some kind of gumption, too,' observed the Judge,
and considered his housekeeper grimly. 'When all's said,' he
added, 'I micht have done waur – I micht have been marriet
upon a skirling Jezebel like you!'

'There's naebody thinking of you, Hermiston!' cried the
offended woman. 'We think of her that's out of her sorrows.
And could *she* have done waur? Tell me that, Hermiston –
tell me that before her clay-cauld corp!'

'Weel, there's some of them gey an' ill to please,' observed
his lordship.

CHAPTER II

FATHER AND SON

MY Lord Justice-Clerk was known to many; the man Adam
Weir perhaps to none. He had nothing to explain or to conceal; he sufficed wholly and silently to himself; and that part of
our nature which goes out (too often with false coin) to acquire
glory or love, seemed in him to be omitted. He did not try to be
loved, he did not care to be; it is probable the very thought
of it was a stranger to his mind. He was an admired lawyer,
a highly unpopular judge; and he looked down upon those
who were his inferiors in either distinction, who were lawyers
of less grasp or judges not so much detested. In all the rest of
his days and doings, not one trace of vanity appeared; and he
went on through life with a mechanical movement, as of the
unconscious, that was almost august.

He saw little of his son. In the childish maladies with which
the boy was troubled, he would make daily inquiries and
daily pay him a visit, entering the sick-room with a facetious
and appalling countenance, letting off a few perfunctory jests,
and going again swiftly, to the patient's relief. Once, a Court
holiday falling opportunely, my lord had his carriage, and
drove the child himself to Hermiston, the customary place of
convalescence. It is conceivable he had been more than usually
anxious, for that journey always remained in Archie's memory
as a thing apart, his father having related to him from beginning to end, and with much detail, three authentic murder
cases. Archie went the usual round of other Edinburgh boys,
the high school and the college; and Hermiston looked on, or
rather looked away, with scarce an affectation of interest in
his progress. Daily, indeed, upon a signal after dinner, he was

brought in, given nuts and a glass of port, regarded sardonically, sarcastically questioned. 'Well, sir, and what have you donn with your book to-day?' my lord might begin, and set him posers in law Latin. To a child just stumbling into Corderius, Papinian and Paul[1] proved quite invincible. But papa had memory of no other. He was not harsh to the little scholar, having a vast fund of patience learned upon the bench, and was at no pains whether to conceal or to express his disappointment. 'Well, ye have a long jaunt before ye yet!' he might observe, yawning, and fall back on his own thoughts (as like as not) until the time came for separation, and my lord would take the decanter and the glass, and be off to the back chamber looking on the Meadows, where he toiled on his cases till the hours were small. There was no 'fuller man' on the Bench; his memory was marvellous, though wholly legal; if he had to 'advise' extempore, none did it better; yet there was none who more earnestly prepared. As he thus watched in the night, or sat at table and forgot the presence of his son, no doubt but he tasted deeply of recondite pleasures. To be wholly devoted to some intellectual exercise is to have succeeded in life; and perhaps only in law and the higher mathematics may this devotion be maintained, suffice to itself without reaction, and find continual rewards without excitement. This atmosphere of his father's sterling industry was the best of Archie's education. Assuredly it did not attract him; assuredly it rather rebutted and depressed. Yet it was still present, unobserved like the ticking of a clock, an arid ideal, a tasteless stimulant in the boy's life.

But Hermiston was not all of one piece. He was, besides, a mighty toper; he could sit at wine until the day dawned, and pass directly from the table to the Bench with a steady hand and a clear head. Beyond the third bottle, he showed the plebeian in a larger print; the low, gross accent, the low, foul mirth, grew broader and commoner; he became less formidable, and infinitely more disgusting. Now, the boy had inherited from Jean Rutherford a shivering delicacy, unequally mated with potential violence. In the playing-fields, and amongst his own companions, he repaid a coarse expression with a blow; at his father's table (when the time came for him to join these revels) he turned pale and sickened in silence. Of all the guests whom he there encountered, he had toleration for only one: David Keith Carnegie, Lord Glenalmond. Lord Glenalmond was tall and emaciated, with long features and long delicate hands. He was often compared with the statue of Forbes of Culloden[2] in the Parliament House; and his blue eye, at more than sixty, preserved some of the fire of youth. His exquisite disparity with any of his fellow-guests, his appearance as of an artist and an aristocrat stranded in rude company, riveted the boy's attention; and as curiosity and interest are the things in the world that are the most immediately and certainly rewarded, Lord Glenalmond was attracted to the boy.

'And so this is your son, Hermiston?' he asked, laying his hand on Archie's shoulder. 'He's getting a big lad.'

'Hout!' said the gracious father, 'just his mother over again – daurna say boo to a goose!'

But the stranger retained the boy, talked to him, drew him out, found in him a taste for letters, and a fine, ardent, modest, youthful soul; and encouraged him to be a visitor on Sunday evenings in his bare, cold, lonely dining-room, where he sat and read in the isolation of a bachelor grown old in refinement. The beautiful gentleness and grace of the old Judge, and the delicacy of his person, thoughts, and language, spoke to Archie's heart in its own tongue. He conceived the ambition to be such another; and, when the day came for him to choose a profession, it was in emulation of Lord Glenalmond, not of Lord Hermiston, that he chose the Bar. Hermiston looked on at this friendship with some secret pride, but openly with the intolerance of scorn. He scarce lost an opportunity to put them down with a rough jape; and, to say truth, it was not difficult, for they were neither of them quick. He had a word of contempt for the whole crowd of poets, painters, fiddlers, and their admirers, the bastard race of amateurs, which was continually on his lips. 'Signor Feedle-eerie!' he would say. 'Oh, for Goad's sake, no more of the Signor!'

'You and my father are great friends, are you not?' asked Archie once.

'There is no man that I more respect, Archie,' replied Lord Glenalmond. 'He is two things of price. He is a great lawyer, and he is upright as the day.'

'You and he are so different,' said the boy, his eyes dwelling on those of his old friend, like a lover's on his mistress's.

'Indeed so,' replied the Judge; 'very different. And so I fear are you and he. Yet I would like it very ill if my young friend were to misjudge his father. He has all the Roman virtues: Cato and Brutus[3] were such; I think a son's heart might well be proud of such an ancestry of one.'

'And I would sooner he were a plaided herd,' cried Archie, with sudden bitterness.

'And that is neither very wise, nor I believe entirely true,' returned Glenalmond. 'Before you are done you will find some of these expressions rise on you like a remorse. They are merely literary and decorative; they do not aptly express your thought, nor is your thought clearly apprehended, and no doubt your father (if he were here) would say "Signor Feedle-eerie!"'

With the infinitely delicate sense of youth, Archie avoided the subject from that hour. It was perhaps a pity. Had he but talked – talked freely – let himself gush out in words (the way youth loves to do and should), there might have been no tale to write upon the Weirs of Hermiston. But the shadow of a threat of ridicule sufficed; in the slight tartness of these words he read a prohibition; and it is likely that Glenalmond meant it so.

Besides the veteran, the boy was without confidant or friend. Serious and eager, he came through school and college, and moved among a crowd of the indifferent, in the seclusion of his shyness. He grew up handsome, with an open, speaking countenance, with graceful, youthful ways; he was clever, he took prizes, he shone in the Speculative Society.* It should

* A famous debating society of the students of Edinburgh University.

seem he must become the centre of a crowd of friends; but something that was in part the delicacy of his mother, in part the austerity of his father, held him aloof from all. It is a fact, and a strange one, that among his contemporaries Hermiston's son was thought to be a chip of the old block. 'You're a friend of Archie Weir's?' said one to Frank Innes; and Innes replied, with his usual flippancy and more than his usual insight: 'I know Weir, but I never met Archie.' No one had met Archie, a malady most incident to only sons. He flew his private signal, and none heeded it; it seemed he was abroad in a world from which the very hope of intimacy was banished; and he looked round about him on the concourse of his fellow-students, and forward to the trivial days and acquaintances that were to come, without hope or interest.

As time went on, the tough and rough old sinner felt himself drawn to the son of his loins and sole continuator of his new family, with softnesses of sentiment that he could hardly credit and was wholly impotent to express. With a face, voice, and manner trained through forty years to terrify and repel, Rhadamanthus may be great, but he will scarce be engaging. It is a fact that he tried to propitiate Archie, but a fact that cannot be too lightly taken; the attempt was so unconspicuously made, the failure so stoically supported. Sympathy is not due to these steadfast iron natures. If he failed to gain his son's friendship, or even his son's toleration, on he went up the great, bare staircase of his duty, uncheered and undepressed. There might have been more pleasure in his relations with Archie, so much he may have recognised at moments; but pleasure was a by-product of the singular chemistry of life, which only fools expected.

An idea of Archie's attitude, since we are all grown up and have forgotten the days of our youth, it is more difficult to convey. He made no attempt whatsoever to understand the man with whom he dined and breakfasted. Parsimony of pain, glut of pleasure, these are the two alternating ends of youth; and Archie was of the parsimonious. The wind blew cold out of a certain quarter – he turned his back upon it; stayed as little as was possible in his father's presence; and when there, averted his eyes as much as was decent from his father's face. The lamp shone for many hundred days upon these two at table – my lord ruddy, gloomy, and unreverent; Archie with a potential brightness that was always dimmed and veiled in that society; and there were not, perhaps, in Christendom two men more radically strangers. The father, with a grand simplicity, either spoke of what interested himself, or maintained an unaffected silence. The son turned in his head for some topic that should be quite safe, that would spare him fresh evidences either of my lord's inherent grossness or of the innocence of his inhumanity; treading gingerly the ways of intercourse, like a lady gathering up her skirts in a by-path. If he made a mistake, and my lord began to abound in matter of offence, Archie drew himself up, his brow grew dark, his share of the talk expired; but my lord would faithfully and cheerfully continue to pour out the worst of himself before his silent and offended son.

'Well, it's a poor hert that never rejoices,' he would say, at the conclusion of such a nightmare' interview. 'But I must get to my plew-stilts.' And he would seclude himself as usual in the back room, and Archie go forth into the night and the city, quivering with animosity and scorn.

CHAPTER III

IN THE MATTER OF THE HANGING
OF DUNCAN JOPP

IT chanced in the year 1813 that Archie strayed one day into
the Judiciary Court. The macer made room for the son of the
presiding judge. In the dock, the centre of men's eyes, there
stood a whey-coloured, misbegotten caitiff, Duncan Jopp, on
trial for his life. His story, as it was raked out before him in
that public scene, was one of disgrace and vice and cowardice,
the very nakedness of crime; and the creature heard and it
seemed at times as though he understood – as if at times he
forgot the horror of the place he stood in, and remembered
the shame of what had brought him there. He kept his head
bowed and his hands clutched upon the rail; his hair dropped
in his eyes and at times he flung it back; and now he glanced
about the audience in a sudden fellness of terror, and now
looked in the face of his judge and gulped. There was pinned
about his throat a piece of dingy flannel; and this it was perhaps
that turned the scale in Archie's mind between disgust and pity.
The creature stood in a vanishing point; yet a little while, and
he was still a man, and had eyes and apprehension; yet a little
longer, and with a last sordid piece of pageantry, he would
cease to be. And here, in the meantime, with a trait of human
nature that caught at the beholder's breath, he was tending
a sore throat.

Over against him, my Lord Hermiston occupied the bench
in the red robes of criminal jurisdiction, his face framed in
the white wig. Honest all through, he did not affect the virtue
of impartiality; this was no case for refinement; there was a
man to be hanged, he would have said, and he was hanging
him. Nor was it possible to see his lordship, and acquit him of

gusto in the task. It was plain he gloried in the exercise of his trained faculties, in the clear sight which pierced at once into the joint of fact, in the rude, unvarnished gibes with which he demolished every figment of defence. He took his ease and jested, unbending in that solemn place with some of the freedom of the tavern; and the rag of man with the flannel round his neck was hunted gallowsward with jeers.

Duncan had a mistress, scarce less forlorn and greatly older than himself, who came up, whimpering and curtseying, to add the weight of her betrayal. My lord gave her the oath in his most roaring voice, and added an intolerant warning. 'Mind what ye say now, Janet,' said he. 'I have an e'e upon ye; I'm ill to jest with.'

Presently, after she was tremblingly embarked on her story, 'And what made ye do this, ye auld runt?' the Court interposed. 'Do ye mean to tell me ye was the panel's mistress?'

'If you please, ma loard,' whined the female.

'Godsake! ye made a bonny couple,' observed his lordship; and there was something so formidable and ferocious in his scorn that not even the galleries thought to laugh.

The summing up contained some jewels. 'These two peetiable creatures seem to have made up thegither, it's not for us to explain why.' – 'The panel, who (whatever else he may be) appears to be equally ill set-out in mind and boady.' – 'Neither the panel nor yet the old wife appears to have had so much common sense as even to tell a lie when it was necessary.' And in the course of sentencing, my lord had this *obiter dictum*: 'I have been the means, under God, of haanging a great number, but never just such a disjaskit rascal as yourself.' The words were strong in themselves: the light and heat and detonation of their delivery, and the savage pleasure of the speaker in his task, made them tingle in the ears.

When all was over, Archie came forth again into a changed world. Had there been the least redeeming greatness in the crime, any obscurity, any dubiety, perhaps he might have understood. But the culprit stood, with his sore throat, in the sweat of his mortal agony, without defence or excuse; a thing to cover up with blushes; a being so much sunk beneath the zones of sympathy that pity might seem harmless. And the judge had pursued him with a monstrous, relishing gaiety, horrible to be conceived, a trait for nightmares. It is one thing to spear a tiger, another to crush a toad; there are æsthetics even of the slaughter-house; and the loathsomeness of Duncan Jopp enveloped and infected the image of his judge.

Archie passed by his friends in the High Street with incoherent words and gestures. He saw Holyrood in a dream, remembrance of its romance awoke in him and faded; he had a vision of the old radiant stories, of Queen Mary and Prince Charlie, of the hooded stag,[1] of the splendour and crime, the velvet and bright iron of the past; and dismissed them with a cry of pain. He lay and moaned in the Hunter's Bog, and the heavens were dark above him and the grass of the field an offence. 'This is my father,' he said. 'I draw my life from him; the flesh upon my bones is his, the bread I am fed with is the wages of these horrors.' He recalled his mother, and ground his forehead in the earth. He thought of flight, and where was he to flee to? of other lives, but was there any life worth living in this den of savage and jeering animals?

The interval before the execution was like a violent dream. He met his father; he would not look at him, he could not speak to him. It seemed there was no living creature but must have been swift to recognise that imminent animosity; but the hide of the Lord Justice-Clerk remained impenetrable. Had my lord been talkative, the truce could never have subsisted; but he was by fortune in one of his humours of sour silence; and under the very guns of his broadside Archie nursed the enthusiasm of rebellion. It seemed to him, from the top of his nineteen years' experience, as if he were marked at birth to be the perpetrator of some signal action, to set back fallen Mercy, to overthrow the usurping devil that sat, horned and hoofed, on her throne. Seductive Jacobin figments, which he had often refuted at the Speculative, swam up in his mind and startled him as with voices; and he seemed to himself to walk accompanied by an almost tangible presence of new beliefs and duties.

On the named morning he was at the place of execution. He saw the fleering rabble, the flinching wretch produced. He looked on for a while at a certain parody of devotion, which seem to strip the wretch of his last claim to manhood. Then followed the brutal instant of extinction, and the paltry dangling of the remains like a broken jumping-jack. He had been prepared for something terrible, not for this tragic meanness. He stood a moment silent, and then – 'I denounce this God-defying murder,' he shouted; and his father, if he must have disclaimed the sentiment, might have owned the stentorian voice with which it was uttered.

Frank Innes dragged him from the spot. The two handsome lads followed the same course of study and recreation, and felt a certain mutual attraction, founded mainly on good looks. It had never gone deep; Frank was by nature a thin, jeering creature, not truly susceptible whether of feeling or inspiring friendship; and the relation between the pair was altogether on the outside, a thing of common knowledge and the pleasantries that spring from a common acquaintance. The more credit to Frank that he was appalled by Archie's outburst, and at least conceived the design of keeping him in sight, and, if possible, in hand, for the day. But Archie, who had just defied – was it God or Satan? – would not listen to the word of a college companion.

'I will not go with you,' he said. 'I do not desire your company, sir; I would be alone.'

'Here, Weir, man, don't be absurd,' said Innes, keeping a tight hold upon his sleeve. 'I will not let you go until I know what you mean to do with yourself; it's no use brandishing that staff.' For indeed at that moment Archie had made a sudden – perhaps a warlike – movement. 'This has been the most insane affair; you know it has. You know very well that I'm playing the good Samaritan. All I wish is to keep you quiet.'

'If quietness is what you wish, Mr Innes,' said Archie, 'and you will promise to leave me entirely to myself, I will tell you so much, that I am going to walk in the country and admire the beauties of nature.'

'Honour bright?' asked Frank.

'I am not in the habit of lying, Mr Innes,' retorted Archie. 'I have the honour of wishing you good-day.'

'You won't forget the Spec.?' asked Innes.

'The Spec.?' said Archie. 'Oh no, I won't forget the Spec.'

And the one young man carried his tortured spirit forth of the city and all the day long, by one road and another, in an endless pilgrimage of misery; while the other hastened smilingly to spread the news of Weir's access of insanity, and to drum up for that night a full attendance at the Speculative, where further eccentric developments might certainly be looked for. I doubt if Innes had the least belief in his prediction: I think it flowed rather from a wish to make the story as good and the scandal as great as possible; not from any ill-will to Archie – from the mere pleasure of beholding interested faces. But for all that his words were prophetic. Archie did not forget the Spec.; he put in an appearance there at the due time, and, before the evening was over, had dealt a memorable shock to his companions.[2] It chanced he was the president of the night. He sat in the same room where the Society still meets – only the portraits were not there; the men who afterwards sat for them were then but beginning their career. The same lustre of many tapers shed its light over the meeting; the same chair, perhaps, supported him that so many of us have sat in since. At times he seemed to forget the business of the evening, but even in these periods he sat with a great air of energy and determination. At times he meddled bitterly and launched with defiance those fines which are the precious and rarely used artillery of the president. He little thought, as he did so, how he resembled his father, but his friends remarked upon it, chuckling. So far, in his high place above his fellow-students, he seemed set beyond the possibility of any scandal; but his mind was made up – he was determined to fulfil the sphere of his offence. He signed to Innes (whom he had just fined, and who had just impeached his ruling) to succeed him in the chair, stepped down from the platform, and took his place by the chimney-piece, the shine of many wax tapers from above illuminating his pale face, the glow of the great red fire relieving from behind his slim figure. He had to propose, as an amendment to the next subject in the case-book, 'Whether capital punishment be consistent with God's will or man's policy?'

A breath of embarrassment, of something like alarm, passed round the room, so daring did these words appear upon the lips of Hermiston's only son. But the amendment was not seconded; the previous question was promptly moved and unanimously voted, and the momentary scandal smuggled by. Innes triumphed in the fulfilment of his prophecy. He and Archie were now become the heroes of the night; but whereas every one crowded about Innes, when the meeting broke up, but one of all his companions came to speak to Archie.

'Weir, man! that was an extraordinary raid of yours!' observed this courageous member, taking him confidentially by the arm as they went out.

'I don't think it a raid,' said Archie grimly. 'More like a war. I saw that poor brute hanged this morning, and my gorge rises at it yet.'

'Hut-tut!' returned his companion, and, dropping his arm like something hot, he sought the less tense society of others.

Archie found himself alone. The last of the faithful – or was it only the boldest of the curious? – had fled. He watched the black huddle of his fellow-students draw off down and up the street, in whispering or boisterous gangs. And the isolation of the moment weighed upon him like an omen and an emblem of his destiny in life. Bred up in unbroken fear of himself, among trembling servants, and in a house which (at the least ruffle in the master's voice) shuddered into silence, he saw himself on the brink of the red valley of war, and measured the danger and length of it with awe. He made a détour in the glimmer and shadow of the streets, came into the back stable lane, and watched for a long while the light burn steady in the Judge's room. The longer he gazed upon that illuminated window-blind, the more blank became the picture of the man who sat behind it, endlessly turning over sheets of process, pausing to sip a glass of port, or rising and passing heavily about his book-lined walls to verify some reference. He could not combine the brutal judge and the industrious, dispassionate student; the connecting link escaped him; from such a dual nature, it was impossible he should predict behaviour; and he asked himself if he had done well to plunge into a business of which the end could not be foreseen; and presently after, with a sickening decline of confidence, if he had done loyally to strike his father. For he had struck him – defied him twice over and before a cloud of witnesses – struck him a public buffet before crowds. Who had called him to judge his father in these precarious and high questions? The office was usurped. It might have become a stranger; in a son – there was no blinking it – in a son, it was disloyal. And now, between these two natures so antipathetic, so hateful to each other, there was depending an unpardonable affront: and the providence of God alone might foresee the manner in which it would be resented by Lord Hermiston.

These misgivings tortured him all night and arose with him in the winter's morning; they followed him from class to class, they made him shrinkingly sensitive to every shade of manner in his companions, they sounded in his ears through the current voice of the professor; and he brought them home with him at night unabated and indeed increased. The cause of this increase lay in a chance encounter with the celebrated Dr Gregory.[3] Archie stood looking vaguely in the lighted window of a book shop, trying to nerve himself for the approaching ordeal. My lord and he had met and parted in the morning as they had now done for long, with scarcely the ordinary civilities of life; and it was plain to the son that nothing had yet reached the father's ears. Indeed, when he recalled the awful countenance of my lord, a timid hope sprang up in him that perhaps there would be found no one bold enough to carry tales. If this were so, he asked himself, would he begin again? and he found no answer. It was at this moment that a hand was laid upon his arm, and a voice said in his ear, 'My dear Mr Archie, you had better come and see me.'

He started, turned around, and found himself face to face with Dr Gregory. 'And why should I come to see you?' he asked, with the defiance of the miserable.

'Because you are looking exceeding ill,' said the doctor, 'and you very evidently want looking after, my young friend. Good folk are scarce, you know; and it is not every one that would be quite so much missed as yourself. It is not every one that Hermiston would miss.'

And with a nod and a smile, the doctor passed on.

A moment after, Archie was in pursuit, and had in turn, but more roughly, seized him by the arm.

'What do you mean? what did you mean by saying that? What makes you think that Hermis – my father would have missed me?'

The doctor turned about and looked him all over with a clinical eye. A far more stupid man than Dr Gregory might have guessed the truth; but ninety-nine out of a hundred, even if they had been equally inclined to kindness, would have blundered by some touch of charitable exaggeration. The doctor was better inspired. He knew the father well; in that white face of intelligence and suffering, he divined something of the son; and he told, without apology or adornment, the plain truth.

'When you had the measles, Mr Archibald, you had them gey and ill; and I thought you were going to slip between my fingers,' he said. 'Well, your father was anxious. How did I know it? says you. Simply because I am a trained observer. The sign that I saw him make ten thousand would have missed; and perhaps – *perhaps*, I say, because he's a hard man to judge of – but perhaps he never made another. A strange thing to consider! It was this. One day I came to him: "Hermiston," said I, "there's a change." He never said a word, just glowered at me (if ye'll pardon the phrase) like a wild beast. "A change for the better," said I. And I distinctly heard him take his breath.'

The doctor left no opportunity for anti-climax; nodding his cocked hat (a piece of antiquity to which he clung) and repeating 'Distinctly' with raised eyebrows, he took his departure, and left Archie speechless in the street.

The anecdote might be called infinitely little, and yet its meaning for Archie was immense. 'I did not know the old man had so much blood in him.' He had never dreamed this sire of his, this aboriginal antique, this adamantine Adam, had even so much of a heart as to be moved in the least degree for another – and that other himself, who had insulted him! With the generosity of youth, Archie was instantly under arms upon the other side: had instantly created a new image of Lord Hermiston, that of a man who was all iron without and all sensibility within. The mind of the vile jester, the tongue that had pursued Duncan Jopp with unmanly insults, the unbeloved countenance that he had known and feared for so long, were all forgotten; and he hastened home, impatient to confess his misdeeds, impatient to throw himself on the mercy of this imaginary character.

He was not to be long without a rude awakening. It was in the gloaming when he drew near the doorstep of the lighted house, and was aware of the figure of his father approaching from the opposite side. Little daylight lingered; but on the door being opened, the strong yellow shine of the lamp gushed out upon the landing and shone full on Archie, as he stood, in the old-fashioned observance of respect, to yield precedence. The Judge came without haste, stepping stately and firm; his chin raised, his face (as he entered the lamplight) strongly illumined, his mouth set hard. There was never a wink of change in his expression; without looking to the right or left, he mounted the stair, passed close to Archie, and entered the house. Instinctively, the boy, upon his first coming, had made a movement to meet him; instinctively, he recoiled against the railing, as the old man swept by him in a pomp of indignation. Words were needless; he knew all – perhaps more than all – and the hour of judgment was at hand.

It is possible that, in this sudden revulsion of hope and before these symptoms of impending danger, Archie might have fled. But not even that was left to him. My lord, after hanging up his cloak and hat, turned round in the lighted entry, and made him an imperative and silent gesture with his thumb, and with the strange instinct of obedience, Archie followed him into the house.

All dinner time there reigned over the Judge's table a palpable silence, and as soon as the solids were despatched he rose to his feet.

'M'Killop, tak' the wine into my room,' said he; and then to his son : 'Archie, you and me has to have a talk.'

It was at this sickening moment that Archie's courage, for the first and last time, entirely deserted him. 'I have an appointment,' said he.

'It'll have to be broken, then,' said Hermiston, and led the way into his study.

The lamp was shaded, the fire trimmed to a nicety, the table covered deep with orderly documents, the backs of law books made a frame upon all sides that was only broken by the window and the doors.

For a moment Hermiston warmed his hands at the fire, presenting his back to Archie; then suddenly disclosed on him the terrors of the Hanging Face.

'What's this I hear of ye?' he asked.

There was no answer possible to Archie.

'I'll have to tell ye, then,' pursued Hermiston. 'It seems ye've been skirling against the father that begot ye, and one of His Maijesty's Judges in this land; and that in the public street, and while an order of the Court was being executit. Forbye which, it would appear that ye've been airing your opeenions in a Coallege Debatin' Society!' he paused a moment: and, then, with extraordinary bitterness, added : 'Ye damned eediot.'

'I had meant to tell you,' stammered Archie. 'I see you are well informed.'

'Muckle obleeged to ye,' said his lordship, and took his usual seat. 'And so you disapprove of Caapital Punishment?' he added.

'I am sorry, sir, I do,' said Archie.

'I am sorry, too,' said his lordship. 'And now, if you please, we shall approach this business with a little more parteecularity. I hear that at the hanging of Duncan Jopp – and, man! ye had a fine client there – in the middle of all the riffraff of the ceety, ye thought fit to cry out, "This is a damned murder, and my gorge rises at the man that haangit him." '

'No, sir, these were not my words,' cried Archie.

'What were yer words, then?' asked the Judge.

'I believe I said, "I denounce it as a murder!" ' said the son, 'I beg your pardon – a God-defying murder. I have no wish to conceal the truth,' he added, and looked his father for a moment in the face.

'God, it would only need that of it next!' cried Hermiston. 'There was nothing about your gorge rising, then?'

'That was afterwards, my lord, as I was leaving the Speculative. I said I had been to see the miserable creature hanged, and my gorge rose at it.'

'Did ye, though?' said Hermiston. 'And I suppose ye knew who haangit him?'

'I was present at the trial; I ought to tell you that, I ought to explain. I ask your pardon beforehand for any expression that may seem undutiful. The position in which I stand is wretched,' said the unhappy hero, now fairly face to face with the business he had chosen. 'I have been reading some of your cases. I was present while Jopp was tried. It was a hideous business. Father, it was a hideous thing! Grant he was vile, why should you hunt him with a vileness equal to his own? It was done with glee – that is the word – you did it with glee, and I looked on, God help me! with horror.'

'You're a young gentleman that doesna approve of Caapital Punishment,' said Hermiston. 'Weel, I'm an auld man that does. I was glad to get Jopp haangit, and what for would I pretend I wasna? You're all for honesty, it seems; you couldna even steik your mouth on the public street. What for should I steik mines upon the bench, the King's officer, bearing the sword, a dreid to evil-doers, as I was from the beginning, and as I will be to the end! Mair than enough of it! Heedious! I never gave twa thoughts to heediousness, I have no call to be bonny. I'm a man that gets through with my day's business, and let that suffice.'

The ring of sarcasm had died out of his voice as he went on; the plain words became invested with some of the dignity of the Justice-seat.

'It would be telling you if you could say as much,' the speaker resumed. 'But ye cannot. Ye've been reading some of my cases, ye say. But it was not for the law in them, it was to spy out your faither's nakedness, a fine employment in a son. You're splairging; you're running at lairge in life like a wild nowt. It's impossible you should think any longer of coming to the Bar. You're not fit for it; no splairger is. And another thing: son of mines or no son of mines, you have flung fylement in public on one of the Senators of the Coallege of Justice, and I would make it my business to see that ye were never admitted there yourself. There is a kind of a decency to be observit. Then comes the next of it – what am I to do with ye next? Ye'll have to find some kind of a trade, for I'll never support ye in idleset. What do ye fancy ye'll be fit for? The pulpit? Na, they could never get diveenity into that bloackhead. Him that the law of man whammles is no' likely to do muckle better by the law of God. What would ye make of hell? Wouldna your gorge rise at that? Na, there's no room for splairgers under the fower quarters of John Calvin. What else is there? Speak up. Have ye got nothing of your own?'

'Father, let me go to the Peninsula,'[4] said Archie. 'That's all I'm fit for – to fight.'

'All? quo' he!' returned the Judge. 'And it would be enough too, if I thought it. But I'll never trust ye so near the French, you that's so Frenchifeed.'

'You do me injustice there, sir,' said Archie. 'I am loyal; I will not boast; but any interest I may have ever felt in the French –'

'Have ye been so loyal to me?' interrupted his father.

There came no reply.

'I think not,' continued Hermiston. 'And I would send no man to be a servant of the King, God bless him! that has proved

86

such a shauchling son to his own faither. You can splairge here on Edinburgh street, and where's the hairm? It doesna play buff on me! And if there were twenty thousand eediots like yourself, sorrow a Duncan Jopp would hang the fewer. But there's no splairging possible in a camp; and if you were to go to it, you would find out for yourself whether Lord Well'n'ton approves of caapital punishment or not. You a sodger!' he cried, with a sudden burst of scorn. 'Ye auld wife, the sodgers would bray at ye like cuddies!'

As at the drawing of a curtain, Archie was aware of some illogicality in his position, and stood abashed. He had a strong impression, besides, of the essential valour of the old gentleman before him, how conveyed it would be hard to say.

'Well, have ye no other proposeetion?' said my lord again.

'You have taken this so calmly, sir, that I cannot but stand ashamed,' began Archie.

'I'm nearer voamiting, though, than you would fancy,' said my lord.

The blood rose to Archie's brow.

'I beg your pardon, I should have said that you had accepted my affront ... I admit it was an affront; I did not think to apologise, but I do, I ask your pardon; it will not be so again, I pass you my word of honour ... I should have said that I admired your magnanimity with – this – offender,' Archie concluded with a gulp.

'I have no other son, ye see,' said Hermiston. 'A bonny one I have gotten! But I must just do the best I can wi' him, and what am I to do? If ye had been younger, I would have wheepit ye for this rideeculous exhibeetion. The way it is, I have just to grin and bear. But one thing is to be clearly understood. As a faither, I must grin and bear it; but if I had been the Lord Advocate instead of the Lord Justice-Clerk, son or no son, Mr Erchibald Weir would have been in a jyle the night.'

Archie was now dominated. Lord Hermiston was coarse and cruel; and yet the son was aware of a bloomless nobility, an ungracious abnegation of the man's self in the man's office. At every word, this sense of the greatness of Lord Hermiston's spirit struck more home; and along with it that of his own impotence, who had struck – and perhaps basely struck – at his own father, and not reached so far as to have even nettled him.

'I place myself in your hands without reserve,' he said.

'That's the first sensible word I've had of ye the night,' said Hermiston. 'I can tell ye, that would have been the end of it, the one way or the other; but it's better ye should come there yourself, than what I would have had to hirstle ye. Weel, by my way of it – and my way is the best – there's just the one thing it's possible that ye might be with decency, and that's a laird. Ye'll be out of hairm's way at the least of it. If ye have to rowt, ye can rowt amang the kye; and the maist feck of the caapital punishment ye're like to come across'll be guddling trouts. Now, I'm for no idle lairdies; every man has to work, if it's only at peddling ballants; to work, or to be wheepit, or to be haangit. If I set ye down at Hermiston, I'll have to see you work that place the way it has never been workit yet; ye must ken about the sheep like a herd; ye must be my grieve there, and I'll see that I gain by ye. Is that understood?'

'I will do my best,' said Archie.

'Well, then, I'll send Kirstie word the morn, and ye can go yourself the day after,' said Hermiston. 'And just try to be less of an eediot!' he concluded, with a freezing smile, and turned immediately to the papers on his desk.

CHAPTER IV

OPINIONS OF THE BENCH

LATE the same night, after a disordered walk, Archie was admitted into Lord Glenalmond's dining-room where he sat, with a book upon his knee, beside three frugal coals of fire. In his robes upon the bench, Glenalmond had a certain air of burliness: plucked of these, it was a may-pole of a man that rose unsteadily from his chair to give his visitor welcome. Archie had suffered much in the last days, he had suffered again that evening; his face was white and drawn, his eyes wild and dark. But Lord Glenalmond greeted him without the least mark of surprise or curiosity.

'Come in, come in,' said he. 'Come in and take a seat. Carstairs' (to his servant), 'make up the fire, and then you can bring a bit of supper,' and again to Archie, with a very trivial accent: 'I was half expecting you,' he added.

'No supper,' said Archie. 'It is impossible that I should eat.'

'Not impossible,' said the tall old man, laying his hand upon his shoulder, 'and, if you will believe me, necessary.'

'You know what brings me?' said Archie, as soon as the servant had left the room.

'I have a guess, I have a guess,' replied Glenalmond. 'We will talk of it presently – when Carstairs has come and gone, and you have had a piece of my good Cheddar cheese and a pull at the porter tankard: not before.'

'It is impossible I should eat,' repeated Archie.

'Tut, tut!' said Lord Glenalmond. 'You have eaten nothing to-day, and, I venture to add, nothing yesterday. There is no case that may not be made worse; this may be a very disagreeable business, but if you were to fall sick and die, it would be still more so, and for all concerned – for all concerned.'

'I see you must know all,' said Archie. 'Where did you hear it?'

'In the mart of scandal, in the Parliament House,' said Glenalmond. 'It runs riot below among the bar and the public, but it sifts up to us upon the bench, and rumour has some of her voices even in the divisions.'

Carstairs returned at this moment, and rapidly laid out a little supper; during which Lord Glenalmond spoke at large and a little vaguely on indifferent subjects, so that it might be rather said of him that he made a cheerful noise, than that he contributed to human conversation; and Archie sat upon the other side, not heeding him, brooding over his wrongs and errors.

But so soon as the servant was gone, he broke forth again at once. 'Who told my father? Who dared to tell him? Could it have been you?'

'No, it was not me,' said the Judge; 'although – to be quite frank with you, and after I had seen and warned you – it might have been me. I believe it was Glenkindie.'

'That shrimp!' cried Archie.

'As you say, that shrimp,' returned my lord; 'although really it is scarce a fitting mode of expression for one of the Senators of the College of Justice. We were hearing the parties in a long, crucial case, before the fifteen; Creech was moving at some length for an infeftment; when I saw Glenkindie lean forward to Hermiston with his hand over his mouth and make him a secret communication. No one could have guessed its nature from your father; from Glenkindie, yes, his malice sparked out of him a little grossly. But your father, no. A man of granite. The next moment he pounced upon Creech. "Mr Creech," says he, "I'll take a look of that sasine," and for thirty minutes after,' said Glenalmond, with a smile, 'Messrs Creech and Co. were fighting a pretty uphill battle, which resulted, I need hardly add, in their total rout. The case was dismissed. No, I doubt if ever I heard Hermiston better inspired. He was literally rejoicing *in apicibus juris*.'

Archie was able to endure no longer. He thrust his plate

away and interrupted the deliberate and insignificant stream of talk. 'Here,' he said, 'I have made a fool of myself, if I have not made something worse. Do you judge between us – judge between a father and a son. I can speak to you; it is not like ... I will tell you what I feel and what I mean to do; and you shall be the judge,' he repeated.

'I decline jurisdiction,' said Glenalmond, with extreme seriousness. 'But, my dear boy, if it will do you any good to talk, and if it will interest you at all to hear what I may choose to say when I have heard you, I am quite at your command. Let an old man say it, for once, and not need to blush: I love you like a son.'

There came a sudden sharp sound in Archie's throat. 'Ay,' he cried, 'and there it is! Love! Like a son! And how do you think I love my father?'

'Quietly, quietly,' says my lord.

'I will be very quiet,' replied Archie. 'And I will be baldly frank. I do not love my father; I wonder sometimes if I do not hate him. There's my shame; perhaps my sin; at least, and in the sight of God, not my fault. How was I to love him? He has never spoken to me, never smiled upon me; I do not think he ever touched me. You know the way he talks? You do not talk so, yet you can sit and hear him without shuddering, and I cannot. My soul is sick when he begins with it; I could smite him in the mouth. And all that's nothing. I was at the trial of this Jopp. You were not there, but you must have heard him often; the man's notorious for it, for being – look at my position! he's my father and this is how I have to speak of him – notorious for being a brute and cruel and a coward. Lord Glenalmond, I give you my word, when I came out of that Court, I longed to die – the shame of it was beyond my strength: but I – I –' he rose from his seat and began to pace the room in a disorder. 'Well, who am I? A boy, who have never been tried, have never done anything except this two-penny impotent folly with my father. But I tell you, my lord, and I know myself, I am at least that kind of a man – or that kind of a boy, if you prefer it – that I could die in torments rather than that any one should suffer as that scoundrel suffered. Well, and what have I done? I see it now. I have made a fool of myself, as I said in the beginning; and I have gone back, and asked my father's pardon, and placed myself wholly in his hands – and he has sent me to Hermiston,' with a wretched smile, 'for life, I suppose – and what can I say? he strikes me as having done quite right, and let me off better than I had deserved.'

'My poor, dear boy!' observed Glenalmond. 'My poor, dear and, if you will allow me to say so, very foolish boy! You are only discovering where you are; to one of your temperament, or of mine, a painful discovery. The world was not made for us; it was made for ten hundred millions of men, all different from each other and from us; there's no royal road there, we just have to sclamber and tumble. Don't think that I am at all disposed to be surprised; don't suppose that I ever think of blaming you; indeed I rather admire! But there fall to be offered one or two observations on the case which occur to me and which (if you will listen to them dispassionately) may be the means of inducing you to view the matter more calmly. First of all, I cannot acquit you of a good deal of what is called intolerance. You seem to have been very much offended because your father talks a little sculduddery after dinner, which it is perfectly licit for him to do, and which (although I am not very fond of it myself) appears to be entirely an affair of taste. Your father, I scarcely like to remind you, since it is so trite a commonplace, is older than yourself. At least, he is *major* and *sui juris*, and may please himself in the matter of his conversation. And, do you know, I wonder if he might not have as good an answer against you and me? We say we sometimes find him *coarse*, but I suspect he might retort that he finds us always dull. Perhaps a relevant exception.'

He beamed on Archie, but no smile could be elicited.

'And now,' proceeded the Judge, 'for "Archibald on Capital Punishment." This is a very plausible academic opinion; of course I do not and I cannot hold it; but that's not to say that many able and excellent persons have not done so in the past. Possibly, in the past, also, I may have a little dipped myself in the same heresy. My third client, or possibly my fourth, was the means of a return in my opinions. I never saw the man I more believed in; I would have put my hand in the fire, I would have gone to the cross for him; and when it came to trial he was gradually pictured before me, by undeniable probation, in the light of so gross, so cold-blooded, and so black-hearted a villain, that I had a mind to have cast my brief upon the table. I was then boiling against the man with even a more tropical temperature than I had been boiling for him. But I said to myself: "No, you have taken up his case; and because you have changed your mind it must not be suffered to let drop. All that rich tide of eloquence that you prepared last night with so much enthusiasm is out of place, and yet you must not desert him, you must say something." So I said something, and I got him off. It made my reputation. But an experience of that kind is formative. A man must not bring his passions to the bar – or to the bench.'

This story had slightly rekindled Archie's interest. 'I could never deny,' he began – 'I mean I can conceive that some men would be better dead. But who are we to know all the springs of God's unfortunate creatures? Who are we to trust ourselves where it seems that God himself must think twice before He treads, and to do it with delight? Yes, with delight. *Tigris ut aspera.*'

'Perhaps not a pleasant spectacle,' said Glenalmond. 'And yet, do you know, I think somehow a great one.'

'I've had a long talk with him to-night,' said Archie.

'I was supposing so,' said Glenalmond.

'And he struck me – I cannot deny that he struck me as something very big,' pursued the son. 'Yes, he is big. He never spoke about himself; only about me. I suppose I admired him. The dreadful part – '

'Suppose we did not talk about that,' interrupted Glenalmond. 'You know it very well, it cannot in any way help that you should brood upon it, and I sometimes wonder whether you and I – who are a pair of sentimentalists – are quite good judges of plain men.'

'How do you mean?' asked Archie.

'*Fair* judges, I mean,' replied Glenalmond. 'Can we be just to them? Do we not ask too much? There was a word of yours just now that impressed me a little when you asked me who we were to know all the springs of God's unfortunate creatures. You applied that, as I understood, to capital cases only. But does it – I ask myself – does it not apply all through? Is it any less difficult to judge of a good man or of a half-good man, than of the worst criminal at the bar? And may not each have relevant excuses?'

'Ah, but we do not talk of punishing the good,' cried Archie.

'No, we do not talk of it,' said Glenalmond. 'But I think we do it. Your father, for instance.'

'You think I have punished him?' cried Archie.

Lord Glenalmond bowed his head.

'I think I have,' said Archie. 'And the worst is, I think he feels it! How much, who can tell, with such a being? But I think he does.'

'And I am sure of it,' said Glenalmond.

'Has he spoken to you, then?' cried Archie.

'Oh, no,' replied the Judge.

'I tell you honestly,' said Archie, 'I want to make it up to him. I will go, I have already pledged myself to go, to Hermiston. That was to him. And now I pledge myself to you, in the sight of God, that I will close my mouth on capital punishment and all other subjects where our views may clash, for – how long shall I say? when shall I have sense enough? – ten years. Is that well?'

'It is well,' said my lord.

'As far as it goes,' said Archie. 'It is enough as regards myself, it is to lay down enough of my conceit. But as regards him, whom I have publicly insulted? What am I to do to him? How do you pay attentions to a – an Alp like that?'

'Only in one way,' replied Glenalmond. 'Only by obedience, punctual, prompt, and scrupulous.'

'And I promise that he shall have it,' answered Archie. 'I offer you my hand in pledge of it.'

'And I take your hand as a solemnity,' replied the Judge. 'God bless you, my dear, and enable you to keep your promise. God guide you in the true way, and spare your days, and preserve to you your honest heart.' At that, he kissed the young man upon the forehead in a gracious, distant, antiquated way; and instantly launched, with a marked change of voice, into another subject. 'And now, let us replenish the tankard; and I believe, if you will try my Cheddar again, you would find you had a better appetite. The Court has spoken, and the case is dismissed.'

'No, there is one thing I must say,' cried Archie. 'I must say it in justice to himself. I know – I believe faithfully, slavishly, after our talk – he will never ask me anything unjust. I am proud to feel it, that we have that much in common, I am proud to say it to you.'

The Judge, with shining eyes, raised his tankard. 'And I think perhaps that we might permit ourselves a toast,' said he. 'I should like to propose the health of a man very different from me and very much my superior – a man from whom I have often differed, who has often (in the trivial expression) rubbed me the wrong way, but whom I have never ceased to respect and, I may add, to be not a little afraid of. Shall I give you his name?'

'The Lord Justice-Clerk, Lord Hermiston,' said Archie, almost with gaiety; and the pair drank the toast deeply.

It was not precisely easy to re-establish, after these emotional passages, the natural flow of conversation. But the Judge eked out what was wanting with kind looks, produced his snuff-box (which was very rarely seen) to fill in a pause, and at last, despairing of any further social success, was upon the point of getting down a book to read a favourite passage, when there came a rather startling summons at the front door, and Carstairs ushered in my Lord Glenkindie, hot from a midnight supper. I am not aware that Glenkindie was ever a beautiful object, being short, and gross-bodied and with an expression of sensuality comparable to a bear's. At that moment, coming in hissing from many potations, with a flushed countenance and blurred eyes, he was strikingly contrasted with the tall, pale, kingly figure of Glenalmond. A rush of confused thought came over Archie – of shame that this was one of his father's elect friends; of pride, that at the least of it Hermiston could carry his liquor; and last of all, of rage, that he should have here under his eye the man that had betrayed him. And then that, too, passed away; and he sat quiet, biding his opportunity.

The tipsy senator plunged at once into an explanation with Glenalmond. There was a point reserved yesterday, he had been able to make neither head nor tail of it, and seeing lights in the house, he had just dropped in for a glass of porter – and at this point he became aware of the third person. Archie saw the cod's mouth and the blunt lips of Glenkindie gape at him for a moment, and the recognition twinkle in his eyes.

'Who's this?' said he. 'What? is this possibly you, Don Quickshot? And how are ye? And how's your father? And what's all this we hear of you? It seems you're a most extraordinary leveller, by all tales. No king, no parliaments, and your gorge rises at the macers, worthy men! Hoot, toot! Dear, dear me! Your father's son, too! Most rideeculous!'

Archie was on his feet, flushing a little at the reappearance of his unhappy figure of speech, but perfectly self-possessed. 'My lord – and you, Lord Glenalmond, my dear friend,' he began, 'this is a happy chance for me, that I can make my confession and offer my apologies to two of you at once.'

'Ah, but I don't know about that. Confession? It'll be judeecial, my young friend,' cried the jocular Glenkindie. 'And I'm afraid to listen to ye. Think if ye were to make me a coanvert!'

'If you would allow me, my lord,' returned Archie, 'what I have to say is very serious to me; and be pleased to be humorous after I am gone!'

'Remember, I'll hear nothing against the macers!' put in the incorrigible Glenkindie.

But Archie continued as though he had not spoken. 'I have played, both yesterday and to-day, a part for which I can only offer the excuse of youth. I was so unwise as to go to an execution; it seems I made a scene at the gallows; not content with which, I spoke the same night in a college society against capital punishment. This is the extent of what I have done, and in case you hear more alleged against me, I protest my innocence. I have expressed my regret already to my father, who is so good as to pass my conduct over – in a degree, and upon the condition that I am to leave my law studies' ...

CHAPTER V

WINTER ON THE MOORS

1 At Hermiston[1]

THE road to Hermiston runs for a great part of the way up the valley of a stream, a favourite with anglers and with midges, full of falls and pools, and shaded by willows and natural woods of birch. Here and there, but at great distances, a byway branches off, and a gaunt farmhouse may be descried above in a fold of the hill; but the more part of the time, the road would be quite empty of passage and the hills of habitation. Hermiston parish is one of the least populous in Scotland; and, by the time you came that length, you would scarce be surprised at the inimitable smallness of the kirk, a dwarfish, ancient place seated for fifty, and standing in a green by the burn-side among two-score gravestones. The manse close by, although no more than a cottage, is surrounded by the brightness of a flower-garden and the straw roofs of bees; and the whole colony, kirk and manse, garden and graveyard, finds harbourage in a grove of rowans, and is all the year round in a great silence broken only by the drone of the bees, the tinkle of the burn, and the bell on Sundays. A mile beyond the kirk the road leaves the valley by a precipitous ascent, and brings you a little after to the place of Hermiston, where it comes to an end in the back-yard before the coach-house. All beyond and about is the great field of the hills; the plover, the curlew, and the lark cry there; the wind blows as it blows in a ship's rigging, hard and cold and pure; and the hill-tops huddle one behind another like a herd of cattle into the sunset.

The house was sixty years old, unsightly, comfortable; a farmyard and a kitchen-garden on the left, with a fruit wall where little hard green pears came to their maturity about the end of October.

The policy (as who should say the park) was of some extent, but very ill reclaimed; heather and moorfowl had crossed the boundary wall and spread and roosted within; and it would have tasked a landscape gardener to say where policy ended and unpolicied nature began. My lord had been led by the influence of Mr Sheriff Scott[4] into a considerable design of planting; many acres were accordingly set out with fir, and the little feathery besoms gave a false scale and lent a strange air of a toy-shop to the moors. A great, rooty sweetness of bogs was in the air, and at all seasons an infinite melancholy piping of hill birds. Standing so high and with so little shelter, it was a cold, exposed house, splashed by showers, drenched by continuous rains that made the gutters to spout, beaten upon and buffeted by all the winds of heaven; and the prospect would be often black with tempest, and often white with the snows of winter. But the house was wind and weather proof, the hearths were kept bright, and the rooms pleasant with live fires of peat; and Archie might sit of an evening and hear the squalls bugle on the moorland, and watch the fire prosper in the earthy fuel, and the smoke winding up the chimney, and drink deep of the pleasures of shelter.

Solitary as the place was, Archie did not want neighbours. Every night, if he chose, he might go down to the manse and share a 'brewst' of toddy with the minister – a hare-brained ancient gentleman, long and light and still active, though his knees were loosened with age, and his voice broke continually in childish trebles – and his lady wife, a heavy, comely dame, without a word to say for herself beyond good-even and good-day. Harum-scarum, clodpole young lairds of the neighbourhood paid him the compliment of a visit. Young Hay of Romanes rode down to call, on his crop-eared pony; young Pringle of Drumanno came up on his bony grey. Hay remained on the hospitable field, and must be carried to bed; Pringle got somehow to his saddle about 3 A.M., and (as Archie stood with the lamp on the upper doorstep) lurched, uttered a senseless viewholloa, and vanished out of the small circle of illumination like a wraith. Yet a minute or two longer the clatter of his break-neck flight was audible, then it was cut off by the intervening steepness of the hill; and again, a great while after, the renewed beating of phantom horse-hoofs, far in the valley of the Hermiston, showed that the horse at least, if not his rider, was still on the homeward way.

There was a Tuesday Club at the 'Cross-keys' in Crossmichael, where the young bloods of the countryside congregated and drank deep on a percentage of the expense, so that he was left gainer who should have drunk the most. Archie had no great mind to this diversion, but he took it like a duty laid upon him, went with a decent regularity, did his manfullest with the liquor, held up his head in the local jests, and got home again and was able to put up his horse, to the admiration of Kirstie and the lass that helped her. He dined at Driffel, supped at Windielaws. He went to the new year's ball at Huntsfield and was made welcome, and thereafter rode to hounds with my Lord Muirfell, upon whose name, as that of a legitimate Lord of Parliament, in a work so full of Lords of Session, my pen should pause reverently. Yet the same fate attended him here as in Edinburgh. The habit of solitude tends to perpetuate itself, and an austerity of which he was quite unconscious, and a pride which seemed arrogance, and perhaps was chiefly shyness, discouraged and offended his new companions. Hay did not return more than twice, Pringle never at all, and there came a time when Archie even desisted from the Tuesday Club, and became in all things – what he had had the name of almost from the first – the Recluse of Hermiston. High-nosed Miss Pringle of Drumanno and high-stepping Miss Marshall of the Mains were understood to have had a difference of opinion about him the day after the ball – he was none the wiser, he could not suppose himself to be remarked by these entrancing ladies. At the ball itself my Lord Muirfell's daughter, the Lady Flora, spoke to him twice, and the second time with a touch of appeal, so that her colour rose and her voice trembled a little in his ear, like a passing grace in music. He stepped back with a heart on fire, coldly and not ungracefully excused himself, and a little after watched her dancing with young Drumanno of the empty laugh, and was harrowed at the sight, and raged to himself that this was a world in which it was given to Drumanno to please, and to himself only to stand aside and envy. He seemed excluded, as of right, from the favour of such society – seemed to extinguish mirth wherever he came, and was quick to feel the wound, and desist, and retire into solitude. If he had but understood the figure he presented, and the impression he made on these bright eyes and tender hearts; if he had but guessed that the Recluse of Hermiston, young, graceful, well spoken, but always cold, stirred the maidens of the county with the charm of Byronism when Byronism was new, it may be questioned whether his destiny might not even yet have been modified. It may be questioned, and I think it should be doubted. It was in his horoscope to be parsimonious of pain to himself, or of the chance of pain, even to the avoidance of any opportunity of pleasure; to have a Roman sense of duty, an instinctive aristocracy of manners and taste; to be the son of Adam Weir and Jean Rutherford.

2 Kirstie

Kirstie was now over fifty, and might have sat to a sculptor. Long of limb, and still light of foot, deep-breasted, robust-loined, her golden hair not yet mingled with any trace of silver, the years had but caressed and embellished her. By the lines of a rich and vigorous maternity, she seemed destined to be the bride of heroes and the mother of their children; and behold, by the iniquity of fate, she had passed through her youth alone, and drew near to the confines of age, a childless woman. The tender ambitions that she had received at birth had been, by time and disappointment, diverted into a certain barren zeal of industry and fury of interference. She carried her thwarted ardours into housework, she washed floors with her empty heart. If she could not win the love of one with love, she must dominate all by her temper. Hasty, wordy, and

wrathful, she had a drawn quarrel with most of her neighbours, and with the others not much more than armed neutral-
ity. The grieve's wife had been 'sneisty'; the sister of the
gardener who kept house for him had shown herself 'upsitten';
and she wrote to Lord Hermiston about once a year demanding
the discharge of the offenders, and justifying the demand by
much wealth of detail. For it must not be supposed that the
quarrel rested with the wife and did not take in the husband
also – or with the gardener's sister, and did not speedily include
the gardener himself. As the upshot of all this petty quarrelling
and intemperate speech, she was practically excluded (like a
lightkeeper on his tower) from the comforts of human association; except with her own indoor drudge, who, being but
a lassie and entirely at her mercy, must submit to the shifty
weather of 'the mistress's' moods without complaint, and be
willing to take buffets or caresses according to the temper of
the hour. To Kirstie, thus situate and in the Indian summer of
her heart, which was slow to submit to age, the gods sent this
equivocal good thing of Archie's presence. She had known him
in the cradle and paddled him when he misbehaved; and yet,
as she had not so much as set eyes on him since he was eleven
and had his last serious illness, the tall, slender, refined, and
rather melancholy young gentleman of twenty came upon
.her with the shock of a new acquaintance. He was 'Young
Hermiston,' 'the laird himsel'': he had an air of distinctive
superiority, a cold straight glance of his black eyes, that abashed
the woman's tantrums in the beginning, and therefore the
possibility of any quarrel was excluded. He was new, and
therefore immediately aroused her curiosity; he was reticent,
and kept it awake. And lastly he was dark and she fair, and he
was male and she female, the everlasting fountains of interest.

Her feeling partook of the loyalty of a clanswoman, the hero-
worship of a maiden aunt, and the idolatry due to a god. No
matter what he had asked of her, ridiculous or tragic, she
would have done it and joyed to do it. Her passion, for it was
nothing less, entirely filled her. It was a rich physical pleasure
to make his bed or light his lamp for him when he was absent,

to pull off his wet boots or wait on him at dinner when he returned. A young man who should have so doted on the idea, moral and physical, of any woman, might be properly described as being in love, head and heels, and would have behaved himself accordingly. But Kirstie – though her heart leaped at his coming footsteps – though, when he patted her shoulder, her face brightened for the day – had not a hope or thought beyond the present moment and its perpetuation to the end of time. Till the end of time she would have had nothing altered, but still continue delightedly to serve her idol, and be repaid (say twice in the month) with a clap on the shoulder.

I have said her heart leaped – it is the accepted phrase. But rather, when she was alone in any chamber of the house, and heard his foot passing on the corridors, something in her bosom rose slowly until her breath was suspended, and as slowly fell again with a deep sigh, when the steps had passed and she was disappointed of her eyes' desire. This perpetual hunger and thirst of his presence kept her all day on the alert. When he went forth at morning, she would stand and follow him with admiring looks. As it grew late and drew to the time of his return, she would steal forth to a corner of the policy wall and be seen standing there sometimes by the hour together, gazing with shaded eyes, waiting the exquisite and barren pleasure of his view a mile off on the mountains. When at night she had trimmed and gathered the fire, turned down his bed, and laid out his night-gear – when there was no more to be done for the king's pleasure, but to remember him fervently in her usually very tepid prayers, and go to bed brooding upon his perfections, his future career, and what she should give him the next day for dinner – there still remained before her one more opportunity; she was still to take in the tray and say goodnight. Sometimes Archie would glance up from his book with a preoccupied nod and a perfunctory salutation which was in truth a dismissal; sometimes – and by degrees more often – the volume would be laid aside, he would meet her coming with a look of relief; and the conversation would be engaged, last out the supper, and be prolonged till the small hours by the waning fire. It was no wonder that Archie was fond of company after his solitary days; and Kirstie, upon her side, exerted all the arts of her vigorous nature to ensnare his attention. She would keep back some piece of news during dinner to be fired off with the entrance of the supper tray, and form as it were the *lever de rideau* of the evening's entertainment. Once he had heard her tongue wag, she made sure of the result. From one subject to another she moved by insidious transitions, fearing the least silence, fearing almost to give him time for an answer lest it should slip into a hint of separation. Like so many people of her class, she was a brave narrator; her place was on the hearthrug and she made it a rostrum, mimeing her stories as she told them, fitting them with vital detail, spinning them out with endless 'quo' he's' and 'quo' she's,' her voice sinking into a whisper over the supernatural or the horrific; until she would suddenly spring up in affected surprise, and pointing to the clock, 'Mercy, Mr Archie!' she would say, 'whatten a time o' night is this of it! God forgive me for a daft wife!' So it befell, by good management, that she was not only the first to begin these nocturnal conversations, but invariably the first to break them off; so she managed to retire and not to be dismissed.

3   A Border Family

Such an unequal intimacy has never been uncommon in Scotland, where the clan spirit survives; where the servant tends to spend her life in the same service, a helpmeet at first, then a tyrant, and at last a pensioner; where, besides, she is not necessarily destitute of the pride of birth, but is, perhaps, like Kirstie, a connection of her master's, and at least knows the legend of her own family, and may count kinship with some illustrious dead. For that is the mark of the Scot of all classes: that he stands in an attitude towards the past unthinkable to Englishmen, and remembers and cherishes the memory of his forebears, good or bad; and there burns alive in him a sense of identity with the dead even to the twentieth generation. No more characteristic instance could be found than in the family of Kirstie Elliott. They were all, and Kirstie the first of all, ready and eager to pour forth the particulars of their genealogy, embellished with every detail that memory had handed down or fancy fabricated; and, behold! from every ramification of that tree there dangled a halter. The Elliotts themselves have had a chequered history; but these Elliotts deduced, besides, from three of the most unfortunate of the border clans – the Nicksons, the Ellwalds, and the Crozers. One ancestor after another might be seen appearing a moment out of the rain and the hill mist upon his furtive business, speeding home, perhaps, with a paltry booty of lame horses and lean kine, or squealing and dealing death in some moorland feud of the ferrets and the wild cats. One after another closed his obscure adventures in mid-air, triced up to the arm of the royal gibbet or the Baron's dule-tree. For the rusty blunderbuss of Scots criminal justice, which usually hurt nobody but jury-men, became a weapon of precision for the Nicksons, the Ellwalds, and the Crozers. The exhilaration of their exploits seemed to haunt the memories of their descendants alone, and the shame to be forgotten. Pride glowed in their bosoms to publish their relationship to 'Andrew Ellwald of the Laverock-stanes, called "Unchancy Dand," who was justified wi' seeven mair of the same name at Jeddart in the days of King James the Sax.' In all this tissue of crime and misfortune, the Elliotts of Cauldstaneslap had one boast which must appear legitimate: the males were gallows-birds, born outlaws, petty thieves, and deadly brawlers, but, according to the same tradition, the females were all chaste and faithful. The power of ancestry on the character is not limited to the inheritance of cells. If I buy ancestors by the gross from the benevolence of Lyon King of Arms,[2] my grandson (if he is Scottish) will feel a quickening emulation of their deeds. The men of the Elliotts were proud, lawless, violent as of right, cherishing and prolonging a tradition. In like manner with the women. And the woman, essentially passionate and reckless, who crouched on the rug, in the shine of the peat fire, telling these tales, had cherished through life a wild integrity of virtue.

Her father Gilbert had been deeply pious, a savage disciplinarian in the antique style, and withal a notorious smuggler. 'I mind when I was a bairn getting mony a skelp and being shoo'd to bed like pou'try,' she would say. 'That would be when the lads and their bit kegs were on the road. We've had the riffraff of two-three counties in our kitchen, mony's the time, betwix' the twelve and the three; and their lanterns would be standing in the forecourt, ay, a score o' them at once. But there was nae ungodly talk permitted at Cauldstaneslap. My faither was a consistent man in walk and conversation; just let slip an aith, and there was the door to ye! He had that zeal for the Lord, it was a fair wonder to hear him pray, but the family has aye had a gift that way.' This father was twice married, once to a dark woman of the old Ellwald stock, by whom he had Gilbert, presently of Cauldstaneslap; and, secondly, to the mother of Kirstie. 'He was an auld man when he married her, a fell auld man wi' a muckle voice – you could hear him rowting from the top o' the Kye-skairs,' she said; 'but for her, it appears she was a perfit wonder. It was gentle blood she had, Mr Archie, for it was your ain. The countryside gaed gyte about her and her gowden hair. Mines is no to be mentioned wi' it, and there's few weemen has mair hair than what I have, or yet a bonnier colour. Often would I tell my dear Miss Jeannie – that was your mother, dear, she was cruel ta'en up about her hair, it was unco' tender, ye see – "Houts, Miss Jeannie," I would say, "just fling your washes and your French dentifrishes in the back o' the fire, for that's the place for them; and awa' down to a burn side, and wash yersel' in cauld hill water, and dry your bonny hair in the caller wind o' the muirs, the way that my mother aye washed hers, and that I have aye made it a practice to have wishen mines – just you do what I tell ye, my dear, and ye'll give me news of it! Ye'll have hair, and routh of hair, a pigtail as thick's my arm," I said, "and the bonniest colour like the clear gowden guineas, so as the lads in kirk'll no can keep their eyes off it!" Weel, it lasted out her time, puir thing! I cuttit a lock of it upon her corp that was lying there sae cauld. I'll show it ye some of thir days if ye're good. But, as I was sayin', my mither —'

On the death of the father there remained golden-haired Kirstie, who took service with her distant kinsfolk, the Ruther-fords, and black-a-vised Gilbert, twenty years older, who farmed the Cauldstaneslap, married, and begot four sons between 1773 and 1784, and a daughter, like a postscript in '97, the year of Camperdown and Cape St Vincent.[3] It seemed it was a tradition in the family to wind up with a belated girl. In 1804, at the age of sixty, Gilbert met an end that might be called heroic. He was due home from market any time from eight at night till five in the morning, and in any condition from the quarrelsome to the speechless, for he maintained to that age the goodly customs of the Scots farmer. It was known on this occasion that he had a good bit of money to bring home; the word had gone round loosely. The laird had shown his guineas, and if anybody had but noticed it, there was an ill-looking, vagabond crew, the scum of Edinburgh, that drew out of the market long ere it was dusk and took the hill-road by Hermiston, where it was not to be believed that they had lawful business. One of the countryside, one Dickieson, they took with them to be their guide, and dear he paid for it! Of a sudden in the ford of the Broken Dykes, this vermin clan fell on the laird, six to one, and him three parts asleep, having drunk hard. But it is ill to catch an Elliott. For a while, in the night and the black water that was deep as to his saddle-girths, he wrought with his staff like a smith at his stithy, and great was the sound of oaths and blows. With that the ambuscade was burst, and he rode for home with a pistol-ball in him, three knife wounds, the loss of his front teeth, a broken rib and bridle, and a dying horse. That was a race with death that the laird rode! In the mirk night, with his broken bridle and his head swimming, he dug his spurs to the rowels in the horse's side, and the horse, that was even worse off than himself, the poor creature! screamed out loud like a person as he went, so that the hills echoed with it, and the folks at Cauldstaneslap got to their feet about the table and looked at each other with white faces. The horse fell dead at the yard gate, the laird won the length of the house and fell there on the threshold. To the son that raised him he gave the bag of money. 'Hae,' said he. All the way up the thieves had seemed to him to be at his heels, but now the hallucination left him – he saw them again in the place of the ambuscade – and the thirst of vengeance seized on his dying mind. Raising himself and pointing with an imperious finger into the black night from which he had come, he uttered the single command, 'Brocken Dykes,' and fainted. He had never been loved, but he had been feared in honour. At that sight, at that word, gasped out at them from a toothless and bleeding mouth, the old Elliott spirit awoke with a shout in the four sons. 'Wanting the hat,' continues my author, Kirstie, whom I but haltingly follow, for she told this tale like one inspired, 'wanting guns, for there wasna twa grains o' pouder in the house, wi' nae mair weepons than their sticks into their hands, the fower o' them took the road. Only Hob, and that was the eldest, hunkered at the doorsill where the blood had rin, fyled his hand wi' it, and haddit it up to Heeven in the way o' the auld Border aith. "Hell shall have her ain again this nicht!" he raired, and rode forth upon his earrand.' It was three miles to Broken Dykes, down hill, and a sore road. Kirstie has seen men from Edinburgh dismounting there in plain day to lead their horses. But the four brothers rode it as if Auld Hornie were behind and Heaven in front. Come to the ford, and there was Dickieson. By all tales, he was not dead, but breathed and reared upon his elbow, and cried out to them for help. It was at a graceless face that he asked mercy. As soon as Hob saw, by the glint of the lantern, the eyes shining and the whiteness of the teeth in the man's face, 'Damn you!' says he; 'ye hae your teeth, hae ye?' and rode his horse to and fro upon that human remnant. Beyond that, Dandie must dismount with the lantern to be their guide; he was the youngest son, scarce twenty at the time. 'A' nicht long they gaed in the wet heath and jennipers, and whaur they gaed they neither knew nor cared, but just followed the bluid

stains and the footprints o' their faither's murderers. And a'
nicht Dandie had his nose to the grund like a tyke, and the
ithers followed and spak' naething, neither black nor white.
There was nae noise to be heard, but just the sough of the
swalled burns, and Hob, the dour yin, risping his teeth as he
gaed.' With the first glint of the morning they saw they were
on the drove road, and at that the four stopped and had a dram
to their breakfasts, for they knew that Dand must have guided
them right, and the rogues could be but little ahead, hot foot
for Edinburgh by the way of the Pentland Hills. By eight o'clock
they had word of them – a shepherd had seen four men 'uncoly
mishandled' go by in the last hour. 'That's yin a piece,' says
Clem, and swung his cudgel. 'Five o' them!' says Hob. 'God's
death, but the faither was a man! And him drunk!' And then
there befell them what my author termed 'a sair misbegowk,'
for they were overtaken by a posse of mounted neighbours
come to aid in the pursuit. Four sour faces looked on the
reinforcement. 'The deil's broughten you!' said Clem, and they
rode thenceforward in the rear of the party with hanging
heads. Before ten they had found and secured the rogues, and
by three of the afternoon, as they rode up the Vennel with their
prisoners, they were aware of a concourse of people bearing
in their midst something that dripped. 'For the boady of the
saxt,' pursued Kirstie, 'wi' his head smashed like a hazel-nit,
had been a' that nicht in the chairge o' Hermiston Water, and
it dunting it on the stanes, and grunding it on the shallows,
and flinging the deid thing heels-ower-hurdie at the Fa's o'
Spango; and in the first o' the day Tweed had got a hold o'
him and carried him off like a wind, for it was uncoly swalled,
and raced wi' him, bobbing under brae-sides, and was long
playing with the creature in the drumlie lynns under the castle,
and at the hinder end of all cuist him up on the sterling of
Crossmichael brig. Sae there they were a' thegither at last (for
Dickieson had been brought in on a cart long syne), and folk
could see what mainner o' man my brither had been that had
held his head again' sax and saved the siller, and him drunk!'
Thus died of honourable injuries and in the savour of fame

Gilbert Elliott of the Cauldstaneslap; but his sons had scarce less glory out of the business. Their·savage haste, the skill with which Dand had found and followed the trail, the barbarity to the wounded Dickieson (which was like an open secret in the county) and the doom which it was currently supposed they had intended for the others, struck and stirred popular imagination. Some century earlier the last of the minstrels might have fashioned the last of the ballads out of that Homeric fight and chase; but the spirit was dead, or had been reincarnated already in Mr Sheriff Scott, and the degenerate moorsmen must be content to tell the tale in prose and to make of the 'Four Black Brothers' a unit after the fashion of the 'Twelve Apostles' or the 'Three Musketeers.'

Robert, Gilbert, Clement, and Andrew – in the proper Border diminutives Hob, Gib, Clem, and Dand Elliott – these ballad heroes, had much in common; in particular, their high sense of the family and the family honour; but they went diverse ways, and prospered and failed in different businesses. According to Kirstie, 'they had a' bees in their bonnets but Hob.' Hob the laird was, indeed, essentially a decent man. An elder of the Kirk, nobody had heard an oath upon his lips, save, perhaps, thrice or so at the sheep-washing, since the chase of his father's murderers. The figure he had shown on that eventful night disappeared as if swallowed by a trap. He who had ecstatically dipped his hand in the red blood, he who had ridden down Dickieson, became, from that moment on, a stiff and rather graceless model of the rustic proprieties; cannily profiting by the high war prices, and yearly stowing away a little nest-egg in the bank against calamity; approved of and sometimes consulted by the greater lairds for the massive and placid sense of what he said, when he could be induced to say anything; and particularly valued by the minister, Mr Torrance, as a right-hand man in the parish, and a model to parents. The transfiguration had been for the moment only; some Barbarossa, some old Adam of our ancestors, sleeps in all of us till the fit circumstance shall call it into action; and for as sober as he now seemed, Hob had given once for all the measure of the devil that haunted him. He was married, and, by reason of the effulgence of that legendary night, was adored by his wife. He had a mob of little lusty, barefoot children who marched in a caravan the long miles to school, the stages of whose pilgrimage were marked by acts of spoliation and mischief, and who were qualified in the countryside as 'fair pests.' But in the house, if 'faither was in,' they were quiet as mice. In short, Hob moved through life in a great peace – the reward of any one who shall have killed his man, with any formidable and figurative circumstance, in the midst of a country gagged and swaddled with civilisation.

It was a current remark that the Elliotts were 'guid and bad, like sanguishes'; and certainly there was a curious distinction, the men of business coming alternately with the dreamers. The second brother, Gib, was a weaver by trade, had gone out early into the world to Edinburgh, and come home again with his wings singed. There was an exaltation in his nature which had led him to embrace with enthusiasm the principles of the French Revolution, and had ended by bringing him under the hawse of my Lord Hermiston in that furious onslaught of his upon the Liberals, which sent Muir and Palmer[5] into exile and dashed the party into chaff. It was whispered that my lord, in his great scorn for the movement and prevailed upon a little by a sense of neighbourliness, had given Gib a hint. Meeting him one day in the Potter-row, my lord had stopped in front of him. 'Gib, ye eediot,' he had said, 'what's this I hear of you? Poalitics, poalitics, poalitics, weaver's poalitics, is the way of it, I hear. If ye arena a' thegither dozened with eediocy, ye'll gang your ways back to Cauldstaneslap, and ca' your loom, and ca' your loom, man!' And Gilbert had taken him at the word and returned, with an expedition almost to be called flight, to the house of his father. The clearest of his inheritance was that family gift of prayer of which Kirstie had boasted; and the baffled politician now turned his attention to religious matters – or, as others said, to heresy and schism. Every Sunday morning he was in Crossmichael, where he had gathered together, one by one, a sect of about a dozen persons, who called themselves 'God's Remnant of the True Faithful,' or, for short, 'God's Remnant.' To the profane, they were known as 'Gib's Deils.' Bailie Sweedie, a noted humorist in the town, vowed that the proceedings always opened to the tune of 'The Deil Fly Away with the Excise-man,' and that the sacrament was dispensed in the form of hot whisky-toddy; both wicked hits at the evangelist, who had been suspected of smuggling in his youth, and had been overtaken (as the phrase went) on the streets of Crossmichael one Fair day. It was known that every Sunday they prayed for a blessing on the arms of Bonaparte. For this, 'God's Remnant,' as they were 'skailing' from the cottage that did duty for a temple, had been repeatedly stoned by the bairns, and Gib himself hooted by a squadron of Border volunteers in which his own brother, Dand, rode in a uniform and with a drawn sword. The 'Remnant' were believed, besides, to be 'antinomian in principle,' which might otherwise have been a serious charge, but the way public opinion then blew it was quite swallowed up and forgotten in the scandal about Bonaparte. For the rest, Gilbert had set up his loom in an outhouse at Cauldstaneslap, where he laboured assiduously six days of the week. His brothers, appalled by his political opinions, and willing to avoid dissension in the household, spoke but little to him; he less to them, remaining absorbed in the study of the Bible and almost constant prayer. The gaunt weaver was dry-nurse at Cauldstaneslap, and the bairns loved him dearly. Except when he was carrying an infant in his arms, he was rarely seen to smile – as, indeed, there were few smilers in that family. When his sister-in-law rallied him, and proposed that he should get a wife and bairns of his own, since he was so fond of them, 'I have no clearness of mind upon that point,' he would reply. If nobody called him in to dinner, he stayed out. Mrs Hob, a hard, unsympathetic woman, once tried the experiment. He went without food all day, but at dusk, as the light began to fail him, he came into the house of his own accord, looking puzzled. 'I've had a great gale of prayer upon my speerit,' said he. 'I canna mind sae muckle's what I had for denner.' The creed of God's Remnant was justified in the life of its founder. 'And yet I dinna ken,' said Kirstie. 'He's maybe no more stockfish than his neeghbours! He rode wi' the rest o' them, and had a good stamach to the work, by a' that I hear! God's Remnant! The deil's clavers! There wasna muckle Christianity in the way Hob guided Johnny Dickieson, at the least of it; but Guid kens! Is he a Christian even? He might be a Mahommedan or a Deevil or a Fire-worshipper, for what I ken.'

The third brother had his name on a doorplate, no less, in the city of Glasgow. 'Mr Clement Elliott,' as long as your arm. In his case, that spirit of innovation which had shown itself timidly in the case of Hob by the admission of new manures, and which had run to waste with Gilbert in subversive politics and heretical religions, bore useful fruit in many ingenious mechanical improvements. In boyhood, from his addiction to strange devices of sticks and string, he had been counted the most eccentric of the family. But that was all by now; and he was a partner of his firm, and looked to die a bailie. He too had married, and was rearing a plentiful family in the smoke and din of Glasgow; he was wealthy, and could have bought out his brother, the cock-laird, six times over, it was whispered; and when he slipped away to Cauldstaneslap for a well-earned holiday, which he did as often as he was able, he astonished the neighbours with his broadcloth, his beaver hat, and the ample plies of his neck-cloth. Though an eminently solid man at bottom, after the pattern of Hob, he had contracted a certain Glasgow briskness and *aplomb* which set him off. All the other Elliotts were as lean as a rake, but Clement was laying on fat, and he panted sorely when he must get into his boots. Dand said, chuckling : 'Ay, Clem has the elements of a corporation.' 'A provost and corporation,' returned Clem. And his readiness was much admired.

The fourth brother, Dand, was a shepherd to his trade, and by starts, when he could bring his mind to it, excelled in the business. Nobody could train a dog like Dandie; nobody, through the peril of great storms in the winter time, could do more gallantly. But if his dexterity were exquisite, his diligence was but fitful; and he served his brother for bed and board, and a trifle of pocket-money when he asked for it. He loved money well enough, knew very well how to spend it, and could make a shrewd bargain when he liked. But he preferred a vague knowledge that he was well to windward to any counted coins in the pocket; he felt himself richer so. Hob would expostulate: 'I'm an amature herd,' Dand would reply: 'I'll keep your sheep to you when I'm so minded, but I'll keep my liberty, too. Thir's no man can coandescend on what I'm worth.' Clem would expound to him the miraculous results of compound interest, and recommend investments. 'Ay, man?' Dand would say, 'and do you think, if I took Hob's siller, that I wouldna drink it or wear it on the lassies? And, anyway, my kingdom is no' of this world. Either I'm a poet or else I'm nothing.' Clem would remind him of old age. 'I'll die young, like Robbie Burns,'[6] he would say stoutly. No question but he had a certain accomplishment in minor verse. His 'Hermiston Burn,' with its pretty refrain –

> I love to gang thinking whaur ye gang linking
> Hermiston burn, in the home;

his 'Auld, auld Elliotts, clay-cauld Elliotts, dour, bauld Elliotts of auld,' and his really fascinating piece about the Praying Weaver's Stone, had gained him in the neighbourhood the reputation, still possible in Scotland, of a local bard; and, though not printed himself, he was recognised by others who were and who had become famous. Walter Scott owed to Dandie the text of the 'Raid of Wearie' in the *Minstrelsy* and made him welcome at his house, and appreciated his talents, such as they were, with all his usual generosity. The Ettrick Shepherd[7] was his sworn crony; they would meet, drink to excess, roar out their lyrics in each other's faces, and quarrel and make it up again till bedtime. And besides these recognitions, almost to be called official, Dandie was made welcome for the sake of his gift through the farmhouses of several contiguous dales, and was thus exposed to manifold temptations which he rather sought than fled. He had figured on the stool of repentance,[8] for once fulfilling to the letter the tradition of his hero and model. His humorous verses to Mr Torrance on that occasion – 'Kenspeckle here my lane I stand' – unfortunately too indelicate for further citation, ran through the country like a fiery cross; they were recited, quoted, paraphrased and laughed over as far away as Dumfries on the one hand and Dunbar on the other.

These four brothers were united by a close bond, the bond of that mutual admiration – or rather mutual hero-worship – which is so strong among the members of secluded families who have much ability and little culture. Even the extremes admired each other. Hob, who had as much poetry as the tongs, professed to find pleasure in Dand's verses; Clem, who had no more religion than Claverhouse, nourished a heartfelt, at least an open-mouthed, admiration of Gib's prayers; and Dandie followed with relish the rise of Clem's fortunes. Indulgence followed hard on the heels of admiration. The laird, Clem, and Dand, who were Tories and patriots of the hottest quality, excused to themselves, with a certain bashfulness, the radical and revolutionary heresies of Gib. By another division of the family, the laird, Clem, and Gib, who were men exactly virtuous, swallowed the dose of Dand's irregularities as a kind of clog or drawback in the mysterious providence of God affixed to bards, and distinctly probative of poetical genius. To appreciate the simplicity of their mutual admiration, it was necessary to hear Clem, arrived upon one of his visits, and dealing in a spirit of continuous irony with the affairs and personalities of that great city of Glasgow where he lived and transacted business. The various personages, ministers of the church, municipal officers, mercantile big-wigs, whom he had occasion to introduce, were all alike denigrated, all served but as reflectors to cast back a flattering side-light on the house of Cauldstaneslap. The Provost, for whom Clem by exception entertained a measure of respect, he would liken to Hob. 'He minds me o' the laird there,' he would say. 'He has some of

Hob's grand, whunstane sense, and the same way with him of steiking his mouth when he's no' very pleased.' And Hob, all unconscious, would draw down his upper lip and produce, as if for comparison, the formidable grimace referred to. The unsatisfactory incumbent of St Enoch's Kirk was thus briefly dismissed: 'If he had but twa fingers o' Gib's he would waken them up.' And Gib, honest man! would look down and secretly smile. Clem was a spy whom they had sent out into the world of men. He had come back with the good news that there was nobody to compare with the Four Black Brothers, no position that they would not adorn, no official that it would not be well they should replace, no interest of mankind, secular or spiritual, which would not immediately bloom under their supervision. The excuse of their folly is in two words: scarce the breadth of a hair divided them from the peasantry. The measure of their sense is this: that these symposia of rustic vanity were kept entirely within the family, like some secret ancestral practice. To the world their serious faces were never deformed by the suspicion of any simper of self-contentment. Yet it was known. 'They hae a guid pride o' themsel's!' was the word in the countryside.

Lastly, in a Border story, there should be added their 'to-names.' Hob was The Laird. 'Roy ne puis, prince ne daigne'; he was the laird of Cauldstaneslap – say fifty acres – *ipsissimus*. Clement was Mr Elliott, as upon his door-plate, the earlier Dafty having been discarded as no longer applicable, and indeed only a reminder of misjudgment and the imbecility of the public; and the youngest, in honour of his perpetual wanderings, was known by the sobriquet of Randy Dand.

It will be understood that not all this information was communicated by the aunt, who had too much of the family failing herself to appreciate it thoroughly in others. But as time went on, Archie began to observe an omission in the family chronicle.

'Is there not a girl too?' he asked.

'Ay. Kirstie. She was named from me, or my grandmother at least – it's the same thing,' returned the aunt, and went on

again about Dand, whom she secretly preferred by reason of
his gallantries.

'But what is your niece like?' said Archie at the next opportunity.

'Her? As black's your hat! But I dinna suppose she would
maybe be what you would ca' *ill-looked* a' thegither. Na, she's
a kind of a handsome jaud – a kind o' gipsy,' said the aunt, who
had two sets of scales for men and women – or perhaps it
would be more fair to say that she had three, and the third
and the most loaded was for girls.

'How comes it that I never see her in church?' said Archie.

''Deed, and I believe she's in Glesgie with Clem and his
wife. A heap good she's like to get of it! I dinna say for men
folk, but where weemen folk are born, there let them bide.
Glory to God, I was never far'er from here than Crossmichael.'

In the meantime it began to strike Archie as strange, that
while she thus sang the praises of her kinsfolk, and manifestly
relished their virtues and (I may say) their vices like a thing
creditable to herself, there should appear not the least sign of
cordiality between the house of Hermiston and that of Cauldstaneslap. Going to church of a Sunday, as the lady housekeeper stepped with her skirts kilted, three tucks of her white
petticoat showing below, and her best India shawl upon her
back (if the day were fine) in a pattern of radiant dyes, she
would sometimes overtake her relatives preceding her more
leisurely in the same direction. Gib of course was absent: by
skreigh of day he had been gone to Crossmichael and his
fellow heretics; but the rest of the family would be seen march-
ing in open order: Hob and Dand, stiff-necked, straight-backed
six-footers, with severe dark faces, and their plaids about their
shoulders; the convoy of children scattering (in a state of high
polish) on the wayside, and every now and again collected by
the shrill summons of the mother; and the mother herself, by
a suggestive circumstance which might have afforded matter
of thought to a more experienced observer than Archie, wrapped in a shawl nearly identical with Kirstie's but a thought
more gaudy and conspicuously newer. At the sight, Kirstie

grew more tall – Kirstie showed her classical profile, nose in air and nostril spread, the pure blood came in her cheek evenly in a delicate living pink.

'A braw day to ye, Mistress Elliott,' said she, and hostility and gentility were nicely mingled in her tones. 'A fine day, mem,' the laird's wife would reply with a miraculous curtsey, spreading the while her plumage – setting off, in other words, and with arts unknown to the mere man, the pattern of her India shawl. Behind her, the whole Cauldstaneslap contingent marched in closer order, and with an indescribable air of being in the presence of the foe; and while Dandie saluted his aunt with a certain familiarity as of one who was well in court, Hob marched on in awful immobility. There appeared upon the face of this attitude in the family the consequences of some dreadful feud. Presumably the two women had been principals in the original encounter, and the laird had probably been drawn into the quarrel by the ears, too late to be included in the present skin-deep reconciliation.

'Kirstie,' said Archie one day, 'what is this you have against your family?'

'I dinna complean,' said Kirstie, with a flush. 'I say naething.'

'I see you do not – not even good-day to your own nephew,' said he.

'I hae naething to be ashamed of,' said she. 'I can say the Lord's Prayer with a good grace. If Hob was ill, or in preeson or poverty, I would see to him blithely. But for curtchying and complimenting and colloguing, thank ye kindly!'

Archie had a bit of a smile: he leaned back in his chair. 'I think you and Mrs Robert are not very good friends,' says he slyly, 'when you have your India shawls on?'

She looked upon him in silence, with a sparkling eye but an indecipherable expression; and that was all that Archie was ever destined to learn of the battle of the India shawls.

'Do none of them ever come here to see you?' he inquired.

'Mr Archie,' said she, 'I hope that I ken my place better. It would be a queer thing, I think, if I was to clamjamfry up your faither's house – that I should say it! – wi' a dirty, black-a-vised clan, no ane o' them it was worth while to mar soap upon but just mysel'! Na, they're all damnifeed wi' the black Ellwalds. I have nae patience wi' black folk.' Then, with a sudden consciousness of the case of Archie, 'No' that it maitters for men sae muckle,' she made haste to add, 'but there's naebody can deny that it's unwomanly. Long hair is the ornament o' woman ony way; we've good warrandise for that – it's in the Bible – and wha can doubt that the Apostle had some gowden-haired lassie in his mind – Apostle and all, for what was he but just a man like yersel'?'

CHAPTER VI

A LEAF FROM CHRISTINA'S
PSALM-BOOK

ARCHIE was sedulous at church. Sunday after Sunday he sat down and stood up with that small company, heard the voice of Mr Torrance leaping like an ill-played clarionet from key to key, and had an opportunity to study his moth-eaten gown and the black thread mittens that he joined together in prayer, and lifted up with a reverent solemnity in the act of benediction. Hermiston pew was a little square box, dwarfish in proportion with the kirk itself, and enclosing a table not much bigger than a footstool. There sat Archie an apparent prince, the only undeniable gentleman and the only great heritor in the parish, taking his ease in the only pew, for no other in the kirk had doors. Thence he might command an undisturbed view of that congregation of solid plaided men, strapping wives and daughters, oppressed children, and uneasy sheep-dogs. It was strange how Archie missed the look of race; except the dogs, with their refined foxy faces and inimitably curling tails, there was no one present with the least claim to gentility. The Cauldstaneslap party was scarcely an exception; Dandie perhaps, as he amused himself making verses through the interminable burden of the service, stood out a little by the glow in his eye and a certain superior animation of face and alertness of body; but even Dandie slouched like a rustic. The rest of the congregation, like so many sheep, oppressed him with a sense of hob-nailed routine, day following day – of physical labour in the open air, oatmeal porridge, peas bannock, the somnolent fire-side in the evening, and the night-long nasal slumbers in a box-bed. Yet he knew many of them to be shrewd and humorous, men of character, notable women, making a bustle in the world and radiating an influence from their low-browed doors. He knew besides they were like other men; below the crust of custom, rapture found a way; he had heard them beat the timbrel before Bacchus – had heard them shout and carouse over their whisky-toddy; and not the most Dutch-bottomed and severe faces among them all, not even the solemn elders themselves, but were capable of singular gambols at the voice of love. Men drawing near to an end of life's adventurous journey – maids thrilling with fear and curiosity on the threshold of entrance – women who had borne and perhaps buried children, who could remember the clinging of the small dead hands and the patter of the little feet now silent – he marvelled that among all those faces there should be no face of expectation, none that was mobile, none into which the rhythm and poetry of life had entered. 'O for a live face,' he thought; and at times he had a memory of Lady Flora; and at times he would study the living gallery before him with despair, and would see himself go on to waste his days in that joyless, pastoral place, and death come to him, and his grave be dug under the rowans, and the Spirit of the Earth laugh out in a thunder-peal at the huge fiasco.

On this particular Sunday, there was no doubt but that the spring had come at last. It was warm, with a latent shiver in the air that made the warmth only the more welcome. The shallows of the stream glittered and tinkled among bunches of primose. Vagrant scents of the earth arrested Archie by the way with moments of ethereal intoxication. The grey, Quaker-ish dale was still only awakened in places and patches from the sobriety of its wintry colouring; and he wondered at its beauty; an essential beauty of the old earth it seemed to him, not resident in particulars but breathing to him from the whole. He surprised himself by a sudden impulse to write poetry – he did so sometimes, loose, galloping octosyllabics in the vein of Scott – and when he had taken his place on a boulder, near some fairy falls and shaded by a whip of a tree that was already radiant with new leaves, it still more surprised him that he should find nothing to write. His heart perhaps beat in time

to some vast in-dwelling rhythm of the universe. By the time
he came to a corner of the valley and could see the kirk, he
had so lingered by the way that the first psalm was finishing.
The nasal psalmody, full of turns and trills and graceless graces,
seemed the essential voice of the kirk itself upraised in thanksgiving. 'Everything's alive,' he said; and again cries it aloud,
'Thank God, everything's alive!' He lingered yet a while in the
kirk-yard. A tuft of primroses was blooming hard by the leg
of an old, black table tombstone, and he stopped to contemplate
the random apologue. They stood forth on the cold earth with a
trenchancy of contrast; and he was struck with a sense of
incompleteness in the day, the season, and the beauty that
surrounded him – the chill there was in the warmth, the gross
black clods about the opening primroses, the damp earthy
smell that was everywhere intermingled with the scents. The
voice of the aged Torrance within rose in an ecstasy. And he
wondered if Torrance also felt in his old bones the joyous
influence of the spring morning; Torrance, or the shadow of
what once was Torrance, that must come so soon to lie outside
here in the sun and rain with all his rheumatisms, while a new
minister stood in his room and thundered from his own
familiar pulpit? The pity of it, and something of the chill of
the grave, shook him for a moment as he made haste to enter.

He went up the aisle reverently and took his place in the
pew with lowered eyes, for he feared he had already offended
the kind old gentleman in the pulpit, and was sedulous to
offend no further. He could not follow the prayer, not even
the heads of it. Brightness of azure, clouds of fragrance, a tinkle
of falling water and singing birds, rose like exhalations from
some deeper, aboriginal memory, that was not his, but belonged
to the flesh on his bones. His body remembered; and it seemed
to him that his body was in no way gross, but ethereal and
perishable like a strain of music; and he felt for it an exquisite
tenderness as for a child, an innocent, full of beautiful instincts
and destined to an early death. And he felt for old Torrance –
of the many supplications, of the few days – a pity that was
near to tears. The prayer ended. Right over him was a tablet

in the wall, the only ornament in the roughly masoned chapel
– for it was no more; the tablet commemorated, I was about
to say the virtues, but rather the existence of a former Rutherford of Hermiston; and Archie, under that trophy of his long
descent and local greatness, leaned back in the pew and contemplated vacancy with the shadow of a smile between playful
and sad, that became him strangely. Dandie's sister, sitting by
the side of Clem in her new Glasgow finery, chose that moment
to observe the young laird. Aware of the stir of his entrance,
the little formalist had kept her eyes fastened and her face
prettily composed during the prayer. It was not hypocrisy, there
was no one further from a hypocrite. The girl had been taught
to behave: to look up, to look down, to look unconscious, to
look seriously impressed in church, and in every conjuncture
to look her best. That was the game of female life, and she
played it frankly. Archie was the one person in church who
was of interest, who was somebody new, reputed eccentric,
known to be young, and a laird, and still unseen by Christina.
Small wonder that, as she stood there in her attitude of pretty
decency, her mind should run upon him! If he spared a glance
in her direction, he should know she was a well-behaved young
lady who had been to Glasgow. In reason he must admire her
clothes, and it was possible that he should think her pretty.
At that her heart beat the least thing in the world; and she
proceeded, by way of a corrective, to call up and dismiss a
series of fancied pictures of the young man who should now,
by rights, be looking at her. She settled on the plainest of them,
a pink short young man with a dish face and no figure, at
whose admiration she could afford to smile; but for all that,
the consciousness of his gaze (which was really fixed on Torrance and his mittens) kept her in something of a flutter till
the word Amen. Even then, she was far too well-bred to gratify
her curiosity with any impatience. She resumed her seat lan-
guidly – this was a Glasgow touch – she composed her dress,
rearranged her nosegay of primroses, looked first in front, then
behind upon the other side, and at last allowed her eyes to
move, without hurry, in the direction of the Hermiston pew.

For a moment, they were riveted. Next she had plucked her gaze home again like a tame bird who should have meditated flight. Possibilities crowded on her; she hung over the future and grew dizzy; the image of this young man, slim, graceful, dark, with the inscrutable half-smile, attracted and repelled her like a chasm. 'I wonder, will I have met my fate?' she thought, and her heart swelled.

Torrance was got some way into his first exposition, positing a deep layer of texts as he went along, laying the foundations of his discourse, which was to deal with a nice point in divinity, before Archie suffered his eyes to wander. They fell first of all on Clem, looking insupportably prosperous and patronising Torrance with the favour of a modified attention, as of one who was used to better things in Glasgow. Though he had never before set eyes on him, Archie had no difficulty in identifying him, and no hesitation in pronouncing him vulgar, the worst of the family. Clem was leaning lazily forward when Archie first saw him. Presently he leaned nonchalantly back; and that deadly instrument, the maiden, was suddenly unmasked in profile. Though not quite in the front of the fashion (had anybody cared!), certain artful Glasgow mantua-makers and her own inherent taste, had arrayed her to great advantage. Her accoutrement was, indeed, a cause of heart-burning, and almost of scandal, in that infinitesimal kirk company. Mrs Hob had said her say at Cauldstaneslap. 'Daft-like!' she had pronounced it. 'A jaiket that'll no' meet! Whaur's the sense of a jaiket that'll no' button upon ye, if it should come to be weet? What do ye ca' thir things? Demmy brokens, d'ye say? They'll be brokens wi' a vengeance or ye can win back! Weel, I have naething to do wi' it — it's no' good taste.' Clem, whose purse had thus metamorphosed his sister, and who was not insensible to the advertisement, had come to the rescue with a 'Hoot, woman! What do you ken of good taste that has never been to the ceety?' And Hob, looking on the girl with pleased smiles, as she timidly displayed her finery in the midst of the dark kitchen, had thus ended the dispute: 'The cutty looks weel,' he had said, 'and it's no' very like rain. Wear them the day, hizzie;

but it's no' a thing to make a practice o'.' In the breasts of her
rivals, coming to the kirk very conscious of white underlinen,
and their faces splendid with much soap, the sight of the toilet
had raised a storm of varying emotion, from the mere un-
envious admiration that was expressed in the long-drawn
'Eh!' to the angrier feeling that found vent in an emphatic
'Set her up!' Her frock was of straw-coloured jaconet muslin,
cut low at the bosom and short at the ankle, so as to display
her *demi-broquins* of Regency violet, crossing with many straps
upon a yellow cobweb stocking. According to the pretty fashion
in which our grandmothers did not hesitate to appear, and our
great-aunts went forth armed for the pursuit and capture of our
great-uncles, the dress was drawn up so as to mould the contour
of both breasts, and in the nook between a cairngorm brooch
maintained it. Here, too, surely in a very enviable position,
trembled the nosegay of primroses. She wore on her shoulders
– or rather, on her back and not her shoulders, which it scarcely
passed – a French coat of sarsenet, tied in front with Margate
braces, and of the same colour with her violet shoes. About
her face clustered a disorder of dark ringlets, a little garland
of yellow French roses surmounted her brow, and the whole
was crowned by a village hat of chipped straw. Amongst all
the rosy and all the weathered faces that surrounded her in
church, she glowed like an open flower – girl and raiment, and
the cairngorm that caught the daylight and returned it in a
fiery flash, and the threads of bronze and gold that played in her
hair.

Archie was attracted by the bright thing like a child. He
looked at her again and yet again, and their looks crossed. The
lip was lifted from her little teeth. He saw the red blood work
vividly under her tawny skin. Her eye, which was great as a
stag's, struck and held his gaze. He knew who she must be –
Kirstie, she of the harsh diminutive, his housekeeper's niece,
the sister of the rustic prophet, Gib – and he found in her the
answer to his wishes.

Christina felt the shock of their encountering glances, and
seemed to rise, clothed in smiles, into a region of the vague

and bright. But the gratification was not more exquisite than it was brief. She looked away abruptly, and immediately began to blame herself for that abruptness. She knew what she should have done, too late – turned slowly with her nose in the air. And meantime his look was not removed, but continued to play upon her like a battery of cannon constantly aimed, and now seemed to isolate her alone with him, and now seemed to uplift her, as on a pillory, before the congregation. For Archie continued to drink her in with his eyes, even as a wayfarer comes to a well-head on a mountain, and stoops his face, and drinks with thirst unassuageable. In the cleft of her little breasts the fiery eye of the topaz and the pale florets of primrose fascinated him. He saw the breasts heave, and the flowers shake with the heaving, and marvelled what should so much discompose the girl. And Christina was conscious of his gaze – saw it, perhaps, with the dainty plaything of an ear that peeped among her ringlets; she was conscious of changing colour, conscious of her unsteady breath. Like a creature tracked, run down, surrounded, she sought in a dozen ways to give herself a countenance. She used her handkerchief – it was a really fine one – then she desisted in a panic: 'He would only think I was too warm.' She took to reading in the metrical psalms, and then remembered it was sermon-time. Last she put a 'sugar-bool' in her mouth, and the next moment repented of the step. It was such a homely-like thing! Mr Archie would never be eating sweeties in kirk; and, with a palpable effort, she swallowed it whole, and her colour flamed high. At this signal of distress Archie awoke to a sense of his ill-behaviour. What had he been doing? He had been exquisitely rude in church to the niece of his housekeeper; he had stared like a lackey and a libertine at a beautiful and modest girl. It was possible, it was even likely, he would be presented to her after service in the kirk-yard, and then how was he to look? And there was no excuse. He had marked the tokens of her shame, of her increasing indignation, and he was such a fool that he had not understood them. Shame bowed him down, and he looked resolutely at Mr Torrance; who little supposed, good, worthy man, as he continued to expound justification by faith, what was his true business: to play the part of derivative to a pair of children at the old game of falling in love.

Christina was greatly relieved at first. It seemed to her that she was clothed again. She looked back on what had passed. All would have been right if she had not blushed, a silly fool! There was nothing to blush at, if she *had* taken a sugar-bool. Mrs MacTaggart, the elder's wife in St Enoch's, took them often. And if he had looked at her, what was more natural than that a young gentleman should look at the best-dressed girl in church? And at the same time, she knew far otherwise; she knew there was nothing casual or ordinary in the look, and valued herself on its memory like a decoration. Well, it was a blessing he had found something else to look at! And presently she began to have other thoughts. It was necessary, she fancied, that she should put herself right by a repetition of the incident, better managed. If the wish was father to the thought, she did not know or she would not recognise it. It was simply as a manœuvre of propriety, as something called for to lessen the significance of what had gone before, that she should a second time meet his eyes, and this time without blushing. And at the memory of the blush, she blushed again, and became one general blush burning from head to foot. Was ever anything so indelicate, so forward, done by a girl before? And here she was, making an exhibition of herself before the congregation about nothing! She stole a glance upon her neighbours, and behold! they were steadily indifferent, and Clem had gone to sleep. And still the one idea was becoming more and more potent with her, that in common prudence she must look again before the service ended. Something of the same sort was going forward in the mind of Archie, as he struggled with the load of penitence. So it chanced that, in the flutter of the moment when the last psalm was given out, and Torrance was reading the verse, and the leaves of every psalm-book in church were rustling under busy fingers, two stealthy glances were sent out like antennæ among the pews and on the indifferent and absorbed occupants, and drew timidly nearer to the straight line between Archie and Christina. They met, they lingered together for the least fraction of time, and that was enough. A charge as of electricity passed through Christina, and behold! the leaf of her psalm-book was torn across.

Archie was outside by the gate of the graveyard, conversing with Hob and the minister and shaking hands all round with the scattering congregation, when Clem and Christina were brought up to be presented. The laird took off his hat and bowed to her with grace and respect. Christina made her Glasgow curtsey to the laird, and went on again up the road for Hermiston and Cauldstaneslap, walking fast, breathing hurriedly with a heightened colour, and in this strange frame of mind, that when she was alone she seemed in high happiness, and when any one addressed her she resented it like a contradiction. A part of the way she had the company of some neighbour girls and a loutish young man; never had they seemed so insipid, never had she made herself so disagreeable. But these struck aside to their various destinations or were out-walked and left behind; and when she had driven off with sharp words the proffered convoy of some of her nephews and nieces, she was free to go on alone up Hermiston brae, walking on air, dwelling intoxicated among clouds of happiness. Near to the summit she heard steps behind her, a man's steps, light and very rapid. She knew the foot at once and walked the faster. 'If it's me he's wanting he can run for it,' she thought, smiling.

Archie overtook her like a man whose mind was made up. 'Miss Kirstie,' he began.

'Miss Christina, if you please, Mr Weir,' she interrupted. 'I canna bear the contraction.'

'You forget it has a friendly sound for me. Your aunt is an old friend of mine and a very good one. I hope we shall see much of you at Hermiston?'

'My aunt and my sister-in-law doesna agree very well. Not that I have much ado with it. But still when I'm stopping in the house, if I was to be visiting my aunt, it would not look considerate-like.'

'I am sorry,' said Archie.

'I thank you kindly, Mr Weir,' she said. 'I whiles think myself it's a great peety.'

'Ah, I am sure your voice would always be for peace!' he cried.

'I wouldna be too sure of that,' she said. 'I have my days like other folk, I suppose.'

'Do you know, in our old kirk, among our good old grey dames, you made an effect like sunshine.'

'Ah, but that would be my Glasgow clothes!'

'I did not think I was so much under the influence of pretty frocks.'

She smiled with a half look at him. 'There's more than you!' she said. 'But you see I'm only Cinderella. I'll have to put all these things by in my trunk; next Sunday I'll be as grey as the rest. They're Glasgow clothes, you see, and it would never do to make a practice of it. It would seem terrible conspicuous.'

By that they were come to the place where their ways severed. The old grey moors were all about them; in the midst a few sheep wandered; and they could see on the one hand the straggling caravan scaling the braes in front of them for Cauld-staneslap, and on the other the contingent from Hermiston bending off and beginning to disappear by detachments into the policy gate. It was in these circumstances that they turned to say farewell, and deliberately exchanged a glance as they shook hands. All passed as it should, genteelly; and in Christina's mind, as she mounted the first steep ascent for Cauld-staneslap, a gratifying sense of triumph prevailed over the recollection of minor lapses and mistakes. She had kilted her gown, as she did usually at that rugged pass; but when she spied Archie still standing and gazing after her, the skirts came down again as if by enchantment. Here was a piece of nicety for that upland parish, where the matrons marched with their coats kilted in the rain, and the lasses walked barefoot to kirk through the dust of summer, and went bravely down by the burnside, and sat on stones to make a public toilet before entering! It was perhaps an air wafted from Glasgow; or perhaps it marked a stage of that dizziness of gratified vanity, in which the instinctive act passed unperceived. He was looking after! She unloaded her bosom of a prodigious sigh that was all pleasure, and betook herself to run. When she had over-taken the stragglers of her family, she caught up the niece whom she had so recently repulsed, and kissed and slapped her, and drove her away again, and ran after her with pretty cries and laughter. Perhaps she thought the laird might still be looking! But it chanced the little scene came under the view of eyes less favourable; for she overtook Mrs Hob march-ing with Clem and Dand.

'You're shürely fey,* lass!' quoth Dandie.

'Think shame to yersel', miss!' said the strident Mrs Hob. 'Is this the gait to guide yersel' on the way hame frae kirk? You're shürely no' sponsible the day. And anyway I would mind my guid claes.'

'Hoot!' said Christina, and went on before them, head in air, treading the rough track with the tread of a wild doe.

She was in love with herself, her destiny, the air of the hills, the benediction of the sun. All the way home, she continued under the intoxication of these sky-scraping spirits. At table she could talk freely of young Hermiston; gave her opinion of him offhand and with a loud voice, that he was a handsome young gentleman, real well-mannered and sensible-like, but it was a pity he looked doleful. Only – the moment after – a memory of his eyes in church embarrassed her. But for this inconsider-able check, all through meal-time she had a good appetite, and she kept them laughing at table, until Gib (who had returned before them from Crossmichael and his separative worship) reproved the whole of them for their levity.

Singing 'in to herself' as she went, her mind still in the turmoil of a glad confusion, she rose and tripped upstairs to a little loft, lighted by four panes in the gable, where she slept with one of her nieces. The niece, who followed her, presum-ing on 'Auntie's' high spirits, was flounced out of the apartment

*Unlike yourself, strange, as persons are observed to be in the hour of approaching death or calamity.

with small ceremony, and retired, smarting and half tearful, to bury her woes in the byre among the hay. Still humming, Christina divested herself of her finery, and put her treasures one by one in her great green trunk. The last of these was the psalm-book; it was a fine piece, the gift of Mistress Clem, in distinct old-faced type, on paper that had begun to grow foxy in the warehouse – not by service – and she was used to wrap it in a handkerchief every Sunday after its period of service was over, and bury it end-wise at the head of her trunk. As she now took it in hand the book fell open where the leaf was torn, and she stood and gazed upon that evidence of her bygone discomposure. There returned again the vision of the two brown eyes staring at her, intent and bright, out of that dark corner of the kirk. The whole appearance and attitude, the smile, the suggested gesture of young Hermiston came before her in a flash at the sight of the torn page. 'I was surely fey!' she said, echoing the words of Dandie, and at the suggested doom her high spirits deserted her. She flung herself prone upon the bed, and lay there, holding the psalm-book in her hands for hours, for the more part in a mere stupor of unconsenting pleasure and unreasoning fear. The fear was superstitious; there came up again and again in her memory Dandie's ill-omened words, and a hundred grisly and black tales out of the immediate neighbourhood read her a commentary on their force. The pleasure was never realised. You might say the joints of her body thought and remembered, and were gladdened, but her essential self, in the immediate theatre of consciousness, talked feverishly of something else, like a nervous person at a fire. The image that she most complacently dwelt on was that of Miss Christina in her character of the Fair Lass of Cauldstaneslap, carrying all before her in the straw-coloured frock, the violet mantle, and the yellow cobweb stockings. Archie's image, on the other hand, when it presented itself, was never welcomed – far less welcomed with any ardour, and it was exposed at times to merciless criticism. In the long, vague dialogues she held in her mind, often with imaginary, often with unrealised interlocutors, Archie, if he

were referred to at all, came in for savage handling. He was
described as 'looking like a stirk,' 'staring like a caulf,' 'a face
like a ghaist's.' 'Do you call that manners?' she said; or, 'I
soon put him in his place.' ' "*Miss Christina, if you please, Mr
Weir!*" says I, and just flyped up my skirt tails.' With gabble
like this she would entertain herself long whiles together, and
then her eye would perhaps fall on the torn leaf, and the eyes
of Archie would appear again from the darkness of the wall,
and the voluble words deserted her, and she would lie still and
stupid, and think upon nothing with devotion, and be sometimes raised by a quiet sigh. Had a doctor of medicine come
into that loft, he would have diagnosed a healthy, well-devel-
oped, eminently vivacious lass lying on her face in a fit of the
sulks; not one who had just contracted, or was just contracting,
a mortal sickness of the mind which should yet carry her
towards death and despair. Had it been a doctor of psychology,
he might have been pardoned for divining in the girl a passion
of childish vanity, self-love *in excelsis*, and no more. It is to be
understood that I have been painting chaos and describing the
inarticulate. Every lineament that appears is too precise, almost
every word used too strong. Take a finger-post in the mountains
on a day of rolling mists; I have but copied the names that
appear upon the pointers, the names of definite and famous
cities far distant, and now perhaps basking in sunshine; but
Christina remained all these hours, as it were, at the foot of the
post itself, not moving, and enveloped in mutable and blinding
wreaths of haze.

The day was growing late and the sunbeams long and level,
when she sat suddenly up, and wrapped in its handkerchief
and put by that psalm-book which had already played a part
so decisive in the first chapter of her love-story. In the absence
of the mesmerist's eye, we are told nowadays that the head
of a bright nail may fill his place, if it be steadfastly regarded.
So that torn page had riveted her attention on what might else
have been but little, and perhaps soon forgotten; while the
ominous words of Dandie – heard, not heeded, and still remembered – had lent to her thoughts, or rather to her mood,

a cast of solemnity, and that idea of Fate[1] – a pagan Fate, uncontrolled by any Christian deity, obscure, lawless, and august – moving indissuadably in the affairs of Christian men. Thus even that phenomenon of love at first sight, which is so rare and seems so simple and violent, like a disruption of life's tissue, may be decomposed into a sequence of accidents happily concurring.

She put on a grey frock and a pink kerchief, looked at herself a moment with approval in the small square of glass that served her for a toilet mirror, and went softly downstairs through the sleeping house that resounded with the sound of afternoon snoring. Just outside the door Dandie was sitting with a book in his hand, not reading, only honouring the Sabbath by a sacred vacancy of mind. She came near him and stood still.

'I'm for off up the muirs, Dandie,' she said.

There was something unusually soft in her tones that made him look up. She was pale, her eyes dark and bright; no trace remained of the levity of the morning.

'Ay, lass? Ye'll have yer ups and downs like me, I'm thinkin',' he observed.

'What for do ye say that?' she asked.

'O, for naething,' says Dand. 'Only I think ye're mair like me than the lave of them. Ye've mair of the poetic temper, tho' Guid kens little enough of the poetic taalent. It's an ill gift at the best. Look at yoursel'. At denner you were all sunshine and flowers and laughter, and now you're like the star of evening on a lake.'

She drank in this hackneyed compliment like wine, and it glowed in her veins.

'But I'm saying, Dand' – she came nearer him – 'I'm for the muirs. I must have a braith of air. If Clem was to be speiring for me, try and quaiet him, will ye no'?'

'What way?' said Dandie. 'I ken but the ae way, and that's leein'. I'll say ye had a sair heid, if ye like.'

'But I havena,' she objected.

'I daursay no,' he returned. 'I said I would say ye had; and if ye like to nay-say me when ye come back, it'll no mateerially maitter, for my chara'ter's clean gane a'ready past reca'.'

'O, Dand, are ye a leear?' she asked, lingering.

'Folks say sae,' replied the bard.

'Wha says sae?' she pursued.

'Them that should ken the best,' he responded. 'The lassies, for ane.'

'But Dand, you would never lee to me?' she asked.

'I'll leave that for your pairt of it, ye girzie,' said he. 'Ye'll lee to me fast eneuch, when ye hae gotten a jo. I'm tellin' ye and it's true; when you have a jo, Miss Kirstie, it'll be for guid and ill. I ken: I was made that way mysel', but the deil was in my luck! Here, gang awa wi' ye to your muirs, and let me be; I'm in an hour of inspiraution, ye upsetting tawpie!'

But she clung to her brother's neighbourhood, she knew not why.

'Will ye no gie's a kiss, Dand?' she said. 'I aye likit ye fine.'

He kissed her and considered her a moment; he found something strange in her. But he was a libertine through and through, nourished equal contempt and suspicion of all womankind, and paid his way among them habitually with idle compliments.

'Gae wa' wi' ye!' said he. 'Ye're a dentie baby, and be content wi' that!'

That was Dandie's way; a kiss and a comfit to Jenny – a bawbee and my blessing to Jill – and good-night to the whole clan of ye, my dears! When anything approached the serious, it became a matter for men, he both thought and said. Women, when they did not absorb, were only children to be shoo'd away. Merely in his character of connoisseur, however, Dandie glanced carelessly after his sister as she crossed the meadow. 'The brat's no' that bad!' he thought with surprise, for though he had just been paying her compliments, he had not really looked at her. 'Hey! what's yon?' For the grey dress was cut with short sleeves and skirts, and displayed her trim strong legs clad in pink stockings of the same shade as the kerchief she wore round her shoulders, and that shimmered as she went.

This was not her way in undress; he knew her ways and the ways of the whole sex in the countryside, no one better; when they did not go barefoot, they wore stout 'rig and furrow' woollen hose of an invisible blue mostly, when they were not black outright; and Dandie, at sight of this daintiness, put two and two together. It was a silk handkerchief, then they would be silken hose; they matched – then the whole outfit was a present of Clem's, a costly present, and not something to be worn through bog and briar, or on a late afternoon of Sunday. He whistled. 'My denty May, either your heid's fair turned, or there's some on-goings!' he observed, and dismissed the subject.

She went slowly at first, but ever straighter and faster for the Cauldstaneslap, a pass among the hills to which the farm owed its name. The Slap opened like a doorway between two rounded hillocks; and through this ran the short cut to Hermiston. Immediately on the other side it went down through the Deil's Hags, a considerable marshy hollow of the hill tops, full of springs, and crouching junipers, and pools where the black peat-water slumbered. There was no view from here. A man might have sat upon the Praying Weaver's Stone a half-century, and seen none but the Cauldstaneslap children twice in the twenty-four hours on their way to the school and back again, an occasional shepherd, the irruption of a clan of sheep, or the birds who haunted about the springs, drinking and shrilly piping. So, when she had once passed the Slap, Kirstie was received into seclusion. She looked back a last time at the farm. It still lay deserted except for the figure of Dandie, who was now seen to be scribbling in his lap, the hour of expected inspiration having come to him at last. Thence she passed rapidly through the morass, and came to the farther end of it, where a sluggish burn discharges, and the path for Hermiston accompanies it on the beginning of its downward path. From this corner a wide view was opened to her of the whole stretch of braes upon the other side, still sallow and in places rusty with the winter, with the path marked boldly, here and there by the burnside a tuft of birches, and – three miles off as the crow flies – from its enclosures and young plantations, the windows of Hermiston glittering in the western sun.

Here she sat down and waited, and looked for a long time at these far-away bright panes of glass. It amused her to have so extended a view, she thought. It amused her to see the house of Hermiston – to see 'folk'; and there was an indistinguishable human unit, perhaps the gardener, visibly sauntering on the gravel paths.

By the time the sun was down and all the easterly braes lay plunged in clear shadow, she was aware of another figure coming up the path at a most unequal rate of approach, now half-running, now pausing and seeming to hesitate. She watched him at first with a total suspension of thought. She held her thought as a person holds his breathing. Then she consented to recognise him. 'He'll no' be coming here, he canna be; it's no' possible.' And there began to grow upon her a subdued choking suspense. He *was* coming: his hesitations had quite ceased, his step grew firm and swift; no doubt remained; and the question loomed up before her instant: what was she to do? It was all very well to say that her brother was a laird himself; it was all very well to speak of casual intermarriages and to count cousinship, like Aunt Kirstie. The difference in their social station was trenchant; propriety, prudence, all that she had ever learned, all that she knew, bade her flee. But on the other hand the cup of life now offered to her was too enchanting. For one moment, she saw the question clearly, and definitely made her choice. She stood up and showed herself an instant in the gap relieved upon the sky line; and the next, fled trembling and sat down glowing with excitement on the Weaver's Stone. She shut her eyes, seeking, praying for composure. Her hand shook in her lap, and her mind was full of incongruous and futile speeches. What was there to make a work about? She could take care of herself, she supposed! There was no harm in seeing the laird. It was the best thing that could happen. She would mark a proper distance to him once and for all. Gradually the wheels of her nature ceased to go round so madly, and she sat in passive expectation, a quiet,

solitary figure in the midst of the grey moss. I have said she was
no hypocrite, but here I am at fault. She never admitted to
herself that she had come up the hill to look for Archie. And
perhaps after all she did not know, perhaps came as a stone
falls. For the steps of love in the young, and especially in girls,
are instinctive and unconscious.

In the meantime, Archie was drawing rapidly near, and he
at least was consciously seeking her neighbourhood. The afternoon had turned to ashes in his mouth; the memory of the
girl had kept him from reading and drawn him as with cords;
and at last, as the cool of the evening began to come on, he had
taken his hat and set forth, with a smothered ejaculation, by
the moor path to Cauldstaneslap. He had no hope to find her;
he took the off chance without expectation of result and to
relieve his uneasiness. The greater was his surprise, as he surmounted the slope and came into the hollow of the Deil's Hags,
to see there, like an answer to his wishes, the little womanly
figure in the grey dress and the pink kerchief sitting little, and
low, and lost, and acutely solitary, in these desolate surroundings and on the weather-beaten stone of the dead weaver. Those
things that still smacked of winter were all rusty about her,
and those things that already relished of the spring had put
forth the tender and lively colours of the season. Even in the
unchanging face of the death-stone changes were to be remarked; and in the channelled lettering, the moss began to
renew itself in jewels of green. By an after-thought that was a
stroke of art, she had turned up over her head the back of the
kerchief; so that it now framed becomingly her vivacious and
yet pensive face. Her feet were gathered under her on the one
side, and she leaned on her bare arm, which showed out strong
and round, tapered to a slim wrist, and shimmered in the fading
light.

Young Hermiston was struck with a certain chill. He was
reminded that he now dealt in serious matters of life and death.
This was a grown woman he was approaching, endowed with
her mysterious potencies and attractions, the treasury of the
continued race, and he was neither better nor worse than the

average of his sex and age. He had a certain delicacy which had preserved him hitherto unspotted, and which (had either of them guessed it) made him a more dangerous companion when his heart should be really stirred. His throat was dry as he came near; but the appealing sweetness of her smile stood between them like a guardian angel.

For she turned to him and smiled, though without rising. There was a shade in this cavalier greeting that neither of them perceived; neither he, who simply thought it gracious and charming as herself; nor yet she, who did not observe (quick as she was) the difference between rising to meet the laird and remaining seated to receive the expected admirer.

'Are ye stepping west, Hermiston?' said she, giving him his territorial name after the fashion of the countryside.

'I was,' said he, a little hoarsely, 'but I think I will be about the end of my stroll now. Are you like me, Miss Christina? the house would not hold me. I came here seeking air.'

He took his seat at the other end of the tombstone and studied her, wondering what was she. There was infinite import in the question alike for her and him.

'Ay,' she said. 'I couldna bear the roof either. It's a habit of mine to come up here about the gloaming when it's quaiet and caller.'

'It was a habit of my mother's also,' he said gravely. The recollection half startled him as he expressed it. He looked around. 'I have scarce been here since. It's peaceful,' he said, with a long breath.

'It's no' like Glasgow,' she replied. 'A weary place, yon Glasgow! But what a day have I had for my hamecoming, and what a bonny evening!'

'Indeed, it was a wonderful day,' said Archie. 'I think I will remember it years and years until I come to die. On days like this – I do not know if you feel as I do – but everything appears so brief, and fragile, and exquisite, that I am afraid to touch life. We are here for so short a time; and all the old people before us – Rutherfords of Hermiston, Elliotts of the Cauld-

staneslap – that were here but a while since, riding about and
keeping up a great noise in this quiet corner – making love too,
and marrying – why, where are they now? It's deadly commonplace, but after all, the commonplaces are the great poetic
truths.'

He was sounding her, semi-consciously, to see if she could
understand him; to learn if she were only an animal the colour
of flowers, or had a soul in her to keep her sweet. She, on her
part, her means well in hand, watched, womanlike, for any
opportunity to shine, to abound in his humour, whatever that
might be. The dramatic artist, that lies dormant or only half-
awake in most human beings, had in her sprung to his feet in
a divine fury, and chance had served her well. She looked upon
him with a subdued twilight look that became the hour of the
day and the train of thought; earnestness shone through her
like stars in the purple west; and from the great but controlled
upheaval of her whole nature there passed into her voice, and
rang in her lightest words, a thrill of emotion.

'Have you mind of Dand's song?' she answered. 'I think he'll
have been trying to say what you have been thinking.'

'No, I never heard it,' he said. 'Repeat it to me, can you?'

'It's nothing wanting the tune,' said Kirstie.

'Then sing it me,' said he.

'On the Lord's Day? That would never do, Mr Weir!'

'I am afraid I am not so strict a keeper of the Sabbath, and
there is no one in this place to hear us, unless the poor old
ancient under the stone.'

'No' that I'm thinking that really,' she said. 'By my way of
thinking, it's just as serious as a psalm. Will I sooth it to ye,
then?'

'If you please,' said he, and, drawing near to her on the
tombstone, prepared to listen.

She sat up as if to sing. 'I'll only can sooth it to ye,' she
explained. 'I wouldna like to sing out loud on the Sabbath. I
think the birds would carry news of it to Gilbert,' and she
smiled. 'It's about the Elliotts,' she continued, 'and I think

139

there's few bonnier bits in the book-poets, though Dand has never got printed yet.'

And she began, in the low, clear tones of her half-voice, now sinking almost to a whisper, now rising to a particular note which was her best, and which Archie learned to wait for with growing emotion :

> 'O they rade in the rain, in the days that are gane,
>   In the rain and the wind and the lave,
> They shoutit in the ha' and they routit on the hill,
>   But they're a' quaitit noo in the grave.
> Auld, auld Elliotts, clay-cauld Elliots, dour, bauld Elliotts of auld !'

All the time she sang she looked steadfastly before her, her knees straight, her hands upon her knee, her head cast back and up. The expression was admirable throughout, for had she not learned it from the lips and under the criticism of the author? When it was done, she turned upon Archie a face softly bright, and eyes gently suffused and shining in the twilight, and his heart rose and went out to her with bound-less pity and sympathy. His question was answered. She was a human being tuned to a sense of the tragedy of life; there were pathos and music and a great heart in the girl.

He arose instinctively, she also, for she saw she had gained a point, and scored the impression deeper, and she had wit enough left to flee upon a victory. They were but common-places that remained to be exchanged, but the low, moved voices in which they passed made them sacred in the memory. In the falling greyness of the evening he watched her figure winding through the morass, saw it turn a last time and wave a hand, and then pass through the Slap; and it seemed to him as if something went along with her out of the deepest of his heart. And something surely had come, and come to dwell there. He had retained from childhood a picture, now half-obliterated by the passage of time and the multitude of fresh impressions, of his mother telling him, with the fluttered earnestness of her voice, and often with dropping tears, the tale of the 'Praying

Weaver,' on the very scene of his brief tragedy and long repose. And now there was a companion piece; and he beheld, and he should behold for ever, Christina perched on the same tomb, in the grey colours of the evening, gracious, dainty, perfect as a flower, and she also singing –

> 'Of old, unhappy far-off things,
> And battles long ago,'[2]

– of their common ancestors now dead, of their rude wars composed, their weapons buried with them, and of these strange changelings, their descendants, who lingered a little in their places, and would soon be gone also, and perhaps sung of by others at the gloaming hour. By one of the unconscious arts of tenderness the two women were enshrined together in his memory. Tears, in that hour of sensibility, came into his eyes indifferently at the thought of either, and the girl, from being something merely bright and shapely, was caught up into the zone of things serious as life and death and his dead mother. So that in all ways and on either side, Fate played his game artfully with this poor pair of children. The generations were prepared, the pangs were made ready, before the curtain rose on the dark drama.

In the same moment of time that she disappeared from Archie, there opened before Kirstie's eyes the cup-like hollow in which the farm lay. She saw, some five hundred feet below her, the house making itself bright with candles, and this was a broad hint to her to hurry. For they were only kindled on a Sabbath night with a view to that family worship which rounded in the incomparable tedium of the day and brought on the relaxation of supper. Already she knew that Robert must be within-sides at the head of the table, 'waling the portions'; for it was Robert in his quality of family priest and judge, not the gifted Gilbert who officiated. She made good time accordingly down the steep ascent, and came up to the door panting as the three younger brothers, all roused at last from slumber, stood together in the cool and the dark of the evening with a fry of nephews and nieces about them, chatting and awaiting the expected signal. She stood back; she had no mind to direct attention to her late arrival or to her labouring breath.

'Kirstie, ye have shaved it this time, my lass,' said Clem. 'Whaur were ye?'

'O, just taking a dander by mysel',' said Kirstie.

And the talk continued on the subject of the American war,[3] without further reference to the truant who stood by them in the covert of the dusk, thrilling with happiness and the sense of guilt.

The signal was given, and the brothers began to go in one after another, amid the jostle and throng of Hob's children.

Only Dandie, waiting till the last, caught Kirstie by the arm. 'When did ye begin to dander in pink hosen, Mistress Elliott?' he whispered slyly.

She looked down; she was one blush. 'I maun have forgotten to change them,' said she; and went in to prayers in her turn with a troubled mind, between anxiety as to whether Dand should have observed her yellow stockings at church, and should thus detect her in a palpable falsehood, and shame that she had already made good his prophecy. She remembered the words of it, how it was to be when she had gotten a jo, and that that would be for good and evil. 'Will I have gotten my jo now?' she thought with a secret rapture.

And all through prayers, where it was her principal business to conceal the pink stockings from the eyes of the indifferent Mrs Hob – and all through supper, as she made a feint of eating, and sat at the table radiant and constrained – and again when she had left them and come into her chamber, and was alone with her sleeping niece, and could at last lay aside the armour of society – the same words sounded within her, the same profound note of happiness, of a world all changed and renewed, of a day that had been passed in Paradise, and of a night that was to be heaven opened. All night she seemed to be conveyed smoothly upon a shallow stream of sleep and waking, and through the bowers of Beulah;[4] all night she cherished to her heart that exquisite hope; and if, towards morning, she forgot it a while in a more profound unconsciousness, it was to catch again the rainbow thought with her first moment of awaking.

CHAPTER VII

ENTER MEPHISTOPHELES

Two days later a gig from Crossmichael deposited Frank Innes at the doors of Hermiston. Once in a way, during the past winter, Archie, in some acute phase of boredom, had written him a letter. It had contained something in the nature of an invitation, or a reference to an invitation – precisely what, neither of them now remembered. When Innes had received it, there had been nothing further from his mind than to bury himself in the moors with Archie; but not even the most acute political heads are guided through the steps of life with unerring directness. That would require a gift of prophecy which has been denied to man. For instance, who could have imagined that, not a month after he had received the letter, and turned it into mockery, and put off answering it, and in the end lost it, misfortunes of a gloomy cast should begin to thicken over Frank's career? His case may be briefly stated. His father, a small Morayshire laird with a large family, became recalcitrant and cut off the supplies; he had fitted himself out with the beginnings of quite a good law library, which, upon some sudden losses on the turf, he had been obliged to sell before they were paid for; and his bookseller, hearing some rumour of the event, took out a warrant for his arrest. Innes had early word of it, and was able to take precautions. In this immediate welter of his affairs, with an unpleasant charge hanging over him, he had judged it the part of prudence to be off instantly, had written a fervid letter to his father at Inverauld, and put himself in the coach for Crossmichael. Any port in a storm! He was manfully turning his back on the Parliament House and its gay babble, on porter and oysters, the racecourse and the ring; and manfully prepared, until these clouds should have blown by, to share a living grave with Archie Weir at Hermiston.

To do him justice, he was no less surprised to be going than Archie was to see him come; and he carried off his wonder with an infinitely better grace.

'Well, here I am!' said he, as he alighted. 'Pylades has come to Orestes at last. By the way, did you get my answer? No? How very provoking! Well, here I am to answer for myself, and that's better still.'

'I am very glad to see you, of course,' said Archie. 'I make you heartily welcome, of course. But you surely have not come to stay, with the Courts still sitting; is that not most unwise?'

'Damn the Courts!' says Frank. 'What are the Courts to friendship and a little fishing?'

And so it was agreed that he was to stay, with no term to the visit but the term which he had privily set to it himself – the day, namely, when his father should have come down with the dust, and he should be able to pacify the bookseller. On such vague conditions there began for these two young men (who were not even friends) a life of great familiarity and, as the days grew on, less and less intimacy. They were together at meal-times, together o' nights when the hour had come for whisky-toddy; but it might have been noticed (had there been any one to pay heed) that they were rarely so much together by day. Archie had Hermiston to attend to, multifarious activities in the hills, in which he did not require, and had even refused, Frank's escort. He would be off sometimes in the morning and leave only a note on the breakfast-table to announce the fact; and sometimes, with no notice at all, he would not return for dinner until the hour was long past. Innes groaned under these desertions; it required all his philosophy to sit down to a solitary breakfast with composure, and all his unaffected good-nature to be able to greet Archie with friendliness on the more rare occasions when he came home late for dinner.

'I wonder what on earth he finds to do, Mrs Elliott?' said he one morning, after he had just read the hasty billet and sat down to table.

'I suppose it will be business, sir,' replied the housekeeper dryly, measuring his distance off to him by an indicated curtsey.

'But I can't imagine what business!' he reiterated.

'I suppose it will be *his* business,' retorted the austere Kirstie.

He turned to her with that happy brightness that made the charm of his disposition, and broke into a peal of healthy and natural laughter.

'Well played, Mrs Elliott!' he cried, and the housekeeper's face relaxed into the shadow of an iron smile. 'Well played indeed!' said he. 'But you must not be making a stranger of me like that. Why, Archie and I were at the High School together, and we've been to College together, and we were going to the Bar together, when – you know! Dear me, dear me! what a pity that was! A life spoiled, a fine young fellow as good as buried here in the wilderness with rustics; and all for what? A frolic, silly, if you like, but no more. God, how good your scones are, Mrs Elliott!'

'They're no' mines, it was the lassie made them,' said Kirstie; 'and, saving your presence, there's little sense in taking the Lord's name in vain about idle vivers that you fill your kyte wi'.'

'I daresay you're perfectly right, ma'am,' quoth the imperturbable Frank. 'But, as I was saying, this is a pitiable business, this about poor Archie; and you and I might do worse than put our heads together, like a couple of sensible people, and bring it to an end. Let me tell you, ma'am, that Archie is really quite a promising young man, and in my opinion he would do well at the Bar. As for his father, no one can deny his ability, and I don't fancy any one would care to deny that he has the deil's own temper –'

'If you'll excuse me, Mr Innes, I think the lass is crying on me,' said Kirstie, and flounced from the room.

'The damned, cross-grained old broomstick!' ejaculated Innes.

In the meantime, Kirstie had escaped into the kitchen, and before her vassal gave vent to her feelings.

'Here, ettercap! Ye'll have to wait on yon Innes! I canna haud myself in. "Puir Erchie"! I'd "puir Erchie" him, if I had my way! And Hermiston with the deil's ain temper! God, let him take Hermiston's scones out of his mouth first. There's no' a hair an ayther o' the Weirs that hasna mair spunk and dirdum to it than what he has in his hale dwaibly body! Settin' up his snash to me! Let him gang to the black toon where he's mebbe wantit – birling in a curricle – wi' pimatum on his heid – making a mess o' himsel' wi' nesty hizzies – a fair disgrace!' It was impossible to hear without admiration Kirstie's graduated disgust, as she brought forth, one after another, these somewhat baseless charges. Then she remembered her immediate purpose, and turned again on her fascinated auditor. 'Do ye no' hear me, tawpie? Do ye no' hear what I'm tellin' ye? Will I have to shoo ye in to him? If I come to attend to ye, mistress!' And the maid fled the kitchen, which had become practically dangerous, to attend on Innes's wants in the front parlour.

Tantœne irœ? Has the reader perceived the reason? Since Frank's coming there were no more hours of gossip over the supper tray! All his blandishments were in vain; he had started handicapped on the race for Mrs Elliott's favour.

But it was a strange thing how misfortune dogged him in his efforts to be genial. I must guard the reader against accepting Kirstie's epithets as evidence; she was more concerned for their vigour than for their accuracy. Dwaibly, for instance; nothing could be more calumnious. Frank was the very picture of good looks, good-humour, and manly youth. He had bright eyes with a sparkle and a dance to them, curly hair, a charming smile, brilliant teeth, an admirable carriage of the head, the look of a gentleman, the address of one accustomed to please at first sight and to improve the impression. And with all these advantages, he failed with everyone about Hermiston; with the silent shepherd, with the obsequious grieve, with the groom who was also the ploughman, with the gardener and the gardener's sister – a pious, down-hearted woman with a shawl over her ears – he failed equally and flatly. They did not like him, and they showed it. The little maid, indeed, was an exception; she admired him devoutly, probably dreamed of him in her private hours; but she was accustomed to play the part of silent auditor to Kirstie's tirades and silent recipient of Kirstie's buffets, and she had learned not only to be a very capable girl of her years, but a very secret and prudent one besides. Frank was thus conscious that he had one ally and sympathiser in the midst of that general union of disfavour that surrounded, watched, and waited on him in the house of Hermiston; but he had little comfort or society from that alliance, and the demure little maid (twelve on her last birthday) preserved her own counsel, and tripped on his service, brisk, dumbly responsive, but inexorably unconversational. For the others, they were beyond hope and beyond endurance. Never had a young Apollo been cast among such rustic barbarians. But perhaps the cause of his ill-success lay in one trait which was habitual and unconscious with him, yet diagnostic of the man. It was his practice to approach any one person at the expense of some one else. He offered you an alliance against the some one else; he flattered you by slighting him; you were drawn into a small intrigue against him before you knew how. Wonderful are the virtues of this process generally; but Frank's mistake was in the choice of the some one else. He was not politic in that; he listened to the voice of irritation. Archie had offended him at first by what he had felt to be rather a dry reception; had offended him since by his frequent absences. He was besides the one figure continually present in Frank's eye; and it was to his immediate dependants that Frank could offer the snare of his sympathy. Now the truth is that the Weirs, father and son, were surrounded by a posse of strenuous loyalists. Of my lord they were vastly proud. It was a distinction in itself to be one of the vassals of the 'Hanging Judge,' and his gross, formidable joviality was far from unpopular in the neighbourhood of his home. For Archie they

had, one and all, a sensitive affection and respect which recoiled from a word of belittlement.

Nor was Frank more successful when he went farther afield.
To the Four Black Brothers, for instance, he was antipathetic
in the highest degree. Hob thought him too light, Gib too profane. Clem, who saw him but for a day or two before he went
to Glasgow, wanted to know what the fule's business was, and
whether he meant to stay here all session time! 'Yon's a drone,'
he pronounced. As for Dand, it will be enough to describe
their first meeting, when Frank had been whipping a river
and the rustic celebrity chanced to come along the path.

'I'm told you are quite a poet,' Frank had said.

'Wha tell 't ye that, mannie?' had been the unconciliating
answer.

'O, everybody,' says Frank.

'God! Here's fame!' said the sardonic poet, and he had
passed on his way.

Come to think of it, we have here perhaps a truer explanation of Frank's failures. Had he met Mr Sherriff Scott he could
have turned a neater compliment, because Mr Scott would
have been a friend worth making. Dand, on the other hand,
he did not value sixpence, and he showed it even while he
tried to flatter. Condescension is an excellent thing, but it is
strange how one-sided the pleasure of it is! He who goes fishing among the Scots peasantry with condescension for a bait
will have an empty basket by evening.

In proof of this theory Frank made a great success of it at
the Crossmichael Club, to which Archie took him immediately
on his arrival; his own last appearance on that scene of gaiety.
Frank was made welcome there at once, continued to go
regularly, and had attended a meeting (as the members ever
after loved to tell) on the evening before his death. Young
Hay and young Pringle appeared again. There was another
supper at Windielaws, another dinner at Driffel; and it resulted
in Frank being taken to the bosom of the county people as un-
reservedly as he had been repudiated by the country folk. He
occupied Hermiston after the manner of an invader in a con-

quered capital. He was perpetually issuing from it, as from a base, to toddy parties, fishing parties, and dinner parties, to which Archie was not invited, or to which Archie would not go. It was now that the name of The Recluse became general for the young man. Some say that Innes invented it; Innes, at least, spread it abroad.

'How's all with your Recluse to-day?' people would ask.

'O, reclusing away!' Innes would declare, with his bright air of saying something witty; and immediately interrupt the general laughter which he had provoked much more by his air than his words, 'Mind you, it's all very well laughing, but I'm not very well pleased. Poor Archie is a good fellow, an excellent fellow, a fellow I always liked. I think it small of him to take his little disgrace so hard and shut himself up. "Grant that it is a ridiculous story, painfully ridiculous," I keep telling him. "Be a man! Live it down, man!" But not he. Of course it's just solitude, and shame, and all that. But I confess I'm beginning to fear the result. It would be all the pities in the world if a really promising fellow like Weir was to end ill. I'm seriously tempted to write to Lord Hermiston, and put it plainly to him.'

'I would if I were you,' some of his auditors would say, shaking the head, sitting bewildered and confused at this new view of the matter, so deftly indicated by a single word. 'A capital idea!' they would add, and wonder at the *aplomb* and position of this young man, who talked as a matter of course of writing to Hermiston and correcting him upon his private affairs.

And Frank would proceed, sweetly confidential: 'I'll give you an idea, now. He's actually sore about the way that I'm received and he's left out in the county – actually jealous and sore. I've rallied him and I've reasoned with him, told him that every one was most kindly inclined towards him, told him even that *I* was received merely because I was his guest. But it's no use. He will neither accept the invitations he gets, nor stop brooding about the ones where he's left out. What I'm afraid of is that the wound's ulcerating. He had always one of those dark, secret, angry natures – a little underhand and plenty of bile – you know the sort. He must have inherited it from the Weirs, whom I suspect to have been a worthy family of weavers somewhere; what's the cant phrase! – sedentary occupation. It's precisely the kind of character to go wrong in a false position like what his father's made for him, or he's making for himself, whichever you like to call it. And for my part, I think it a disgrace,' Frank would say generously.

Presently the sorrow and anxiety of this disinterested friend took shape. He began in private, in conversations of two, to talk vaguely of bad habits and low habits. 'I must say I'm afraid he's going wrong altogether,' he would say. 'I'll tell you plainly, and between ourselves, I scarcely like to stay there any longer; only, man, I'm positively afraid to leave him alone. You'll see, I shall be blamed for it later on. I'm staying at a great sacrifice. I'm hindering my chances at the Bar, and I can't blind my eyes to it. And what I'm afraid of is that I'm going to get kicked for it all round before all's done. You see, nobody believes in friendship nowadays.'

'Well, Innes,' his interlocutor would reply, 'it's very good of you, I must say that. If there's any blame going you'll always be sure of *my* good word, for one thing.'

'Well,' Frank would continue, 'candidly, I don't say it's pleasant. He has a very rough way with him; his father's son, you know. I don't say he's rude – of course, I couldn't be expected to stand that – but he steers very near the wind. No, it's not pleasant; but I tell ye, man, in conscience I don't think it would be fair to leave him. Mind you, I don't say there's anything actually wrong. What I say is that I don't like the looks of it, man!' and he would press the arm of his momentary confidant.

In the early stages I am persuaded there was no malice. He talked but for the pleasure of airing himself. He was essentially glib, as becomes the young advocate, and essentially careless of the truth, which is the mark of the young ass; and so he talked at random. There was no particular bias, but that one which is indigenous and universal, to flatter himself and to

please and interest the present friend. And by thus milling air
out of his mouth, he had presently built up a presentation of
Archie which was known and talked of in all corners of the
county. Wherever there was a residential house and a walled
garden, wherever there was a dwarfish castle and a park,
wherever a quadruple cottage by the ruins of a peel-tower
showed an old family going down, and wherever a handsome
villa with a carriage approach and a shrubbery marked the
coming up of a new one – probably on the wheels of machin-
ery – Archie began to be regarded in the light of a dark, perhaps a vicious mystery, and the future developments of his
career to be looked for with uneasiness and confidential whispering. He had done something disgraceful, my dear. What, was
not precisely known, and that good kind young man, Mr
Innes, did his best to make light of it. But there it was. And
Mr Innes was very anxious about him now; he was really
uneasy, my dear; he was positively wrecking his own prospects
because he dared not leave him alone. How wholly we all lie
at the mercy of a single prater, not needfully with any malign
purpose! And if a man but talks of himself in the right spirit,
refers to his virtuous actions by the way, and never applies to
them the name of virtue, how easily his evidence is accepted
in the court of public opinion!

All this while, however, there was a more poisonous ferment
at work between the two lads, which came late indeed to the
surface, but had modified and magnified their dissensions from
the first. To an idle, shallow, easy-going customer like Frank,
the smell of a mystery was attractive. It gave his mind something to play with, like a new toy to a child; and it took him
on the weak side, for like many young men coming to the
Bar, and before they have been tried and found wanting, he
flattered himself he was a fellow of unusual quickness and
penetration. They knew nothing of Sherlock Holmes[1] in these
days, but there was a good deal said of Talleyrand. And if you
could have caught Frank off his guard, he would have con-
fessed with a smirk, that, if he resembled any one, it was the
Marquis de Talleyrand-Périgord.[2] It was on the occasion of

Archie's first absence that this interest took root. It was vastly deepened when Kirstie resented his curiosity at breakfast, and that same afternoon there occurred another scene which clinched the business. He was fishing Swingleburn, Archie accompanying him, when the latter looked at his watch.

'Well, good-bye,' said he. 'I have something to do. See you at dinner.'

'Don't be in such a hurry,' cries Frank. 'Hold on till I get my rod up. I'll go with you; I'm sick of flogging this ditch.'

And he began to reel up his line.

Archie stood speechless. He took a long while to recover his wits under this direct attack; but by the time he was ready with his answer, and the angle was almost packed up, he had become completely Weir, and the hanging face gloomed on his young shoulders. He spoke with a laboured composure, a laboured kindness even; but a child could see that his mind was made up.

'I beg your pardon, Innes; I don't want to be disagreeable, but let us understand one another from the beginning. When I want your company, I'll let you know.'

'Oh!' cries Frank, 'you don't want my company, don't you?'

'Apparently not just now,' replied Archie. 'I even indicated to you when I did, if you'll remember – and that was at dinner. If we two fellows are to live together pleasantly – and I see no reason why we should not – it can only be by respecting each other's privacy. If we begin intruding –'

'Oh, come! I'll take this at no man's hands. Is this the way you treat a guest and an old friend?' cried Innes.

'Just go home and think over what I said by yourself,' continued Archie, 'whether it's reasonable, or whether it's really offensive or not; and let's meet at dinner as though nothing had happened. I'll put it this way, if you like – that I know my own character, that I'm looking forward (with great pleasure, I assure you) to a long visit from you, and that I'm taking precautions at the first. I see the thing that we – that I, if you like – might fall out upon, and I step in and *obsto principiis*. I wager you five pounds you'll end by seeing that I mean friendliness, and I assure you, Francie, I do,' he added, relenting.

Bursting with anger, but incapable of speech, Innes shouldered his rod, made a gesture of farewell, and strode off down the burnside. Archie watched him go without moving. He was sorry, but quite unashamed. He hated to be inhospitable, but in one thing he was his father's son. He had a strong sense that his house was his own and no man else's; and to lie at a guest's mercy was what he refused. He hated to seem harsh. But that was Frank's look-out. If Frank had been commonly discreet, he would have been decently courteous. And there was another consideration. The secret he was protecting was not his own merely; it was hers; it belonged to that inexpressible she who was fast taking possession of his soul, and whom he would soon have defended at the cost of burning cities. By the time he had watched Frank as far as the Swingleburnfoot, appearing and disappearing in the tarnished heather, still stalking at a fierce gait but already dwindled in the distance into less than the smallness of Lilliput, he could afford to smile at the occurrence. Either Frank would go, and that would be a relief – or he would continue to stay, and his host must continue to endure him. And Archie was now free – by devious paths, behind hillocks and in the hollow of burns – to make for the trysting-place where Kirstie, cried about by the curlew and the plover, waited and burned for his coming by the Covenanter's stone.

Innes went off down-hill in a passion of resentment, easy to be understood, but which yielded progressively to the needs of his situation. He cursed Archie for a cold-hearted, unfriendly, rude dog; and himself still more passionately for a fool in having come to Hermiston when he might have sought refuge in almost any other house in Scotland, but the step once taken was practically irretrievable. He had no more ready money to go anywhere else; he would have to borrow from Archie the next club-night; and ill as he thought of his host's manners, he was sure of his practical generosity. Frank's resemblance to Talleyrand strikes me as imaginary; but at least not Talleyrand himself could have more obediently taken his lesson from the facts. He met Archie at dinner without resentment, almost with cordiality. You must take your friends as you find them, he would have said. Archie couldn't help being his father's son, or his grandfather's, the hypothetical weaver's, grandson. The son of a hunks, he was still a hunks at heart, incapable of true generosity and consideration; but he had other qualities with which Frank could divert himself in the meanwhile, and to enjoy which it was necessary that Frank should keep his temper.

So excellently was it controlled that he awoke next morning with his head full of a different, though a cognate subject. What was Archie's little game? Why did he shun Frank's company? What was he keeping secret? Was he keeping tryst with somebody, and was it a woman? It would be a good joke and a fair revenge to discover. To that task he set himself with a great deal of patience, which might have surprised his friends, for he had been always credited not with patience so much as brilliancy; and little by little, from one point to another, he at last succeeding in piecing out the situation. First he remarked that, although Archie set out in all the directions of the compass, he always came home again from some point between the south and west. From the study of a map, and in consideration of the great expanse of untenanted moorland running in that direction towards the sources of the Clyde, he laid his finger on Cauldstaneslap and two other neighbouring farms, Kingsmuirs and Polintarf. But it was difficult to advance farther. With his rod for a pretext, he vainly visited each of them in turn; nothing was to be seen suspicious about this trinity of moorland settlements. He would have tried to follow Archie, had it been the least possible, but the nature of the land precluded the idea. He did the next best, ensconced himself in a quiet corner, and pursued his movements with a telescope. It was equally in vain, and he soon wearied of his futile vigilance, left the telescope at home, and had almost given the matter up in despair, when, on the twenty-seventh day of his visit, he was suddenly confronted with the person whom he sought. The first Sunday Kirstie had managed to stay away from kirk on some pretext of indisposition, which was more truly modesty; the pleasure of beholding Archie seeming too sacred, too vivid for that public place. On the two following, Frank had himself been absent on some of his excursions among the neighbouring families. It was not until the fourth, according-ly, that Frank had occasion to set eyes on the enchantress. With the first look, all hesitation was over. She came with the Cauldstaneslap party; then she lived at Cauldstaneslap. Here was Archie's secret, here was the woman, and more than that – though I have need here of every manageable attenuation of language – with the first look, he had already entered himself as rival. It was a good deal in pique, it was a little in revenge, it was much in genuine admiration: the devil may decide the proportions; I cannot, and it is very likely that Frank could not.

'Mighty attractive milkmaid,' he observed, on the way home.

'Who?' said Archie.

'O, the girl you're looking at – aren't you? Forward there on the road. She came attended by the rustic bard; presumably, therefore, belongs to his exalted family. The single objection! for the Four Black Brothers are awkward customers. If any-thing were to go wrong, Gib would gibber, and Clem would prove inclement; and Dand fly in danders, and Hob blow up in gobbets. It would be a Helliott of a business!'

'Very humorous, I am sure,' said Archie.

'Well, I am trying to be so,' said Frank. 'It's none too easy in this place, and with your solemn society, my dear fellow. But confess that the milkmaid has found favour in your eyes or resign all claim to be a man of taste.'

'It is no matter,' returned Archie.

But the other continued to look at him, steadily and quiz-zically, and his colour slowly rose and deepened under the glance, until not impudence itself could have denied that he was blushing. And at this Archie lost some of his control. He changed his stick from one hand to the other, and – 'O, for God's sake, don't be an ass!' he cried.

'Ass? That's the retort delicate without doubt,' says Frank. 'Beware of the homespun brothers, dear. If they come into the dance, you'll see who's an ass. Think now, if they only applied (say) a quarter as much talent as I have applied to the question of what Mr Archie does with his evening hours, and why he is so unaffectedly nasty when the subject's touched on –'

'You are touching on it now,' interrupted Archie, with a wince.

'Thank you. That was all I wanted, an articulate confession,' said Frank.

'I beg to remind you –' began Archie.

But he was interrupted in turn. 'My dear fellow, don't. It's quite needless. The subject's dead and buried.'

And Frank began to talk hastily on other matters, an art in which he was an adept, for it was his gift to be fluent on anything or nothing. But although Archie had the grace or the timidity to suffer him to rattle on, he was by no means done with the subject. When he came home to dinner, he was greeted with a sly demand, how things were looking 'Cauld-staneslap ways.' Frank took his first glass of port out after dinner to the toast of Kirstie, and later in the evening he returned to the charge again.

'I say, Weir, you'll excuse me for returning again to this affair. I've been thinking it over, and I wish to beg you very seriously to be more careful. It's not a safe business. Not safe, my boy,' said he.

'What?' said Archie.

'Well, it's your own fault if I must put a name on the thing; but really, as a friend, I cannot stand by and see you rushing head down into these dangers. My dear boy,' said he, holding up a warning cigar, 'consider what is to be the end of it?'

'The end of what?' – Archie, helpless with irritation, persisted in this dangerous and ungracious guard.

'Well, the end of the milkmaid; or, to speak more by the card, the end of Miss Christina Elliott of the Cauldstaneslap?'

'I assure you,' Archie broke out, 'this is all a figment of your imagination. There is nothing to be said against that young lady; you have no right to introduce her name into the conversation.'

'I'll make a note of it,' said Frank. 'She shall henceforth be nameless, nameless, nameless, Gregarach! I make a note besides of your valuable testimony to her character. I only want to look at this thing as a man of the world. Admitted she's an angel – but, my good fellow, is she a lady?'

This was torture to Archie. 'I beg your pardon,' he said, struggling to be composed, 'but because you have wormed yourself into my confidence –'

'Oh, come!' cried Frank. 'Your confidence? It was rosy but unconsenting. Your confidence, indeed! Now, look! This is what I must say, Weir, for it concerns your safety and good character, and therefore my honour as your friend. You say I wormed myself into your confidence. Wormed is good. But what have I done? I have put two and two together, just as the parish will be doing to-morrow, and the whole of Tweed-dale in two weeks, and the Black Brothers – well, I won't put a date on that; it will be a dark and stormy morning. Your secret, in other words, is poor Poll's. And I want to ask of you as a friend whether you like the prospect? There are two horns to your dilemma, and I must say for myself I should look mighty ruefully on either. Do you see yourself explaining to the Four Black Brothers? or do you see yourself presenting the milkmaid to papa as the future lady of Hermiston? Do you? I tell you plainly, I don't.'

Archie rose. 'I will hear no more of this,' he said in a trembling voice.

But Frank again held up his cigar. 'Tell me one thing first. Tell me if this is not a friend's part that I am playing?'

'I believe you think it so,' replied Archie. 'I can go as far as that. I can do so much justice to your motives. But I will hear no more of it. I am going to bed.'

'That's right, Weir,' said Frank, heartily. 'Go to bed and think over it; and I say, man, don't forget your prayers! I don't often do the moral – don't go in for that sort of thing – but when I do there's one thing sure, that I mean it.'

So Archie marched off to bed, and Frank sat alone by the table for another hour or so, smiling to himself richly. There was nothing vindictive in his nature; but, if revenge came in his way, it might as well be good, and the thought of Archie's pillow reflections that night was indescribably sweet to him. He felt a pleasant sense of power. He looked down on Archie as on a very little boy whose strings he pulled – as on a horse whom he had backed and bridled by sheer power of intelligence, and whom he might ride to glory or the grave at pleasure. Which was it to be? He lingered long, relishing the details of schemes that he was too idle to pursue. Poor cork upon a torrent, he tasted that night the sweets of omnipotence, and brooded like a deity over the strands of that intrigue which was to shatter him before the summer waned.

CHAPTER VIII

A NOCTURNAL VISIT

KIRSTIE had many causes of distress. More and more as we grow old – and yet more and more as we grow old and are women, frozen by the fear of age – we come to rely on the voice as the single outlet of the soul. Only thus, in the curtailment of our means, can we relieve the straitened cry of the passion within us; only thus, in the bitter and sensitive shyness of advancing years, can we maintain relations with those vivacious figures of the young that still show before us and tend daily to become no more than the moving wallpaper of life. Talk is the last link, the last relation. But with the end of the conversation, when the voice stops and the bright face of the listener is turned away, solitude falls again on the bruised heart. Kirstie had lost her 'cannie hour at e'en'; she could no more wander with Archie, a ghost, if you will, but a happy ghost, in fields Elysian. And to her it was as if the whole world had fallen silent; to him, but an unremarkable change of amusements. And she raged to know it. The effervescency of her passionate and irritable nature rose within her at times to bursting point.

This is the price paid by age for unseasonable ardours of feeling. It must have been so for Kirstie at any time when the occasion chanced; but it so fell out that she was deprived of this delight in the hour when she had most need of it, when she had most to say, most to ask, and when she trembled to recognise her sovereignty not merely in abeyance but annulled. For, with the clairvoyance of a genuine love, she had pierced the mystery that had so long embarrassed Frank. She was conscious, even before it was carried out, even on that Sunday night when it began, of an invasion of her rights; and a voice told her the invader's name. Since then, by arts, by accident, by small things observed, and by the general drift of Archie's humour, she had passed beyond all possibility of doubt. With a sense of justice that Lord Hermiston might have envied, she had that day in church considered and admitted the attractions of the younger Kirstie; and with the profound humanity and sentimentality of her nature, she had recognised the coming of fate. Not thus would she have chosen. She had seen, in imagination, Archie wedded to some tall, powerful, and rosy heroine of the golden locks, made in her own image, for whom she would have strewed the bride-bed with delight; and now she could have wept to see the ambition falsified. But the gods had pronounced, and her doom was otherwise.

She lay tossing in bed that night, besieged with feverish thoughts. There were dangerous matters pending, a battle was toward, over the fate of which she hung in jealousy, sympathy, fear, and alternate loyalty and disloyalty to either side. Now she was reincarnated in her niece, and now in Archie. Now she saw, through the girl's eyes, the youth on his knees to her, heard his persuasive instances with a deadly weakness, and received his over-mastering caresses. Anon, with a revulsion, her temper raged to see such utmost favours of fortune, and love squandered on a brat of a girl, one of her own house, using her own name – a deadly ingredient – and that 'didna ken her ain mind an' was as black's your hat.' Now she trembled lest her deity should plead in vain, loving the idea of success for him like a triumph of nature; anon, with returning loyalty to her own family and sex, she trembled for Kirstie and the credit of the Elliotts. And again she had a vision of herself, the day over for her old-world tales and local gossip, bidding farewell to her last link with life and brightness and love; and behind and beyond, she saw but the blank butt-end where she must crawl to die. Had she then come to the lees? she, so great, so beautiful, with a heart as fresh as a girl's and strong as woman-hood? It could not be, and yet it was so; and for a moment her bed was horrible to her as the sides of the grave. And she looked forward over a waste of hours, and saw herself go on to rage, and tremble, and be softened, and rage again, until the day came and the labours of the day must be renewed.

Suddenly she heard feet on the stairs – his feet, and soon after the sound of a window-sash flung open. She sat up with her heart beating. He had gone to his room alone, and he had not gone to bed. She might again have one of her night cracks; and at the entrancing prospect, a change came over her mind; with the approach of this hope of pleasure, all the baser metal became immediately obliterated from her thoughts. She rose, all woman, and all the best of woman, tender, pitiful, hating the wrong, loyal to her own sex – and all the weakest of that dear miscellany, nourishing, cherishing next her soft heart, voicelessly flattering, hopes that she would have died sooner than have acknowledged. She tore off her night-cap, and her hair fell about her shoulders in profusion. Undying coquetry awoke. By the faint light of her nocturnal rush, she stood before the looking-glass, carried her shapely arms above her head, and gathered up the treasures of her tresses. She was never backward to admire herself; that kind of modesty was a stranger to her nature; and she paused, struck with a pleased wonder at the sight. 'Ye daft auld wife!' she said, answering a thought that was not; and she blushed with the innocent consciousness of a child. Hastily she did up the massive and shining coils, hastily donned a wrapper, and with the rush-light in her hand, stole into the hall. Below stairs she heard the clock ticking the deliberate seconds, and Frank jingling with the decanters in the dining-room. Aversion rose in her, bitter and momentary. 'Nesty, tippling puggy!' she thought; and the next moment she had knocked guardedly at Archie's door and was bidden enter.

Archie had been looking out into the ancient blackness, pierced here and there with a rayless star; taking the sweet air of the moors and the night into his bosom deeply; seeking, perhaps finding, peace after the manner of the unhappy. He turned round as she came in, and showed her a pale face against the window-frame.

'Is that you, Kirstie?' he asked. 'Come in!'

'It's unco' late, my dear,' said Kirstie, affecting unwillingness.
'No, no,' he answered, 'not at all. Come in, if you want a
crack. I am not sleepy, God knows!'

She advanced, took a chair by the toilet-table and the candle,
and set the rush-light at her foot. Something – it might be in
the comparative disorder of her dress, it might be the emotion
that now welled in her bosom – had touched her with a wand
of transformation, and she seemed young with the youth of
goddesses.

'Mr Erchie,' she began, 'what's this that's come to ye?'

'I am not aware of anything that has come,' said Archie,
and blushed and repented bitterly that he had let her in.

'Oh, my dear, that'll no dae!' said Kirstie. 'It's ill to blind the
eyes of love. Oh, Mr Erchie, tak' a thocht ere it's ower late. Ye
shouldna be impatient o' the braws o' life, they'll a' come in
their saison, like the sun and the rain. Ye're young yet; ye've
mony cantie years afore ye. See and dinna wreck yersel' at the
outset like sae mony ithers! Hae patience – they telled me aye
that was the owercome o' life – hae patience, there's a braw day
coming yet. Gude kens it never cam' to me; and here I am wi'
nayther man nor bairn to ca' my ain, wearyin' a' folks wi' my
ill tongue, and you just the first, Mr Erchie!'

'I have a difficulty in knowing what you mean,' said Archie.

'Weel, and I'll tell ye,' she said. 'It's just this, that I'm
feared. I'm feared for ye, my dear. Remember, your faither is
a hard man, reapin' where he hasna sowed and gaitherin' where
he hasna strawed. It's easy speakin', but mind! Ye'll have to
look in the gurly face o'm, where it's ill to look, and vain to
look for mercy. Ye mind me o' a bonny ship pitten oot into
the black and gowsty seas – ye're a' safe still, sittin' quait and
crackin' wi' Kirstie in your lown chalmer; but whaur will ye
be the morn, and in whatten horror o' the fearsome tempest,
cryin' on the hills to cover ye?'

'Why, Kirstie, you're very enigmatical to-night – and very
eloquent,' Archie put in.

'And, my dear Mr Erchie,' she continued, with a change of
voice, 'ye mauna think that I canna sympathise wi' ye. Ye

mauna think that I havena been young mysel'. Lang syne, when
I was a bit lassie, no' twenty yet —' She paused and sighed.
'Clean and callcr, wi' a fit like the hinney bee,' she continued,
'I was aye big and buirdly, ye maun understand; a bonny figure
o' a woman, though I say it that suldna — built to rear bairns
— braw bairns they suld hae been, and grand I would hae likit
it! But I was young, dear, wi' the bonny glint o' youth in my
e'en, and little I dreamed I'd ever be tellin' ye this, an auld,
lanely, rudas wife! Weel, Mr Erchie, there was a lad cam'
courtin' me, as was but naetural. Mony had come before, and
I would nane o' them. But this yin had a tongue to wile the
birds frae the lift and the bees frae the foxglove bells. Deary
me, but it's lang syne. Folk have dee'd sinsyne and been buried,
and are forgotten, and bairns been born and got merrit and
got bairns o' their ain. Sinsyne woods have been plantit, and
have grawn up and are bonny trees, and the joes sit in their
shadow, and sinsyne auld estates have changed hands, and
there have been wars and rumours of wars on the face of the
earth. And here I'm still — like an ould droopit craw — lookin'
on and craikin'. But, Mr Erchie, do ye no' think that I have
mind o' it a' still? I was dwallin' then in my faither's house;
and it's a curious thing that we were whiles trysted in the
Deil's Hags. And do ye no' think that I have mind of the
bonny simmer days, the lang miles o' the bluid-red heather, the
cryin' o' the whaups, and the lad and the lassie that was
trysted? Do ye no' think that I mind how the hilly sweetness
ran about my hairt? Ay, Mr Erchie, I ken the way o' it — fine do
I ken the way — how the grace o' God takes them like Paul
of Tarsus, when they think it least, and drives the pair o'
them into a land which is like a dream, and the world and the
folks in't are nae mair than clouds to the puir lassie, and
Heeven nae mair than windlestraes, if she can but pleesure him!
Until Tam dee'd — that was my story,' she broke off to say, 'he
dee'd, and I wasna at the buryin'. But while he was here, I
could take care o' mysel'. And can yon puir lassie?'

Kirstie, her eyes shining with unshed tears, stretched out
her hand towards him appealingly; the bright and the dull gold

of her hair flashed and smouldered in the coils behind her comely head, like the rays of an eternal youth; the pure colour had risen in her face; and Archie was abashed alike by her beauty and her story. He came towards her slowly from the window, took up her hand in his and kissed it.

'Kirstie,' he said hoarsely, 'you have misjudged me sorely. I have always thought of her, I wouldna harm her for the universe, my woman!'

'Eh, lad, and that's easy sayin',' cried Kirstie, 'but it's nae sae easy doin'! Man, do ye no' comprehend that it's God wull we should be blendit and glamoured, and have nae command over our ain members at a time like that? My bairn,' she cried, still holding his hand, 'think o' the puir lass! have pity upon her, Erchie! and O, be wise for twa! Think o' the risk she rins! I have seen ye, and what's to prevent ithers? I saw ye once in the Hags, in my ain howf, and I was wae to see ye there – in pairt for the omen, for I think there's a weird on the place – and in pairt for puir nakit envy and bitterness o' hairt. It's strange ye should forgather there tae! God! but yon puir, thrawn, auld Covenanter's seen a heap o' human natur since he lookit his last on the musket-barrels, if he never saw nane afore,' she added, with a kind of wonder in her eyes.

'I swear by my honour I have done her no wrong,' said Archie. 'I swear by my honour and the redemption of my soul that there shall none be done her. I have heard of this before. I have been foolish, Kirstie, not unkind, and, above all, not base.'

'There's my bairn!' said Kirstie, rising. 'I'll can trust ye noo, I'll can gang to my bed wi' an easy hairt.' And then she saw in a flash how barren had been her triumph. Archie had promised to spare the girl, and he would keep it; but who had promised to spare Archie? What was to be the end of it? Over a maze of difficulties she glanced, and saw, at the end of every passage, the flinty countenance of Hermiston. And a kind of horror fell upon her at what she had done. She wore a tragic mask. 'Erchie, the Lord peety you, dear, and peety me! I have buildit on this foundation,' – laying her hand heavily on his shoulder – 'and buildit hie, and pit my hairt in the buildin' of it. If the hale hypothec were to fa', I think, laddie, I would dee! Excuse a daft wife that loves ye, and that kenned your mither. And for His name's sake keep yersel' frae inordinate desires; haud your hairt in baith your hands, carry it canny and laigh; dinna send it up like a bairn's kite into the collie-shangie o' the wunds! Mind, Maister Erchie dear, that this life's a disappointment, and a mouthfu' o' mools is the appointed end.'

'Ay, but Kirstie, my woman, you're asking me ower much at last,' said Archie, profoundly moved, and lapsing into the broad Scots. 'Ye're asking what nae man can grant ye, what only the Lord of heaven can grant ye if He see fit. Ay! And can even He? I can promise ye what I shall do, and you can depend on that. But how I shall feel – my woman, that is long past thinking of!'

They were both standing by now opposite each other. The face of Archie wore the wretched semblance of a smile; hers was convulsed for a moment.

'Promise me ae thing,' she cried, in a sharp voice. 'Promise me ye'll never do naething without telling me.'

'No, Kirstie, I canna promise ye that,' he replied. 'I have promised enough, God kens!'

'May the blessing of God lift and rest upon ye, dear!' she said.

'God bless ye, my old friend,' said he.

CHAPTER IX

AT THE WEAVER'S STONE

IT was late in the afternoon when Archie drew near by the hill path to the Praying Weaver's Stone. The Hags were in shadow. But still, through the gate of the Slap, the sun shot a last arrow, which sped far and straight across the surface of the moss, here and there touching and shining on a tussock, and lighted at length on the gravestone and the small figure awaiting him there. The emptiness and solitude of the great moors seemed to be concentrated there, and Kirstie pointed out by that finger of sunshine for the only inhabitant. His first sight of her was thus excruciatingly sad, like a glimpse of a world from which all light, comfort, and society were on the point of vanishing. And the next moment, when she had turned her face to him and the quick smile had enlightened it, the whole face of nature smiled upon him in her smile of welcome. Archie's slow pace was quickened; his legs hasted to her though his heart was hanging back. The girl, upon her side, drew herself together slowly and stood up, expectant; she was all languor, her face was gone white; her arms ached for him, her soul was on tip-toes. But he deceived her, pausing a few steps away, not less white than herself, and holding up his hand with a gesture of denial.

'No, Christina, not to-day,' he said. 'To-day I have to talk to you seriously. Sit ye down, please, there where you were. Please!' he repeated.

The revulsion of feeling in Christina's heart was violent. To have longed and waited these weary hours for him, rehearsing her endearments – to have seen him at last come – to have been ready there, breathless, wholly passive, his to do what he would with – and suddenly to have found herself confronted

167

with a grey-faced, harsh schoolmaster – it was too rude a
shock. She could have wept, but pride withheld her. She sat
down on the stone, from which she had arisen, part with the
instinct of obedience, part as though she had been thrust there.
What was this? Why was she rejected? Had she ceased to
please? She stood here offering her wares, and he would none
of them! And yet they were all his! His to take and keep;
not his to refuse, though! In her quick petulant nature, a
moment ago on fire with hope, thwarted love and wounded
vanity wrought. The schoolmaster that there is in all men, to
the despair of all girls and most women, was now completely
in possession of Archie. He had passed a night of sermons; a
day of reflection; he had come wound up to do his duty; and
the set mouth, which in him only betrayed the effort of his
will, to her seemed the expression of an averted heart. It was
the same with his constrained voice and embarrassed utterance;
and if so – if it was all over – the pang of the thought took
away from her the power of thinking.

He stood before her some way off. 'Kirstie, there's been too
much of this. We've seen too much of each other.' She looked
up quickly and her eyes contracted. 'There's no good ever
comes of these secret meetings. They're not frank, not honest
truly, and I ought to have seen it. People have begun to talk;
and it's not right of me. Do you see?'

'I see somebody will have been talking to ye,' she said sullenly.

'They have, more than one of them,' replied Archie.

'And whae were they?' she cried. 'And what kind o' love
do ye ca' that, that's ready to gang round like a whirligig at
folk talking? Do ye think they havena talked to me?'

'Have they indeed?' said Archie, with a quick breath. 'That
is what I feared. Who were they? Who has dared –'

Archie was on the point of losing his temper.

As a matter of fact, not any one had talked to Christina on
the matter; and she strenuously repeated her own first question
in a panic of self-defence.

'Ah, well! what does it matter?' he said. 'They were good

folk that wished well to us, and the great affair is that there are people talking. My dear girl, we have to be wise. We must not wreck our lives at the outset. They may be long and happy yet, and we must see to it, Kirstie, like God's rational creatures and not like fool children. There is one thing we must see to before all. You're worth waiting for, Kirstie! worth waiting for a generation; it would be enough reward.' – And here he remembered the schoolmaster again, and very unwisely took to following wisdom. 'The first thing that we must see to, is that there shall be no scandal about, for my father's sake. That would ruin all; do ye no' see that?'

Kirstie was a little pleased, there had been some show of warmth of sentiment in what Archie had said last. But the dull irritation still persisted in her bosom; with the aboriginal instinct, having suffered herself, she wished to make Archie suffer.

And besides, there had come out the word she had always feared to hear from his lips, the name of his father. It is not to be supposed that, during so many days with a love avowed between them, some reference had not been made to their conjoint future. It had in fact been often touched upon, and from the first had been the sore point. Kirstie had wilfully closed the eye of thought; she would not argue even with herself; gallant, desperate little heart, she had accepted the command of that supreme attraction like the call of fate and marched blindfold on her doom. But Archie, with his masculine sense of responsibility, must reason; he must dwell on some future good, when the present good was all in all to Kirstie; he must talk – and talk lamely, as necessity drove him – of what was to be. Again and again he had touched on marriage; again and again been driven back into indistinctness by a memory of Lord Hermiston. And Kirstie had been swift to understand and quick to choke down and smother the understanding; swift to leap up in flame at a mention of that hope, which spoke volumes to her vanity and her love, that she might one day be Mrs Weir of Hermiston; swift, also, to recognise in his stumbling or throttled utterance the death-knell of these expectations, and constant, poor girl! in her large-minded madness, to go on and to reck nothing of the future. But these unfinished references, these blinks in which his heart spoke, and his memory and reason rose up to silence it before the words were well uttered, gave her unqualifiable agony. She was raised up and dashed down again bleeding. The recurrence of the subject forced her, for however short a time, to open her eyes on what she did not wish to see; and it had invariably ended in another disappointment. So now again, at the mere wind of its coming, at the mere mention of his father's name – who might seem indeed to have accompanied them in their whole moorland courtship, an awful figure in a wig with an ironical and bitter smile, present to guilty consciousness – she fled from it head down.

'Ye havena told me yet,' she said, 'who was it spoke?'

'Your aunt for one,' said Archie.

'Auntie Kirstie?' she cried. 'And what do I care for my Auntie Kirstie?'

'She cares a great deal for her niece,' replied Archie, in kind reproof.

'Troth, and it's the first I've heard of it,' retorted the girl.

'The question here is not who it is, but what they say, what they have noticed,' pursued the lucid schoolmaster. 'That is what we have to think of in self-defence!'

'Auntie Kirstie, indeed! A bitter, thrawn auld maid that's fomented trouble in the country before I was born, and will be doing it still, I daur say, when I'm deid! It's in her nature; it's as natural for her as it's for a sheep to eat.'

'Pardon me, Kirstie, she was not the only one,' interposed Archie. 'I had two warnings, two sermons, last night, both most kind and considerate. Had you been there, I promise you you would have grat, my dear! And they opened my eyes. I saw we were going a wrong way.'

'Who was the other one?' Kirstie demanded.

By this time Archie was in the condition of a hunted beast. He had come, braced and resolute; he was to trace out a line of conduct for the pair of them in a few cold, convincing sentences; he had now been there some time, and he was still staggering round the outworks and undergoing what he felt to be a savage cross-examination.

'Mr Frank!' she cried. 'What nex', I would like to ken?'

'He spoke most kindly and truly.'

'What like did he say?'

'I am not going to tell you; you have nothing to do with that,' cried Archie, startled to find he had admitted so much.

'Oh, I have naething to do with it!' she repeated, springing to her feet. 'A'body at Hermiston's free to pass their opinions upon me, but I have naething to do wi' it! Was this at prayers like? Did ye ca' the grieve into the consultation? Little wonder if a'body's talking, when you make a'body ye're confidants! But as you say, Mr Weir – most kindly, most considerately, most truly, I'm sure, – I have naething to do with it. And I think I'll better be going. I'll be wishing you good-evening, Mr Weir.' And she made him a stately curtsey, shaking as she did so from head to foot, with the barren ecstasy of temper.

Poor Archie stood dumbfounded. She had moved some steps away from him before he recovered the gift of articulate speech.

'Kirstie!' he cried. 'Oh, Kirstie woman!'

There was in his voice a ring of appeal, a clang of mere astonishment that showed the schoolmaster was vanquished.

She turned round on him. 'What do ye Kirstie me for?' she retorted. 'What have ye to do wi' me? Gang to your ain freends and deave them!'

He could only repeat the appealing 'Kirstie!'

'Kirstie, indeed!' cried the girl, her eyes blazing in her white face. 'My name is Miss Christina Elliott, I would have ye to ken, and I daur ye to ca' me out of it. If I canna get love, I'll have respect, Mr Weir. I'm come of decent people, and I'll have respect. What have I done that ye should lightly me? What have I done? What have I done? Oh, what have I done?' and her voice rose upon the third repetition. 'I thocht – I thocht – I thocht I was sae happy!' and the first sob broke from her like the paroxysm of some mortal sickness.

Archie ran to her. He took the poor child in his arms, and she nestled to his breast as to a mother's, and clasped him in hands that were strong like vices. He felt her whole body shaken by the throes of distress, and had pity upon her beyond speech. Pity, and at the same time a bewildered fear of this explosive engine in his arms, whose works he did not understand, and yet had been tampering with. There arose from before him the curtains of boyhood, and he saw for the first time the ambiguous face of woman as she is. In vain he looked back over the interview; he saw not where he had offended. It seemed unprovoked, a wilful convulsion of brute nature ...

WILL O' THE MILL

THE PLAIN AND THE STARS

THE Mill where Will lived with his adopted parents stood in a falling valley between pine-woods and great mountains. Above, hill after hill soared upwards until they soared out of the depth of the hardiest timber, and stood naked against the sky. Some way up, a long grey village lay like a seam or a rag of vapour on a wooded hillside; and when the wind was favourable, the sound of the church bells would drop down, thin and silvery, to Will. Below, the valley grew ever steeper and steeper, and at the same time widened out on either hand; and from an eminence beside the mill it was possible to see its whole length and away beyond it over a wide plain, where the river turned and shone, and moved on from city to city on its voyage towards the sea. It chanced that over this valley there lay a pass into a neighbouring kingdom, so that, quiet and rural as it was, the road that ran along beside the river was a high thoroughfare between two splendid and powerful societies. All through the summer, travelling-carriages came crawling up, or went plunging briskly downwards past the mill; and as it happened that the other side was very much easier of ascent, the path was not much frequented, except by people going in one direction; and of all the carriages that Will saw go by, five-sixths were plunging briskly downwards and only one-sixth crawling up. Much more was this the case with foot-passengers. All the light-footed tourists, all the pedlars laden with strange wares, were tending downward like the river that accompanied their path. Nor was this all; for when Will was yet a child a disastrous war arose over a great part of the world. The newspapers were full of defeats and victories, the earth rang with cavalry hoofs, and often for days together and

175

for miles around the coil of battle terrified good people from their labours in the field. Of all this, nothing was heard for a long time in the valley; but at last one of the commanders pushed an army over the pass by forced marches, and for three days horse and foot, cannon and tumbril, drum and standard, kept pouring downward past the mill. All day the child stood and watched them on their passage – the rhythmical stride, the pale, unshaven faces tanned about the eyes, the discoloured regimentals and the tattered flags, filled him with a sense of weariness, pity, and wonder; and all night long, after he was in bed, he could hear the cannon pounding and the feet trampling, and the great armament sweeping onward and downward past the mill. No one in the valley ever heard the fate of the expedition, for they lay out of the way of gossip in those troublous times; but Will saw one thing plainly, that not a man returned. Whither had they all gone? Whither went all the tourists and pedlars with strange wares? whither all the brisk barouches with servants in the dicky? whither the water of the stream, ever coursing downward and ever renewed from above? Even the wind blew oftener down the valley, and carried the· dead leaves along with it in the fall. It seemed like a great conspiracy of things animate and inanimate; they all went downward, fleetly and gaily downward, and only he, it seemed, remained behind, like a stock upon the wayside. It sometimes made him glad when he noticed how the fishes kept their heads up stream. They, at least, stood faithfully by him, while all else were posting downward to the unknown world.

One evening he asked the miller where the river went.

'It goes down the valley,' answered he, 'and turns a power of mills – six-score mills, they say, from here to Unterdeck – and it none the wearier after all. And then it goes out into the lowlands, and waters the great corn country, and runs through a sight of fine cities (so they say) where kings live all alone in great palaces, with a sentry walking up and down before the door. And it goes under bridges with stone men upon them, looking down and smiling so curious at the water, and living folks leaning their elbows on the wall and looking over too.

And then it goes on and on, and down through marshes and sands, until at last it falls into the sea, where the ships are that bring parrots and tobacco from the Indies. Ay, it has a long trot before it as it goes singing over our weir, bless its heart!'

'And what is the sea?' asked Will.

'The sea!' cried the miller. 'Lord help us all, it is the greatest thing God made! That is where all the water in the world runs down into a great salt lake. There it lies, as flat as my hand and as innocent-like as a child; but they do say when the wind blows it gets up into water-mountains bigger than any of ours, and swallows down great ships bigger than our mill, and makes such a roaring that you can hear it miles away upon the land. There are great fish in it five times bigger than a bull, and one old serpent as long as our river and as old as all the world, with whiskers like a man, and a crown of silver on her head.'

Will thought he had never heard anything like this, and he kept on asking question after question about the world that lay away down the river, with all its perils and marvels, until the old miller became quite interested himself, and at last took him by the hand and led him to the hill-top that overlooks the valley and the plain. The sun was near setting, and hung low down in a cloudless sky. Everything was defined and glorified in golden light. Will had never seen so great an expanse of country in his life; he stood and gazed with all his eyes. He could see the cities, and the woods and fields, and the bright curves of the river, and far away to where the rim of the plain trenched along the shining heavens. An overmastering emotion seized upon the boy, soul and body; his heart beat so thickly that he could not breathe; the scene swam before his eyes; the sun seemed to wheel round and round, and throw off, as it turned, strange shapes which disappeared with the rapidity of thought, and were succeeded by others. Will covered his face with his hands, and burst into a violent fit of tears; and the poor miller, sadly disappointed and perplexed, saw nothing better for it than to take him up in his arms and carry him home in silence.

From that day forward Will was full of new hopes and longings. Something kept tugging at his heartstrings; the running water carried his desires along with it as he dreamed over its fleeting surface; the wind, as it ran over innumerable treetops, hailed him with encouraging words; branches beckoned downward; the open road, as it shouldered round the angles and went turning and vanishing faster and faster down the valley, tortured him with its solicitations. He spent long whiles on the eminence, looking down the rivershed and abroad on the flat lowlands, and watched the clouds that travelled forth upon the sluggish wind and trailed their purple shadows on the plain; or he would linger by the wayside, and follow the carriages with his eyes as they rattled downward by the river. It did not matter what it was; everything that went that way, were it cloud or carriage, bird or brown water in the stream, he felt his heart flow out after it in an ecstasy of longing.

We are told by men of science that all the ventures of mariners on the sea, all that counter-marching of tribes and races that confounds old history with its dust and rumour, sprang from nothing more abstruse than the laws of supply and demand, and a certain natural instinct for cheap rations. To any one thinking deeply, this will seem a dull and pitiful explanation. The tribes that came swarming out of the North and East, if they were indeed pressed onward from behind by others, were drawn at the same time by the magnetic influence of the South and West. The fame of other lands had reached them; the name of the eternal city rang in their ears; they were not colonists, but pilgrims; they travelled towards wine and gold and sunshine, but their hearts were set on something higher. That divine unrest, that old stinging trouble of humanity that makes all high achievements and all miserable failure, the same that spread wings with Icarus, the same that sent Columbus into the desolate Atlantic, inspired and supported these barbarians on their perilous march. There is one legend which profoundly represents their spirit, of how a flying party of these wanderers encountered a very old man shod with iron. The old man asked them whither they were going; and they answered with one voice: 'To the Eternal City!' He looked upon them gravely. 'I have sought it,' he said, 'over the most part of the world. Three such pairs as I now carry on my feet have I worn out upon this pilgrimage, and now the fourth is growing slender underneath my steps. And all this while I have not found the city.' And he turned and went his own way alone, leaving them astonished.

And yet this would scarcely parallel the intensity of Will's feeling for the plain. If he could only go far enough out there, he felt as if his eyesight would be purged and clarified, as if his hearing would grow more delicate, and his very breath would come and go with luxury. He was transplanted and withering where he was; he lay in a strange country and was sick for home. Bit by bit, he pieced together broken notions of the world below; of the river, ever moving and growing until it sailed forth into the majestic ocean; of the cities, full of brisk and beautiful people, playing fountains, bands of music and marble palaces, and lighted up at night from end to end with artificial stars of gold; of the great churches, wise universities, brave armies, and untold money lying stored in vaults; of the high-flying vice that moved in the sunshine, and the stealth and swiftness of midnight murder. I have said he was sick as if for home: the figure halts. He was like some one lying in twilit, formless pre-existence, and stretching out his hands lovingly towards many-coloured, many-sounding life. It was no wonder he was unhappy, he would go and tell the fish; they were made for their life, wished for no more than worms and running water, and a hole below a falling bank; but he was differently designed, full of desires and aspirations, itching at the fingers, lusting with the eyes, whom the whole variegated world could not satisfy with aspects. The true life, the true bright sunshine, lay far out upon the plain. And O! to see this sunlight once before he died! to move with a jocund spirit in a golden land! to hear the trained singers and sweet church bells, and see the holiday gardens! 'And O fish!' he would cry, 'if you would only turn your noses down stream, you could swim so easily into the fabled waters and see the vast ships passing over your head like clouds, and hear the great water-hills making music over you all day long!' But the fish kept looking patiently in their own direction, until Will hardly knew whether to laugh or cry.

Hitherto the traffic on the road had passed by Will, like something seen in a picture : he had perhaps exchanged saluta-tions with a tourist, or caught sight of an old gentleman in a travelling-cap at a carriage window; but for the most part it had been a mere symbol, which he contemplated from apart and with something of a superstitious feeling. A time came at last when this was to be changed. The miller, who was a greedy man in his way, and never forewent an opportunity of honest profit, turned the mill-house into a little wayside inn, and, several pieces of good fortune falling in opportunely, built stables and got the position of post master on the road. It now became Will's duty to wait upon people, as they sat to break their fasts in the little arbour at the top of the mill garden; and you may be sure that he kept his ears open, and learned many new things about the outside world as he brought the omelette or the wine. Nay, he would often get into con-versation with single guests, and by adroit questions and polite attention, not only gratify his own curiosity, but win the goodwill of the travellers. Many complimented the old couple on their serving-boy; and a professor was eager to take him away with him, and have him properly educated in the plain. The miller and his wife were mightily astonished and even more pleased. They thought it a very good thing that they should have opened their inn. 'You see,' the old man would remark, 'he has a kind of talent for a publican; he never would have made anything else!' And so life wagged on in the valley, with high satisfaction to all concerned but Will. Every car-riage that left the inn-door seemed to take a part of him away with it; and when people jestingly offered him a lift, he could with difficulty command his emotion. Night after night he would dream that he was awakened by flustered servants, and that a splendid equipage waited at the door to carry him down into the plain; night after night; until the dream, which had seemed all jollity to him at first, began to take on a colour of gravity, and the nocturnal summons and waiting equipage occupied a place in his mind as something to be both feared and hoped for.

One day, when Will was about sixteen, a fat young man arrived at sunset to pass the night. He was a contented-looking fellow, with a jolly eye, and carried a knapsack. While dinner was preparing, he sat in the arbour to read a book; but as soon as he had begun to observe Will, the book was laid aside; he was plainly one of those who prefer living people to people made of ink and paper. Will, on his part, although he had not been much interested in the stranger at first sight, soon began to take a great deal of pleasure in his talk, which was full of good-nature and good-sense, and at last conceived a great respect for his character and wisdom. They sat far into the night; and about two in the morning Will opened his heart to the young man, and told him how he longed to leave the valley and what bright hopes he had connected with the cities of the plain. The young man whistled, and then broke into a smile.

'My young friend,' he remarked, 'you are a very curious little fellow, to be sure, and wish a great many things which you will never get. Why, you would feel quite ashamed if you knew how the little fellows in these fairy cities of yours are all after the same sort of nonsense, and keep breaking their hearts to get up into the mountains. And let me tell you, those who go down into the plains are a very short while there before they wish themselves heartily back again. The air is not so light nor so pure; nor is the sun any brighter. As for the beautiful men and women, you would see many of them in rags and many of them deformed with horrible disorders; and a city is so hard a place for people who are poor and sensitive that many choose to die by their own hand.'

'You must think me very simple,' answered Will. 'Although I have never been out of this valley, believe me, I have used my eyes. I know how one thing lives on another; for instance, how the fish hangs in the eddy to catch his fellows; and the shepherd, who makes so pretty a picture carrying home the lamb, is only carrying it home for dinner. I do not expect to find all things right in your cities. That is not what troubles me; it might have been that once upon a time; but although I have lived here always, I have asked many questions and learned a great deal in these last years, and certainly enough to cure me of my old fancies. But you would not have me die like a dog and not see all that is to be seen, and do all that a man can do, let it be good or evil? you would not have me spend all my days between this road here and the river, and not so much as make a motion to be up and live my life? – I would rather die out of hand,' he cried, 'than linger on as I am doing.'

'Thousands of people,' said the young man, 'live and die like you, and are none the less happy.'

'Ah!' said Will, 'if there are thousands who would like, why should not one of them have my place?'

It was quite dark; there was a hanging lamp in the arbour which lit up the table and the faces of the speakers; and along the arch, the leaves upon the trellis stood out illuminated against the night sky, a pattern of transparent green upon a dusky purple. The fat young man rose, and, taking Will by the arm, led him out under the open heavens.

'Did you ever look at the stars?' he asked, pointing upwards.

'Often and often,' answered Will.

'And do you know what they are?'

'I have fancied many things.'

'They are worlds like ours,' said the young man. 'Some of them less; many of them a million times greater; and some of the least sparkles that you see are not only worlds, but whole clusters of worlds turning about each other in the midst of space. We do not know what there may be in any of them; perhaps the answer to all our difficulties or the cure of all our sufferings: and yet we can never reach them; not all the skill of the craftiest of men can fit out a ship for the nearest of these our neighbours, nor would the life of the most aged suffice for such a journey. When a great battle has been lost or a dear friend is dead, when we are hipped or in high spirits, there they are unweariedly shining overhead. We may stand down here, a whole army of us together, and shout until we break our hearts, and not a whisper reaches them. We may climb the highest mountain, and we are no nearer them. All we can do is to stand down here in the garden and take off our hats; the starshine lights upon our heads, and where mine is a little bald, I dare say you can see it glisten in the darkness. The mountain and the mouse. That is like to be all we shall ever have to do with Arcturus or Aldebaran. Can you apply a parable?' he added, laying his hand upon Will's shoulder. 'It is not the same thing as a reason, but usually vastly more convincing.'

Will hung his head a little, and then raised it once more to heaven. The stars seemed to expand and emit a sharper brilliancy; and as he kept turning his eyes higher and higher, they seemed to increase in multitude under his gaze.

'I see,' he said, turning to the young man. 'We are in a rat-trap.'

'Something of that size. Did you ever see a squirrel turning in a cage? and another squirrel sitting philosophically over his nuts? I needn't ask you which of them looked more of a fool.'

The Parson's Marjory

After some years the old people died, both in one winter, very carefully tended by their adopted son, and very quietly mourned when they were gone. People who had heard of his roving fancies supposed he would hasten to sell the property, and go down the river to push his fortunes. But there was never any sign of such an intention on the part of Will. On the contrary, he had the inn set on a better footing, and hired a couple of servants to assist him in carrying it on; and there he settled down, a kind, talkative, inscrutable young man, six feet three in his stockings, with an iron constitution and a friendly voice. He soon began to take rank in the district as a bit of an oddity: it was not much to be wondered at from the first, for he was always full of notions, and kept calling the plainest common sense in question; but what most raised the report upon him was the odd circumstance of his courtship with the parson's Marjory.

The parson's Marjory was a lass about nineteen, when Will would be about thirty; well enough looking, and much better educated than any other girl in that part of the country, as became her parentage. She held her head very high, and had already refused several offers of marriage with a grand air, which had got her hard names among the neighbours. For all that she was a good girl, and one that would have made any man well contented.

Will had never seen much of her; for although the church and parsonage were only two miles from his own door, he was never known to go there but on Sundays. It chanced, however, that the parsonage fell into disrepair, and had to be dismantled; and the parson and his daughter took lodgings for a month or so, on very much reduced terms, at Will's inn. Now, what with the inn, and the mill, and the old miller's savings, our friend was a man of substance; and besides that, he had a name for good temper and shrewdness which make a capital portion in marriage; and so it was currently gossiped, among their ill-wishers, that the parson and his daughter had not chosen their temporary lodging with their eyes shut. Will was about the last man in the world to be cajoled or frightened into marriage. You had only to look into his eyes, limpid and still like pools of water, and yet with a sort of clear light that seemed to come from within, and you would understand at once that here was one who knew his own mind, and would stand to it immovably. Marjory herself was no weakling by her looks, with strong, steady eyes and a resolute and quiet bearing. It might be a question whether she was not Will's match in steadfastness, after all, or which of them would rule the roost in marriage. But Marjory had never given it a thought, and accompanied her father with the most unshaken innocence and unconcern.

The season was still so early that Will's customers were few and far between; but the lilacs were already flowering, and the weather was so mild that the party took dinner under the trellis, with the noise of the river in their ears and the woods ringing about them with the songs of birds. Will soon began to take a particular pleasure in these dinners. The parson was rather a dull companion, with a habit of dozing at table; but nothing rude or cruel ever fell from his lips. And as for the parson's daughter, she suited her surroundings with the best grace imaginable; and whatever she said seemed so pat and pretty that Will conceived a great idea of her talents. He could see her face, as she leaned forward, against a background of rising pinewoods; her eyes shone peaceably; the light lay around her hair like a kerchief; something that was hardly a smile rippled her pale cheeks, and Will could not contain himself from gazing on her in an agreeable dismay. She looked, even in her quietest moments, so complete in herself, and so quick with life down to her finger-tips and the very skirts of her dress, that the remainder of created things became no more than a blot by comparison; and if Will glanced away from her to her surroundings, the trees looked inanimate and senseless, the clouds hung in heaven like dead things, and even the mountain-tops were disenchanted. The whole valley could not compare in looks with this one girl.

Will was always observant in the society of his fellow-creatures; but his observation became almost painfully eager in the case of Marjory. He listened to all she uttered, and read her eyes, at the same time, for the unspoken commentary. Many kind, simple, and sincere speeches found an echo in his heart. He became conscious of a soul beautifully poised upon itself, nothing doubting, nothing desiring, clothed in peace. It was not possible to separate her thoughts from her appearance. The turn of her wrist, the still sound of her voice, the light in her eyes, the lines of her body, fell in tune with her grave and gentle words, like the accompaniment that sustains and harmonises the voice of the singer. Her influence was one thing, not to be divided or discussed, only to be felt with gratitude and joy. To Will, her presence recalled something of his childhood, and the thought of her took its place in his mind beside

that of dawn, of running water, and of the earliest violets
and lilacs. It is the property of things seen for the first time, or
for the first time after long, like the flowers in spring, to re-
awaken in us the sharp edge of sense and that impression of
mystic strangeness which otherwise passes out of life with the
coming of years; but the sight of a loved face is what renews
a man's character from the fountain upwards.

One day after dinner Will took a stroll among the firs; a
grave beatitude possessed him from top to toe, and he kept
smiling to himself and the landscape as he went. The river
ran between the stepping-stones with a pretty wimple; a bird
sang loudly in the wood; the hill-tops looked immeasurably
high, and as he glanced at them from time to time seemed to
contemplate his movements with a beneficent but awful curiosity. His way took him to the eminence which overlooked the
plain; and there he sat down upon a stone, and fell into deep
and pleasant thought. The plain lay abroad with its cities and
silver river; everything was asleep, except a great eddy of
birds which kept rising and falling and going round and round
in the blue air. He repeated Marjory's name aloud, and the
sound of it gratified his ear. He shut his eyes, and her image
sprang up before him, quietly luminous and attended with
good thoughts. The river might run for ever; the birds fly
higher and higher till they touched the stars. He saw it was
empty bustle after all; for here, without stirring a foot, waiting
patiently in his own narrow valley, he also had attained the
better sunlight.

The next day Will made a sort of declaration across the
dinner-table, while the parson was filling his pipe.

'Miss Marjory,' he said, 'I never knew any one I liked so
well as you. I am mostly a cold, unkindly sort of man; not from
want of heart, but out of strangeness in my way of thinking;
and people seem far away from me. 'Tis as if there were a circle
round me, which kept every one out but you; I can hear the
others talking and laughing; but you come quite close. – Maybe
this is disagreeable to you?' he asked.

Marjory made no answer.

'Speak up, girl,' said the parson.

'Nay, now,' returned Will, 'I wouldn't press her, parson. I feel tongue-tied myself, who am not used to it; and she's a woman, and little more than a child, when all is said. But for my part, as far as I can understand what people mean by it, I fancy I must be what they call in love. I do not wish to be held as committing myself; for I may be wrong; but that is how I believe things are with me. And if Miss Marjory should feel any otherwise on her part, mayhap she would be so kind as shake her head.'

Marjory was silent, and gave no sign that she had heard.

'How is that, parson?' asked Will.

'The girl must speak,' replied the parson, laying down his pipe. 'Here's our neighbour who says he loves you, Madge. Do you love him, ay or no?'

'I think I do,' said Marjory, faintly.

'Well then, that's all that could be wished!' cried Will, heartily. And he took her hand across the table, and held it a moment in both of his with great satisfaction.

'You must marry,' observed the parson, replacing his pipe in his mouth.

'Is that the right thing to do, think you?' demanded Will.

'It is indispensable,' said the parson.

'Very well,' replied the wooer.

Two or three days passed away with great delight to Will, although a bystander might scarce have found it out. He continued to take his meals opposite Marjory, and to talk with her and gaze upon her in her father's presence; but he made no attempt to see her alone, nor in any other way changed his conduct towards her from what it had been since the beginning. Perhaps the girl was a little disappointed, and perhaps not unjustly; and yet if it had been enough to be always in the thoughts of another person, and so pervade and alter his whole life, she might have been thoroughly contented. For she was never out of Will's mind for an instant. He sat over the stream, and watched the dust of the eddy, and the poised fish, and straining weeds; he wandered out alone into the purple even, with all the blackbirds piping round him in the wood; he rose early in the morning; and saw the sky turn from grey to gold, and the light leap upon the hill-tops; and all the while he kept wondering if he had never seen such things before, or how it was that they should look so different now. The sound of his own mill-wheel, or of the wind among the trees, confounded and charmed his heart. The most enchanting thoughts presented themselves unbidden in his mind. He was so happy that he could not sleep at night, and so restless that he could hardly sit still out of her company. And yet it seemed as if he avoided her rather than sought her out.

One day, as he was coming home from a ramble, Will found Marjory in the garden picking flowers, and as he came up with her, slackened his pace and continued walking by her side.

'You like flowers?' he said.

'Indeed I love them dearly,' she replied. 'Do you?'

'Why, no,' said he, 'not so much. They are a very small affair, when all is done. I can fancy people caring for them greatly, but not doing as you are just now.'

'How?' she asked, pausing and looking up at him.

'Plucking them,' said he. 'They are a deal better off where they are, and look a deal prettier, if you go to that.'

'I wish to have them for my own,' she answered, 'to carry them near my heart, and keep them in my room. They tempt me when they grow here; they seem to say, "Come and do something with us"; but once I have cut them and put them by, the charm is laid, and I can look at them with quite an easy heart.'

'You wish to possess them,' replied Will, 'in order to think no more about them. It's a bit like killing the goose with the golden eggs. It's a bit like what I wished to do when I was a boy. Because I had a fancy for looking out over the plain, I wished to go down there – where I couldn't look out over it any longer. Was not that fine reasoning? Dear, dear, if they only thought of it, all the world would do like me; and you would let your flowers alone, just as I stay up here in the mountains.' Suddenly he broke off sharp. 'By the Lord!' he cried. And when she asked him what was wrong, he turned the question off, and walked away into the house with rather a humorous expression of face.

He was silent at table; and after the night had fallen and the stars had come out overhead, he walked up and down for hours in the courtyard and garden with an uneven pace. There was still a light in the window of Marjory's room: one little oblong patch of orange in a world of dark blue hills and silver starlight. Will's mind ran a great deal on the window; but his thoughts were not very lover-like. 'There she is in her room,' he thought, 'and there are the stars overhead: – a blessing upon both!' Both were good influences in his life; both soothed and braced him in his profound contentment with the world. And what more should he desire with either? The fat young man and his councils were so present to his mind, that he threw back his head, and, putting his hands before his mouth, shouted aloud to the populous heavens. Whether from the position of his head or the sudden strain of the exertion, he seemed to see a momentary shock among the stars, and a diffusion of frosty light pass from one to another along the sky. At the same instant, a corner of the blind was lifted up and lowered again at once. He laughed a loud ho-ho! 'One and another!' thought Will. 'The stars tremble, and the blind goes up. Why, before Heaven, what a great magician I must be! Now if I were only a fool, should not I be in a pretty way?' And he went off to bed, chuckling to himself: 'If I were only a fool!'

The next morning, pretty early, he saw her once more in the garden, and sought her out.

'I have been thinking about getting married,' he began abruptly; 'and after having turned it all over, I have made up my mind it's not worth while.'

She turned upon him for a single moment; but his radiant, kindly appearance would, under the circumstances, have disconcerted an angel, and she looked down again upon the ground in silence. He could see her tremble.

'I hope you don't mind,' he went on, a little taken aback. 'You ought not. I have turned it all over, and upon my soul there's nothing in it. We should never be one whit nearer than we are just now, and, if I am a wise man, nothing like so happy.'

'It is unnecessary to go round about with me,' she said. 'I very well remember that you refused to commit yourself; and now that I see you were mistaken, and in reality have never cared for me, I can only feel sad that I have been so far misled.'

'I ask your pardon,' said Will stoutly; 'you do not understand my meaning. As to whether I have ever loved you or not, I must leave that to others. But for one thing, my feeling is not changed; and for another, you may make it your boast that you have made my whole life and character something different from what they were. I mean what I say; no less. I do not think getting married is worth while. I would rather you went on living with your father, so that I could walk over and see you once, or maybe twice a week, as people go to church, and then we should both be all the happier between whiles. That's my notion. But I'll marry you if you will,' he added.

'Do you know that you are insulting me?' she broke out.

'Not I, Marjory,' said he; 'if there is anything in a clear conscience, not I. I offer all my heart's best affections; you can take it or want it, though I suspect it's beyond either your power or mine to change what has once been done, and set me fancy-free. I'll marry you, if you like; but I tell you again and again, it's not worth while, and we had best stay friends. Though I am a quiet man I have noticed a heap of things in my life. Trust in me, and take things as I propose; or, if you don't like that, say the word, and I'll marry you out of hand.'

There was a considerable pause, and Will, who began to feel uneasy, began to grow angry in consequence.

'It seems you are too proud to say your mind,' he said. 'Believe me that's a pity. A clean shrift makes simple living. Can a man be more downright or honourable to a woman than I have been? I have said my say, and given you your choice. Do you want me to marry you? or will you take my friendship, as I think best? or have you had enough of me for good?

Speak out for the dear God's sake! You know your father told you a girl should speak her mind in these affairs.'

She seemed to recover herself at that, turned without a word, walked rapidly through the garden, and disappeared into the house, leaving Will in some confusion as to the result. He walked up and down the garden, whistling softly to himself. Sometimes he stopped and contemplated the sky and hill-tops; sometimes he went down to the tail of the weir and sat there, looking foolishly at the water. All this dubiety and perturbation was so foreign to his nature and the life which he had resolutely chosen for himself, that he began to regret Marjory's arrival. 'After all,' he thought, 'I was as happy as a man need be. I could come down here and watch my fishes all day long if I wanted: I was as settled and contented as my old mill.'

Marjory came down to dinner, looking very trim and quiet; and no sooner were all three at table than she made her father a speech, with her eyes fixed upon her plate, but showing no other sign of embarrassment or distress.

'Father,' she began, 'Mr Will and I have been talking things over. We see that we have each made a mistake about our feelings, and he has agreed, at my request, to give up all idea of marriage, and be no more than my very good friend, as in the past. You see, there is no shadow of a quarrel, and indeed I hope we shall see a great deal of him in the future, for his visits will always be welcome in our house. Of course, father, you will know best, but perhaps we should do better to leave Mr Will's house for the present. I believe, after what has passed, we should hardly be agreeable inmates for some days.'

Will, who had commanded himself with difficulty from the first, broke out upon this into an inarticulate noise, and raised one hand with an appearance of real dismay, as if he were about to interfere and contradict. But she checked him at once, looking up at him with a swift glance and an angry flush upon her cheek.

'You will perhaps have the good grace,' she said, 'to let me explain these matters for myself.'

Will was put entirely out of countenance by her expression and the ring of her voice. He held his peace, concluding that there were some things about this girl beyond his comprehension – in which he was exactly right.

The poor parson was quite crestfallen. He tried to prove that this was no more than a true lovers' tiff, which would pass off before night; and when he was dislodged from that position, he went on to argue that where there was no quarrel there could be no call for a separation; for the good man liked both his entertainment and his host. It was curious to see how the girl managed them, saying little all the time, and that very quietly, and yet twisting them round her finger and insensibly leading them wherever she would by feminine tact and generalship. It scarcely seemed to have been her doing – it seemed as if things had merely so fallen out – that she and her father took their departure that same afternoon in a farm-cart, and went farther down the valley, to wait, until their own house was ready for them, in another hamlet. But Will had been observing closely, and was well aware of her dexterity and resolution. When he found himself alone he had a great many curious matters to turn over in his mind. He was very sad and solitary, to begin with. All the interest had gone out of his life, and he might look up at the stars as long as he pleased, he somehow failed to find support or consolation. And then he was in such a turmoil of spirit about Marjory. He had been puzzled and irritated at her behaviour, and yet he could not keep himself from admiring it. He thought he recognised a fine, perverse angel in that still soul which he had never hitherto suspected; and though he saw it was an influence that would fit but ill with his own life of artificial calm, he could not keep himself from ardently desiring to possess it. Like a man who has lived among shadows and now meets the sun, he was both pained and delighted.

As the days went forward he passed from one extreme to another; now pluming himself on the strength of his determination, now despising his timid and silly caution. The former was, perhaps, the true thought of his heart, and represented

the regular tenor of the man's reflections; but the latter burst
forth from time to time with an unruly violence, and then he
would forget all consideration, and go up and down his house
and garden or walk among the fir-woods like one who is
beside himself with remorse. To equable, steady-minded Will
this state of matters was intolerable; and he determined, at
whatever cost, to bring it to an end. So, one warm summer
afternoon he put on his best clothes, took a thorn switch in his
hand, and set out down the valley by the river. As soon as he
had taken his determination, he had regained at a bound his
customary peace of heart, and he enjoyed the bright weather
and the variety of the scene without any admixture of alarm
or unpleasant eagerness. It was nearly the same to him how the
matter turned out. If she accepted him he would have to marry
her this time, which perhaps was all for the best. If she refused
him, he would have done his utmost, and might follow his
own way in the future with an untroubled conscience. He
hoped, on the whole, she would refuse him; and then, again,
as he saw the brown roof which sheltered her, peeping through
some willows at an angle of the stream, he was half inclined to
reverse the wish, and more than half ashamed of himself for
this infirmity of purpose.

Marjory seemed glad to see him, and gave him her hand
without affectation or delay.

'I have been thinking about this marriage,' he began.

'So have I,' she answered. 'And I respect you more and more
for a very wise man. You understand me better than I understood myself; and I am now quite certain that things are all
for the best as they are.'

'At the same time –' ventured Will.

'You must be tired,' she interrupted. 'Take a seat and let me
fetch you a glass of wine. The afternoon is so warm; and I
wish you not to be displeased with your visit. You must come
quite often; once a week, if you can spare the time; I am
always so glad to see my friends.'

'Oh, very well,' thought Will to himself. 'It appears I was
right after all.' And he paid a very agreeable visit, walked home

again in capital spirits, and gave himself no further concern about the matter.

For nearly three years Will and Marjory continued on these terms, seeing each other once or twice a week without any word of love between them; and for all that time I believe Will was nearly as happy as a man can be. He rather stinted himself the pleasure of seeing her; and he would often walk half-way over to the parsonage, and then back again, as if to whet his appetite. Indeed, there was one corner of the road, whence he could see the church-spire wedged into a crevice of the valley between sloping fir-woods, with a triangular snatch of plain by way of background, which he greatly affected as a place to sit and moralise in before returning homewards; and the peasants got so much into the habit of finding him there in the twilight that they gave it the name of 'Will o' the Mill's Corner.'

At the end of the three years Marjory played him a sad trick by suddenly marrying somebody else. Will kept his countenance bravely, and merely remarked that, for as little as he knew of women, he had acted very prudently in not marrying her himself three years before. She plainly knew very little of her own mind, and, in spite of a deceptive manner, was as fickle and flighty as the rest of them. He had to congratulate himself on an escape, he said, and would take a higher opinion of his own wisdom in consequence. But at heart, he was reasonably displeased, moped a good deal for a month or two, and fell away in flesh, to the astonishment of his serving-lads.

It was perhaps a year after this marriage that Will was awakened late one night by the sound of a horse galloping on the road, followed by precipitate knocking at the inn-door. He opened his window and saw a farm servant, mounted and holding a led horse by the bridle, who told him to make what haste he could and go along with him; for Marjory was dying, and had sent urgently to fetch him to her bedside. Will was no horseman, and made so little speed upon the way that the poor young wife was very near her end before he arrived.

But they had some minutes' talk in private, and he was present and wept very bitterly while she breathed her last.

Death

Year after year went away into nothing, with great explosions and outcries in the cities on the plain; red revolt springing up and being suppressed in blood, battle swaying hither and thither, patient astronomers in observatory towers picking out and christening new stars, plays being performed in lighted theatres, people being carried into hospitals on stretchers, and all the usual turmoil and agitation of men's lives in crowded centres. Up in Will's valley only the wind and seasons made an epoch; the fish hung in the swift stream, the birds circled overhead, the pine-tops rustled underneath the stars, the tall hills stood over all; and Will went to and fro, minding his wayside inn, until the snow began to thicken on his head. His heart was young and vigorous; and if his pulses kept a sober time, they still beat strong and steady in his wrists. He carried a ruddy stain on either cheek, like a ripe apple; he stooped a little, but his step was still firm; and his sinewy hands were reached out to all men with a friendly pressure. His face was covered with those wrinkles which are got in open air, and which, rightly looked at, are no more than a sort of permanent sunburning; such wrinkles heighten the stupidity of stupid faces; but to a person like Will, with his clear eyes and smiling mouth, only give another charm by testifying to a simple and easy life. His talk was full of wise sayings. He had a taste for other people; and other people had a taste for him. When the valley was full of tourists in the season, there were merry nights in Will's arbour; and his views, which seemed whimsical to his neighbours, were often enough admired by learned people out of towns and colleges. Indeed, he had a very noble old age, and grew daily better known; so that his fame was heard of in the cities of the plain; and young men who had been summer travellers spoke together in *cafés* of Will o' the Mill and his rough philosophy. Many and many an invitation, you may be sure, he had; but nothing could tempt him from his upland valley. He would shake his head and smile over his tobacco-pipe with a deal of meaning. 'You come too late,' he would answer. 'I am a dead man now: I have lived and died already. Fifty years ago you would have brought my heart into my mouth; and now you do not even tempt me. But that is the object of long living, that man should cease to care about life.' And again: 'There is only one difference between a long life and a good dinner: that, in the dinner, the sweets come last.' Or once more: 'When I was a boy, I was a bit puzzled, and hardly knew whether it was myself or the world that was curious and worth looking into. Now, I know it is myself; and stick to that.'

He never showed any symptom of frailty, but kept stalwart and firm to the last; but they say he grew less talkative towards the end, and would listen to other people by the hour in an amused and sympathetic silence. Only, when he did speak, it was more to the point and more charged with old experience. He drank a bottle of wine gladly; above all, at sunset on the hill-top or quite late at night under the stars in the arbour. The sight of something attractive and unattainable seasoned his enjoyment, he would say; and he professed he had lived long enough to admire a candle all the more when he could compare it with a planet.

One night, in his seventy-second year, he awoke in bed, in such uneasiness of body and mind that he arose and dressed himself and went out to meditate in the arbour. It was pitch dark, without a star; the river was swollen, and the wet woods and meadows loaded the air with perfume. It had thundered during the day, and it promised more thunder for the morrow. A murky, stifling night for a man of seventy-two! Whether it was the weather or the wakefulness, or some little touch of fever in his old limbs, Will's mind was besieged by tumultuous and crying memories. His boyhood, the night with the fat young man, the death of his adopted parents, the summer days with Marjory, and many of those small circumstances, which seem nothing to another, and are yet the very gist of a man's own life to himself – things seen, words heard, books misconstrued – arose from their forgotten corners and usurped his attention. The dead themselves were with him, not merely taking part in this thin show of memory that defiled before his brain, but revisiting his bodily senses as they do in profound and vivid dreams. The fat young man leaned his elbows on the table opposite; Marjory came and went with an apronful of flowers between the garden and the arbour; he could hear the old parson knocking out his pipe or blowing his resonant nose. The tide of his consciousness ebbed and flowed; he was sometimes half asleep and drowned in his recollections of the past; and sometimes he was broad awake, wondering at himself. But about the middle of the night he was startled by the voice of the dead miller calling to him out of the house as he used to do on the arrival of custom. The hallucination was so perfect that Will sprang from his seat and stood listening for the summons to be repeated; and as he listened he became conscious of another noise besides the brawling of the river and the ringing in his feverish ears. It was like the stir of the horses and the creaking of harness, as though a carriage with an impatient team had been brought up upon the road before the courtyard gate. At such an hour, upon this rough and dangerous pass, the supposition was no better than absurd; and Will dismissed it from his mind, and resumed his seat upon the arbour chair; and sleep closed over him again like running water. He was once again awakened by the dead miller's call, thinner and more spectral than before; and once again he heard the noise of an equipage upon the road. And so thrice and four times, the same dream, or the same fancy, presented itself to his senses: until at length, smiling to himself as when one humours a nervous child, he proceeded towards the gate to set his uncertainty at rest.

From the arbour to the gate was no great distance, and yet it took Will some time; it seemed as if the dead thickened around him in the court, and crossed his path at every step. For, first, he was suddenly surprised by an overpowering sweetness of heliotropes; it was as if his garden had been planted with this flower from end to end, and the hot, damp night had drawn forth all their perfumes in a breath. Now the heliotrope had been Marjory's favourite flower, and since her death not one of them had ever been planted on Will's ground.

'I must be going crazy,' he thought. 'Poor Marjory and her heliotropes!'

And with that he raised his eyes towards the window that had once been hers. If he had been bewildered before, he was now almost terrified; for there was a light in the room; the window was an orange oblong as of yore; and the corner of the blind was lifted and let fall as on the night when he stood and shouted to the stars in his perplexity. The illusion only endured an instant; but it left him somewhat unmanned, rubbing his eyes and staring at the outline of the house and the black night behind it. While he thus stood, and it seemed as if he must have stood there quite a long time, there came a renewal of the noises on the road : and he turned in time to meet a stranger, who was advancing to meet him across the court. There was something like the outline of a great carriage discernible on the road behind the stranger, and, above that, a few black pine-tops, like so many plumes.

'Master Will?' asked the new-comer, in brief military fashion.

'That same, sir,' answered Will. 'Can I do anything to serve you?'

'I have heard you much spoken of, Master Will,' returned the other; 'much spoken of, and well. And though I have both hands full of business, I wish to drink a bottle of wine with you in your arbour. Before I go, I shall introduce myself.'

Will led the way to the trellis, and got a lamp lighted and a bottle uncorked. He was not altogether unused to such complimentary interviews, and hoped little enough for this one, being schooled by many disappointments. A sort of cloud had settled on his wits and prevented him from remembering the strangeness of the hour. He moved like a person in his sleep; and it seemed as if the lamp caught fire and the bottle came uncorked with the facility of thought. Still, he had some

curiosity about the appearance of his visitor, and tried in vain
to turn the light into his face; either he handled the lamp
clumsily, or there was a dimness over his eyes; but he could
make out little more than a shadow at table with him. He
stared and stared at this shadow, as he wiped out the glasses,
and began to feel cold and strange about the heart. The
silence weighed upon him, for he could hear nothing now,
not even the river, but the drumming of his own arteries in his
ears.

'Here's to you,' said the stranger, roughly.

'Here is my service, sir,' replied Will, sipping his wine, which
somehow tasted oddly.

'I understand you are a very positive fellow,' pursued the
stranger.

Will made answer with a smile of some satisfaction and a
little nod.

'So am I,' continued the other, 'and it is the delight of my
heart to tramp on people's corns. I will have nobody positive
but myself; not one. I have crossed the whims, in my time,
of kings and generals and great artists. And what would you
say,' he went on, 'if I had come up here on purpose to cross
yours?'

Will had it on his tongue to make a sharp rejoinder; but
the politeness of an old innkeeper prevailed; and he held his
peace and made answer with a civil gesture of the hand.

'I have,' said the stranger. 'And if I did not hold you in a
particular esteem, I should make no words about the matter.
It appears you pride yourself on staying where you are. You
mean to stick by your inn. Now I mean you shall come for a
turn with me in my barouche; and before this bottle's empty,
so you shall.'

'That would be an odd thing, to be sure,' replied Will, with
a chuckle. 'Why, sir, I have grown here like an old oak-tree;
the devil himself could hardly root me up: and for all I perceive you are a very entertaining old gentleman, I would
wager you another bottle you lose your pains with me.'

The dimness of Will's eyesight had been increasing all this

while; but he was somehow conscious of a sharp and chilling scrutiny which irritated and yet overmastered him.

'You need not think,' he broke out suddenly, in an explosive, febrile manner that startled and alarmed himself, 'that I am a stay-at-home, because I fear anything under God. God knows I am tired enough of it all; and when the time comes for a longer journey than ever you dream of, I reckon I shall find myself prepared.'

The stranger emptied his glass and pushed it away from him. He looked down for a little, and then, leaning over the table, tapped Will three times upon the forearm with a single finger. 'The time has come!' he said solemnly.

An ugly thrill spread from the spot he touched. The tones of his voice were dull and startling, and echoed strangely in Will's heart.

'I beg your pardon,' he said, with some discomposure. 'What do you mean?'

'Look at me, and you will find your eyesight swim. Raise your hand; it is dead-heavy. This is your last bottle of wine, Master Will, and your last night upon the earth.'

'You are a doctor?' quavered Will.

'The best that ever was,' replied the other; 'for I cure both mind and body with the same prescription. I take away all pain and I forgive all sins; and where my patients have gone wrong in life, I smooth out all complications and set them free again upon their feet.'

'I have no need of you,' said Will.

'A time comes for all men, Master Will,' replied the doctor, 'when the helm is taken out of their hands. For you, because you were prudent and quiet, it has been long of coming, and you have had long to discipline yourself for its reception. You have seen what is to be seen about your mill; you have sat close all your days like a hare in its form; but now that is at an end; and,' added the doctor, getting on his feet, 'you must arise and come with me.'

'You are a strange physician,' said Will, looking steadfastly upon his guest.

'I am a natural law,' he replied, 'and people call me Death.'

'Why did you not tell me so at first?' cried Will. 'I have been waiting for you these many years. Give me your hand, and welcome.'

'Lean upon my arm,' said the stranger, 'for already your strength abates. Lean on me heavily as you need; for though I am old, I am very strong. It is but three steps to my carriage, and there all your trouble ends. Why, Will,' he added, 'I have been yearning for you as if you were my own son; and of all the men that ever I came for in my long days, I have come for you most gladly. I am caustic, and sometimes offend people at first sight; but I am a good friend at heart to such as you.'

'Since Marjory was taken,' returned Will, 'I declare before God you were the only friend I had to look for.'

So the pair went arm-in-arm across the courtyard.

One of the servants awoke about this time and heard the noise of horses pawing before he dropped asleep again; all down the valley that night there was a rushing as of a smooth and steady wind descending towards the plain; and when the world rose next morning, sure enough Will o' the Mill had gone at last upon his travels.

THRAWN JANET

THE Reverend Murdoch Soulis was long minister of the moorland parish of Balweary, in the vale of Dule. A severe, bleak-faced old man, dreadful to his hearers, he dwelt in the last years of his life, without relative or servant or any human company, in the small and lonely manse under the Hanging Shaw. In spite of the iron composure of his features, his eye was wild, scared, and uncertain; and when he dwelt, in private admonition, on the future of the impenitent, it seemed as if his eye pierced through the storms of time to the terrors of eternity. Many young persons, coming to prepare themselves against the season of the Holy Communion, were dreadfully affected by his talk. He had a sermon on 1st Peter v. and 8th, 'The devil as a roaring lion,' on the Sunday after every seventeenth of August, and he was accustomed to surpass himself upon that text both by the appalling nature of the matter and the terror of his bearing in the pulpit. The children were frightened into fits, and the old looked more than usually oracular, and were, all that day, full of those hints that Hamlet deprecated. The manse itself, where it stood by the water of Dule among some thick trees, with the Shaw overhanging it on the one side, and on the other many cold, moorish hill-tops rising toward the sky, had begun, at a very early period of Mr Soulis's ministry, to be avoided in the dusk hours by all who valued themselves upon their prudence; and guidmen sitting at the clachan alehouse shook their heads together at the thought of passing late by that uncanny neighbourhood. There was one spot, to be more particular, which was regarded with especial awe. The manse stood between the highroad and the water of Dule, with a gable to each; its back was towards the kirktown of Balweary, nearly half a mile away; in front of it, a bare garden, hedged with thorn, occupied the land between the river and the road. The house was two stories high, with two large rooms on each. It opened not directly on the garden, but on a causewayed path, or passage, giving on the road on the one hand, and closed on the other by the tall willows and elders that bordered on the stream. And it was this strip of causeway that enjoyed among the young parishioners of Balweary so infamous a reputation. The minister walked there often after dark, sometimes groaning aloud in the instancy of his unspoken prayers; and when he was from home, and the manse door was locked, the more daring schoolboys ventured, with beating hearts, to 'follow my leader' across that legendary spot.

This atmosphere of terror, surrounding, as it did, a man of God of spotless character and orthodoxy, was a common cause of wonder and subject of inquiry among the few strangers who were led by chance or business into that unknown, outlying country. But many even of the people of the parish were ignorant of the strange events which had marked the first year of Mr Soulis's ministrations; and among those who were better informed, some were naturally reticent, and others shy of that particular topic. Now and again, only, one of the older folk would warm into courage over his third tumbler, and recount the cause of the minister's strange looks and solitary life.

Fifty years syne,[1] when Mr Soulis cam' first into Ba'weary, he was still a young man – a callant, the folk said – fu' o' book-learnin' an' grand at the exposition, but, as was natural in sae young a man, wi' nae leevin' experience in religion. The younger sort were greatly taken wi' his gifts and his gab; but auld, concerned, serious men and women were moved even to prayer for the young man, whom they took to be a self-deceiver, and the parish that was like to be sae ill-supplied. It was before the days o' the moderates – weary fa' them; but ill things are like guid – they baith come bit by bit, a pickle at a time; and there were folk even then that said the Lord had left the college professors to their ain devices, an' the lads that went to study wi' them wad hae done mair an' better sittin' in a peat-bog, like their forbears of the persecution, wi' a Bible under their oxter an' a speerit o' prayer in their heart. There was nae doubt onyway, but that Mr Soulis had been ower lang at the college. He was careful and troubled for mony things besides the ae thing needful. He had a feck o' books wi' him – mair than had ever been seen before in a' that presbytery; and a sair wark the carrier had wi' them, for they were a' like to have smoored in the De'il's Hag between this and Kilmackerlie. They were books o' divinity, to be sure, or so they ca'd them; but the serious were o' opinion there was little service for sae mony, when the hail o' God's Word would gang in the neuk o' a plaid. Then he wad sit half the day and half the nicht forbye, which was scant decent – writin', nae less; an' first they were feared he wad read his sermons; an' syne it proved he was writin' a book himsel', which was surely no' fittin' for ane o' his years an' sma' experience.

Onyway it behoved him to get an auld, decent wife to keep the manse for him an' see to his bit denners; an' he was recommended to an auld limmer – Janet M'Clour, they ca'd her – an' sae far left to himsel' as to be ower persuaded. There was mony advised him to the contrar, for Janet was mair than suspeckit by the best folk in Ba'weary. Lang or that, she had had a wean to a dragoon; she hadna come forrit* for maybe thretty year; and bairns had seen her mumblin' to hersel' up on Key's Loan in the gloamin', whilk was an unco time an' place for a God-fearin' woman. Howsoever, it was the laird himsel' that had first tauld the minister o' Janet; an' in thae days he wad hae gane a far gate to pleesure the laird. When folk tauld him that Janet was sib to the de'il, it was a' superstition by his way o' it; an' when they cast up the Bible to him an' the witch of Endor,[2] he wad threep it doun their thrapples that thir days were a' gane by, an' the de'il was mercifully restrained.

Weel, when it got about the clachan that Janet M'Clour was to be servant at the manse, the folk were fair mad wi' her an'

*To come forrit' – to offer oneself as a communicant.

him thegither; an' some o' the guidwives had nae better to dae than get round her door-cheeks and chairge her wi' a' that was ken't again' her, frae the sodger's bairn to John Tamson's twa kye. She was nae great speaker; folk usually let her gang her ain gate, an' she let them gang theirs, wi' neither Fair-guid-een nor Fair-guid-day; but when she buckled to, she had a tongue to deave the miller. Up she got, an' there wasna an auld story in Ba'weary but she gart somebody lowp for it that day; they couldna say ae thing but she could say twa to it; till, at the hinder end, the guidwives up an' claught haud of her, an' clawed the coats aff her back, and pu'd her doun the clachan to the water o' Dule, to see if she were a witch or no, soom or droun. The carline skirled till ye could hear at the Hangin' Shaw, an' she focht like ten; there was mony a guidwife bure the mark o' her neist day an' mony a lang day after; an' just in the hettest o' the collieshangie, wha suld come up (for his sins) but the new minister!

'Women,' said he (an' he had a grand voice), 'I charge you in the Lord's name to let her go.'

Janet ran to him – she was fair wud wi' terror – an' clang to him, an' prayed him, for Christ's sake, save her frae the cummers; an' they, for their pairt, tauld him a' that was ken't, an' maybe mair.

'Woman,' says he to Janet, 'is this true?'

'As the Lord sees me,' says she, 'as the Lord made me, no' a word o't. Forbye the bairn,' says she, 'I've been a decent woman a' my days.'

'Will you,' says Mr Soulis, 'in the name of God, and before me, His unworthy minister, renounce the devil and his works?'

Weel, it wad appear that when he askit that, she gave a girn that fairly frichit them that saw her, an' they could hear her teeth play dirl thegither in her chafts; but there was naething for it but the ae way or the ither; an' Janet lifted up her hand an' renounced the de'il before them a'.

'And now,' says Mr Soulis to the guidwives, 'home with ye, one and all, and pray to God for His forgiveness.'

An' he gied Janet his arm, though she had little on her but a sark, and took her up the clachan to her ain door like a leddy o' the land; an' her screighin' an' laughin' as was a scandal to be heard.

There were mony grave folk lang ower their prayers that nicht; but when the morn cam' there was sic a fear fell upon a' Ba'weary that the bairns hid theirsels, an' even the menfolk stood an' keekit frae their doors. For there was Janet comin' doun the clachan – her or her likeness, nane could tell – wi' her neck thrawn, an' her heid on ae side, like a body that has been hangit, an' a girn on her face like an unstreakit corp. By an' by they got used wi' it, an' even sneered at her to ken what was wrang; but frae that day forth she couldna speak like a Christian woman, but slavered an' played click wi' her teeth like a pair o' shears; an' frae that day forth the name o' God cam' never on her lips. Whiles she wad try to say it, but it michtna be. Them that kenned best said least; but they never gied that Thing the name o' Janet M'Clour; for the auld Janet, by their way o't, was in muckle hell that day. But the minister was neither to haud nor to bind; he preached about naething but the folk's cruelty that had gi'en her a stroke of the palsy; he skelpit the bairns that meddled her; an' he had her up to the manse that same nicht, an' dwalled there a' his lane wi' her under the Hangin' Shaw.

Weel, time gaed by : and the idler sort commenced to think mair lichtly o' that black business. The minister was weel thocht o'; he was aye late at the writing, folk wad see his can'le doon by the Dule water after twal' at e'en; and he seemed pleased wi' himsel' an' upsitten as at first, though a' body could see that he was dwining. As for Janet she cam' an' she gaed; if she didna speak muckle afore, it was reason she should speak less then; she meddled naebody; but she was an eldritch thing to see, an' nane wad hae mistrysted wi' her for Ba'weary glebe.

About the end o' July there cam' a spell o' weather, the like o't never was in that country-side; it was lown an' het an' heartless; the herds couldna win up the Black Hill, the bairns were ower weariet to play; an' yet it was gousty too, wi' claps o' het wund that rumm'led in the glens, and bits o' shouers that slockened naething. We aye thocht it büt to thun'er on the morn; but the morn cam', an' the morn's morning, an' it was aye the same uncanny weather, sair on folks and bestial. O' a' that were the waur, nane suffered like Mr Soulis; he could neither sleep nor eat, he tauld his elders; an' when he wasna writin' at his weary book, he wad be stravaguin' ower a' the country-side like a man possessed, when a' body else was blithe to keep caller ben the house.

Abune Hangin' Shaw, in the bield o' the Black Hill, there's a bit enclosed grund wi' an iron yett: an' it seems, in the auld days, that was the kirkyaird o' Ba'weary, an' consecrated by the Papists before the blessed licht shone upon the kingdom. It was a great howff, o' Mr Soulis's onyway; there he wad sit an' consider his sermons; an' indeed it's a bieldy bit. Weel, as he cam' ower the wast end o' the Black Hill, ae day, he saw first twa, an' syne fower, an' syne seeven corbie craws fleein' round an' round abune the auld kirkyaird. They flew laigh an' heavy, an' squawked to ither as they gaed; an' it was clear to Mr Soulis that something had put them frae their ordinar. He wasna easy fleyed, an' gaed straucht up to the wa's; an' what suld he find there but a man, or the appearance o' a man, sittin' in the inside upon a grave. He was of a great stature, an' black as hell, and his e'en were singular to see.* Mr Soulis had heard tell o' black men, mony's the time; but there was something unco about this black man that daunted him.[3] Het as he was, he took a kind o' cauld grue in the marrow o' his banes; but up he spak for a' that; an' says he: 'My friend, are you a stranger in this place?' The black man answered never a word; he got upon his feet, an' begoud on to hirsle to the wa' on the far side; but he aye lookit at the minister; an' the minister stood an' lookit back; till a' in a meenit the black man was ower the wa' an' rinnin' for the bield o' the trees. Mr Soulis,

* It was a common belief in Scotland that the devil appeared as a black man. This appears in several witch trials and I think in Law's *Memorials*, that delightful storehouse of the quaint and grisly.

he hardly kenned why, ran after him; but he was fair forjeskit wi' his walk an' the het, unhalesome weather; an' rin as he likit, he got nae mair than a glisk o' the black man amang the birks, till he won doun to the foot o' the hillside, an' there he saw him ance mair, gaun, hap-step-an'-lawp, ower Dule water to the manse.

Mr Soulis wasna weel pleased that this fearsome gangrel suld mak' sae free wi' Ba'weary manse; an' he ran the harder, an', wet shoon, ower the burn, an' up the walk; but the de'il a black man was there to see. He stepped out upon the road, but there was naebody there; he gaed a' ower the garden, but na, nae black man. At the hinder end, an' a bit feared as was but natural, he lifted the hasp an' into the manse; and there was Janet M'Clour before his e'en, wi' her thrawn craig, an' nane sae pleased to see him. An' he aye minded sinsyne, when first he set his e'en upon her, he had the same cauld and deidly grue.

'Janet,' says he, 'have you seen a black man?'

'A black man!' quo' she. 'Save us a'! Ye're no wise, minister. There's nae black man in a' Ba'weary.'

But she didna speak plain, ye maun understand; but yam-yammered, like a powney wi' the bit in its moo.

'Weel,' says he, 'Janet, if there was nae black man, I have spoken with the Accuser of the Brethren.'

An' he sat doun like ane wi' a fever, an' his teeth chittered in his heid.

'Hoots,' says she, 'think shame to yoursel', minister'; an' gied him a drap brandy that she keept aye by her.

Syne Mr Soulis gaed into his study amang a' his books. It's a lang, laigh, mirk chalmer, perishin' cauld in winter, an' no' very dry even in the top o' the simmer, for the manse stands near the burn. Sae doun he sat, and thocht of a' that had come an' gane since he was in Ba'weary, an' his hame, an' the days when he was a bairn an' ran daffin' on the braes; an' that black man aye ran in his heid like the owercome of a sang. Aye the mair he thocht, the mair he thocht o' the black man. He tried the prayer, an' the words wouldna come to him; an' he tried, they say, to write at his book, but he couldna mak' nar mair o' that. There was whiles he thocht the black man was at his oxter, an' the swat stood upon him cauld as well-water; and there was ither whiles, when he cam' to himsel' like a christened bairn an' minded naething.

The upshot was that he gaed to the window an' stood glowrin' at Dule water. The trees are unco thick, an' the water lies deep an' black under the manse; an' there was Janet washin' the cla'es wi' her coats kilted. She had her back to the minister, an' he, for his pairt, hardly kenned what he was lookin' at. Syne she turned round, an' shawed her face; Mr Soulis had the same cauld grue as twice that day afore, an' it was borne in upon him what folk said, that Janet was deid lang syne, an' this was a bogle in her clay-cauld flesh. He drew back a pickle and he scanned her narrowly. She was tramp-trampin' in the cla'es croonin' to hersel'; and eh! Gude guide us, but it was a fearsome face. Whiles she sang louder, but there was nae man born o' woman that could tell the words o' her sang; an' whiles she lookit side-lang doun, but there was naething there for her to look at. There gaed a scunner through the flesh upon his banes; an' that was Heeven's advertisement. But Mr Soulis just blamed himsel', he said, to think sae ill o' a puir, auld afflicted wife that hadna a freend forbye himsel'; an' he put up a bit prayer for him an' her, an' drank a little caller water – for his heart rose again' the meat – an' gaed up to his naked bed in the gloamin'.

That was a nicht that has never been forgotten in Ba'weary, the nicht o' the seeventeenth o' August, seeventeen hun'er' an' twal'. It had been het afore, as I hae said, but that nicht it was hetter than ever. The sun gaed doun amang unco-lookin' clouds; it fell as mirk as the pit; no' a star, no' a breath o' wund; ye couldna see your han' afore your face, an' even the auld folk cuist the covers frae their beds an' lay pechin' for their breath. Wi' a' that he had upon his mind, it was gey an' unlikely Mr Soulis wad get muckle sleep. He lay an' he tummled; the gude, caller bed that he got into brunt his very banes; whiles he slept, an' whiles he waukened; whiles he heard the time o' nicht, an' whiles a tyke yowlin' up the muir, as if somebody was deid; whiles he thocht he heard bogles claverin' in his lug, an' whiles he saw spunkies in the room. He behoved, he judged, to be sick; an' sick he was – little he jaloosed the sickness.

At the hinder end, he got a clearness in his mind, sat up in his sark on the bed-side, an' fell thinkin' ance mair o' the black man an' Janet. He couldna weel tell how – maybe it was the cauld to his feet – but it cam' in upon him wi' a spate that there was some connection between thir twa, an' that either or baith o' them were bogles. An' just at that moment, in Janet's room, which was neist to his, there cam' a stramp o' feet as if men were wars'lin', an' then a loud bang; an' then a wund gaed reishling round the fower quarters o' the house; an' then a' was ance mair as seelent as the grave.

Mr Soulis was feared for neither man nor de'il. He got his tinder-box, an' lit a can'le, an' made three steps o't ower to Janet's door. It was on the hasp, an' he pushed it open, an' keeked bauldly in. It was a big room, as big as the minister's ain, an' plenished wi' grand, auld solid gear, for he had naething else. There was a fower-posted bed wi' auld tapestry; an' a braw cabinet o' aik, that was fu' o' the minister's divinity books, an' put there to be out o' the gate; an' a wheen duds o' Janet's lying here an' there about the floor. But nae Janet could Mr Soulis see; nor ony sign o' a contention. In he gaed (an' there's few that wad hae followed him) an' lookit a' round, an' listened. But there was naething to be heard, neither inside the manse nor in a' Ba'weary parish, an' naething to be seen but the muckle shadows turnin' round the can'le. An' then, a' at aince, the minister's heart played dunt an' stood stock-still; an' a cauld wund blew amang the hairs o' his heid. Whaten a weary sicht was that for the puir man's e'en! For there was Janet hangin' frae a nail beside the auld aik cabinet: her heid aye lay on her shouther, her e'en were steekit, the tongue projected frae her mouth, an' her heels were twa feet clear abune the floor.

'God forgive us all!' thocht Mr Soulis, 'poor Janet's dead.'

He cam' a step nearer to the corp; an' then his heart fair

whammled in his inside. For by what cantrip it wad ill beseem
a man to judge, she was hangin' frae a single nail an' by a
single wursted thread for darnin' hose.

It 's a awfu' thing to be your lane at nicht wi' siccan prodigies
o' darkness; but Mr Soulis was strong in the Lord. He turned
an' gaed his ways oot o' that room, an' lockit the door ahint
him; an' step by step, doun the stairs, as heavy as leed; and
set doun the can'le on the table at the stairfoot. He couldna
pray, he couldna think, he was dreepin' wi' caul' swat, an'
naething could he hear but the dunt-dunt-duntin' o' his ain
heart. He micht maybe hae stood there an hour, or maybe twa,
he minded sae little; when a' o' a sudden, he heard a laigh,
uncanny steer up-stairs; a foot gaed to an' fro in the chalmer
whaur the corp was hangin'; syne the door was opened, though
he minded weel that he had lockit it; an' syne there was a step
upon the landin', an' it seemed to him as if the corp was lookin'
ower the rail and doun upon him whaur he stood.

He took up the can'le again (for he couldna want the licht),
an' as saftly as ever he could, gaed straucht out o' the manse
an' to the far end o' the causeway. It was aye pit-mirk; the
flame o' the can'le, when he set it on the grund, brunt steedy
and clear as in a room; naething moved, but the Dule water
seepin' and sabbin' doun the glen, an' yon unhaly footstep
that cam' ploddin' doun the stairs inside the manse. He kenned
the foot ower weel, for it was Janet's; an' at ilka step that cam' a
wee thing nearer, the cauld got deeper in his vitals. He com-
mended his soul to Him that made an' keepit him; 'and, O Lord,'
said he, 'give me strength this night to war against the powers
of evil.'

By this time the foot was comin' through the passage for
the door; he could hear a hand skirt alang the wa', as if the
fearsome thing was feelin' for its way. The saughs tossed an'
maned thegither, a long sigh cam' ower the hills, the flame o'
the can'le was blawn aboot; an' there stood the corp of Thrawn
Janet, wi her grogram goun an' her black mutch, wi' the heid
aye upon the shouther, an' the girn still upon the face o't –

leevin', ye wad hae said – deid, as Mr Soulis weel kenned – upon
the threshold o' the manse.

It 's a strange thing that the soul of a man should be that
thirled into his perishable body; but the minister saw that, an'
his heart didna break.

She didna stand there lang; she began to move again an'
cam' slowly towards Mr Soulis whaur he stood under the
saughs. A' the life o' his body, a' the strength o' his speerit,
were glowerin' frae his e'en. It seemed she was gaun to speak,
but wanted words, an' made a sign wi' the left hand. There
cam' a clap o' wund, like a cat's fuff; oot gaed the can'le, the
saughs skreighed like folk; an' Mr Soulis kenned that, live or
die, this was the end o't.

'Witch, beldame, devil!' he cried, 'I charge you, by the
power of God, begone – if you be dead, to the grave – if you
be damned, to hell.'

An' at that moment the Lord's ain hand out o' the Heevens
struck the Horror whaur it stood; the auld, deid, desecrated
corp o' the witch-wife, sae lang keepit frae the grave and
hirsled round by de'ils, lowed up like a brunstane spunk an' fell
in ashes to the grund; the thunder followed, peal on dirlin'
peal, the rairin' rain upon the back o' that; and Mr Soulis
lowped through the garden hedge, an' ran, wi' skelloch upon
skelloch, for the clachan.

That same mornin', John Christie saw the Black Man pass
the Muckle Cairn as it was chappin' six; before eicht, he gaed
by the change-house at Knockdow; an' no' lang after, Sandy
M'Lellan saw him gaun linkin' doun the braes frae Kilmackerlie. There 's little doubt but it was him that dwalled sae lang in
Janet's body; but he was awa' at last; an' sinsyne the de'il has
never fashed us in Ba'weary.

But it was a sair dispensation for the minister; lang, lang
he lay ravin' in his bed; an' frae that hour to this, he was the
man ye ken the day.

THE MISADVENTURES OF
JOHN NICHOLSON

CHAPTER I

IN WHICH JOHN SOWS THE WIND

JOHN VAREY NICHOLSON was stupid; yet, stupider men than he are now sprawling in Parliament, and lauding themselves as the authors of their own distinction. He was of a fat habit, even from boyhood, and inclined to a cheerful and cursory reading of the face of life; and possibly this attitude of mind was the original cause of his misfortunes. Beyond this hint philosophy is silent on his career, and superstition steps in with the more ready explanation that he was detested of the gods.

His father – that iron gentleman – had long ago enthroned himself on the heights of the Disruption Principles.[1] What these are (and in spite of their grim name they are quite innocent) no array of terms would render thinkable to the merely English intelligence; but to the Scot they often prove unctuously nourishing, and Mr Nicholson found in them the milk of lions. About the period when the Churches convene at Edinburgh in their annual assemblies, he was to be seen descending the Mound in the company of divers red-headed clergymen: these voluble, he only contributing oracular nods, brief negatives, and the austere spectacle of his stretched upper lip. The names of Candlish and Begg were frequent in these interviews, and occasionally the talk ran on the Residuary Establishment and the doings of one Lee.[2] A stranger to the tight little theological kingdom of Scotland might have listened and gathered literally nothing. And Mr Nicholson (who was not a dull man) knew that, and raged at it. He knew there was a vast world outside, to whom Disruption Principles were as the chatter of tree-top apes,[3] the paper brought him chill whiffs from it; he had met Englishmen who had asked lightly if he did not belong to the Church of

Scotland, and then had failed to be much interested by his elucidation of that nice point; it was an evil, wild, rebellious world, lying sunk in *dozenedness*, for nothing short of a Scot's word will paint this Scotsman's feelings. And when he entered his own house in Randolph Crescent (south side), and shut the door behind him, his heart swelled with security. Here, at least, was a citadel unassailable by right-hand defections or left-hand extremes. Here was a family where prayers came at the same hour, where the Sabbath literature was unimpeachably selected, where the guest who should have leaned to any false opinion was instantly set down, and over which there reigned all week, and grew denser on Sundays, a silence that was agreeable to his ear, and gloom that he found comfortable.

Mrs Nicholson had died about thirty, and left him with three children: a daughter two years and a son about eight years younger than John; and John himself, the unfortunate protagonist of the present history. The daughter, Maria, was a good girl – dutiful, pious, dull, but so easily startled that to speak to her was quite a perilous enterprise. 'I don't think I care to talk about that, if you please,' she would say, and strike the boldest speechless by her unmistakable pain; this upon all topics – dress, pleasure, morality, politics, in which the formula was changed to 'my papa thinks otherwise,' and even religion, unless it was approached with a particular whining tone of voice. Alexander, the younger brother, was sickly, clever, fond of books and drawing, and full of satirical remarks. In the midst of these, imagine that natural, clumsy, unintelligent, and mirthful animal, John; mighty well-behaved in comparison with other lads, although not up to the mark of the house in Randolph Crescent; full of a sort of blundering affection, full of caresses which were never very warmly received; full of sudden and loud laughter which rang out in that still house like curses. Mr Nicholson himself had a great fund of humour, of the Scots order – intellectual, turning on the observation of men; his own character, for instance – if he could have seen it in another – would have been a rare feast to him; but his son's empty guffaws over a broken plate, and empty, almost light-hearted remarks, struck him with pain as the indices of a weak mind.

Outside the family John had early attached himself (much as a dog may follow a marquess) to the steps of Alan Houston, a lad about a year older than himself, idle, a trifle wild, the heir to a good estate which was still in the hands of a rigorous trustee, and so royally content with himself that he took John's devotion as a thing of course. The intimacy was gall to Mr Nicholson; it took his son from the house, and he was a jealous parent; it kept him from the office, and he was a martinet; lastly, Mr Nicholson was ambitious for his family (in which, and the Disruption Principles, he entirely lived), that he hated to see a son of his play second fiddle to an idler. After some hesitation, he ordered that the friendship should cease – an unfair command, though seemingly inspired by the spirit of prophecy; and John, saying nothing, continued to disobey the order under the rose.

John was nearly nineteen when he was one day dismissed rather earlier than usual from his father's office, where he was studying the practice of the law. It was Saturday; and except that he had a matter of four hundred pounds in his pocket which it was his duty to hand over to the British Linen Company's Bank, he had the whole afternoon at his disposal. He went by Princes Street, enjoying the mild sunshine, and the little thrill of easterly wind that tossed the flags along that terrace of palaces, and tumbled the green trees in the garden. The band was playing down in the valley under the castle; and when it came to the turn of the pipers, he heard their wild sounds with a stirring of the blood. Something distantly martial awoke in him; and he thought of Miss Mackenzie, whom he was to meet that day at dinner in his father's house.

Now, it is undeniable that he should have gone directly to the bank, but right in the way stood the billiard-room of the hotel where Alan was almost certain to be found; and the temptation proved too strong. He entered the billiard-room, and was instantly greeted by his friend, cue in hand.

'Nicholson,' said he, 'I want you to lend me a pound or two till Monday.'

'You've come to the right shop, haven't you?' returned John. 'I have twopence.'

'Nonsense,' said Alan. 'You can get some. Go and borrow at your tailor's; they all do it. Or I'll tell you what: pop your watch.'

'Oh, yes, I daresay,' said John. 'And how about my father?'

'How is he to know? He doesn't wind it up for you at night, does he?' inquired Alan, at which John guffawed. 'No, seriously; I am in a fix,' continued the tempter. 'I have lost some money to a man here. I'll give it you to-night, and you can get the heirloom out again on Monday. Come; it's a small service, after all. I would do a good deal more for you.'

Whereupon John went forth, and pawned his gold watch under the assumed name of John Froggs, 85 Pleasance. But the nervousness that assailed him at the door of that inglorious haunt – a pawnshop – and the effort necessary to invent the pseudonym (which somehow seemed to him a necessary part of the procedure), had taken more time than he imagined; and when he returned to the billiard-room with the spoils, the bank had already closed its doors.

This was a shrewd knock. 'A piece of business had been neglected.' He heard these words in his father's trenchant voice, and trembled, and then dodged the thought. After all, who was to know? He must carry four hundred pounds about with him till Monday, when the neglect could be surreptitiously repaired; and meanwhile, he was free to pass the afternoon on the encircling divan of the billiard-room, smoking his pipe, sipping a pint of ale, and enjoying to the mast-head the modest pleasures of admiration.

None can admire like a young man. Of all youth's passions and pleasures, this is the most common and least alloyed; and every flash of Alan's black eyes; every aspect of his curly head; every graceful reach, and easy, stand-off attitude of waiting, everything about him down even to his shirt-sleeves and wrist-links, were seen by John through a luxurious glory. He valued himself by the possession of that royal friend, hugged himself upon the thought, and swam in warm azure; his own defects, like vanquished difficulties, becoming things on which to plume himself. Only when he thought of Miss Mackenzie there fell upon his mind a shadow of regret; that young lady was worthy of better things than plain John Nicholson, still known among schoolmates by the derisive name of 'Fatty'; and he felt that if he could chalk a cue or stand at ease, with such a careless grace as Alan, he could approach the object of his sentiments with a less crushing sense of inferiority.

Before they parted, Alan made a proposal that was startling in the extreme. He would be at Collette's that night about twelve, he said. Why should not John come there and get the money? To go to Collette's was to see life, indeed; it was wrong; it was against the laws; it partook, in a very dingy manner, of adventure. Were it known, it was the sort of exploit that disconsidered a young man for good with the more serious classes, but gave him a standing with the riotous. And yet Collette's was not a hell; it could not come, without vaulting hyperbole, under the rubric of a gilded saloon; and, if it was a sin to go there, the sin was merely local and municipal. Collette's (whose name I do not know how to spell, for I was never in epistolary communication with that hospitable outlaw) was simply an unlicensed publican, who gave suppers after eleven at night, the Edinburgh hour of closing. If you belonged to a club, you could get a much better supper at the same hour, and lose not a jot in public esteem. But if you lacked that qualification, and were an-hungered, or inclined towards conviviality at unlawful hours, Collette's was your only port. You were very ill-supplied. The company was not recruited from the Senate or the Church, though the Bar was very well represented on the only occasion on which I flew in the face of my country's laws, and, taking my reputation in my hand, penetrated into that grim supper-house. And Collette's frequenters, thrillingly conscious of wrong-doing and 'that two-handed engine (the policeman) at the door,' were perhaps inclined to somewhat feverish excess. But the place was in no sense a very bad one; and it is somewhat strange to me, at this distance of time, how it had acquired its dangerous repute.

In precisely the same spirit as a man may debate a project to ascend the Matterhorn or to cross Africa, John considered Alan's proposal, and, greatly daring, accepted it. As he walked home, the thoughts of this excursion out of the safe places of life into the wild and arduous, stirred and struggled in his imagination with the image of Flora Mackenzie – incongruous and yet kindred thoughts, for did not each imply unusual tightening of the pegs of resolution? did not each woo him forth and warn him back again into himself?

Between these two considerations, at least, he was more than usually moved; and when he got to Randolph Crescent, he quite forgot the four hundred pounds in the inner pocket of his great-coat, hung up the coat, with its rich freight, upon his particular pin of the hat-stand; and in the very action sealed his doom.

CHAPTER II

IN WHICH JOHN REAPS
THE WHIRLWIND

ABOUT half-past ten it was John's brave good fortune to offer his arm to Miss Mackenzie, and escort her home. The night was chill and starry; all the way eastward the trees of the different gardens rustled and looked black. Up the stone gully of Leith Walk, when they came to cross it, the breeze made a rush and set the flames of the street-lamps quavering; and when at last they had mounted to the Royal Terrace, where Captain Mackenzie lived, a great salt freshness came in their faces from the sea. These phases of the walk remained written on John's memory, each emphasised by the touch of that light hand on his arm; and behind all these aspects of the nocturnal city he saw, in his mind's eye, a picture of the lighted drawing-room at home where he had sat talking with Flora; and his father, from the other end, had looked on with a kind and ironical smile. John had read the significance of that smile, which might have escaped a stranger. Mr Nicholson had remarked his son's entanglement with satisfaction, tinged by humour; and his smile, if it still was a thought contemptuous, had implied consent.

At the captain's door the girl held out her hand, with a certain emphasis; and John took it and kept it a little longer, and said, 'Good-night, Flora, dear,' and was instantly thrown into much fear by his presumption. But she only laughed, ran up the steps, and rang the bell; and while she was waiting for the door to open, kept close in the porch, and talked to him from that point as out of a fortification. She had a knitted shawl over her head; her blue Highland eyes took the light from the neighbouring street-lamp and sparkled; and when the door opened and closed upon her, John felt cruelly alone.

He proceeded slowly back along the terrace in a tender glow; and when he came to Greenside Church, he halted in a doubtful mind. Over the crown of the Calton Hill, to his left, lay the way to Collette's, where Alan would soon be looking for his arrival, and where he would now have no more consented to go than he would have wilfully wallowed in a bog; the touch of the girl's hand on his sleeve, and the kindly light in his father's eyes, both loudly forbidding. But right before him was the way home, which pointed only to bed, a place of little ease for one whose fancy was strung to the lyrical pitch, and whose not very ardent heart was just then tumultuously moved. The hill-top, the cool air of the night, the company of the great monuments, the sight of the city under his feet, with its hills and valleys and crossing files of lamps, drew him by all he had of the poetic, and he turned that way; and by that quite innocent deflection, ripened the crop of his venial errors for the sickle of destiny.

On a seat on the hill above Greenside he sat for perhaps half an hour, looking down upon the lamps of Edinburgh, and up at the lamps of heaven. Wonderful were the resolves he formed; beautiful and kindly were the vistas of future life that sped before him. He uttered to himself the name of Flora in so many touching and dramatic keys, that he became at length fairly melted with tenderness, and could have sung aloud. At that juncture the sound of a certain creasing in his greatcoat caught his ear. He put his hand into his pocket, pulled forth the envelope that held the money, and sat stupefied. The Calton Hill, about this period, had an ill name of nights; and to be sitting there with four hundred pounds that did not belong to him was hardly wise. He looked up. There was a man in a very bad hat a little on one side of him, apparently looking at the scenery; from a little on the other a second night-walker was drawing very quietly near. Up jumped John. The envelope fell from his hands; he stooped to get it, and at the same moment both men ran in and closed with him.

A little after, he got to his feet very sore and shaken, the poorer by a purse which contained exactly one penny postage-stamp, by a cambric handkerchief, and by the all-important envelope.

Here was a young man on whom, at the highest point of loverly exaltation, there had fallen a blow too sharp to be supported alone; and not many hundred yards away his greatest friend was sitting at supper – ay, and even expecting him. Was it not in the nature of man that he should run there? He went in quest of sympathy – in quest of that droll article that we all suppose ourselves to want when in a strait, and have agreed to call advice; and he went, besides, with vague but rather splendid expectations of relief. Alan was rich, or would be so when he came of age. By a stroke of the pen he might remedy this misfortune, and avert that dreaded interview with Mr Nicholson, from which John now shrunk in imagination as the hand draws back from fire.

Close under the Calton Hill there runs a certain narrow avenue, part street, part by-road. The head of it faces the doors of the prison; its tail descends into the sunless slums of the Low Calton. On one hand it is overhung by the crags of the hill, on the other by an old grave-yard. Between these two the road-way runs in a trench, sparsely lighted at night, sparsely frequented by day, and bordered, when it has cleared the place of tombs, by dingy and ambiguous houses. One of these was the house of Collette; and at this door our ill-starred John was presently beating for admittance. In an evil hour he satisfied the jealous inquiries of the contraband hotelkeeper; in an evil hour he penetrated into the somewhat unsavoury interior. Alan, to be sure, was there, seated in a room lighted by noisy gas-jets, beside a dirty table-cloth, engaged on a coarse meal, and in the company of several tipsy members of the junior bar. But Alan was not sober; he had lost a thousand pounds upon a horse-race, had received the news at dinner-time, and was now, in default of any possible means of extrication, drowning the memory of his predicament. He to help John! The thing was impossible; he couldn't help himself.

'If you have a beast of a father,' said he, 'I can tell you I have a brute of a trustee.'

'I'm not going to hear my father called a beast,' said John, with a beating heart, feeling that he risked the last sound rivet of the chain that bound him to life.

But Alan was quite good-natured.

'All right, old fellow,' said he. 'Mos' respec'able man your father.' And he introduced his friend to his companions as 'old Nicholson the what-d'ye-call-um's son.'

John sat in dumb agony. Collette's foul walls and maculate table-linen, and even down to Collette's villainous casters, seemed like objects in a nightmare. And just then there came a knock and a scurrying; the police, so lamentably absent from the Calton Hill, appeared upon the scene; and the party, taken *flagrante delicto*, with their glasses at their elbow, were seized, marched up to the police office, and all duly summoned to appear as witnesses in the consequent case against that arch-shebeener, Collette.

It was a sorrowful and a mightily sobered company that came forth again. The vague terror of public opinion weighed generally on them all; but there were private and particular horrors on the minds of individuals. Alan stood in dread of his trustee, already sorely tried. One of the group was the son of a country minister, another of a judge; John, the unhappiest of all, had David Nicholson to father, the idea of facing whom on such a scandalous subject was physically sickening. They stood a while consulting under the buttresses of Saint Giles; thence they adjourned to the lodgings of one of the number in North Castle Street, where (for that matter) they might have had quite as good a supper, and far better drink, than in the dangerous paradise from which they had been routed. There, over an almost tearful glass, they debated their position. Each explained he had the world to lose if the affair went on, and he appeared as a witness. It was remarkable what bright prospects were just then in the very act of opening before each of that little company of youths, and what pious consideration for the feelings of their families began now to well from them. Each, moreover, was in an odd state of destitution. Not one could bear his share of the fine; not one but evinced a wonderful twinkle of hope that each of the others (in succession) was the very man who could step in to make good the deficit. One took a high hand; he could not pay his share; if it went to a trial, he should bolt; he had always felt the English Bar to be his true sphere. Another branched out into touching details about his family, to which no one listened. John, in the midst of this disorderly competition of poverty and meanness, sat stunned, contemplating the mountain bulk of his misfortunes.

At last, upon a pledge that each should apply to his family with a common frankness, this convention of unhappy young asses broke up, went down the common stair, and in the grey of the spring morning, with the streets lying dead empty all about them, the lamps burning on into the daylight in diminished lustre, and the birds beginning to sound premonitory notes from the groves of the town gardens, went each his own way with bowed head and echoing footfall.

The rooks were awake in Randolph Crescent; but the windows looked down, discreetly blinded, on the return of the prodigal. John's pass-key was a recent privilege; this was the first time it had been used; and, oh! with what a sickening sense of his unworthiness he now inserted it into the well-oiled lock and entered that citadel of the proprieties! All slept; the gas in the hall had been left faintly burning to light his return; a dreadful stillness reigned, broken by the deep ticking of the eight-day clock. He put the gas out, and sat on a chair in the hall, waiting and counting the minutes, longing for any human countenance. But when at last he heard the alarm-clock spring its rattle in the lower story, and the servants begin to be about, he instantly lost heart, and fled to his own room, where he threw himself upon the bed.

CHAPTER III

IN WHICH JOHN ENJOYS
THE HARVEST HOME

SHORTLY after breakfast, at which he assisted with a highly tragical countenance, John sought his father where he sat, presumably in religious meditation, on the Sabbath mornings. The old gentleman looked up with that sour, inquisitive expression that came so near to smiling and was so different in effect.

'This is a time when I do not like to be disturbed,' he said.

'I know that,' returned John; 'but I have – I want – I've made a dreadful mess of it,' he broke out, and turned to the window.

Mr Nicholson sat silent for an appreciable time, while his unhappy son surveyed the poles in the back green, and a certain yellow cat that was perched upon the wall. Despair sat upon John as he gazed; and he raged to think of the dreadful series of his misdeeds, and the essential innocence that lay behind them.

'Well,' said his father, with an obvious effort, but in very quiet tones, 'what is it?'

'Maclean gave me four hundred pounds to put in the bank, sir,' began John; 'and I'm sorry to say that I've been robbed of it!'

'Robbed of it?' cried Mr Nicholson, with a strong rising inflection. 'Robbed? Be careful what you say, John!'

'I can't say anything else, sir; I was just robbed of it,' said John, in desperation, sullenly.

'And where and when did this extraordinary event take place?' inquired the father.

'On the Calton Hill about twelve last night.'

'The Calton Hill?' repeated Mr Nicholson. 'And what were you doing there at such a time of the night?'

'Nothing, sir,' says John.

Mr Nicholson drew in his breath.

'And how came the money in your hands at twelve last night?' he asked, sharply.

'I neglected that piece of business,' said John, anticipating comment; and then in his own dialect: 'I clean forgot all about it.'

'Well,' said his father, 'it's a most extraordinary story. Have you communicated with the police?'

'I have,' answered poor John, the blood leaping to his face. 'They think they know the men that did it. I daresay the money will be recovered, if that was all,' said he, with a desperate indifference, which his father set down to levity; but which sprang from the consciousness of worse behind.

'Your mother's watch, too?' asked Mr Nicholson.

'Oh, the watch is all right!' cried John. 'At least, I mean I was coming to the watch – the fact is, I am ashamed to say, I – I had pawned the watch before. Here is the ticket; they didn't find that; the watch can be redeemed; they don't sell pledges.' The lad panted out these phrases, one after another, like minute-guns; but at the last word, which rang in that stately chamber like an oath, his heart failed him utterly; and the dreaded silence settled on father and son.

It was broken by Mr Nicholson picking up the pawn-ticket: 'John Froggs, 85 Pleasance,' he read; and then turning upon John, with a brief flash of passion and disgust, 'Who is John Froggs?' he cried.

'Nobody,' said John. 'It was just a name.'

'An *alias*,' his father commented.

'Oh! I think scarcely quite that,' said the culprit; 'it's a form, they all do it, the man seemed to understand, we had a great deal of fun over the name –'

He paused at that, for he saw his father wince at the picture like a man physically struck; and again there was silence.

'I do not think,' said Mr Nicholson, at last, 'that I am an ungenerous father. I have never grudged you money within reason, for any avowable purpose; you had just to come to me and speak. And now I find that you have forgotten all decency and all natural feeling, and actually pawned – pawned – your mother's watch. You must have had some temptation; I will do you the justice to suppose it was a strong one. What did you want with this money?'

'I would rather not tell you, sir,' said John. 'It will only make you angry.'

'I will not be fenced with,' cried his father. 'There must be an end of disingenuous answers. What did you want with this money?'

'To lend it to Houston, sir,' says John.

'I thought I had forbidden you to speak to that young man?' asked his father.

'Yes, sir,' said John; 'but I only met him.'

'Where?' came the deadly question.

And 'in a billiard-room' was the damning answer. Thus, had John's single departure from the truth brought instant punishment. For no other purpose but to see Alan would he have entered a billiard-room; but he had desired to palliate the fact of his disobedience, and now it appeared that he frequented these disreputable haunts upon his own account.

Once more Mr Nicholson digested the vile tidings in silence; and when John stole a glance at his father's countenance, he was abashed to see the marks of suffering.

'Well,' said the old gentleman, at last, 'I cannot pretend not to be simply bowed down. I rose this morning what the world calls a happy man – happy, at least, in a son of whom I thought I could be reasonably proud –'

But it was beyond human nature to endure this longer, and John interrupted almost with a scream. 'Oh, wheest!' he cried, 'that's not all, that's not the worst of it – it's nothing! How could I tell you were proud of me? Oh! I wish, I wish that I had known; but you always said I was such a disgrace! And the dreadful thing is this: we were all taken up last night, and we have to pay Collette's fine among the six, or we'll be had up for evidence – shebeening it is. They made me swear to tell you; but for my part,' he cried, bursting into tears, 'I just wish that

I was dead!' And he fell on his knees before a chair and hid his face.

Whether his father spoke, or whether he remained long in the room or at once departed, are points lost to history. A horrid turmoil of mind and body; bursting sobs; broken, vanishing thoughts, now of indignation, now of remorse; broken elementary whiffs of consciousness, of the smell of the horsehair on the chair bottom, of the jangling of church bells that now began to make day horrible throughout the confines of the city, of the hard floor that bruised his knees, of the taste of tears that found their way into his mouth: for a period of time, the duration of which I cannot guess, while I refuse to dwell longer on its agony, these were the whole of God's world for John Nicholson.

When at last, as by the touching of a spring, he returned again to clearness of consciousness and even a measure of composure, the bells had but just done ringing, and the Sabbath silence was still marred by the patter of belated feet. By the clock above the fire, as well as by these more speaking signs, the service had not long begun; and the unhappy sinner, if his father had really gone to church, might count on near two hours of only comparative unhappiness. With his father, the superlative degree returned infallibly. He knew it by every shrinking fibre in his body, he knew it by the sudden dizzy whirling of his brain, at the mere thought of that calamity. An hour and a half, perhaps an hour and three quarters, if the doctor was longwinded, and then would begin again that active agony from which, even in the dull ache of the present, he shrunk as from the bite of fire. He saw, in a vision, the family pew, the somnolent cushions, the Bibles, the Psalm-books, Maria with her smelling-salts, his father sitting spectacled and critical; and at once he was struck with indignation, not unjustly. It was inhuman to go off to church, and leave a sinner in suspense, unpunished, unforgiven. And at the very touch of criticism, the paternal sanctity was lessened; yet the paternal terror only grew; and the two strands of feeling pushed him in the same direction.

And suddenly there came upon him a mad fear lest his father should have locked him in. The notion had no ground in sense; it was probably no more than a reminiscence of similar calamities in childhood, for his father's room had always been the chamber of inquisition and the scene of punishment; but it struck so rigorously in his mind that he must instantly approach the door and prove its untruth. As he went, he struck upon a drawer left open in the business table. It was the money-drawer, a measure of his father's disarray : the money-drawer – perhaps a pointing providence! Who is to decide, when even divines differ between a providence and a temptation? or who, sitting calmly under his own vine, is to pass a judgement on the doings of a poor, hunted dog, slavishly afraid, slavishly rebellious, like John Nicholson on that particular Sunday? His hand was in the drawer, almost before his mind had conceived the hope; and rising to his new situation, he wrote, sitting in his father's chair and using his father's blotting-pad, his pitiful apology and farewell :

MY DEAR FATHER, – I have taken the money, but I will pay it back as soon as I am able. You will never hear of me again. I did not mean any harm by anything, so I hope you will try and forgive me. I wish you would say good-bye to Alexander and Maria, but not if you don't want to. I could not wait to see you, really. Please try to forgive me. Your affectionate son.

JOHN NICHOLSON

The coins abstracted and the missive written, he could not· be gone too soon from the scene of these transgressions; and remembering how his father had once returned from church, on some slight illness, in the middle of the second psalm, he durst not even make a packet of a change of clothes. Attired as he was, he slipped from the paternal doors, and found himself in the cool spring air, the thin spring sunshine, and the great Sabbath quiet of the city, which was now only pointed by the cawing of the rooks. There was not a soul in Randolph Crescent, nor a soul in Queensferry Street; in this out-door privacy and the sense of escape, John took heart again; and with a pathetic sense of leave-taking, he even ventured up the lane and stood a while, a strange peri at the gates of a quaint paradise, by the west end of St George's Church. They were singing within; and by a strange chance, the tune was 'St George's, Edinburgh,' which bears the name, and was first sung in the choir of that church. 'Who is this King of Glory?' went the voices from within; and to John this was like the end of all Christian observances, for he was now to be a wild man like Ishmael, and his life was to be cast in homeless places and with godless people.

It was thus, with no rising sense of the adventurous, but in mere desolation and despair, that he turned his back on his native city, and set out on foot for California, with a more immediate eye to Glasgow.

CHAPTER IV

THE SECOND SOWING

IT is no part of mine to narrate the adventures of John Nicholson, which were many, but simply his more momentous misadventures, which were more than he desired, and, by human
standards, more than he deserved; how he reached California,
how he was rooked, and robbed, and beaten, and starved; how
he was at last taken up by charitable folk, restored to some
degree of self-complacency, and installed as a clerk in a bank
in San Francisco, it would take too long to tell; nor in these
episodes were there any marks of the peculiar Nicholsonic destiny, for they were just such matters as befell some thousands
of other young adventurers in the same days and places.[1] But
once posted in the bank, he fell for a time into a high degree of
good fortune, which, as it was only a longer way about to fresh
disaster, it behoves me to explain.

It was his luck to meet a young man in what is technically
called a 'dive,' and thanks to his monthly wages, to extricate
this new acquaintance from a position of present disgrace and
possible danger in the future. This young man was the nephew
of one of the Nob Hill magnates, who run the San Francisco
Stock Exchange, much as more humble adventurers, in the
corner of some public park at home, may be seen to perform
the simple artifice of pea and thimble: for their own profit,
that is to say, and the discouragement of public gambling. It
was thus in his power – and, as he was of grateful temper, it
was among the things that he desired – to put John in the way
of growing rich; and thus, without thought or industry, or so
much as even understanding the game at which he played, but
by simply buying and selling what he was told to buy and sell,
that plaything of fortune was presently at the head of between

eleven and twelve thousand pounds, or, as he reckoned it, of upward of sixty thousand dollars.

How he had come to deserve this wealth, any more than how he had formerly earned disgrace at home, was a problem beyond the reach of his philosophy. It was true that he had been industrious at the bank, but no more so than the cashier, who had seven small children and was visibly sinking in decline. Nor was the step which had determined his advance – a visit to a dive with a month's wages in his pocket – an act of such transcendent virtue, or even wisdom, as to seem to merit the favour of the gods. From some sense of this, and of the dizzy see-saw – heaven-high, hell-deep – on which men sit clutching; or perhaps fearing that the sources of his fortune might be insidiously traced to some root in the field of petty cash; he stuck to his work, said not a word of his new circumstances, and kept his account with a bank in a different quarter of the town. The concealment, innocent as it seems, was the first step in the second tragi-comedy of John's existence.

Meanwhile, he had never written home. Whether from diffidence or shame, or a touch of anger, or mere procrastination, or because (as we have seen) he had no skill in literary arts, or because (as I am sometimes tempted to suppose) there is a law in human nature that prevents young men – not otherwise beasts – from the performance of this simple act of piety – months and years had gone by, and John had never written. The habit of not writing, indeed, was already fixed before he had begun to come into his fortune; and it was only the difficulty of breaking this long silence that withheld him from an instant restitution of the money he had stolen or (as he preferred to call it) borrowed. In vain he sat before paper, attending on inspiration; that heavenly nymph, beyond suggesting the words, 'my dear father,' remained obstinately silent; and presently John would crumple up the sheet and decide, as soon as he had 'a good chance,' to carry the money home in person. And this delay, which is indefensible, was his second step into the snares of fortune.

Ten years had passed, and John was drawing near to thirty.

He had kept the promise of his boyhood, and was now of a lusty frame, verging toward corpulence; good features, good eyes, a genial manner, a ready laugh, a long pair of sandy whiskers, a dash of an American accent, a close familiarity with the great American joke, and a certain likeness to a R-y-l P-rs-n-ge, who shall remain nameless for me, made up the man's externals as he could be viewed in society. Inwardly, in spite of his gross body and highly masculine whiskers, he was more like a maiden lady than a man of twenty-nine.

It chanced one day, as he was strolling down Market Street on the eve of his fortnight's holiday, that his eye was caught by certain railway bills, and in very idleness of mind he calculated that he might be home for Christmas if he started on the morrow. The fancy thrilled him with desire, and in one moment he decided he would go.

There was much to be done; his portmanteau to be packed, a credit to be got from the bank where he was a wealthy customer, and certain offices to be transacted for that other bank in which he was an humble clerk; and it chanced, in conformity with human nature, that out of all this business it was the last that came to be neglected. Night found him, not only equipped with money of his own, but once more (as on that former occasion) saddled with a considerable sum of other people's.

Now it chanced there lived in the same boarding-house a fellow-clerk of his, an honest fellow, with what is called a weakness for drink – though it might, in this case, have been called a strength, for the victim had been drunk for weeks together without the briefest intermission. To this unfortunate John intrusted a letter with an inclosure of bonds, addressed to the bank manager. Even as he did so he thought he perceived a certain haziness of eye and speech in his trustee; but he was too hopeful to be stayed, silenced the voice of warning in his bosom, and with one and the same gesture committed the money to the clerk, and himself into the hands of destiny.

I dwell, even at the risk of tedium, on John's minutest errors, his case being so perplexing to the moralist; but we have done

with them now, the roll is closed, the reader has the worst of
our poor hero, and I leave him to judge for himself whether he
or John has been the less deserving. Henceforth we have to
follow the spectacle of a man who was a mere whip-top for
calamity; on whose unmerited misadventures not even the
humourist can look without pity, and not even the philosopher
without alarm.

That same night the clerk entered upon a bout of drunken-
ness so consistent as to surprise even his intimate acquaintance.
He was speedily ejected from the boarding-house; deposited his
portmanteau with a perfect stranger, who did not even catch
his name; wandered he knew not where, and was at last hove-
to, all standing, in a hospital at Sacramento. There, under the
impenetrable *alias* of the number of his bed, the crapulous being
lay for some more days unconscious of all things, and of one
thing in particular : that the police were after him. Two months
had come and gone before the convalescent in the Sacramento
hospital was identified with Kirkman, the absconding San Francisco clerk; even then, there must elapse nearly a fortnight more
till the perfect stranger could be hunted up, the portmanteau
recovered, and John's letter carried at length to its destination,
the seal still unbroken, the enclosure still intact.

Meanwhile, John had gone upon his holidays without a word,
which was irregular; and there had disappeared with him a
certain sum of money, which was out of all bounds of palliation.
But he was known to be careless, and believed to be honest;
the manager besides had a regard for him; and little was said,
although something was no doubt thought, until the fortnight
was finally at an end, and the time had come for John to re-
appear. Then, indeed, the affair began to look black; and when
inquiries were made, and the penniless clerk was found to have
amassed thousands of dollars, and kept them secretly in a rival
establishment, the stoutest of his friends abandoned him, the
books were overhauled for traces of ancient and artful fraud,
and though none were found, there still prevailed a general
impression of loss. The telegraph was set in motion; and the
correspondent of the bank in Edinburgh, for which place it

was understood that John had armed himself with extensive credits, was warned to communicate with the police.

Now this correspondent was a friend of Mr Nicholson's: he was well acquainted with the tale of John's calamitous disappearance from Edinburgh; and putting one thing with another, hasted with the first word of this scandal, not to the police, but to his friend. The old gentleman had long regarded his son as one dead; John's place had been taken, the memory of his faults had already fallen to be one of those old aches, which awaken again indeed upon occasion, but which we can always vanquish by an effort of the will; and to have the long lost resuscitated in a fresh disgrace was doubly bitter.

'MacEwen,' said the old man, 'this must be hushed up, if possible. If I give you a check for this sum, about which they are certain, could you take it on yourself to let the matter rest?'

'I will,' said MacEwen. 'I will take the risk of it.'

'You understand,' resumed Mr Nicholson, speaking precisely, but with ashen lips, 'I do this for my family, not for that unhappy young man. If it should turn out that these suspicions are correct, and he has embezzled large sums, he must lie on his bed as he has made it.' And then looking up at MacEwen with a nod, and one of his strange smiles: 'Good-bye,' said he; and MacEwen, perceiving the case to be too grave for consolation, took himself off and blessed God on his way home that he was childless.

CHAPTER V

THE PRODIGAL'S RETURN

By a little after noon on the eve of Christmas, John had left his portmanteau in the cloak-room, and stepped forth into Princes Street with a wonderful expansion of the soul, such as men enjoy in the completion of long-nourished schemes. He was at home again, incognito and rich; presently he could enter his father's house by means of the pass-key, which he had piously preserved through all his wanderings; he would throw down the borrowed money; there would be a reconciliation, the details of which he frequently arranged; and he saw himself, during the next month, made welcome in many stately houses at many frigid dinner-parties, taking his share in the conversation with the freedom of the man and the traveller, and laying down the law upon finance with the authority of the successful investor. But this programme was not to be begun before evening — not till just before dinner, indeed, at which meal the reassembled family were to sit roseate, and the best wine (the modern fatted calf) should flow for the prodigal's return.

Meanwhile he walked familiar streets, merry reminiscences crowding round him, sad ones also, both with the same surprising pathos. The keen frosty air; the low, rosy, wintery sun; the castle, hailing him like an old acquaintance; the names of friends on door-plates; the sight of friends whom he seemed to recognise, and whom he eagerly avoided, in the streets; the pleasant chant of the north country accent; the dome of St George's reminding him of his last penitential moments in the lane, and of that King of Glory whose name had echoed ever since in the saddest corner of his memory; and the gutters where he had learned to slide, and the shop where he had bought his skates, and the stones on which he had trod, and the railings in which he had rattled his clachan as he went to school; and all those thousand and one nameless particulars, which the eye sees without noting, which the memory keeps indeed yet without knowing, and which, taken one with another, build up for us the aspect of the place that we call home: and all these besieged him, as he went, with both delight and sadness.

His first visit was for Houston, who had a house on Regent's Terrace, kept for him in old days by an aunt. The door was opened (to his surprise) upon the chain, and a voice asked him from within what he wanted.

'I want Mr Houston – Mr Alan Houston,' said he.

'And who are ye?' said the voice.

'This is most extraordinary,' thought John; and then aloud he told his name.

'No, young Mr John?' cried the voice, with a sudden increase of Scottish accent, testifying to a friendlier feeling.

'The very same,' said John.

And the old butler removed his defences, remarking only, 'I thocht ye were that man.' But his master was not there; he was staying, it appeared, at the house in Murrayfield; and though the butler would have been glad enough to have taken his place and given all the news of the family, John, struck with a little chill, was eager to be gone. Only, the door was scarce closed again, before he regretted that he had not asked about 'that man.'

He was to pay no more visits till he had seen his father and made all well at home; Alan had been the only possible exception, and John had not time to go as far as Murrayfield. But here he was on Regent's Terrace; there was nothing to prevent him going round the end of the hill, and looking from without on the Mackenzies' house. As he went, he reflected that Flora must now be a woman of near his own age, and it was within the bounds of possibility that she was married; but this dishonourable doubt he damned down.

There was the house, sure enough; but the door was of another colour, and what was this – two door-plates? He drew nearer; the top one bore, with dignified simplicity the words, 'Mr Proudfoot'; the lower one was more explicit, and informed

the passer-by that here was likewise the abode of 'Mr J. A. Dun-
lop Proudfoot, Advocate.' The Proudfoots must be rich, for no
advocate could look to have much business in so remote a
quarter; and John hated them for their wealth and for their
name, and for the sake of the house they desecrated with their
presence. He remembered a Proudfoot he had seen at school,
not known : a little, whey-faced urchin, the despicable member
of some lower class. Could it be this abortion that had climbed
to be an advocate, and now lived in the birthplace of Flora and
the home of John's tenderest memories? The chill that had
first seized upon him when he heard of Houston's absence deepened and struck inward. For a moment, as he stood under the
doors of that estranged house, and looked east and west along
the solitary pavement of the Royal Terrace, where not a cat
was stirring, the sense of solitude and desolation took him by
the throat, and he wished himself in San Francisco.

And then the figure he made, with his decent portliness, his
whiskers, the money in his purse, the excellent cigar that he
now lighted, recurred to his mind in consolatory comparison
with that of a certain maddened lad who, on a certain spring
Sunday ten years before, and in the hour of church-time
silence, had stolen from that city by the Glasgow road. In the
face of these changes, it were impious to doubt fortune's kindness. All would be well yet; the Mackenzies would be found,
Flora, younger and lovelier and kinder than before; Alan would
be found, and would have so nicely discriminated his behaviour
as to have grown, on the one hand, into a valued friend of Mr
Nicholson's, and to have remained, upon the other, of that exact
shade of joviality which John desired in his companions. And
so, once more, John fell to work discounting the delightful
future; his first appearance in the family pew; his first visit to
his uncle Greig, who thought himself so great a financier, and
on whose purblind Edinburgh eyes John was to let in the
dazzling daylight of the West; and the details in general of
that unrivalled transformation scene, in which he was to display
to all Edinburgh a portly and successful gentleman in the shoes
of the derided fugitive.

The time began to draw near when his father would have returned from the office, and it would be the prodigal's cue to enter. He strolled westward by Albany Street, facing the sunset embers, pleased, he knew not why, to move in that cold air and indigo twilight, starred with street-lamps. But there was one more disenchantment waiting him by the way.

At the corner of Pitt Street he paused to light a fresh cigar; the vesta threw, as he did so, a strong light upon his features, and a man of about his own age stopped at sight of it.

'I think your name must be Nicholson,' said the stranger.

It was too late to avoid recognition; and besides, as John was now actually on the way home, it hardly mattered, and he gave way to the impulse of his nature.

'Great Scott!' he cried, 'Beatson!' and shook hands with warmth. It scarce seemed he was repaid in kind.

'So you're home again?' said Beatson. 'Where have you been all this long time?'

'In the States,' said John – 'California. I've made my pile though; and it suddenly struck me it would be a noble scheme to come home for Christmas.'

'I see,' said Beatson. 'Well, I hope we'll see something of you now you're here.'

'Oh, I guess so,' said John, a little frozen.

'Well, ta-ta,' concluded Beatson, and he shook hands again and went.

This was a cruel first experience. It was idle to blink facts: here was John home again, and Beatson – Old Beatson – did not care a rush. He recalled Old Beatson in the past – that merry and affectionate lad – and their joint adventures and mishaps, the window they had broken with a catapult in India Place, the escalade of the Castle rock, and many another inestimable bond of friendship; and his hurt surprise grew deeper. Well, after all, it was only on a man's own family that he could count; blood was thicker than water, he remembered; and the net result of this encounter was to bring him to the doorstep of his father's house, with tenderer and softer feelings.

The night had come; the fanlight over the door shone bright;

the two windows of the dining-room where the cloth was being laid, and the three windows of the drawing-room where Maria would be waiting dinner, glowed softlier through yellow blinds. It was like a vision of the past. All this time of his absence, life had gone forward with an equal foot, and the fires and the gas had been lighted, and the meals spread, at the accustomed hours. At the accustomed hour, too, the bell had sounded thrice to call the family to worship. And at the thought a pang of regret for his demerit seized him; he remembered the things that were good and that he had neglected and the things that were evil and that he had loved; and it was with a prayer upon his lips that he mounted the steps and thrust the key into the key-hole.

He stepped into the lighted hall, shut the door softly behind him, and stood there fixed in wonder. No surprise of strangeness could equal the surprise of that complete familiarity. There was the bust of Chalmers near the stair railings, there was the clothes-brush in the accustomed place; and there, on the hat-stand, hung hats and coats that must surely be the same as he remembered. Ten years dropped from his life, as a pin may slip between the fingers; and the ocean and the mountains, and the mines, and crowded marts and mingled races of San Francisco, and his own fortune and his own disgrace, became, for that one moment, the figures of a dream that was over.

He took off his hat, and moved mechanically towards the stand; and there he found a small change that was a great one to him. The pin that had been his from boyhood, where he had flung his balmoral hat when he loitered home from the academy, and his first hat when he came briskly back from college or the office – his pin was occupied. 'They might have at least respected my pin!' he thought, and he was moved as by a slight, and began at once to recollect that he was here an interloper, in a strange house, which he had entered almost by a burglary, and where at any moment he might be scandalously challenged.

He moved at once, his hat still in his hand, to the door of his father's room, opened it, and entered. Mr Nicholson sat in the same place and posture as on that last Sunday morning; only he was older, and greyer, and sterner; and as he now glanced up and caught the eye of his son, a strange commotion and a dark flush sprang into his face.

'Father,' said John, steadily, and even cheerfully, for this was a moment against which he was long ago prepared, 'father, here I am, and here is the money that I took from you. I have come back to ask your forgiveness, and to stay Christmas with you and the children.'

'Keep your money,' said the father, 'and go!'

'Father!' cried John; 'For God's sake don't receive me this way. I've come for –'

'Understand me,' interrupted Mr Nicholson; 'you are no son of mine; and in the sight of God, I wash my hands of you. One last thing I will tell you; one warning I will give you; all is discovered, and you are being hunted for your crimes; if you are still at large it is thanks to me; but I have done all that I mean to do; and from this time forth I would not raise one finger – not one finger – to save you from the gallows! And now,' with a low voice of absolute authority, and a single weighty gesture of the finger 'and now – go!'

CHAPTER VI

THE HOUSE AT MURRAYFIELD

How John passed the evening, in what windy confusion of mind, in what squalls of anger and lulls of sick collapse, in what pacing of streets and plunging into public-houses, it would profit little to relate. His misery, if it were not progressive, yet tended in no way to diminish; for in proportion as grief and indignation abated, fear began to take their place. At first, his father's menacing words lay by in some safe drawer of memory, biding their hour. At first, John was all thwarted affection and blighted hope; next bludgeoned vanity raised its head again, with twenty mortal gashes: and the father was disowned even as he had disowned the son. What was this regular course of life, that John should have admired it? what were these clock-work virtues, from which love was absent? Kindness was the test, kindness the aim and soul; and judged by such a standard, the discarded prodigal – now rapidly drowning his sorrows and his reason in successive drams – was a creature of a lovelier morality than his self-righteous father. Yes, he was the better man; he felt it, glowed with the consciousness, and entering a public-house at the corner of Howard Place (whither he had somehow wandered) he pledged his own virtues in a glass – perhaps the fourth since his dismissal. Of that he knew nothing, keeping no account of what he did or where he went; and in the general crashing hurry of his nerves, unconscious of the approach of intoxication. Indeed, it is a question whether he were really growing intoxicated, or whether at first the spirits did not even sober him. For it was even as he drained this last glass that his father's ambiguous and menacing words – popping from their hiding-place in memory – startled him like a hand laid upon his shoulder. 'Crimes, hunted, the gallows.' They were ugly words; in the ears of an innocent man, perhaps all the uglier; for if some judicial error were in act against him, who should set a limit to its grossness or to how far it might be pushed? Not John, indeed; he was no believer in the powers of innocence, his cursed experience pointing in quite other ways; and his fears, once wakened, grew with every hour and hunted him about the city streets.

It was perhaps nearly nine at night; he had eaten nothing since lunch, he had drunk a good deal, and he was exhausted by emotion, when the thought of Houston came into his head. He turned, not merely to the man as a friend, but to his house as a place of refuge. The danger that threatened him was still so vague that he knew neither what to fear nor where he might expect it; but this much at least seemed indeniable, that a private house was safer than a public inn. Moved by these counsels, he turned at once to the Caledonian Station, passed (not without alarm) into the bright lights of the approach, redeemed his portmanteau from the cloak-room, and was soon whirling in a cab along the Glasgow road. The change of movement and position, the sight of the lamps twinkling to the rear, and the smell of damp and mould and rotten straw which clung about the vehicle, wrought in him strange alternations of lucidity and mortal giddiness.

'I have been drinking,' he discovered; 'I must go straight to bed, and sleep.' And he thanked Heaven for the drowsiness that came upon his mind in waves.

From one of these spells he was wakened by the stoppage of the cab; and, getting down, found himself in quite a country road, the last lamp of the suburb shining some way below, and the high walls of a garden rising before him in the dark. The Lodge (as the place was named), stood, indeed, very solitary. To the south it adjoined another house, but standing in so large a garden as to be well out of cry; on all other sides, open fields stretched upward to the woods of Corstorphine Hill, or backward to the dells of Ravelston, or downward toward the valley of the Leith. The effect of seclusion was aided by the great height of the garden walls, which were, indeed, conventual, and, as John had tested in former days, defied the climbing schoolboy. The lamp of the cab threw a gleam upon the door and the not brilliant handle of the bell.

'Shall I ring for ye?' said the cabman, who had descended from his perch and was slapping his chest, for the night was bitter.

'I wish you would,' said John, putting his hand to his brow in one of his accesses of giddiness.

The man pulled at the handle, and the clanking of the bell replied from farther in the garden; twice and thrice he did it, with sufficient intervals; in the great, frosty silence of the night, the sounds fell sharp and small.

'Does he expect ye?' asked the driver, with that manner of familiar interest that well became his port-wine face; and when John had told him no, 'Well, then,' said the cabman, 'if ye'll tak' my advice of it, we'll just gang back. And that's disinterested, mind ye, for my stables are in the Glesgie road.'

'The servants must hear,' said John.

'Hout!' said the driver. 'He keeps no servants here, man. They're a' in the town house; I drive him often; it's just a kind of hermitage, this.'

'Give me the bell,' said John; and he plucked at it like a man desperate.

The clamour had not yet subsided before they heard steps upon the gravel, and a voice of singular nervous irritability cried to them through the door, 'Who are you, and what do you want?'

'Alan,' said John, 'it's me – it's Fatty – John, you know. I'm just come home, and I've come to stay with you.'

There was no reply for a moment, and then the door was opened.

'Get the portmanteau down,' said John to the driver.

'Do nothing of the kind,' said Alan; and then to John, 'Come in here a moment. I want to speak to you.'

John entered the garden, and the door was closed behind him. A candle stood on the gravel walk, winking a little in the draughts; it threw inconstant sparkles on the clumped holly, struck the light and darkness to and fro like a veil on Alan's features, and set his shadow hovering behind him. All beyond was inscrutable; and John's dizzy brain rocked with the shadow. Yet even so, it struck him that Alan was pale, and his voice, when he spoke, unnatural.

'What brings you here to-night?' he began. 'I don't want, God knows, to seem unfriendly; but I cannot take you in, Nicholson; I cannot do it.'

'Alan,' said John, 'you've just got to! You don't know the mess I'm in; the governor's turned me out, and I daren't show my face in an inn, because they're down on me for murder or something!'

'For what?' cried Alan, starting.

'Murder, I believe,' says John.

'Murder!' repeated Alan, and passed his hand over his eyes. 'What was that you were saying?' he asked again.

'That they were down on me,' said John. 'I'm accused of murder, by what I can make out; and I've really had a dreadful day of it, Alan, and I can't sleep on the road-side on a night like this – at least, not with a portmanteau,' he pleaded.

'Hush!' said Alan, with his head on one side; and then, 'did you hear nothing?' he asked.

'No,' said John, thrilling, he knew not why, with communicated terror. 'No, I heard nothing; why?' And then, as there was no answer, he reverted to his pleading: 'But I say, Alan, you've just got to take me in. I'll go right away to bed if you have anything to do. I seem to have been drinking; I was that knocked over. I wouldn't turn you away, Alan, if you were down on your luck.'

'No?' returned Alan. 'Neither will I you, then. Come and let's get your portmanteau.'

The cabman was paid, and drove off down the long, lamp-lit hill, and the two friends stood on the side-walk beside the portmanteau till the last rumble of the wheels had died in silence. It seemed to John as though Alan attached importance to this departure of the cab; and John, who was in no state to criticise, shared profoundly in the feeling.

When the stillness was once more perfect, Alan shouldered the portmanteau, carried it in, and shut and locked the garden door; and then, once more, abstraction seemed to fall upon him, and he stood with his hand on the key, until the cold began to nibble at John's fingers.

'Why are we standing here?' asked John.

'Eh?' said Alan, blankly.

'Why, man, you don't seem yourself,' said the other.

'No, I'm not myself,' said Alan; and he sat down on the portmanteau and put his face in his hands.

John stood beside him swaying a little, and looking about him at the swaying shadows, the flitting sparkles, and the steady stars overhead, until the windless cold began to touch him through his clothes on the bare skin. Even in his bemused intelligence, wonder began to awake.

'I say, let's come on to the house,' he said at last.

'Yes, let's come on to the house,' repeated Alan.

And he rose at once, re-shouldered the portmanteau, and taking the candle in his other hand, moved forward to the Lodge. This was a long, low building, smothered in creepers; and now, except for some chinks of light between the dining-room shutters, it was plunged in darkness and silence.

In the hall Alan lighted another candle, gave it to John, and opened the door of a bedroom.

'Here,' said he; 'go to bed. Don't mind me, John. You'll be sorry for me when you know.'

'Wait a bit,' returned John; 'I've got so cold with all that standing about. Let's go into the dining-room a minute. Just one glass to warm me, Alan.'

On the table in the hall stood a glass, and a bottle with a whisky label on a tray. It was plain that the bottle had just been opened, for the cork and corkscrew lay beside it.

'Take that,' said Alan, passing John the whisky, and then with a certain roughness pushed his friend into the bedroom, and closed the door behind him.

John stood amazed; then he shook the bottle, and, to his further wonder, found it partly empty. Three or four glasses

were gone. Alan must have uncorked a bottle of whisky and
drank three or four glasses one after the other, without sitting
down, for there was no chair, and that in his own cold lobby
on this freezing night! It fully explained his eccentricities, John
reflected sagely, as he mixed himself a grog. Poor Alan! He was
drunk; and what a dreadful thing was drink, and what a slave
to it poor Alan was, to drink in this unsociable, uncomfortable
fashion! The man who would drink alone, except for health's
sake – as John was now doing – was a man utterly lost. He took
the grog out, and felt hazier, but warmer. It was hard work
opening the portmanteau and finding his night things; and before he was undressed, the cold had struck home to him once
more. 'Well,' said he; 'just a drop more. There's no sense in
getting ill with all this other trouble.' And presently dreamless
slumber buried him.

When John awoke it was day. The low winter sun was already in the heavens, but his watch had stopped, and it was
impossible to tell the hour exactly. Ten, he guessed it, and made
haste to dress, dismal reflections crowding on his mind. But it
was less from terror than from regret that he now suffered;
and with his regret there were mingled cutting pangs of penitence. There had fallen upon him a blow, cruel, indeed, but yet
only the punishment of old misdoing; and he had rebelled and
plunged into fresh sin. The rod had been used to chasten, and
he had bit the chastening fingers. His father was right; John
had justified him; John was no guest for decent people's houses,
and no fit associate for decent people's children. And had a
broader hint been needed, there was the case of his old friend.
John was no drunkard, though he could at times exceed; and
the picture of Houston drinking neat spirits at his hall-table
struck him with something like disgust. He hung from meeting
his old friend. He could have wished he had not come to him;
and yet, even now, where else was he to turn?

These musings occupied him while he dressed and accompanied him into the lobby of the house. The door stood open on
the garden; doubtless, Alan had stepped forth; and John did as
he supposed his friend had done. The ground was hard as iron,

the frost still rigorous as he brushed among the hollies, icicles jingled and glittered in their fall; and wherever he went, a volley of eager sparrows followed him. Here were Christmas weather and Christmas morning duly met, to the delight of children. This was the day of reunited families, the day to which he had so long looked forward, thinking to awake in his own bed in Randolph Crescent, reconciled with all men and repeating the foot-prints of his youth; and here he was alone, pacing the alleys of a wintery garden and filled with penitential thoughts.

And that reminded him: why was he alone? and where was Alan? The thought of the festal morning and the due salutations reawakened his desire for his friend, and he began to call for him by name. As the sound of his voice died away, he was aware of the greatness of the silence that environed him. But for the twittering of the sparrows and the crunching of his own feet upon the frozen snow, the whole windless world of air hung over him entranced, and the stillness weighed upon his mind with a horror of solitude.

Still calling, at intervals, but now with a moderated voice, he made the hasty circuit of the garden, and finding neither man nor trace of man in all its evergreen coverts, turned at last to the house. About the house the silence seemed to deepen strangely. The door, indeed, stood open as before; but the windows were still shuttered, the chimneys breathed no stain into the bright air, there sounded abroad none of the low stir (perhaps audible rather to the ear of the spirit than to the ear of the flesh) by which a house announces and betrays its human lodgers. And yet Alan must be there – Alan locked in drunken slumbers, forgetful of the return of day, of the holy season, and of the friend whom he had so coldly received and was now so churlishly neglecting. John's disgust redoubled at the thought; but hunger was beginning to grow stronger than repulsion, and as a step to breakfast, if nothing else, he must find and arouse the sleeper.

He made the circuit of the bedroom quarters. All, until he came to Alan's chamber, were locked from without, and bore the marks of a prolonged disuse. But Alan's was a room in commission, filled with clothes, knick-knacks, letters, books, and the conveniences of a solitary man. The fire had been lighted; but it had long ago burned out, and the ashes were stone cold. The bed had been made, but it had not been slept in.

Worse and worse, then; Alan must have fallen where he sat, and now sprawled brutishly, no doubt, upon the dining-room floor.

The dining-room was a very long apartment, and was reached through a passage; so that John, upon his entrance, brought but little light with him, and must move toward the windows with spread arms, groping and knocking on the furniture. Suddenly he tripped and fell his length over a prostrate body. It was what he had looked for, yet it shocked him; and he marvelled that so rough an impact should not have kicked a groan out of the drunkard. Men had killed themselves ere now in such excesses, a dreary and degraded end had made John shudder. What if Alan were dead? There would be a Christmas Day!

By this, John had his hand upon the shutters, and flinging them back, beheld once again the blessed face of the day. Even by that light the room had a discomfortable air. The chairs were scattered, and one had been overthrown; the table-cloth, laid as if for dinner, was twitched upon one side, and some of the dishes had fallen to the floor. Behind the table lay the drunkard, still unaroused, only one foot visible to John.

But now that light was in the room, the worst seemed over; it was a disgusting business, but not more than disgusting; and it was with no great apprehension that John proceeded to make the circuit of the table: his last comparatively tranquil moment for that day. No sooner had he turned the corner, no sooner had his eye alighted on the body, than he gave a smothered, breathless cry, and fled out of the room and out of the house.

It was not Alan who lay there, but a man well up in years, of stern countenance and iron-grey locks; and it was no drunkard, for the body lay in a black pool of blood, and the open eyes stared upon the ceiling.

To and fro walked John before the door. The extreme sharpness of the air acted on his nerves like an astringent, and braced them swiftly. Presently, he not relaxing in his disordered walk, the images began to come clearer and stay longer in his fancy; and next the power of thought came back to him, and the horror and danger of his situation rooted him to the ground.

He grasped his forehead, and staring on one spot of gravel, pieced together what he knew and what he suspected. Alan had murdered some one: possibly 'that man' against whom the butler chained the door in Regent's Terrace; possibly another; some one at least: a human soul, whom it was death to slay and whose blood lay spilled upon the floor. This was the reason of the whisky drinking in the passage, of his unwillingness to welcome John, of his strange behaviour and bewildered words; this was why he had started at and harped upon the name of murder; this was why he had stood and hearkened, or sat and covered his eyes, in the black night. And now he was gone, now he had basely fled; and to all his perplexities and dangers John stood heir.

'Let me think – let me think,' he said, aloud, impatiently, even pleadingly, as if to some merciless interrupter. In the turmoil of his wits, a thousand hints and hopes and threats and terrors dinning continuously in his ears, he was like one plunged in the hubbub of a crowd. How was he to remember – he, who had not a thought to spare – that he was himself the author, as well as the theatre, of so much confusion? But in the hours of trial the junto of man's nature is dissolved, and anarchy succeeds.

It was plain he must stay no longer where he was, for here was a new Judicial Error in the very making. It was not so plain where he must go, for the old Judicial Error, vague as a cloud, appeared to fill the habitable world; whatever it might be, it watched for him, full-grown, in Edinburgh; it must have had its birth in San Francisco; it stood guard no doubt, like a dragon, at the bank where he should cash his credit; and though there were doubtless many other places, who should say in which of them it was not ambushed? No, he could not tell where he was to go; he must not lose time on these insolubilities. Let him go back to the beginning. It was plain he must stay no longer where he was. It was plain, too, that he must not flee as he was, for he could not carry his portmanteau, and to flee and leave it, was to plunge deeper in the mire. He must go, leave the house unguarded, find a cab, and return – return after an absence? Had he courage for that?

And just then he spied a stain about a hand's breadth on his trouser-leg, and reached his finger down to touch it. The finger was stained red; it was blood; he stared upon it with disgust, and awe, and terror, and in the sharpness of the new sensation, fell instantly to act.

He cleansed his finger in the snow, returned into the house, drew near with hushed footsteps to the dining-room door, and shut and locked it. Then he breathed a little freer, for here at least was an oaken barrier between himself and what he feared. Next, he hastened to his room, tore off the spotted trousers which seemed in his eyes a link to bind him to the gallows, flung them in a corner, donned another pair, breathlessly crammed his night things into his portmanteau, locked it, swung it with an effort from the ground, and with a rush of relief, came forth again under the open heavens.

The portmanteau, being of Occidental build, was no featherweight; it had distressed the powerful Alan; and as for John, he was crushed under its bulk, and the sweat broke upon him thickly. Twice he must set it down to rest before he reached the gate; and when he had come so far, he must do as Alan did, and take his seat upon one corner. Here, then, he sat a while and panted; but now his thoughts were sensibly lightened; now, with the trunk standing just inside the door, some part of his dissociation from the house of crime had been effected, and the cabman need not pass the garden wall. It was wonderful how that relieved him; for the house, in his eyes, was a place to strike the most cursory beholder with suspicion, as though the very windows had cried murder.

But there was to be no remission of the strokes of fate. As he thus sat, taking breath in the shadow of the wall and hopped about by sparrows, it chanced that his eye roved to the fastening of the door; and what he saw plucked him to his feet. The thing locked with a spring; once the door was closed, the bolt shut of itself; and without a key, there was no means of entering from without.

He saw himself obliged to one of two distasteful and perilous alternatives; either to shut the door altogether and set his portmanteau out upon the way-side, a wonder to all beholders; or to leave the door ajar, so that any thievish tramp or holiday school-boy might stray in and stumble on the grisly secret. To the last, as the least desperate, his mind inclined; but he must first insure himself that he was unobserved. He peered out, and down the long road: it lay dead empty. He went to the corner of the by-road that comes by way of Dean; there also not a passenger was stirring. Plainly it was, now or never, the high tide of his affairs; and he drew the door as close as he durst, slipped a pebble in the chink, and made off down hill to find a cab.

Half-way down a gate opened, and a troop of Christmas children sallied forth in the most cheerful humour, followed more soberly by a smiling mother.

'And this is Christmas Day!' thought John; and could have laughed aloud in tragic bitterness of heart.

CHAPTER VII

A TRAGI-COMEDY IN A CAR

IN front of Donaldson's Hospital, John counted it good fortune to perceive a cab a great way off, and by much shouting and waving of his arm to catch the notice of the driver. He counted it good fortune, for the time was long to him till he should have done for ever with the Lodge; and the farther he must go to find a cab, the greater the chance that the inevitable discovery had taken place, and that he should return to find the garden full of angry neighbours. Yet when the vehicle drew up he was sensibly chagrined to recognise the port-wine cabman of the night before. 'Here,' he could not but reflect, 'here is another link in the Judicial Error.'

The driver, on the other hand, was pleased to drop again upon so liberal a fare; and as he was a man – the reader must already have perceived – of easy, not to say familiar manners, he dropped at once into a vein of friendly talk, commenting on the weather, on the sacred season, which struck him chiefly in the light of a day of liberal gratuities, on the chance which had reunited him to a pleasing customer, and on the fact that John had been (as he was pleased to call it) visibly 'on the randan' the night before.

'And ye look driedful bad the-day, sir, I must say that,' he continued. 'There's nothing like a dram for ye – if ye'll take my advice of it; and bein' as it's Christmas, I'm no' saying,' he added, with a fatherly smile, 'but what I would join ye mysel'.'

John had listened with a sick heart.

'I'll give you a dram when we've got through,' said he, affecting a sprightliness which sat on him most unhandsomely, 'and not a drop till then. Business first, and pleasure afterward.'

With this promise the jarvey was prevailed upon to clamber

to his place and drive, with hideous deliberation, to the door of the Lodge. There were no signs as yet of any public emotion; only, two men stood not far off in talk, and their presence, seen from afar, set John's pulses buzzing. He might have spared himself his fright, for the pair were lost in some dispute of a theological complexion, and with lengthened upper lip and enumerating fingers, pursued the matter of their difference, and paid no heed to John.

But the cabman proved a thorn in the flesh. Nothing would keep him on his perch; he must clamber down, comment upon the pebble in the door (which he regarded as an ingenious but unsafe device), help John with the portmanteau, and enliven matters with a flow of speech, especially of questions, which I thus condense:

'He'll no' be here himsel', will he? No? Well, he's an eccentric man – a fair oddity – if ye ken the expression. Great trouble with his tenants, they tell me. I've driven the fam'ly for years. I drove a cab at his father's waddin'. What'll your name be? – I should ken your face. Baigrey, ye say? There were Baigreys about Gilmerton; ye'll be one of that lot? Then this'll be a friend's portmantie, like? Why? Because the name upon it's Nucholson! Oh, if ye're in a hurry, that's another job. Waverley Brig'? Are ye for away?'

So the friendly toper prated and questioned and kept John's heart in a flutter. But to this also, as to other evils under the sun, there came a period; and the victim of circumstances began at last to rumble towards the railway terminus at Waverley Bridge. During the transit, he sat with raised glasses in the frosty chill and mouldy fetor of his chariot, and glanced out sidelong on the holiday face of things, the shuttered shops, and the crowds along the pavement, much as the rider in the Tyburn cart may have observed the concourse gathering to his execution.

At the station his spirits rose again; another stage of his escape was fortunately ended – he began to spy blue water. He called a railway porter, and bade him carry the portmanteau to the cloak-room: not that he had any notion of delay; flight,

instant flight was his design, no matter whither; but he had
determined to dismiss the cabman ere he named, or even chose
his destination, thus possibly balking the Judicial Error of
another link. This was his cunning aim, and now with one foot
on the road-way, and one still on the coach-step, he made haste
to put the thing in practice, and plunged his hand into his
trousers pocket.

There was nothing there!

Oh, yes; this time he was to blame. He should have remembered, and when he deserted his blood-stained pantaloons,
he should not have deserted along with them his purse. Make
the most of his error, and then compare it with the punishment! Conceive his new position, for I lack words to picture it;
conceive him condemned to return to that house, from the
very thought of which his soul revolted, and once more to
expose himself to capture on the very scene of the misdeed:
conceive him linked to the mouldy cab and the familiar cabman. John cursed the cabman silently, and then it occurred
to him that he must stop the incarceration of his portmanteau;
that, at least, he must keep close at hand, and he turned to
recall the porter. But his reflections, brief as they had appeared,
must have occupied him longer than he supposed, and there
was the man already returning with the receipt.

Well, that was settled; he had lost his portmanteau also; for
the sixpence with which he had paid the Murrayfield Toll was
one that had strayed alone into his waistcoat pocket, and unless he once more successfully achieved the adventure of the
house of crime, his portmanteau lay in the cloak-room in
eternal pawn, for lack of a penny fee. And then he remembered
the porter, who stood aggressively attentive, words of gratitude
hanging on his lips.

John hunted right and left; he found a coin – prayed God
that it was a sovereign – drew it out, beheld a half-penny, and
offered it to the porter.

The man's jaw dropped.

'It's only a halfpenny!' he said, startled out of railway
decency.

'I know that,' said John, piteously.

And here the porter recovered the dignity of man.

'Thank you, sir,' said he, and would have returned the base gratuity. But John, too, would none of it; and as they struggled, who must join in but the cabman?

'Hoots, Mr Baigrey,' said he, 'you surely forget what day it is!'

'I tell you I have no change!' cried John.

'Well,' said the driver, 'and what then? I would rather give a man a shillin' on a day like this than put him off with a derision like a baw-bee. I'm surprised at the like of you, Mr Baigrey!'

'My name is not Baigrey!' broke out John, in mere childish temper and distress.

'Ye told me it was yoursel',' said the cabman.

'I know I did; and what the devil right had you to ask?' cried the unhappy one.

'Oh, very well,' said the driver. 'I know my place if you know yours – if you know yours!' he repeated, as one who should imply grave doubt; and muttered inarticulate thunders, in which the grand old name of gentleman was taken seemingly in vain.

Oh, to have been able to discharge this monster, whom John now perceived, with tardy clear-sightedness, to have begun betimes the festivities of Christmas! But far from any such ray of consolation visiting the lost, he stood bare of help and helpers, his portmanteau sequestered in one place, his money deserted in another and guarded by a corpse; himself, so sedulous of privacy, the cynosure of all men's eyes about the station; and, as if these were not enough mischances, he was now fallen in ill-blood with the beast to whom his poverty had linked him! In ill-blood, as he reflected dismally, with the witness who perhaps might hang or save him. There was no time to be lost; he durst not linger any longer in that public spot; and whether he had recourse to dignity or conciliation, the remedy must be applied at once. Some happily surviving element of manhood moved him to the former.

'Let us have no more of this,' said he, his foot once more upon the step. 'Go back to where we came from.'

He had avoided the name of any destination, for there was now quite a little band of railway folk about the cab, and he still kept an eye upon the Court of Justice, and laboured to avoid concentric evidence. But here again the fatal jarvey outmanœuvred him.

'Back to the Ludge?' cried he, in shrill tones of protest.

'Drive on at once!' roared John, and slammed the door behind him, so that the crazy chariot rocked and jingled.

Forth trundled the cab into the Christmas streets, the fare within plunged in the blackness of a despair that neighboured on unconsciousness, the driver on the box digesting his rebuke and his customer's duplicity. I would not be thought to put the pair in competition; John's case was out of all parallel. But the cabman, too, is worth the sympathy of the judicious; for he was a fellow of genuine kindliness and a high sense of personal dignity incensed by drink; and his advances had been cruelly and publicly rebuffed. As he drove, therefore, he counted his wrongs, and thirsted for sympathy and drink. Now, it chanced he had a friend, a publican, in Queensferry Street, from whom, in view of the sacredness of the occasion, he thought he might extract a dram. Queensferry Street lies something off the direct road to Murrayfield. But then there is the hilly cross-road that passes by the valley of the Leith and the Dean Cemetery; and Queensferry Street is on the way to that. What was to hinder the cabman, since his horse was dumb, from choosing the cross-road, and calling on his friend in passing? So it was decided; and the charioteer, already somewhat molified, turned aside his horse to the right.

John, meanwhile, sat collapsed, his chin sunk upon his chest, his mind in abeyance. The smell of the cab was still faintly present to his senses, and a certain leaden chill about his feet; all else had disappeared in one vast oppression of calamity and physical faintness. It was drawing on to noon – two-and-twenty hours since he had broken bread; in the interval, he had suffered tortures of sorrow and alarm, and been partly tipsy;

and though it was impossible to say he slept, yet when the cab stopped and the cabman thrust his head into the window, his attention had to be recalled from depths of vacancy.

'If you'll no' *stand* me a dram,' said the driver, with a well-merited severity of tone and manner, 'I daresay ye'll have no objection to my taking one mysel'?'

'Yes – no – do what you like,' returned John; and then, as he watched his tormenter mount the stairs and enter the whisky-shop, there floated into his mind a sense as of something long ago familiar. At that he started fully awake, and stared at the shop-fronts. Yes, he knew them; but when? and how? Long since, he thought; and then, casting his eye through the front glass, which had been recently occluded by the figure of the jarvey, he beheld the tree-tops of the rookery in Randolph Crescent. He was close to home – home, where he had thought, at that hour, to be sitting in the well-remembered drawing-room in friendly converse; and, instead –!

It was his first impulse to drop into the bottom of the cab; his next, to cover his face with his hands. So he sat, while the cabman toasted the publican, and the publican toasted the cabman, and both reviewed the affairs of the nation; so he still sat, when his master condescended to return, and drive off at last down-hill, along the curve of Lynedoch Place; but even so sitting, as he passed the end of his father's street, he took one glance from between shielding fingers, and beheld a doctor's carriage at the door.

'Well, just so,' thought he; 'I'll have killed my father! And this is Christmas Day!'

If Mr Nicholson died, it was down this same road he must journey to the grave; and down this road, on the same errand, his wife had preceded him years before; and many other leading citizens, with the proper trappings and attendance of the end. And now, in that frosty, ill-smelling, straw-carpeted, and ragged-cushioned cab, with his breath congealing on the glasses, where else was John himself advancing to?

The thought stirred his imagination, which began to manufacture many thousand pictures, bright and fleeting, like the shapes in a kaleidoscope; and now he saw himself, ruddy and comfortered, sliding in the gutter; and, again, a little woe-begone, bored urchin tricked forth in crape and weepers, descending this same hill at the foot's-pace of mourning coaches, his mother's body just preceding him; and yet again, his fancy, running far in front, showed him the house at Murrayfield – now standing solitary in the low sunshine, with the sparrows hopping on the threshold and the dead man within staring at the roof – and now, with a sudden change, thronged about with white-faced, hand-uplifting neighbours, and doctor bursting through their midst and fixing his stethoscope as he went, the policeman shaking a sagacious head beside the body. It was to this he feared that he was driving; in the midst of this he saw himself arrive, heard himself stammer faint explanations, and felt the hand of the constable upon his shoulder. Heavens! how he wished he had played the manlier part; how he despised himself that he had fled that fatal neighbourhood when all was quiet, and should now be tamely travelling back when it was thronging with avengers!

Any strong degree of passion lends, even to the dullest, the forces of the imagination. And so now as he dwelt on what was probably awaiting him at the end of this distressful drive – John, who saw things little, remembered them less and could not have described them at all, beheld in his mind's eye the garden of the Lodge, detailed as in a map; he went to and fro in it, feeding his terrors; he saw the hollies, the snowy borders, the paths where he had sought Alan, the high, conventual walls, the shut door – what! was the door shut? Ay, truly, he had shut it – shut in his money, his escape, his future life – shut it with these hands, and none could now open it! He heard the snap of the spring-lock like something bursting in his brain, and sat astonied.

And then he woke again, terror jarring through his vitals. This was no time to be idle; he must be up and doing, he must think. Once at the end of this ridiculous cruise, once at the Lodge door, there would be nothing for it but to turn the cab and trundle back again. Why, then, go so far? why add

another feature of suspicion to a case already so suggestive?
why not turn at once? It was easy to say, turn; but whither?
He had nowhere now to go to; he could never – he saw it in
letters of blood – he could never pay that cab; he was saddled
with that cab for ever. Oh, that cab! his soul yearned to be rid
of it. He forgot all other cares. He must first quit himself and
this ill-smelling vehicle and of the human beast that guided it –
first do that; do that at least; do that at once.

And just then the cab suddenly stopped, and there was his
persecutor rapping on the front glass. John let it down, and
beheld the port-wine countenance inflamed with intellectual
triumph.

'I ken wha ye are!' cried the husky voice. 'I mind ye now.
Ye're a Nucholson. I drove ye to Hermiston to a Christmas
party, and ye came back on the box, and I let ye drive.'

It is a fact. John knew the man; they had been even friends.
His enemy, he now remembered, was a fellow of great good-
nature – endless good-nature – with a boy; why not with a man?
Why not appeal to his better side? He grasped at the new
hope.

'Great Scott! and so you did,' he cried, as if in a transport
of delight, his voice sounding false in his own ears. 'Well, if
that's so, I've something to say to you. I'll just get out, I guess.
Where are we, anyway?'

The driver had fluttered his ticket in the eyes of the branch
toll-keeper, and they were now brought to on the highest and
most solitary part of the by-road. On the left, a row of field-
side trees beshaded it; on the right, it was bordered by naked
fallows, undulating down-hill to the Queensferry Road; in
front, Corstorphine Hill raised its snow-bedabbled, darkling
woods against the sky. John looked all about him, drinking
the clear air like wine; then his eyes returned to the cabman's
face as he sat, not ungleefully, awaiting John's communication,
with the air of one looking to be tipped.

The features of that face were hard to read, drink had so
swollen them, drink had so painted them, in tints that varied
from brick red to mulberry. The small grey eyes blinked, the

lips moved, with greed; greed was the ruling passion; and though there was some good-nature, some genuine kindliness, a true human touch, in the old toper, his greed was now so set afire by hope, that all other traits of character lay dormant. He sat there a monument of gluttonous desire.

John's heart slowly fell. He had opened his lips, but he stood there and uttered naught. He sounded the well of his courage, and it was dry. He groped in his treasury of words, and it was vacant. A devil of dumbness had him by the throat; the devil of terror babbled in his ears; and suddenly, without a word uttered, with no conscious purpose formed in his will, John whipped about, tumbled over the road-side wall, and began running for his life across the fallows.

He had not gone far, he was not past the midst of the first field, when his whole brain thundered within him, 'Fool! You have your watch!' The shock stopped him, and he faced once more towards the cab. The driver was leaning over the wall, brandishing his whip, his face empurpled, roaring like a bull. And John saw (or thought) that he had lost the chance. No watch would pacify the man's resentment now; he would cry for vengeance also. John would be under the eye of the police; his tale would be unfolded, his secret plumbed, his destiny would close on him at last, and for ever.

He uttered a deep sigh; and just as the cabman, taking heart of grace, was beginning at last to scale the wall, his defaulting customer fell again to running, and disappeared into the farther fields.

CHAPTER VIII

SINGULAR INSTANCE OF THE UTILITY OF PASS-KEYS

WHERE he ran at first, John never very clearly knew; nor yet how long a time elapsed ere he found himself in the by-road near the lodge of Ravelston, propped against the wall, his lungs heaving like bellows, his legs leaden-heavy, his mind possessed by one sole desire – to lie down and be unseen. He remembered the thick coverts round the quarry-hole pond, an untrodden corner of the world where he might surely find concealment till the night should fall. Thither he passed down the lane; and when he came there, behold! he had forgotten the frost, and the pond was alive with young people skating, and the pond-side coverts were thick with lookers-on. He looked on a while himself. There was one tall, graceful maiden, skating hand in hand with a youth, on whom she bestowed her bright eyes perhaps too patently; and it was strange with what anger John beheld her. He could have broken forth in curses; he could have stood there, like a mortified tramp, and shaken his fist and vented his gall upon her by the hour – or so he thought; and the next moment his heart bled for the girl. 'Poor creature, it's little she knows!' he sighed. 'Let her enjoy herself while she can!' But was it possible, when Flora used to smile at him on the Braid ponds, she could have looked so fulsome to a sick-hearted bystander?

The thought of one quarry, in his frozen wits, suggested another; and he plodded off towards Craig Leith. A wind had sprung up out of the north-west; it was cruel keen, it dried him like a fire, and racked his finger-joints. It brought clouds, too; pale, swift, hurrying clouds, that blotted heaven and shed gloom upon the earth. He scrambled up among the hazelled rubbish heaps that surround the caldron of the quarry, and lay flat upon the stones. The wind searched close along the earth, the stones were cutting and icy, the bare hazels wailed about him; and soon the air of the afternoon began to be vocal with those strange and dismal harpings that herald snow. Pain and misery turned in John's limbs to a harrowing impatience and blind desire of change; now he would roll in his harsh lair, and when the flints abraded him, was almost pleased; now he would crawl to the edge of the huge pit and look dizzily down. He saw the spiral of the descending roadway, the steep crags, the clinging bushes, the peppering of snow-wreaths, and far down in the bottom, the diminished crane. Here, no doubt, was a way to end it. But it somehow did not take his fancy.

And suddenly he was aware that he was hungry; ay, even through the tortures of the cold, even through the frosts of despair, a gross, desperate longing after food, no matter what, no matter how, began to wake and spur him. Suppose he pawned his watch? But no, on Christmas Day – this was Christmas Day! – the pawn-shop would be closed. Suppose he went to the public-house close by at Blackhall, and offered the watch, which was worth ten pounds, in payment for a meal of bread and cheese? The incongruity was too remarkable; the good folks would either put him to the door, or only let him in to send for the police. He turned his pockets out one after another; some San Francisco tram-car checks, one cigar, no lights, the pass-key to his father's house, a pocket-handkerchief, with just a touch of scent: no, money could be raised on none of these. There was nothing for it but to starve; and after all, what mattered it? That also was a door of exit.

He crept close among the bushes, the wind playing round him like a lash; his clothes seemed thin as paper, his joints burned, his skin curdled on his bones. He had a vision of a high-lying cattle-drive in California, and the bed of a dried stream with one muddy pool, by which the vaqueros had encamped: splendid sun over all, the big bonfire blazing, the strips of cow browning and smoking on a skewer of wood; how warm it was, how savoury the steam of scorching meat! And then again he remembered his manifold calamities, and burrowed and wallowed in the sense of his disgrace and shame. And next he was entering Frank's restaurant in Montgomery Street, San Francisco; he had ordered a pan-stew and venison chops, of which he was immoderately fond, and as he sat waiting, Munroe, the good attendant, brought him a whisky punch; he saw the strawberries float on the delectable cup, he heard the ice chink about the straws. And then he woke again to his detested fate, and found himself sitting, humped together in a windy combe of quarry refuse – darkness thick about him, thin flakes of snow flying here and there like rags of paper, and the strong shuddering of his body clashing his teeth like a hiccough.

We have seen John in nothing but the stormiest condition; we have seen him reckless, desperate, tried beyond his moderate powers; of his daily self, cheerful, regular, not unthrifty, we have seen nothing; and it may thus be a surprise to the reader, to learn that he was studiously careful of his health. This favourite preoccupation now awoke. If he were to sit there and die of cold, there would be mighty little gained; better the police cell and the chances of a jury trial, than the miserable certainty of death at a dike side before the next winter's dawn, or death a little later in the gas-lighted wards of an infirmary.

He rose on aching legs, and stumbled here and there among the rubbish-heaps, still circumvented by the yawning crater of the quarry; or perhaps he only thought so, for the darkness was already dense, the snow was growing thicker, and he moved like a blind man, and with a blind man's terrors. At last he climbed a fence, thinking to drop into the road, and found himself staggering, instead, among the iron furrows of a ploughland, endless, it seemed, as a whole county. And next he was in a wood, beating among young trees; and then he was aware of a house with many lighted windows, Christmas carriages waiting at the doors, and Christmas drivers (for Christmas has a double edge) becoming swiftly hooded with snow. From this glimpse of human cheerfulness, he fled like Cain; wandered in the night, unpiloted, careless of whither he went; fell, and lay, and then rose again and wandered farther; and at last, like a transformation scene, behold him in the lighted jaws of the city, staring at a lamp which had already donned the tilted night-cap of the snow. It came thickly now, a 'Feeding Storm'; and while he yet stood blinking at the lamp, his feet were buried. He remembered something like it in the past, a street-lamp crowned and caked upon the windward side with snow, the wind uttering its mournful hoot, himself looking on, even as now; but the cold had struck too sharply on his wits, and memory failed him as to the date and sequel of the reminiscence.

His next conscious moment was on the Dean Bridge; but whether he was John Nicholson of a bank in a California street, or some former John, a clerk in his father's office, he had now clean forgotten. Another blank, and he was thrusting his pass-key into the door-lock of his father's house.

Hours must have passed. Whether crouched on the cold stones or wandering in the fields among the snow, was more than he could tell; but hours had passed. The finger of the hall clock was close on twelve; a narrow peep of gas in the hall-lamp shed shadows; and the door of the back room – his father's room – was open and emitted a warm light. At so late an hour, all this was strange; the lights should have been out, the doors locked, the good folk safe in bed. He marvelled at the irregularity, leaning on the hall table; and marvelled to himself there; and thawed and grew once more hungry, in the warmer air of the house.

The clock uttered its premonitory catch; in five minutes Christmas Day would be among the days of the past – Christmas! – what a Christmas! Well, there was no use waiting; he had come into that house, he scarce knew how; if they were to thrust him forth again, it had best be done at once; and he moved to the door of the back room and entered.

Oh, well, then he was insane, as he had long believed.

There, in his father's room, at midnight, the fire was roaring and the gas blazing; the papers, the sacred papers – to lay a hand on which was criminal – had all been taken off and piled along the floor; a cloth was spread, and a supper laid, upon the business table; and in his father's chair a woman, habited like a nun, sat eating. As he appeared in the doorway, the nun rose, gave a low cry, and stood staring. She was a large woman, strong, calm, a little masculine, her features marked with courage and good sense; and as John blinked back at her, a faint resemblance dodged about his memory, as when a tune haunts us, and yet will not be recalled.

'Why, it's John!' cried the nun.

'I daresay I'm mad,' said John, unconsciously following King Lear; 'but, upon my word, I do believe you're Flora.'

'Of course I am,' replied she.

And yet it is not Flora at all, thought John; Flora was slender, and timid, and of changing colour, and dewy-eyed; and had Flora such an Edinburgh accent? But he said none of these things, which was perhaps as well. What he said was, 'Then why are you a nun?'

'Such nonsense!' said Flora. 'I'm a sick-nurse; and I am here nursing your sister, with whom, between you and me, there is precious little the matter. But that is not the question. The point is: How do you come here? and are you not ashamed to show yourself?'

'Flora,' said John, sepulchrally, 'I haven't eaten anything for three days. Or, at least, I don't know what day it is; but I guess I'm starving.'

'You unhappy man!' she cried. 'Here, sit down and eat my supper; and I'll just run upstairs and see my patient, not but what I doubt she's fast asleep; for Maria is a *malade imaginaire*.'

With this specimen of the French, not of Stratford-atte-Bowe, but of a finishing establishment in Moray Place, she left John alone in his father's sanctum. He fell at once upon the food; and it is to be supposed that Flora had found her patient wakeful, and been detained with some details of nursing, for he had time to make a full end of all there was to eat, and not only to empty the teapot, but to fill it again from a kettle that was fitfully singing on his father's fire. Then he sat torpid, and pleased, and bewildered; his misfortunes were then half forgotten; his mind considering, not without regret, this unsentimental return to his old love.

He was thus engaged, when that bustling woman noiselessly re-entered.

'Have you eaten?' said she. 'Then tell me all about it.'

It was a long and (as the reader knows) a pitiful story; but Flora heard it with compressed lips. She was lost in none of those questionings of human destiny that have, from time to time, arrested the flight of my own pen; for women, such as she, are no philosophers, and behold the concrete only. And women, such as she, are very hard on the imperfect man.

'Very well,' said she, when he had done; 'then down upon your knees at once, and beg God's forgiveness.'

And the great baby plumped upon his knees, and did as he was bid; and none the worse for that! But while he was heartily enough requesting forgiveness on general principles, the rational side of him distinguished, and wondered if, perhaps, the apology were not due upon the other part. And when he rose again from that becoming exercise, he first eyed the face of his old love doubtfully, and then, taking heart, uttered his protest.

'I must say, Flora,' said he, 'in all this business, I can see very little fault of mine.'

'If you had written home,' replied the lady, 'there would have been none of it. If you had even gone to Murrayfield reasonably sober, you would never have slept there, and the worst would not have happened. Besides, the whole thing began years ago. You got into trouble, and when your father, honest man, was disappointed, you took the pet, or got afraid, and ran away from punishment. Well, you've had your own way of it, John, and I don't suppose you like it.'

'I sometimes fancy I'm not much better than a fool,' sighed John.

'My dear John,' said she, 'not much!'

He looked at her, and his eye fell. A certain anger rose within him; here was a Flora he disowned; she was hard; she was of a set colour; a settled, mature, undecorative manner;

plain of speech, plain of habit – he had come near saying, plain of face. And this changeling called herself by the same name as the many-coloured, clinging maid of yore; she of the frequent laughter, and the many sighs, and the kind, stolen glances. And to make all worse, she took the upper hand with him, which (as John knew well) was not the true relation of the sexes. He steeled his heart against this sick-nurse.

'And how do you come to be here?' he asked.

She told him how she had nursed her father in his long illness, and when he died, and she was left alone, had taken to nurse others, partly from habit, partly to be of some service in the world; partly, it might be, for amusement. 'There's no accounting for taste,' said she. And she told him how she went largely to the houses of old friends, as the need arose; and how she was thus doubly welcome, as an old friend first, and then as an experienced nurse, to whom doctors would confide the gravest cases.

'And, indeed, it's a mere farce my being here for poor Maria,' she continued; 'but your father takes her ailments to heart, and I cannot always be refusing him. We are great friends, your father and I; he was very kind to me long ago – ten years ago.'

A strange stir came in John's heart. All this while had he been thinking only of himself? All this while, why had he not written to Flora? In penitential tenderness, he took her hand, and, to his awe and trouble, it remained in his, compliant. A voice told him this was Flora, after all – told him so quietly, yet with a thrill of singing.

'And you never married?' said he.

'No, John, I never married,' she replied.

The hall clock striking two recalled them to the sense of time.

'And now,' said she, 'you have been fed and warmed, and I have heard your story, and now it's high time to call your brother.'

'Oh!' cried John, chap-fallen; 'do you think that absolutely necessary?'

'*I* can't keep you here; I am a stranger,' said she. 'Do you want to run away again? I thought you had enough of that.'

He bowed his head under the reproof. She despised him, he reflected, as he sat once more alone; a monstrous thing for a woman to despise a man; and strangest of all, she seemed to like him. Would his brother despise him, too? And would his brother like him?

And presently the brother appeared, under Flora's escort; and, standing afar off beside the door-way, eyed the hero of this tale.

'So this is you?' he said, at length.

'Yes, Alick, it's me – it's John,' replied the elder brother, feebly.

'And how did you get in here?' inquired the younger.

'Oh, I had my pass-key,' says John.

'The deuce you had!' said Alexander. 'Ah, you lived in a better world! There are no pass-keys going now.'

'Well, father was always averse to them,' sighed John.

And the conversation then broke down, and the brothers looked askance at one another in silence.

'Well, and what the devil are we to do?' said Alexander. 'I suppose if the authorities got wind of you, you would be taken up?'

'It depends on whether they've found the body or not,' returned John. 'And then there's that cabman, to be sure!'

'Oh, bother the body!' said Alexander. 'I mean about the other thing. That's serious.'

'Is that what my father spoke about?' asked John. 'I don't even know what it is.'

'About your robbing your bank in California, of course,' replied Alexander.

It was plain, from Flora's face, that this was the first she had heard of it; it was plainer still, from John's, that he was innocent.

'I!' he exclaimed. 'I rob my bank! My God! Flora, this is too much; even you must allow that.'

'Meaning you didn't?' asked Alexander.

'I never robbed a soul in all my days,' cried John: 'except

my father, if you call that robbery; and I brought him back the money in this room, and he wouldn't even take it!'

'Look here, John,' said his brother; 'let us have no misunderstanding upon this. MacEwen saw my father; he told him a bank you had worked for in San Francisco was wiring over the habitable globe to have you collared – that it was supposed you had nailed thousands; and it was dead certain you had nailed three hundred. So MacEwen said, and I wish you would be careful how you answer. I may tell you also, that your father paid the three hundred on the spot.'

'Three hundred?' repeated John. 'Three hundred pounds, you mean? That's fifteen hundred dollars. Why, then, it's Kirkman!' he broke out. 'Thank Heaven! I can explain all that. I gave them to Kirkman to pay for me the night before I left – fifteen hundred dollars, and a letter to the manager. What do they suppose I would steal fifteen hundred dollars for? I'm rich; I struck it rich in stocks. It's the silliest stuff I ever heard of. All that's needful is to cable to the manager : Kirkman has the fifteen hundred – find Kirkman. He was a fellow-clerk of mine, and a hard case; but to do him justice, I didn't think he was as hard as this.'

'And what do you say to that, Alick?' asked Flora.

'I say the cablegram shall go to-night!' cried Alexander, with energy. 'Answer prepaid, too. If this can be cleared away – and upon my word I do believe it can – we shall all be able to hold up our heads again. Here, you John, you stick down the address of your bank manager. You, Flora, you can pack John into my bed, for which I have no further use to-night. As for me, I am off to the post-office, and thence to the High Street about the dead body. The police ought to know, you see, and they ought to know through John; and I can tell them some rigmarole about my brother being a man of highly nervous organisation, and the rest of it. And then, I'll tell you what, John – did you notice the name upon the cab?'

John gave the name of the driver, which, as I have not been able to commend the vehicle, I here suppress.

'Well,' resumed Alexander, 'I'll call round at their place

before I come back, and pay your shot for you. In that way, before breakfast-time, you'll be as good as new.'

John murmured inarticulate thanks. To see his brother thus energetic in his service moved him beyond expression; if he could not utter what he felt, he showed it legibly in his face; and Alexander read it there, and liked it the better in that dumb delivery.

'But there's one thing,' said the latter, 'cablegrams are dear; and I daresay you remember enough of the governor to guess the state of my finances.'

'The trouble is,' said John, 'that all my stamps are in that beastly house.'

'All your what?' asked Alexander.

'Stamps – money,' explained John. 'It's an American expression; I'm afraid I contracted one or two.'

'I have some,' said Flora. 'I have a pound-note upstairs.'

'My dear Flora,' returned Alexander, 'a pound-note won't see us very far; and besides, this is my father's business, and I shall be very much surprised if it isn't my father who pays for it.'

'I would not apply to him yet; I do not think that can be wise,' objected Flora.

'You have a very imperfect idea of my resources, and none at all of my effrontery,' replied Alexander. 'Please observe.'

He put John from his way, chose a stout knife among the supper things, and with surprising quickness broke into his father's drawer.

'There's nothing easier when you come to try,' he observed, pocketing the money.

'I wish you had not done that,' said Flora. 'You will never hear the last of it.'

'Oh, I don't know,' returned the young man; 'the governor is human after all. And now, John, let me see your famous pass-key. Get into bed, and don't move for anyone till I come back. They won't mind you not answering when they knock; I generally don't myself.'

CHAPTER IX

IN WHICH MR NICHOLSON CONCEDES
THE PRINCIPLE OF AN ALLOWANCE

In spite of the horrors of the day and the tea-drinking of the night, John slept the sleep of infancy. He was awakened by the maid, as it might have been ten years ago, tapping at the door. The winter sunrise was painting the east; and as the window was to the back of the house, it shone into the room with many strange colours of refracted light. Without, the houses were all cleanly roofed with snow; the garden walls were coped with it a foot in height; the greens lay glittering. Yet strange as snow had grown to John during his years upon the Bay of San Francisco, it was what he saw within that most affected him. For it was to his own room that Alexander had been promoted; there was the old paper with the device of flowers, in which a cunning fancy might yet detect the face of Skinny Jim, of the Academy, John's former dominie; there was the old chest of drawers; there were the chairs – one, two, three – three as before. Only the carpet was new, and the litter of Alexander's clothes and books and drawing materials, and a pencil-drawing on the wall, which (in John's eyes) appeared a marvel of proficiency.

He was thus lying, and looking, and dreaming, hanging, as it were, between two epochs of his life, when Alexander came to the door, and made his presence known in a loud whisper. John let him in, and jumped back into the warm bed.

'Well, John,' said Alexander, 'the cablegram is sent in your name, and twenty words of answer paid. I have been to the cab-office and paid your cab, even saw the old gentleman himself, and properly apologised. He was mighty placable, and indicated his belief you had been drinking. Then I knocked up old

MacEwen out of bed, and explained affairs to him as he sat and shivered in a dressing-gown. And before that I had been to the High Street, where they have heard nothing of your dead body, so that I incline to the idea that you dreamed it.'

'Catch me!' said John.

'Well, the police never do know anything,' assented Alexander; 'and at any rate, they have dispatched a man to inquire and to recover your trousers and your money, so that really your bill is now fairly clean; and I see but one lion in your path – the governor.'

'I'll be turned out again, you'll see,' said John, dismally.

'I don't imagine so,' returned the other; 'not if you do what Flora and I have arranged; and your business now is to dress, and lose no time about it. Is your watch right? Well, you have a quarter of an hour. By five minutes before the half-hour you must be at table, in your old seat, under Uncle Duthie's picture. Flora will be there to keep you countenance; and we shall see what we shall see.'

'Wouldn't it be wiser for me to stay in bed?' said John.

'If you mean to manage your own concerns, you can do precisely what you like,' replied Alexander; 'but if you are not in your place five minutes before the half-hour I wash my hands of you, for one.'

And thereupon he departed. He had spoken warmly, but the truth is, his heart was somewhat troubled. And as he hung over the banisters, watching for his father to appear, he had hard ado to keep himself braced for the encounter that must follow.

'If he takes it well, I shall be lucky,' he reflected. 'If he takes it ill, why it'll be a herring across John's tracks, and perhaps all for the best. He's a confounded muff, this brother of mine, but he seems a decent soul.'

At that stage a door opened below with a certain emphasis, and Mr Nicholson was seen solemnly to descend the stairs, and pass into his own apartment. Alexander followed, quaking inwardly, but with a steady face. He knocked, was bidden to enter, and found his father standing in front of the forced drawer, to which he pointed as he spoke.

'This is a most extraordinary thing,' said he; 'I have been robbed!'

'I was afraid you would notice it,' observed his son; 'it made such a beastly hash of the table.'

'You were afraid I would notice it?' repeated Mr Nicholson. 'And, pray, what may that mean?'

'That I was a thief, sir,' returned Alexander. 'I took all the money in case the servants should get hold of it; and here is the change, and a note of my expenditure. You were gone to bed, you see, and I did not feel at liberty to knock you up; but I think when you have heard the circumstances, you will do me justice. The fact is, I have reason to believe there has been some dreadful error about my brother John; the sooner it can be cleared up the better for all parties; it was a piece of business, sir – and so I took it, and decided, on my own responsibility, to send a telegram to San Francisco. Thanks to my quickness we may hear to-night. There appears to be no doubt, sir, that John has been abominably used.'

'When did this take place?' asked the father.

'Last night, sir, after you were asleep,' was the reply.

'It's most extraordinary,' said Mr Nicholson. 'Do you mean to say you have been out all night?'

'All night, as you say, sir. I have been to the telegraph and the police-office, and Mr MacEwen's. Oh, I had my hands full,' said Alexander.

'Very irregular,' said the father. 'You think of no one but yourself.'

'I do not see that I have much to gain in bringing back my elder brother,' returned Alexander, shrewdly.

The answer pleased the old man; he smiled. 'Well, well, I will go into this after breakfast,' said he.

'I'm sorry about the table,' said the son.

'The table is a small matter; I think nothing of that,' said the father.

'It's another example,' continued the son, 'of the awkward-
ness of a man having no money of his own. If I had a proper
allowance, like other fellows of my age, this would have been
quite unnecessary.'

'A proper allowance!' repeatd his father, in tones of blighting
sarcasm, for the expression was not new to him. 'I have never
grudged you money for any proper purpose.'

'No doubt, no doubt,' said Alexander, 'but then you see
you ar'n't always on the spot to have the thing explained to
you. Last night for instance –'

'You could have wakened me last night,' interrupted his
father.

'Was it not some similar affair that first got John into a mess?'
asked the son, skilfully evading the point.

But the father was not less adroìt. 'And pray, sir, how did
you come and go out of the house?' he asked.

'I forgot to lock the door, it seems,' replied Alexander.

'I have had cause to complain of that too often,' said Mr
Nicholson. 'But still I do not understand. Did you keep the
servants up?'

'I propose to go into all that at length after breakfast,' returned
Alexander. 'There is the half-hour going; we must not keep
Miss Mackenzie waiting.'

And greatly daring, he opened the door.

Even Alexander, who it must have been perceived, was on
terms of comparative freedom with his parent; even Alexander
had never before dared to cut short an interview in this high-
handed fashion. But the truth is the very mass of his son's
delinquencies daunted the old gentleman. He was like the man
with the cart of apples – this was beyond him! That Alexander
should have spoiled his table, taken his money, stayed out all
night, and then coolly acknowledged all, was something un-
dreamed of in the Nicholsonian philosophy, and transcended
comment. The return of the change, which the old gentleman
still carried in his hand, had been a feature of imposing imped-
ence; it had dealt him a staggering blow. Then there was the

reference to John's original flight – a subject which he always
kept resolutely curtained in his own mind; for he was a man
who loved to have made no mistakes, and when he feared
he might have made one kept the papers sealed. In view of
all these surprises and reminders, and of his son's composed
and masterful demeanour, there began to creep on Mr Nicholson a sickly misgiving. He seemed beyond his depth; if he did
or said anything, he might come to regret it. The young man,
besides, as he had pointed out himself, was playing a generous
part. And if wrong had been done – and done to one who was,
after, and in spite of, all, a Nicholson – it should certainly be
righted.

All things considered, monstrous as it was to be cut short
in his inquiries, the old gentleman submitted, pocketed the
change, and followed his son into the dining-room. During
these few steps he once more mentally revolted, and once
more, and this time finally, laid down his arms : a still, small
voice in his bosom having informed him authentically of a piece
of news; that he was afraid of Alexander. The strange thing
was that he was pleased to be afraid of him. He was proud
of his son; he might be proud of him; the boy had character
and grit, and knew what he was doing.

These were his reflections as he turned the corner of the
dining-room door. Miss Mackenzie was in the place of honour,
conjuring with a teapot and a cozy; and, behold! there was
another person present, a large, portly, whiskered man of a
very comfortable and respectable air, who now rose from his
seat and came forward, holding out his hand.

'Good-morning, father,' said he.

Of the contention of feeling that ran high in Mr Nicholson's
starched bosom, no outward sign was visible; nor did he delay
long to make a choice of conduct. Yet in that interval he had
reviewed a great field of possibilities both past and future;
whether it was possible he had not been perfectly wise in
his treatment of John; whether it was possible that John was
innocent; whether, if he turned John out a second time, as his

outraged authority suggested, it was possible to avoid a scandal; and whether, if he went to that extremity, it was possible that Alexander might rebel.

'Hum!' said Mr Nicholson, and put his hand, limp and dead, into John's.

And then, in an embarrassed silence, all took their places; and even the paper – from which it was the old gentleman's habit to suck mortification daily, as he marked the decline of our institutions – even the paper lay furled by his side.

But presently Flora came to the rescue. She slid into the silence with a technicality, asking if John still took his old inordinate amount of sugar. Thence it was but a step to the burning question of the day; and in tones a little shaken, she commented on the interval since she had last made tea for the prodigal, and congratulated him on his return. And then addressing Mr Nicholson, she congratulated him also in a manner that defied his ill-humour; and from that launched into the tale of John's misadventures not without some suitable suppressions.

Gradually Alexander joined; between them, whether he would or no, they forced a word or two from John; and these fell so tremulously, and spoke so eloquently of a mind oppressed with dread, that Mr Nicholson relented. At length even he contributed a question: and before the meal was at an end all four were talking even freely.

Prayers followed, with the servants gaping at this newcomer whom no one had admitted; and after prayers there came that moment on the clock which was the signal for Mr Nicholson's departure.

'John,' said he, 'of course you will stay here. Be very careful not to excite Maria, if Miss Mackenzie thinks it desirable that you should see her. – Alexander, I wish to speak with you alone.' And then, when they were both in the back-room: 'You need not come to the office to-day,' said he; 'you can stay and amuse your brother, and I think it would be respectful to call on Uncle Greig. And by-the-by' (this spoken with a certain – dare we say? – bashfulness), 'I agree to concede the principle of an allowance; and I will consult with Dr Durie, who is quite a man of the world and has sons of his own, as to the amount. And, my fine fellow, you may consider yourself in luck!' he added, with a smile.

'Thank you,' said Alexander.

Before noon a detective had restored to John his money, and brought news, sad enough in truth, but perhaps the least sad possible. Alan had been found in his own house in Regent's Terrace, under care of the terrified butler. He was quite mad, and instead of going to prison, had gone to Morningside Asylum. The murdered man, it appeared, was an evicted tenant who had for nearly a year pursued his late landlord with threats and insults; and beyond this, the cause and details of the tragedy were lost.

When Mr Nicholson returned for dinner they were able to put a dispatch into his hands: 'John V. Nicholson, Randolph Crescent, Edinburgh. – Kirkman has disappeared; police looking for him. All understood. Keep mind quite easy. – Austin.' Having had this explained to him, the old gentleman took down the cellar key and departed for two bottles of the 1820 port. Uncle Greig dined there that day, and Cousin Robina, and, by an odd chance, Mr MacEwen; and the presence of these strangers relieved what might have been otherwise a somewhat strained relation. Ere they departed, the family was welded once more into a fair semblance of unity.

In the end of April John led Flora – or, let us say, as more descriptive, Flora led John – to the altar, if altar that may be called which was indeed the drawing-room mantel-piece in Mr Nicholson's house, with the Reverend Dr Durie posted on the hearth-rug in the guise of Hymen's priest.

The last I saw of them, on a recent visit to the north, was at a dinner-party in the house of my old friend Gellatly Macbride; and after we had, in classic phrase, 'rejoined the ladies,' I had an opportunity to overhear Flora conversing with another married woman on the much canvassed matter of a husband's tobacco.

'Oh, yes!' said she; 'I only allow Mr Nicholson four cigars

a day. Three he smokes at fixed times – after a meal, you know, my dear; and the fourth he can take when he likes with any friend.'

'Bravo!' thought I to myself; 'this is the wife for my friend John!'

THE HOUSE OF ELD

So soon as the child began to speak, the gyve was riveted; and the boys and girls limped about their play like convicts. Doubtless it was more pitiable to see and more painful to bear in youth; but even the grown folk, besides being very unhandy on their feet, were often sick with ulcers.

About the time when Jack was ten years old, many strangers began to journey through that country. These he beheld going lightly by on the long roads, and the thing amazed him. 'I wonder how it comes,' he asked, 'that all these strangers are so quick afoot, and we must drag about our fetter?'

'My dear boy,' said his uncle, the catechist, 'do not complain about your fetter, for it is the only thing that makes life worth living. None are happy, none are good, none are respectable, that are not gyved like us. And I must tell you, besides, it is very dangerous talk. If you grumble of your iron, you will have no luck; if ever you take it off, you will be instantly smitten by a thunderbolt.'

'Are there no thunderbolts for these strangers?' asked Jack.

'Jupiter is longsuffering to the benighted,' returned the catechist.

'Upon my word, I could wish I had been less fortunate,' said Jack. 'For if I had been born benighted, I might now be going free; and it cannot be denied the iron is inconvenient, and the ulcer hurts.'

'Ah!' cried his uncle, 'do not envy the heathen! Theirs is a sad lot! Ah, poor souls, if they but knew the joys of being fettered! Poor souls, my heart yearns for them. But the truth is they are vile, odious, insolent, ill-conditioned, stinking brutes, not truly human – for what is a man without a fetter? – and

287

you cannot be too particular not to touch or speak with them.'

After this talk, the child would never pass one of the un-fettered on the road but what he spat at him and called him names, which was the practice of the children in that part.

It chanced one day, when he was fifteen, he went into the woods, and the ulcer pained him. It was a fair day, with a blue sky; all the birds were singing; but Jack nursed his foot. Pres-ently, another song began; it sounded like the singing of a person, only far more gay; at the same time there was a beat-ing on the earth. Jack put aside the leaves; and there was a lad of his own village, leaping, and dancing and singing to himself in a green dell; and on the grass beside him lay the dancer's iron.

'Oh!' cried Jack, 'you have your fetter off!'

'For God's sake, don't tell your uncle!' cried the lad.

'If you fear my uncle,' returned Jack, 'why do you not fear the thunderbolt?'

'That is only an old wives' tale,' said the other. 'It is only told to children. Scores of us come here among the woods and dance for nights together, and are none the worse.'

This put Jack in a thousand new thoughts. He was a grave lad; he had no mind to dance himself; he wore his fetter man-fully, and tended his ulcer without complaint. But he loved the less to be deceived or to see others cheated. He began to lie in wait for heathen travellers, at covert parts of the road, and in the dusk of the day, so that he might speak with them unseen; and these were greatly taken with their wayside questioner, and told him things of weight. The wearing of gyves (they said) was no command of Jupiter's. It was the con-trivance of a white-faced thing, a sorcerer, that dwelt in that country in the Wood of Eld. He was one like Glaucus that could change his shape, yet he could be always told; for when he was crossed, he gobbled like a turkey. He had three lives; but the third smiting would make an end of him indeed; and with that his house of sorcery would vanish, the gyves fall, and the villagers take hands and dance like children.

'And in your country?' Jack would ask.

But at this the travellers, with one accord, would put him

off; until Jack began to suppose there was no land entirely happy. Or, if there were, it must be one that kept its folk at home; which was natural enough.

But the case of the gyves weighed upon him. The sight of the children limping stuck in his eyes; the groans of such as dressed their ulcers haunted him. And it came at last in his mind that he was born to free them.

There was in that village a sword of heavenly forgery, beaten upon Vulcan's anvil. It was never used but in the temple, and then the flat of it only; and it hung on a nail by the catechist's chimney. Early one night, Jack rose, and took the sword, and was gone out of the house and the village in the darkness.

All night he walked at a venture; and when day came, he met strangers going to the fields. Then he asked after the Wood of Eld and the house of sorcery; and one said north, and one south; until Jack saw that they deceived him. So then, when he asked his way of any man, he showed the bright sword naked; and at that the gyve on the man's ankle rang, and answered in his stead; and the word was still *Straight on.* But the man, when his gyve spoke, spat and struck at Jack, and threw stones at him as he went away; so that his head was broken.

So he came to that wood, and entered in, and he was aware of a house in a low place, where funguses grew, and the trees met, and the steaming of the marsh arose about it like a smoke. It was a fine house, and a very rambling; some parts of it were ancient like the hills, and some but of yesterday, and none finished; and all the ends of it were open, so that you could go in from every side. Yet it was in good repair, and all the chimneys smoked.

Jack went in through the gable; and there was one room after another, all bare, but all furnished in part, so that a man could dwell there; and in each there was a fire burning, where a man could warm himself, and a table spread where he might eat. But Jack saw nowhere any living creature; only the bodies of some stuffed.

'This is a hospitable house,' said Jack; 'but the ground must be quaggy underneath, for at every step the building quakes.'

He had gone some time in the house, when he began to be hungry. Then he looked at the food, and at first he was afraid; but he bared the sword, and by the shining of the sword, it seemed the food was honest. So he took the courage to sit down and eat, and he was refreshed in mind and body.

'This is strange,' thought he, 'that in the house of sorcery there should be food so wholesome.'

As he was yet eating, there came into that room the appearance of his uncle, and Jack was afraid because he had taken the sword. But his uncle was never more kind, and sat down to meat with him, and praised him because he had taken the sword. Never had these two been more pleasantly together, and Jack was full of love to the man.

'It was very well done,' said his uncle, 'to take the sword and come yourself into the House of Eld; a good thought and a brave deed. But now you are satisfied; and we may go home to dinner arm in arm.'

'Oh, dear, no!' said Jack. 'I am not satisfied yet.'

'How!' cried his uncle. 'Are you not warmed by the fire? Does not this food sustain you?'

'I see the food to be wholesome,' said Jack; 'and still it is no proof that a man should wear a gyve on his right leg.'

Now at this the appearance of his uncle gobbled like a turkey.

'Jupiter!' cried Jack, 'is this the sorcerer?'

His hand held back and his heart failed him for the love he bore his uncle; but he heaved up the sword and smote the appearance on the head; and it cried out aloud with the voice of his uncle; and fell to the ground; and a little bloodless white thing fled from the room.

The cry rang in Jack's ears, and his knees smote together, and conscience cried upon him; and yet he was strengthened, and there woke in his bones the lust of that enchanter's blood. 'If the gyves are to fall,' said he, 'I must go through with this, and when I get home I shall find my uncle dancing.'

So he went on after the bloodless thing. In the way, he met the appearance of his father; and his father was incensed, and railed upon him, and called to him upon his duty, and bade him be home, while there was yet time. 'For you can still,' said he, 'be home by sunset; and then all will be forgiven.'

'God knows,' said Jack, 'I fear your anger; but yet your anger does not prove that a man should wear a gyve on his right leg.'

And at that the appearance of his father gobbled like a turkey.

'Ah, heaven,' cried Jack, 'the sorcerer again!'

The blood ran backward in his body and his joints rebelled against him for the love he bore his father; but he heaved up the sword, and plunged it in the heart of the appearance; and the appearance cried out aloud with the voice of his father; and fell to the ground; and a little bloodless white thing fled from the room.

The cry rang in Jack's ears, and his soul was darkened; but now rage came to him. 'I have done what I dare not think upon,' said he. 'I will go to an end with it, or perish. And when I get home, I pray God this may be a dream, and I may find my father dancing.'

So he went on after the bloodless thing that had escaped; and in the way he met the appearance of his mother, and she wept. 'What have you done?' she cried. 'What is this that you have done? Oh, come home (where you may be by bedtime) ere you do more ill to me and mine; for it is enough to smite my brother and your father.'

'Dear mother, it is not these that I have smitten,' said Jack; 'it was but the enchanter in their shape. And even if I had, it would not prove that a man should wear a gyve on his right leg.'

And at this the appearance gobbled like a turkey.

He never knew how he did that; but he swung the sword on the one side, and clove the appearance through the midst; and it cried out aloud with the voice of his mother; and fell to the ground; and with the fall of it, the house was gone from over Jack's head, and he stood alone in the woods, and the gyve was loosened from his leg.

'Well,' said he, 'the enchanter is now dead, and the fetter gone.' But the cries rang in his soul, and the day was like night to him. 'This has been a sore business,' said he. 'Let me get forth out of the wood, and see the good that I have done to others.'

He thought to leave the fetter where it lay, but when he turned to go, his mind was otherwise. So he stooped and put the gyve in his bosom; and the rough iron galled him as he went, and his bosom bled.

Now when he was forth of the wood upon the highway, he met folk returning from the field; and those he met had no fetter on the right leg, but, behold! they had one upon the left. Jack asked them what it signified; and they said, 'that was the new wear, for the old was found to be a superstition.' Then he looked at them nearly; and there was a new ulcer on the left ankle, and the old one on the right was not yet healed.

'Now, may God forgive me!' cried Jack. 'I would I were well home.'

And when he was home, there lay his uncle smitten on the head, and his father pierced through the heart, and his mother cloven through the midst. And he sat in the lone house and wept beside the bodies.

MORAL

> Old is the tree and the fruit good,
> Very old and thick the wood.
> Woodman, is your courage stout?
> Beware! the root is wrapped about
> Your mother's heart, your father's bones;
> And like the mandrake comes with groans.

APPENDIX

What was to happen in *Weir of Hermiston?*

Extract from Sir Sidney Colvin's Editorial Note to the novel (1896):

Archie persists in his good resolution of avoiding further conduct compromising to young Kirstie's good name. Taking advantage of the situation thus created, and of the girl's unhappiness and wounded vanity, Frank Innes pursues his purpose of seduction; and Kirstie, though still caring for Archie in her heart, allows herself to become Frank's victim. Old Kirstie is the first to perceive something amiss with her, and believing Archie to be the culprit, accuses him, thus making him aware for the first time that mischief has happened. He does not at once deny the charge, but seeks out and questions young Kirstie, who confesses the truth to him; and he, still loving her, promises to protect and defend her in her trouble. He then has an interview with Frank Innes on the moor, which ends in a quarrel and in Archie killing Frank beside the Weaver's Stone. Meanwhile the Four Black Brothers, having become aware of their sister's betrayal, are bent on vengeance against Archie as her supposed seducer. They are about to close in upon him with this purpose, when he is arrested by the officers of the law for the murder of Frank. He is tried before his own father, the Lord Justice-Clerk, found guilty, and condemned to death. Meanwhile the elder Kirstie, having discovered from the girl how matters really stand, informs her nephews of the truth and they, in a great revulsion of feeling in Archie's favour, determine on an action after the ancient manner of their house. They gather a following, and after a great fight break the prison where Archie lies confined, and rescue him. He and young Kirstie thereafter escape to America. But the ordeal of taking part in the trial of his own son has been too much for the Lord Justice-Clerk, who dies of the shock.

APPENDIX

This is based on notes taken by Stevenson's stepdaughter, Bella Strong, when acting as amanuensis during composition of the novel.

GLOSSARY

ae one

antinomian one of a sect which holds that the moral law is not obligatory to one who is God's chosen

Auld Hornie the Devil

ballant ballad
bauchles old shoes
bauld bold
begoud began
bield shelter
bieldy sheltered
birks birches
birling whirling
black-a-vised dark-complexioned
bogle apparition
bonnet-laird yeoman
bool sugarplum
brae rising ground
brig bridge
brumstane brimstone
buff, play buff on make a fool of
burn stream
butt end end of a cottage
byre cow-house

ca' drive
callant lad
caller fresh

canna cannot
canny careful, shrewd
cantie cheerful
cantrip witch's trick
carline old woman
chafts jaws
chalmer chamber
change-house ale-house
chapping striking
claes clothes
clamjamfry crowd
clavers idle talk
cock-laird yeoman
collieshangie turmoil
crack converse
craig throat, neck
cuddy donkey
cuist cast
cummers gossips
cutty brat

daffing romping
dander saunter
danders cinders
daurna dare not
deave deafen
dentie dainty
dirdum vigour
disjaskit worn-out, disreputable-looking
doer land-agent

door-cheeks door-posts,
  thresholds
drumlie dark
duds clothes
dule-tree the tree of lamentation,
  the hanging-tree; *dule* is also
  Scots for boundary, and it
  may mean the boundary-tree
  or tree on which interlopers
  hung by the baron
dunting knocking
dwaibly infirm, rickety
dwining wasting away,
  declining in health

earrand errand
eldritch ghastly, frightful,
  uncanny
ettercap vixen

fashed troubled
fechting fighting
feck quantity, portion
feckless feeble, powerless
fell strong and fiery
fey unlike yourself, strange,
  as persons are observed to be
  in the hour of approaching
  death
fit foot
flit depart
flyped turned up or inside out
forbye in addition to
forgather to fall in with
forjeskit jaded, fatigued
fower four
fuff (of cats) spit, hiss
fule fool
füshionless weak
fyle to soil, defile
fylement defilement

gaed went
gang go
gangrel vagrant, vagabond,
  vermin
gart made, compelled
gey an' very
gigot leg of mutton
girn grin
girzie diminutive of Grizel, and
  so a playful nickname
glaur mud
glint glance, sparkle
glisk glimpse
gloaming twilight
glower scowl
gobbets small lumps
gousty stormy
gowden golden
gowsty gusty
grat wept
grieve land-steward
grogam coarse fabric of mohair
  and wool
guddle to catch fish with the
  hands by groping under the
  stones or banks
gurley stormy, surly
gyte beside itself

haddit held
hag marshy moorland
haud squall
heels-ower-hurdie head over
  heels
hinney honey
hirsle move, glide resting on
  the hams
hirstle bustle
hizzie wench
howe hollow

296

howf haunt

hunkered crouched

hypothec term used in Scots law meaning the security given by a tenant to a landlord, as furniture, produce etc. Colloquially this has come to mean 'the whole structure', 'the whole affair'

idleset idleness

infeftment a term in Scots law synonymous with investiture

jaloose suspect

jaud jade

jeely-piece a slice of bread and jam or jelly

jennipers juniper

jo sweetheart

justifeed executed, made the victim of justice

jyle jail

kebbuck cheese

keek look out, pry

kenspeckle conspicuous

kilted tucked up

kyte belly

laigh low

laird landed proprietor

lane alone

lave rest, remainder

limmer loose woman

linking tripping

loup leap, run off

lown lonely, still, calm

lynn cataract

macers officers of the supreme court

menseful well-mannered

mirk dark

misbegowk deception, disappointment

mools earth

muckle much, great, big

mutch cap

my lane by myself

neist next

neuk corner

nowt black cattle

owercome refrain, chorus

oxter armpit

palmering walking infirmly

panel in Scots law, the accused person in a criminal action, the prisoner

peching short coughing

peel a fortified watch-tower

plew-stilts plough-handles

policy ornamental grounds of a country mansion

puddock frog

quean wench

rair roar

reishling beating

risping grating

rowt to roar, rant

rowth abundance

rudas haggard old woman

sab sob

sanguishes sandwiches

sark chemise, nightdress

sasine in Scots law the act of giving legal possession of feudal property or in

colloquial use the deed by
which that possession is
approved
saughs willows
sclamber scramble
screighing screeching,
screaming
scunner shudder
session the Court of Session, the
Supreme Court of Scotland
shauchling shuffling
sic kin
siller money
sinsyne since then
skailing dispersing
skelloch scream
skelp slap
skirling screaming
skirt move stealthily
skreigh-o'day daybreak
smoored drowned
snash abuse
sneisty supercilious
sooth hum
sough sound, murmur
speir to ask
speldering sprawling
splairge to splash
spunk spirit, fire
spunkie will o' the wisp
steer commotion
steik, steek to shut
stirk a young bullock
stockfish hard, savourless
sugar-bool sugarplum
syne since

tawpie a slow, foolish slut
telling you a good thing for you
thir these
thirl subject to, dependent on
thrapple neck
thrawn twisted, disjointed
threep assert persistently
tummle tumble
two-names local sobriquets in
addition to patronymic
tyke dog

unchancy unlucky
unco strange, extraordinary,
very
unstreakit (of corpse) not laid
out for burial
upsitten impertinent

vivers victuals

wae sad, unhappy
waling choosing
warrandise warranty
war'sling wrestling
waur worse
weird destiny
whammle upset
whaup curlew
wheen a few
windlestrae crested dog's tail
grass
wund wind

yett gate
yin one

NOTES

WEIR OF HERMISTON

Introductory

1. (p. 55) By opening with a description of the Weaver's Stone, Stevenson both directs our attention to the violent act at the centre of the novel (the last sentence clearly refers to the never-written scene of Archie's killing of Frank Innes) and also gives his story the appropriate context in Scottish culture and history. The Stone has many Covenanter associations.

The Covenanters take their name from a document, the National Covenant, drawn up and sworn to in February 1638. By this time Scotland had been united with England through a common king for thirty-five years. The current king, Charles I, was unpopular in Scotland; he displayed little knowledge of or interest in Scottish affairs, and his High Church sympathies antagonized a nation whose Protestantism was Calvinist rather than modified Lutheran. Scottish extremists, angered by Charles's attempts to impose his ideas on their country, became increasingly convinced of a divinely-appointed duty to ensure the domination, indeed the regulation of all aspects of life by their own Church – and this, not only in Scotland but in England too. A second Covenant, generally known as the Solemn League and Covenant, was undertaken in September 1643. The Scots placed great hopes in the Commonwealth, hopes that were to be disappointed. After the Restoration of Charles II, the majority of Scots, though still adhering to their own faith, accepted the situation of the coexistence of religious difference. There were, however, some, particularly in the south-west of Scotland (Galloway), who felt that this acceptance was compromise with the ungodly, and who considered themselves bound by the Covenant to protest actively against a worldly Government. It is to these last-ditch upholders of the promises of the *second* Covenant that the term Covenanter usually refers.

Claverhouse: John Graham of Claverhouse, Viscount Dundee

(1648–89). 'Bonnie Dundee' has been branded by folk-history as the bloody and implacable enemy of the Covenanters, and it is to this that Stevenson is appealing with his picture of the man-of-war slaying a harmless religious craftsman. After a career in both the French and Dutch armies Claverhouse was appointed in 1678 Captain of one of the three cavalry troops ordered to take action against the Covenanters, and was present with his troop at the famous Covenanter defeat, the Battle of Bothwell Brigg (22 June 1679), an event that the sixteen-year-old Stevenson movingly described in his first book *The Pentland Rising* (1866). From 1682–5 Claverhouse directed operations against the Covenanter diehards, and though ruthless in his approach did not go in for the indiscriminate killings his reputation would suggest, being probably only directly responsible for ten deaths. He supported James VII of Scotland and II of England against William of Orange and received his mortal wound at the Battle of Killiecrankie (27 July 1689).

Balweary: As mentioned in the Introduction to this volume, Stevenson set no fewer than three stories in this village: *Thrawn Janet, Heathercat,* and *Weir,* and the three interrelate in references. This seems to me an indication of the influence of Balzac on Stevenson and to reveal a wish for his mature fiction to amount to a unified picture, comparable to Balzac's, of Scottish history and life.

Old Mortality: The strange figure of Robert Paterson (1715–1801), 'Old Mortality', is memorably evoked in the introduction to Walter Scott's Covenanter novel of the same name (1816). The son of a farmer near Hawick, Robert Paterson came early under the influences of the extreme Covenanters, and his experience of the Catholic Jacobite supporters in 1745–6 only intensified his already ardent and austere Puritan faith. Though married and with a family, Robert Paterson devoted his life from 1758 onwards to travelling round Galloway, Ayrshire and Dumfriesshire, erecting and looking after monuments to fallen Covenanter heroes. He was not a skilled engraver but practised his art for love alone, receiving no fee or reward.

Cameronian: The Cameronians were the extreme wing of the Covenanters who considered it direst sin even to contemplate a *modus vivendi* with the Government. They take their name from Richard Cameron (1648–80), who was responsible for creating a rift among the Covenanters by his whole-hearted denunciation of any clergyman who had accepted the position of toleration offered by the Government under the Indulgences. The denunciation was later surpassed by another, even more vehement one of the King's authority – on 20 June 1680 at Sanquhar. This speech, not surprisingly, led to a price being put on his head and to his being pursued to the death by members of the military. The phrase 'gave his life ... in a glorious folly and without comprehension or regret' suggests the fanaticism of Cameron's followers.

It should be noted that a Weaver's Stone can be found in the vicinity of Buckstane near Edinburgh. Compton Mackenzie in his short study of Stevenson (1968) tells how he heard from the owner of a farmhouse near Buckstane that as a young man Stevenson had been a frequent visitor there and had fallen in love with the youngest daughter of the family called – like the heroine of *Weir* – Christina. A favourite rendezvous of the young lovers was this Weaver's Stone.

2. (p. 55) *Francie's Cairn*: Presumably the Francie referred to here is Frank Innes, the young man to be killed in the hollow.

Chapter I

1. (p. 56) *Lord Justice-Clerk*: Originally clerk of the central criminal court and later a judge, Braxfield became Lord Justice-Clerk in 1798, and thereby effective head of the criminal court.

2. (p. 56) Jean Rutherford certainly comes from a lawless, reckless old family. *Flodden*: One of the greatest defeats of the Scots by the English (1513). Considering roughly 15,000 Scots were killed at this battle near the Tweed, it is no great disgrace for one of the Rutherfords to have been killed there.

Hanged at his peel door by James the Fifth: James V (1512–42) made a concerted drive against the power and general disregard for law and order that prevailed among the great Border families and their retainers. In 1530 he went down to the Border country, and in order to subdue the unruly area of Liddersdale, a possible setting for *Weir*, hanged Johnnie Armstrong, together with other members of the Armstrong family, outside his home. The ballad of Johnnie Armstrong is one of the most famous of all Border ballads. Such a man as Johnnie Armstrong was this particular 'riding Rutherford'.

Tom Dalyell: General Sir Thomas Dalyell (1599–1685). Again an implacable military foe of the Covenanters, Dalyell's was a wild and colourful career. He was captured by the Cromwellians and imprisoned in the Tower from which he escaped. He then served abroad, becoming indeed General under the Czar of Russia; he is thought to have brought the thumbscrew from Russia to Britain. Charles II gave him, in 1666, command of all his forces in Scotland and he defeated the Covenanters at Rullion Green, referred to elsewhere in the novel. He was later appointed Commissioner of the Justiciary for tackling the problem of recalcitrant Covenanters.

The relation of the women to the men in the Rutherford family much resembles that in the Stevenson family as described by Robert Louis Stevenson in his unfinished *Records of a Family of Engineers*. Stevenson's great-grandmother and grandmother were both called Jean and both bear some resemblance, in their piety, their quietness and their rather muddled attempts to keep house, to Mrs Weir. The later anecdote about the food Jean's cook serves up to my Lord Hermiston is paralleled in stories of Stevenson's own paternal grandmother:

> My grandmother remained to the end devout and unambitious, occupied with her Bible, her children, and her house; easily shocked, and associating largely with a clique of godly parasites ... The cook was a godly woman, the butcher a Christian man, and the table suffered. The scene has been often described to me of my grandfather sawing with a darkened countenance at some indissoluble joint – 'Preserve me, my dear, what kind of ruddy, stringy beast is this?' – of the joint removed, the pudding substituted and uncovered; and of my grandmother's anxious glance and hasty, deprecatory comment, 'Just mismanaged!' Yet with the invincible obstinacy of soft natures, she would adhere to the godly woman and the Christian man, or find others of the same kidney to replace them.

Again Jean's attitude to Archie has an antecedent in Stevenson's own family. Of his great-grandmother Stevenson wrote: 'like so many other ... Scotswomen, she vowed her son should wag his head in a pulpit'.

3. (p. 57) *Lord Advocate:* The Crown Prosecutor in Scotland.

4. (p. 61) The *'Letters'* (published 1664) are the best-known work of Samuel Rutherford (1600–61) and formed part of the staple devotional reading for Scots for many generations. Rutherford had a distinguished career; he held the Professorship of Divinity at St Andrews University and became one of the Scottish Commissioners

to the Westminster Assembly, which discussed the relationship
between the Scottish and English Churches. But Rutherford connected himself with the more extreme wing of the Covenanters.
Jean's thoughts on religious matters reflect the violent and near-
erotic imagery of Rutherford's writings.

Scougal: Henry Scougal (1650–78). One of the saints of the Scottish
church who became Professor of Divinity at Aberdeen University
at a remarkably young age. The only work of his to be published
in his lifetime was *The Life of God in the Soul of Man* (1677), a
work which became a Scottish religious classic. Scougal died of
consumption at the age of twenty-eight.

5. (p. 61) Here are three more enemies of the Covenanters. Jean
Rutherford/Weir is surely justified in thinking that her ungodly,
successful husband would have been of their number.

Bloody Mackenzie: Sir George Mackenzie of Rosehaugh (1636–81)
was one of those ambiguous, divided personalities who so fascinated
Stevenson. His story indeed can cast a light on my Lord Hermiston's.
Mackenzie's, too, was a brilliant legal mind. He was made Lord
Advocate in 1677, and in this capacity conducted prosecutions
against the Covenanters, conducting them moreover without an
exception successfully. It was his relentlessness in these cases that
earned him his nickname. It should be remembered however that
he was also a highly literary man, author of many works of prose,
founder of the Advocates' Library of Scotland, and a distinguished
political philosopher. His name should arouse in the reader a
sense of the equivocal nature of the Law and its practitioners, a
theme which runs centrally through the novel.

Lauderdale: John Maitland, 2nd Earl and 1st Duke of Lauderdale
(1616–82). Rightly called 'politic' by Stevenson, Lauderdale was in
fact one of the original drafters of the Solemn League and Covenant
itself. He moved however towards the Royalist party and was
captured after the Battle of Worcester (1651) as a supporter of
Charles II. After the Restoration he was appointed Secretary of
State for Scotland, and this former Covenanter then proceeded to
associate himself with punitive action against men of his old
persuasion. To be fair it must be said that he favoured more lenient
policies than did most of his colleagues.

Rothes: John Leslie, 7th Earl and 1st Duke of Rothes (1630–81). His
career has much in common with Lauderdale's. He was a Covenanter leader in 1638, though always of the faction that supported
Royalist claims. Like Lauderdale he closely associated himself with

Charles II and was captured after the Battle of Worcester. After
Charles' return he became King's Commissioner to the Scottish
Parliament and conducted the Anti-Covenanter activities that provoked the Pentland Rising in 1666. His later years were spent
in rivalry to Lauderdale.

6. (p. 63) These lines played an important role in Stevenson's own
imaginative development. He wrote in an essay 'Rosa Quo Locorum'
about his literary tastes as a very young child:

> I had ... under the same influence – that of my dear
> nurse – a favourite author: it is possible that the reader has
> never heard of him – the Rev. Robert Murray McCheyne.
> My nurse and I admired his name exceedingly, so that I
> must have been taught the love of beautiful sounds before I
> was breeched; and I remember two specimens of his muse
> until this day:

> > Behind the hills of Naphatali,
> > The sun went slowly down,
> > Leaving on mountain, tower and tree,
> > A tinge of golden brown.

7. (p. 65) Archie, we can work out from the facts Stevenson gives us,
was born in 1794. Revolution broke out in France in 1789; 1792 was
the Year One of the new order. At the time of the action of the
novel proper, France was under Napoleonic domination and is
associated throughout its course with anarchy and atheism. We
can see this in Chapter III when Lord Hermiston says to his son:
'But I'll never trust ye so near the French, ye that's so Frenchifeed.'

Chapter II

1. (p. 70) *Papinian and Paul:* Roman lawyers. The Scottish law
system is far more closely tied to the Roman than the English.
Papinian (A.D. 140–212). Roman jurist who served under Marcus
Aurelius. He was the author of thirty-seven books of 'Quaestiones'
and nineteen of 'Responsa', excerpts from which were included in
Justinian's *Digest.*
Paul (floruit A.D. 540). Officer in Justinian's household and author
of many epigrams. These references reflect Stevenson's own successful training for the Scottish bar.
2. (p. 71) *Forbes of Culloden:* Comparison of Lord Glenalmond to
the statue of Duncan Forbes (1685–1747) provides the appropriate con-

text in which to view Archie's friend and mentor. Forbes, member of Parliament for Inverness Burgh, was made Lord Advocate in 1726. He played a noble role in the tragic affair of the Porteous riots, defying the proposal that severe measures should be taken against Edinburgh after a mob of its townfolk had hanged the Captain of the City Guards, John Porteous. They had killed him because he had fired on members of a crowd who had made open protest at a public execution of a contrabandist. The similarity between this historical episode (obliquely referred to here) and Archie's own protest at the hanging of Duncan Jopp shows how Stevenson's mind was operating while at work on *Weir*. At the time of the 1745 Jacobite uprising Forbes exerted the influence of his own personality to stop the majority of the northern clans from joining it. For all his honourable service to the Government's cause, Cumberland despised Forbes for his humanitarianism and in the relation of these two men one to another can be seen perhaps the contrast we are intended to make for ourselves between Weir of Hermiston and Glenalmond.

3. (p. 72) *Cato and Brutus:*
Marcus Porcius Cato, Cato the Censor (234–149 B.C.). He held the post of Censor from 184 B.C. onwards and devoted himself to purging the Roman nobility of their loose morality. He was a brilliant orator, perhaps most famous for his address to the Senate in which he urged the destruction of Carthage with the words: *'Carthago delenda est'*.

Lucius Junius Brutus (floruit 510 B.C.). Leader of the uprising against the infamous Tarquins, the corrupt kings of Rome, and subsequently one of the first two consuls of the Roman Republic. His sons conspired against him by trying to restore the Tarquins and as a result were condemned by their father to death. The reference here is, of course, a deliberate device on Stevenson's part to point to the horrifying (unwritten) climax of the novel. Lord Hermiston is to follow Brutus' example and condemn a cherished son to death. And in his espousal of radical and, in his father's eyes, subversive attitudes, Archie can be seen as running a course parallel to that of the sons of Brutus who were so anxious to overthrow the structure their father had helped to build. It is indeed possible that Stevenson derived further inspiration for his theme from David's (1748–1825) painting 'The Lictors bringing Brutus the Bodies of his Sons' – which hangs in the Louvre and dates from 1789, the year of the French Revolution. An irony can be seen here : it is the father who is carrying out justice so intransigently, so against instinctive feeling, who is acting in a French manner, not the son whom he criticizes for being 'Frenchifeed'.

Chapter III

1. (p. 77) *Holyrood:* the Palace of Holyroodhouse.
Queen Mary: Mary, Queen of Scots (1542–87).
Prince Charlie: 'Bonnie Prince Charlie' (1720–88). The Young Pretender held court at Holyrood in September–October 1745 before setting out for London. Stevenson planned a novel *The Young Chevalier* about Prince Charlie in his exile years – one and a half chapters survive.
the hooded stag: King David I was hunting near Arthur's Seat when his life was put in danger by the charge of a huge stag. Miraculously the king found a fragment of the Holy Rood placed in his hand, and at this, the stag fled away.

2. (p. 79) Stevenson was a member of the Spec. during his student days at Edinburgh University. He himself tried to organize a debate in the Society on the morality of capital punishment. Papers that Stevenson did successfully read at the Spec. provide interesting evidence of the seriousness of his mind at the very time when he was being branded by Edinburgh society as an idler : 'Two Questions on the Relations between Christ's Teaching and Modern Christianity', 'The Influence of the Covenanting Persecution on the Scottish Mind', 'Law and Free Will'.

3. (p. 81) *Dr Gregory:* James Gregory (1753–1821). He became in 1790 Professor of the Practice of Medicine at Edinburgh University and Chief of the Edinburgh Medical School. Perhaps the best-known of his publications was the *Conspectus* (1780–82), very widely read in both Britain and Europe, in particular for its therapeutics. He was a brilliant lecturer and a tireless and often vituperative controversialist.

4. (p. 86) *the Peninsula:* Peninsula War (1808–14). British forces joined Spanish and Portuguese armies to oppose Napoleon's armies in the Iberian Peninsula.

Chapter V

1. (p. 98) The question of the locality of Hermiston is best answered by a quotation from Sir Sidney Colvin's editorial note to the novel (1896) :

If the reader seeks, further, to know whether the scenery of Hermiston can be identified with any one special place familiar to the writer's early experience, the answer, I think, must be in the negative. Rather it is distilled from a number of different haunts and associations among the moorlands of southern Scotland. In the dedication and in a letter to me he indicates the Lammermuirs as the scene of his tragedy, and Mrs Stevenson (his mother) told me that she thought he was inspired by recollections of a visit paid in boyhood to an uncle living at a remote farmhouse in that district called Overshiels, in the parish of Stow. But although he may have thought of the Lammermuirs in the first instance, we have already found him drawing his description of the kirk and manse from another haunt of his youth, namely Glencorse in the Pentlands. And passages in chapters V and VIII point explicitly to a third district, that is, the country bordering upon Upper Tweeddale, with the country stretching thence to the headwaters of the Clyde. With this country also holiday rides and excursions from Peebles had made him familiar as a boy; and this seems the most natural scene of the story, if only from its proximity to the proper home of the Elliots, which of course is the heart of the Border, especially Teviotdale and Ettrick. Some of the geographical names mentioned are clearly not meant to furnish literal indications. The Spango, for instance, is a water running, I believe, not into the Tweed but into the Nith, and Crossmichael as the name of a town is borrowed from Galloway; but it may be taken to all intents and purposes as standing for Peebles, where ... there existed in the early years of the century a well-known club of the same character as that described in the story. Lastly the name of Hermiston itself is taken from a farm on the Water of Ale, between Ettrick and Teviotdale, and close to the proper country of the Elliotts.

2. (p. 105) *Lyon King of Arms:* the chief of the Court of Heraldry in Scotland.

3. (p. 107) *Camperdown:* British naval defeat of the Dutch which averted an invasion of Ireland.

Cape St Vincent: British naval victory over a superior Spanish fleet, Spain being then allied to revolutionary France.

4. (p. 99) *Mr Sheriff Scott:* Walter Scott (1771–1832). Scott was appointed Sheriff-Depute of Selkirkshire in 1799. An inveterate explorer of the Border country, he had a keen interest in its old tales and ballads ever since his earliest childhood. During the course of his travels he collected many such, a mammoth collection of them appearing between 1802–3 in the three-volume *Minstrelsy of the Scottish Border.* Some of the ballads had been supplied by James Hogg (see below), the real-life counterpart of Dand Elliott. Scott's first novel *Waverley* was published anonymously in 1814.

5. (p. 111) *Muir and Palmer:* Members of the Friends of the People and victims of Lord Braxfield's most infamous carrying out of 'justice'. Thomas Muir (1765–98) was indeed perhaps the most celebrated man to be sentenced by Braxfield – after a mockery of a fair trial to fourteen years' transportation to Botany Bay. Muir, born in Glasgow and educated there at Grammar School and University, was moved by the French Revolution and the subsequent publication of Tom Paine's *Rights of Man* (1791) to work for suffrage reform in Britain. He formed close ties with French revolutionaries and became a leading member of the Edinburgh Convention of Delegates of Friends of the People. During the Anglo-French War of 1793, Muir fell obviously under suspicion and, a trained lawyer himself of great ability, was tried in the High Court of Edinburgh for treasonous activities. In point of fact he enjoyed preferential treatment in Australia and only stayed there for two years before being rescued by an American ship. He died in France.

6. (p. 114) *Robbie Burns* (1759–96): Though Stevenson greatly loved Burns' poems, his attitude to Burns the man was more ambiguous, as after close study of his life, he found himself repelled by his particular form of sensuality, by his compulsive womanizing. And this aspect of Burns' life he stressed in his own essay on him, a piece which offended many Scottish (in particular Edinburgh) readers. Stevenson was probably irritated by the fact that Edinburgh society, which he personally had found lamentably lacking in compassion where sexual mores were concerned, was prepared to forget Burns' grosser misdeeds on account of his romantic fame.

7. (p. 114) *The Ettrick Shepherd:* James Hogg (1770–1835). Scottish poet and novelist. Born in that part of the Border country known as Ettrick Forest, Hogg became a shepherd when still a boy (hence his nickname). Throughout his life he combined farming and literary work. His shepherding, his closeness to the traditional life of the Border folk and something of his personality make their

way into the portrait of Dand Elliott. Like Dand, Hogg was friendly
with Scott, to whom he supplied ballads and of whom he wrote a
memoir *Domestic Manners and Private Life of Sir Walter Scott*
(1834). Hogg and Dand Elliott were both heavy drinkers – Hogg
indulged from time to time in protracted wild drinking bouts.
Hogg's best-known works are his long poem 'The Queen's Wake'
(1813) which first made him famous, and *The Confessions of a
Justified Sinner* (1834), a terrifying study of an Antinomian, a
young man who commits a series of murders under the conviction
that as he is one of God's elect he is in no danger of divine dis-
approval or punishment for them.

8. (p. 115) A picture by David Allan reproduced in T. C. Smout's excellent *A History of the Scottish People 1560–1830* (1969) is worth
looking at in order to get a full idea of the humiliation of the *stool of
repentance*. The elders of the kirk, and therefore moral arbiters of
the community, chiefly sentenced offenders for sexual peccadilloes;
the guilty person was made to stand in a public place set aside for
the purpose inside the church so that all the congregation could
look at him/her and be duly horrified. In fact, as Burns recorded,
people were increasingly apt to feel sympathy for the victim and
outrage at the petty cruelty of the kirk elders. Throughout the
latter part of the eighteenth century fines became a more wide-
spread punishment than the kirk-stool, and indeed, by the time in
which *Weir* is set, even fines were on the decrease.

Chapter VI

1. (p. 133) *that idea of Fate:* These words and the passage that follows
cannot help but remind us of Hardy. The concept of the characters
as helplessly in the grip of destiny is present elsewhere in the
novel, most particularly in the *Introductory* section and in the
paragraph with which the novel breaks off. Stevenson's admiration of Hardy had led him to pay the novelist a visit in his Dor-
chester home in 1885. In thinking of Hardy in relation to *Weir*
one's mind travels first to *Tess* (1891) since the love of Archie and
Kirstie bears distinct resemblance to that of Angel and Tess, and
Kirstie too is to be a virtuous girl who, almost in spite of herself,
falls victim to a seducer's powers. Indeed Stevenson compares
Kirstie to Tess in a letter to Barrie of 1 November 1892: 'Suffice it to
breathe in your ear that she was what Hardy calls (and others in
their plain way don't) a Pure Woman.' Colvin adds as a footnote
that this 'allusion to *Tess of the d'Urbervilles* a book R.L.S. did

not like'. My own impression, however, is otherwise. It was in a letter to Stevenson that Henry James made his famous remark: 'The good little Thomas Hardy has scored a great success with *Tess of the d'Urbervilles* which is chock-full of faults and falsity and yet has a singular beauty and charm'; Stevenson's reply to this letter has been lost, yet he must have defended both Hardy and *Tess* since later James wrote to Stevenson: 'I grant you Hardy with all my heart ... so I bowed my head and let *Tess of the D's* pass.'

2. (p. 141) A quotation from Wordsworth's beautiful lyric poem 'The Solitary Reaper'.

3. (p. 142) *the American war*: Anglo-American War of 1812–14, which originated in the strained relations of the two countries during Britain's struggle against Napoleon. Peace was signed in Ghent, Belgium in December 1814 but news of this did not reach the United States until February 1815 shortly after a decisive American victory by Andrew Jackson.

4. (p. 142) From the land of *Beulah*, the *Pilgrim's Progress* tells us, pilgrims could see the Celestial City. Beulah was remarkable for its profusion of flowers which continually sprung up.

Chapter VII

1. (p. 152) *Sherlock Holmes*: Sherlock Holmes' first appearance was in *Study in Scarlet* (1887).

2. (p. 152) *Talleyrand*: Charles Maurice de Tallyrand-Périgord (1754–1838). French statesman who held a high position both in revolutionary France and under Napoleon. He enjoyed the company of wits and beauties, and in both private and public life was distinguished by his total lack of principle and his overweening egotism.

1. (p. 206) *Fifty years syne:* See Introduction for historical placing of the story. The main events of *Thrawn Janet* take place at the end of the great period of ardent witch-hunting. Prevalent all over Europe throughout the seventeenth century, the persecution of witches reached greater and more horrific proportions in Scotland during that time than anywhere else. The interested reader is referred to the relevant passages in T. C. Smout's fascinating and authoritative work: *A History of the Scottish People 1560–1830:*

> in the years between 1560 and 1707 considerably more than 3,000 people, and perhaps as many as 4,500 perished horribly because their contemporaries thought they were witches. In England, with a population five times as large, only about a thousand were killed as witches.

There was, Smout continues:

> ... a peculiarity of Scottish witch-hunting; the landed classes and the wealthiest burgesses were seldom or never accused of witchcraft, whereas in Europe no class was exempt. Scottish victims were mainly women, the wives of farmers, country and town craftsmen and cottars or poor old widows ...

Also of particular value to readers of this story is this:

> The power of the preachers on a simple rural population should not be underestimated – Sunday by Sunday they poured their fierce and eloquent sermons into the souls of their hearers – dreadful warnings and vivid descriptions of hellfire and the personal devil, a piercing insistence on pre-destination, and on the hopelessness of man ever attempting to earn redemption by his own efforts and spiritual strivings. It is not surprising that some in the congregation came to believe they were irretrievably damned, and being damned were the devil's own servants, and as servants should become witches and learn to imitate the rites which were so widely publicised by confessions at witchcraft trials.

2. (p. 207) *the witch of Endor:* was consulted by Saul, who ironic-

ally had banned witches, and from her he learned of his imminent death.

3. (p. 210) The devil and black men were intimately associated in the Scottish mind. K. M. Briggs, the eminent folklorist, has told me that in Scottish witchcraft ceremonies ritual dancers would blacken their faces in the devil's honour and those witches who practised against James VI/I described their master as a great black man who preached them a sermon in a church.

THE MISADVENTURES OF JOHN NICHOLSON

Chapter I

1. (p. 219) *Disruption Principles:* In 1843 the Scottish Church suffered its famous Disruption in which 470 ministers broke with the established State Church of Scotland and founded the Free Church, itself later to experience further disruptions. Those who broke away from the Church of Scotland did so in the name of Protestantism which, they felt, was being compromised by the ecclesiastical establishment. The quarrel which decided the break was two-fold: over the relationship between the civil and the church courts, and over the right (anciently upheld in Scotland) of the congregation to have a say in the appointment of its ministers.

2. (p. 219) *Candlish:* Robert Candlish (1806–73). Minister of the most influential congregation in Edinburgh, St George's, who threw himself into conflict with the civil courts. Candlish believed passionately in the right of the Scottish people to an effective voice in the appointment of ministers and too in the independent jurisdiction of the church in spiritual matters. He proposed a motion in the Assembly that seven ministers be suspended because they had disregarded church injunction and obeyed that of the Civil Court, a deliberate throwing down of the gauntlet. In 1843 his party supported him in his declaration that he could no longer belong to the Established Church from which they therefore officially withdrew to found the Free Church. Candlish was a leading light in the subsequent organization of the Free Church.

Begg: James Begg (1808–83), Free Church Minister. He supported Candlish's faction in 1843, and was activated by his extreme evangelical faith which he felt demanded his withdrawal from a time-serving state church. He believed in restoration of the old Scottish Sabbath prohibitions, in popular education and in the evils of the Roman Catholic hierarchy in their country.

Lee: John Lee (1779–1859), Principal at Edinburgh University. When the Disruption took place Lee remained faithful to the Established Church, undertook to conduct the Divinity Classes at the University and was shortly afterwards made Professor of Divinity.

Residuary Establishment: Those ministers who remained faithful to the State Church.

3. (p. 219) *as the chatter of tree-top apes:* note the deliberate Darwinian simile!

Chapter IV

1. (p 236) John's journey to California has much in common with Louis Stevenson's own. In 1879 against the advice of his friends he left Britain for America to join Fanny Osbourne whom he had heard was severely ill in California. And he left his parents only a cursory note, dwelling mostly on his own unhappiness, and lacking in any proper information about his whereabouts, future plans or even ultimate intentions. He experienced a hellish train journey across the States and arrived in San Francisco in a state close to mental and physical collapse. From there he started to make his way south to Monterey where Fanny was living with her sister. His strength gave out on the way there however and he was found lying under a tree in a near-stupor by two old frontiersmen who nursed him back to health. Stevenson's miseries in California – however solaced by the beauty he found in Monterey and by the spirit of picaresque adventure he found still abroad in San Francisco on his second visit there – were not really eased until a forgiving telegram arrived from his father. Stevenson married Fanny in San Francisco on 19 May 1880.

Discover more about our forthcoming books through Penguin's FREE newspaper...

READ MORE IN PENGUIN

In every corner of the world, on every subject under the sun, Penguin represents quality and variety – the very best in publishing today.

For complete information about books available from Penguin – including Puffins, Penguin Classics and Arkana – and how to order them, write to us at the appropriate address below. Please note that for copyright reasons the selection of books varies from country to country.

In the United Kingdom: Please write to *Dept. JC, Penguin Books Ltd, FREEPOST, West Drayton, Middlesex UB7 0BR*

If you have any difficulty in obtaining a title, please send your order with the correct money, plus ten per cent for postage and packaging, to *PO Box No. 11, West Drayton, Middlesex UB7 0BR*

In the United States: Please write to *Penguin USA Inc., 375 Hudson Street, New York, NY 10014*

In Canada: Please write to *Penguin Books Canada Ltd, 10 Alcorn Avenue, Suite 300, Toronto, Ontario M4V 3B2*

In Australia: Please write to *Penguin Books Australia Ltd, 487 Maroondah Highway, Ringwood, Victoria 3134*

In New Zealand: Please write to *Penguin Books (NZ) Ltd, 182–190 Wairau Road, Private Bag, Takapuna, Auckland 9*

In India: Please write to *Penguin Books India Pvt Ltd, 706 Eros Apartments, 56 Nehru Place, New Delhi 110 019*

In the Netherlands: Please write to *Penguin Books Netherlands B.V., Keizersgracht 231 NL–1016 DV Amsterdam*

In Germany: Please write to *Penguin Books Deutschland GmbH, Friedrichstrasse 10–12, W–6000 Frankfurt/Main 1*

In Spain: Please write to *Penguin Books S. A., C. San Bernardo 117–6° E–28015 Madrid*

In Italy: Please write to *Penguin Italia s.r.l., Via Felice Casati 20, I–20124 Milano*

In France: Please write to *Penguin France S. A., 17 rue Lejeune, F–31000 Toulouse*

In Japan: Please write to *Penguin Books Japan, Ishikiribashi Building, 2–5–4, Suido, Tokyo 112*

In Greece: Please write to *Penguin Hellas Ltd, Dimocritou 3, GR–106 71 Athens*

In South Africa: Please write to *Longman Penguin Southern Africa (Pty) Ltd, Private Bag X08, Bertsham 2013*

READ MORE IN PENGUIN

A CHOICE OF CLASSICS

Matthew Arnold	**Selected Prose**
Jane Austen	**Emma**
	Lady Susan/ The Watsons/ Sanditon
	Mansfield Park
	Northanger Abbey
	Persuasion
	Pride and Prejudice
	Sense and Sensibility
Anne Brontë	**Agnes Grey**
	The Tenant of Wildfell Hall
Charlotte Brontë	**Jane Eyre**
	Shirley
	Villette
Emily Brontë	**Wuthering Heights**
Samuel Butler	**Erewhon**
	The Way of All Flesh
Thomas Carlyle	**Selected Writings**
Arthur Hugh Clough	**Selected Poems**
Wilkie Collins	**The Moonstone**
	The Woman in White
Charles Darwin	**The Origin of Species**
	The Voyage of the Beagle
Benjamin Disraeli	**Sybil**
George Eliot	**Adam Bede**
	Daniel Deronda
	Felix Holt
	Middlemarch
	The Mill on the Floss
	Romola
	Scenes of Clerical Life
	Silas Marner
Elizabeth Gaskell	**Cranford and Cousin Phillis**
	The Life of Charlotte Brontë
	Mary Barton
	North and South
	Wives and Daughters

READ MORE IN PENGUIN

A CHOICE OF CLASSICS

Charles Dickens	**American Notes for General Circulation**
	Barnaby Rudge
	Bleak House
	The Christmas Books (in two volumes)
	David Copperfield
	Dombey and Son
	Great Expectations
	Hard Times
	Little Dorrit
	Martin Chuzzlewit
	The Mystery of Edwin Drood
	Nicholas Nickleby
	The Old Curiosity Shop
	Oliver Twist
	Our Mutual Friend
	The Pickwick Papers
	Selected Short Fiction
	A Tale of Two Cities
Edward Gibbon	**The Decline and Fall of the Roman Empire**
George Gissing	**New Grub Street**
William Godwin	**Caleb Williams**
Thomas Hardy	**The Distracted Preacher and Other Tales**
	Far from the Madding Crowd
	Jude the Obscure
	The Mayor of Casterbridge
	A Pair of Blue Eyes
	The Return of the Native
	Tess of the d'Urbervilles
	The Trumpet-Major
	Under the Greenwood Tree
	The Woodlanders

READ MORE IN PENGUIN

A CHOICE OF CLASSICS

Thomas Macaulay	**The History of England**
Henry Mayhew	**London Labour and the London Poor**
John Stuart Mill	**The Autobiography**
	On Liberty
William Morris	**News from Nowhere and Selected Writings and Designs**
Robert Owen	**A New View of Society and Other Writings**
Walter Pater	**Marius the Epicurean**
John Ruskin	**'Unto This Last' and Other Writings**
Walter Scott	**Ivanhoe**
Robert Louis Stevenson	**Dr Jekyll and Mr Hyde and Other Stories**
William Makepeace Thackeray	**The History of Henry Esmond**
	The History of Pendennis
	Vanity Fair
Anthony Trollope	**Barchester Towers**
	Can You Forgive Her?
	The Eustace Diamonds
	Framley Parsonage
	The Last Chronicle of Barset
	Phineas Finn
	The Small House at Allington
	The Warden
Mary Wollstonecraft	**A Vindication of the Rights of Woman**
Dorothy and William Wordsworth	**Home at Grasmere**